Praise for *USA Today* bestseller
A SEAL in Wolf's Clothing

"Excitement, hot and sexy love scenes, and situational humor that has me laughing out loud."

—Fresh Fiction

"A nonstop, action-packed romance with kick, growls, and sexy attitude."

—Long and Short Reviews

"A delightful and tantalizing read. The characters are spirited and realistic... You'll be captivated."

—Thoughts in Progress

Praise for *Dreaming of the Wolf*

"Fascinating characters and exciting action-packed crime drama plot. A great fantasy twist and yet another way to interpret the legend of weres."

—RT Book Reviews, 4 Stars

"The queen of werewolf dramas Terry Spear provides a powerful tale as she makes her mythos seem real... a great tale of love and war."

—Midwest Book Review

"Intense and swoon-inducing... The chemistry is steamy and hot."

—*USA Today Happy Ever After*

Praise for *Heart of the Highland Wolf*

"A high-powered romance that satisfies on every level... *Heart of the Highland Wolf* embraces the best of what romance has to offer with characters that jump off the pages and into a reader's heart."

—*Long and Short Reviews*

"Fast paced and completely and utterly fascinating... The chemistry between the characters was brilliant."

—*Royal Reviews*

"This novel has it all... Hot doesn't even begin to describe it."

—*Love Romance Passion*

Praise for *Wolf Fever*

"Another great story sure to amaze and intrigue readers... sensual, passionate, and very well written... Terry Spear's writing is pure entertainment."

—*Long and Short Reviews*

"Riveting and entertaining... makes one want to devour all of the rest of Terry Spear's books."

—*Fresh Fiction*

"Full of nail-biting suspense, sexy scenes, and plenty of hot alphas... Terry Spear knows exactly how to extract emotions from her readers... and keep them riveted."

—*Love Romance Passion*

Praise for *Seduced by the Wolf*

"Gently laced with just enough wolf detail and werewolf lore, this action-packed story crackles with mystery, adventure, violence, and passion; a worthy addition to Spear's beautifully imagined werewolf world."

—*Library Journal*

"Ms. Spear's werewolf stories keep getting better and better. You will find yourself lusting after the sexy alpha hero and cheering for the heroine."

—*Night Owl Romance*

Praise for *Legend of the White Wolf*

"No one does tales of the wolf better than Terry Spear."

—*Genre Go Round Reviews*

"Spear's latest novel is bursting with romance, suspense, and heart-pounding excitement... *Legend of the White Wolf* will leave you howling for more!"

—*Love Romance Passion*

"Hooked me from the start, with its action and mystery woven together against the backdrop of a scenic Maine winter. This book has it all; fantasy, suspense, and romance with a touch of the paranormal to boot."

—*Literary Escapism*

Praise for *To Tempt the Wolf*

"Where this book truly shines is the werewolf society and the group dynamics amongst them. The sparring between the alpha leaders is top-notch and it's fascinating to see how wolf habits transcend into human behavior."

—*Medieval Bookworm*

"Do not attempt to start reading this book unless you have a full two hours to sit and be held spellbound... With absolute fascination and intrigue, I was held captive and unable to put this book down... with a quick slash of the pen, author Terry Spear will have you caught up and panting for more."

—*The Romance Studio*

"Chilling suspense and sizzling romance meet in this page-turner. The dark, sexy alpha hero will capture you—body, mind, and soul."

—Nicole North, author of *Devil in a Kilt*

"A paranormal romp that sizzles! Action-packed romance and suspense-filled plot add up to pure magic. I couldn't turn the pages fast enough. Terry Spear is a great addition to the paranormal genre!"

—*Armchair Interviews*

Praise for *Destiny of the Wolf*

"Terry Spear weaves paranormal, suspense, and romance together in one nonstop roller coaster of passion and adventure."

—*Love Romance Passion*

"A werewolf tale that will have you believing they live among us! This is a definite keeper on my shelf!"

—*Paranormal Romance Reviews*

"What I love most about these werewolves is that they read books about werewolves... The thought that some werewolf out there is reading this book added a whole new dimension of delight for me..."

—*Armchair Interviews*

A HOWL for a HIGHLANDER

TERRY SPEAR

sourcebooks
casablanca

Published by Sourcebooks Casablanca, an imprint of Sourcebooks, Inc.
P.O. Box 4410, Naperville, Illinois 60567-4410
(630) 961-3900
FAX: (630) 961-2168
www.sourcebooks.com

Printed and bound in Canada
WC 10 9 8 7 6 5 4 3 2 1

*This book is dedicated to
those who love men in kilts!*

Chapter 1

NEWLY ARRIVED ON GRAND CAYMAN ISLAND WITH A carry-on bag slung over his shoulder and wearing black jeans, a black T-shirt, and black boots—his usual attire when in his commando warrior mode—Duncan MacNeill was ready to locate and deal as harshly as he needed to with Salisbury Silverman, the American gray wolf most knew as Sal.

The financial wizard had stolen Duncan's clan's money along with the investments of countless others. If the rumor was true, Silverman had holed up at his home on the island. At least that was the latest word Duncan had received after months of trying to track the financier down. As far as Duncan was concerned, and as werewolves would have it, the law wasn't needed in a case like this.

None of their kind could go to prison—not when they could shift to wolf during the appearance of the moon, unless the werewolf was a royal—so a werewolf had to take care of the matter in a werewolf's way. With barely any human roots, the royals could shift at will but they would still feel the compelling urge to shift at some point over the year, even if the moon didn't dictate the need.

Warrants in several countries were out for the man's arrest. Unbeknownst to Silverman, he had made the fatal mistake of going after a *werewolf pack's* investments this time. That mistake could get him killed faster than anything else. The notoriety of the case—if the authorities charged him for all the fraud he'd committed, he most likely would be found guilty and sentenced to prison—put all werewolves at risk. It was best that Duncan recover his clan's funds, make the rest of the stolen money available to the others whom Silverman had fleeced, and ensure that the crook quietly disappeared for good.

Duncan had every intention of returning to his native Scotland, to his ancestral home at Argent Castle, and to his gray wolf pack and clan with all possible haste. He was thinking that a trip to the island paradise was a waste of time, except for catching the bastard, when he breathed in the scent of a *female wolf*.

A woman would *not* divert him from this mission or any other, no matter how interested he might be in an unmated female wolf of the right age. Yet, instinctively, he surveyed the newly arrived passengers, looking for the woman. She hadn't taken his connecting flight from Miami or he would have smelled her, located her, and let her know she was in the company of another wolf if she was traveling alone and needed his protection from human types—or *other* wolves, no matter her age or mate status.

His own conscience wouldn't allow otherwise. Now that he'd reached his destination, he told himself he had no need to track a female wolf for any reason. He hadn't smelled any male in the vicinity that indicated one had come to meet her at the airport or was accompanying her. Which was why, he suspected, it was as though the devil was goading him to search for her instead of getting in the line for customs and immigration checks, signing for his rental car, and locating his hotel. Then, he'd find Silverman, who was supposed to have come in on an earlier flight in his own plane—paid for by all those he'd bilked, of course.

Duncan surveyed the crowded airport, didn't see any female who looked like she could be a wolf, and let out his breath.

His older quadruplet brother by four and a half minutes, Guthrie, the financial genius who had gotten them into this investment mess in the first place, had been sure Duncan wouldn't use subtle enough tactics in going after the crook. True, subtlety wasn't a part of Duncan's makeup. Not with three older quadruplet brothers. It didn't matter that they had been born only minutes apart. They'd known from birth who would be in charge when their *da* died.

Being the youngest of the bunch, Duncan didn't have much hope of ever ruling the pack or clan. So he made up for his birth order by never wavering in the face of danger and being the best warrior the clan could have. In this day and age, which was centuries later than when they'd been born, he still had to prove he had what it took to protect the clan.

Once they reached puberty, *lupus garous* aged approximately one year for every thirty, healing quickly when injured, though some injuries could cause death. They weren't immortal. Drowning, bleeding out, or massive injuries could prevent their healing genetics from taking them out of risk and be enough to cause their deaths. More died in those ways than from being the victim of a silver bullet. Truth of the matter was that anyone, werewolf or human, could die from ingesting silver or being struck by a silver slug. Most werewolves preferred other, more honorable methods of killing their enemies, like through hand-to-hand—or teeth-to-teeth—combat or in a battle of the fittest, just like in nature.

Duncan wished he could have brought his claymore with him. However, with tight airport security everywhere, he didn't believe airport authorities would think kindly of him if he attempted to carry a broadsword on board the plane. Since he was traveling light, he had no bags other than a carry-on. His cousin Heather had teased him about not taking swim trunks. But when did a wolf wear a swimsuit?

Besides, he wasn't here to swim in the aqua waters surrounding the sun-kissed Caribbean islands. Heather had warned him that the islands didn't allow nude swimming, though. He'd snorted at that. He did *not* plan to swim. Unless Silverman leapt into the water and attempted to swim away from him. They'd most likely be clothed in their wolf coats anyway.

Duncan again breathed in the air-conditioned molecules at the airport, smelling the odor of humanity: men, women, colognes, perfumes, coconut suntan oils on departing island guests, pine floor cleaners, and *her*—the wolf.

He stalked over to the baggage claim area, surveyed the new passengers grabbing their suitcases off the conveyor belt, and spotted her. She was of average height, and yet something about her stood out. Maybe the way she was dressed to have fun—in silver sandals, as if proving silver couldn't harm their kind, and satiny pale-blue capris that showed off shapely tanned calves and ankles. A well-toned ass made him take a second look as she leaned over the conveyor belt to grab a black-and-white floral bag.

He swore she didn't wear panties, as he could see no telltale sign of panty lines under the fabric stretched tight over her derriere as she bent over.

She set her bag on the floor next to her and watched the suitcases on the carousel wind their way around as men and women grabbed bags off the conveyor belt on either side of her. His gaze traveled up her body to her narrow waist and the sassy silver chain threaded through the belt loops. He almost smiled at her tenaciousness in wearing so much faux silver.

He could envision tugging on that chain.

He looked higher to a pale-blue, cotton scoop-necked shirt. The Rampant Lion, known also as the Scottish lion, was emblazoned in glittery silver across the front of it and caressed nice-sized breasts. His gaze shot up to her face. Was she a Scottish lass? Had Celtic roots? Or just liked the shirt?

He liked the shirt. Or at least the way the lion dipped and dove over her well-endowed bust.

Quickly, he chastised himself for thinking along those lines. He was here to do a job, and a slip of a she-wolf wasn't going to thwart him from getting started on his mission. He didn't have the reputation of being a steadfast warrior who took no prisoners and vanquished the enemy for nothing. Women never sidetracked him.

Hell, who was he kidding? This time, he couldn't give any really good reason why, but the woman definitely *was* distracting him, fascinating him in a wolfish way.

Jade eyes suddenly caught his studious gaze, and the

woman's naturally soft, rosy lips parted. She must have
really been concentrating on getting her bags to have
missed that a predator like him was so avidly watching
her. Most of their kind were wary but curious about all
things. So caught up in finding her bags, she hadn't been
paying attention to anything else.

Maybe she was so interested in a vacation in paradise that she'd never considered she'd have any trouble.
Probably had never suspected another wolf would catch
her here. Most likely, she was a royal who didn't have
to be too concerned about shifting and was just here to
have some fun. At least, she didn't look like she was on
a business trip. Until he noticed the laptop sitting on the
floor next to her right foot.

Her tanned cheeks flushed beautifully as her gaze
fixed on his. He couldn't remember a time when he'd
made a woman blush from his attentions. He should
have looked away, indicating he had just glimpsed her
and acknowledging that his interest was only that he
appreciated seeing one of his kind on foreign soil. But
damned if his alpha male tendencies didn't roar to the
forefront, and instead he challenged her to break eye
contact first, to prove she wasn't as intrigued with him
as he was with her.

When she didn't immediately look away, he gave
her an appreciative smile, damn his cockiness. He'd
meant to show no interest in her at all, yet Guthrie was
right. When it came to being subtle, Duncan didn't
have the gene.

She still didn't look away—not demurely as a beta
would or with annoyance like an alpha might. But he
didn't think her expression showed challenge as much

as utter disbelief. Without consciously allowing it, his smile widened.

Shit.

He was known to be rather severe so that his clansmen and wolf pack wouldn't think he was weaker than his brothers. And yet here he was, grinning like a fool at a beautiful wolf. He was glad none of them saw him like this. He would *never* have lived it down.

She glanced at the bag over his shoulder. She had to know he hadn't been on the same flight or she would have smelled him. She had to wonder then if he was going to be a problem, the way he watched her. He already had his bag, and should have left the area by now but instead was full-out ogling her.

With the utmost difficulty, he bowed his head a little to her in greeting, turned, and stalked off, entering the line of travelers waiting to have their customs and immigration forms processed. He swore she was boring holes into his back as she watched him walk away. If he cast a look over his shoulder, he knew he'd see her scrutinizing him. Making sure he was leaving her well enough alone.

He hadn't planned on checking to see if she was observing him further once he had settled in line, either. At least that was the plan. But the line was backed up, and he couldn't help himself. He glanced back at the baggage claim area. Sure enough, she was studying him; only this time, she quickly turned away. Caught in the act. Maybe not wanting to show she was worried about him or intrigued. No, not intrigued. Just troubled as to what his intentions were toward her.

He had *no* intentions toward her. So why couldn't he take his eyes off her?

"Sir?" the man behind him said, waving to the line as it had moved up. The man's sharp tone instantly pulled Duncan's attention away from the classy wolf.

He needed to get laid.

Chapter 2

GETTING LAID, YEAH, DUNCAN THOUGHT GRUMPILY. But *not* by a female wolf. They played for keeps. One mating was all it took to be committed to another wolf for life.

He made a concerted effort to keep his eyes forward while he was in the customs line, watching it move slowly toward the customs agent and not looking back to see if the silver-adorned female wolf might be joining him in line soon. He really tried hard. But he couldn't help himself. She was definitely alone, at least for now, and that bothered him.

He had to admit that if she'd been an elderly female, it wouldn't have bothered him in quite the same way.

He glanced back to see if she was anywhere in sight. *No*. Just as well.

Telling himself that didn't help. It bugged him that he didn't know where she'd gone. He considered what might have occurred. Either she'd lost a bag and was not in line yet, or she was waiting until *he* cleared out of the airport.

He finally managed to reach the agent and tell the immigrations officer which hotel he was staying at. Then he was on his way to the car rental area in the center of the terminal.

He had just paid for his car hire and was heading outside when he saw her pulling her bag to the taxi stand where palm fronds danced overhead in the hot, humid breeze.

Passengers were waiting impatiently in line, some scowling, tired from their extended flights and ready to settle into hotels, villas, or other destinations throughout the island. One tapped his foot on the ground; another complained grouchily into a cell phone about the delay.

Duncan's lady wolf looked at the long line of disgruntled passengers waiting for a taxi, and her whole body drooped a little in the heat. Her expression was one of resignation, not annoyance like most of the other passengers. He didn't blame them, though. Patience definitely wasn't one of his virtues, either.

He knew his next move was not a good one. Not that he minded rescuing a damsel in distress on occasion, but he was afraid he'd want much more than that with her, and he couldn't afford it—either emotionally or financially. But he couldn't just leave her there waiting for a taxi when he had a rental car, unless she preferred that to his giving her a ride.

He swung his bag over his shoulder and stalked toward her, immediately catching her eye. Her wilted form quickly stiffened, and her eyes narrowed a little with suspicion.

"I've hired a car," he offered, trying to show he meant her no trouble.

She raised her brows a little. "Scottish?"

"Aye. American?" he asked.

"Yep."

Just like the woman his oldest brother had mated, Julia Wildthorn, werewolf romance author. After the American, Silverman, had stolen their funds, Duncan hadn't thought he'd care for Americans in the flesh, but Ian's mate was definitely the exception.

Passengers waiting for taxis turned to stare at the two of them. Several gave them brilliant smiles. Love in the making in paradise. If only their observers knew what a disaster that could be between wolves if they weren't careful.

One silver-haired man said, "I suppose the offer doesn't stand for a couple of old codgers like us, does it, young man?" Looking as though he was ready for fun in paradise, he was wearing a floral shirt over a well-rounded belly and standing with his wife, who was dressed in a pink blouse that matched her pink hair.

The female wolf's green eyes gleamed with amusement. "You can drop me off at my villa, if you don't mind... if it wouldn't be too much trouble to take them to their rental also," she said to Duncan. A glimmer of a smile perched on her lips, enticing him to take the bait. Her voice, lightly seductive, instantly snagged him to do her bidding.

The woman would be his undoing.

Duncan gave a little huff of a laugh at the way she'd played the game. Did she think the older couple would protect her from the big, bad wolf? He seized the elderly couple's bags and said, "Sure, the more the merrier." *Not*.

But he was determined to take the female wolf to her place last, wherever it was, so that he'd have a moment alone with her and could learn if she was meeting someone or was by herself for the duration of her trip... during which he shouldn't involve himself in any way in her affairs.

"Where are you staying?" he asked the older man.

The man looked back at the female wolf, as if knowing that she needed him to be her knight, and motioned to her. "Where did you need to go?"

The tourist wasn't an alpha, reminding Duncan more of a fatherly type who was trying his best to be chivalrous and protect the young woman. He couldn't help but admire that quality in the older man and wondered if he had grown daughters of his own.

"A private oceanfront villa. That way, north on Seven Mile Beach," she said, waving her arm. "About seven miles from the airport."

"Private villa?" Duncan figured the she-wolf had some money. "And where did you need to go?" he again asked the older couple.

The older man motioned south. "To one of the hotels in that direction on Seven Mile Beach. But you can drop the young lady off first."

"That's all right," Duncan said. "My place is near hers, so it would make things more convenient if I dropped you off first." In truth, he had no idea where his hotel was. Only that it was the only cheap one that had been available on such short notice.

The older man looked at the female wolf as if trying to read her concern. She shrugged. "That'll be fine with me."

Yet Duncan swore she didn't mean it at all.

After dropping the couple off at their hotel with everyone wishing everyone else a fun time on the island, and another look from the older man that said he wished he could go with them to ensure the lady's safety, Duncan left the couple behind.

Driving north, he said to his very quiet wolf passenger,

whose hint of a floral and female wolf fragrance drifted about him, "I'm Duncan MacNeill, and you are?"

"Shelley Campbell."

"Of Scottish descent," he remarked, glancing at the Scottish lion on her shirt, getting another eyeful of the shape of her beautiful breasts, and wondering what they would look like without the Scottish lion guarding them.

"Yes, I am. And you're from there still?"

As if all Highlanders had left the country for some other place. For some reason the notion irked him. "Some of us stayed in Scotland, aye, lass."

A hint of annoyance flashed across her pretty features. "Hmm," she said softly, but he heard the irritation in her voice. "Well, my family members were crofters, replaced by sheep in the old days. *Fuadach nan Gàidheal*, the expulsion of the Gael in the 1700s."

Well, he'd walked right into that one. He cleared his throat. He knew that his ancestors had displaced families in the same way during the Highland Clearances. She wouldn't like that he was from one of the ruling families that had done so. She definitely wouldn't be sympathetic to the fact he and his family were in financial trouble and could once again be on the verge of losing their castle if he didn't get the money back from Silverman.

When he had cleared his throat but didn't say anything, she gave a tiny disgruntled laugh under her breath. "So, does that mean your family was just more fortunate than mine? Followed a clan who took care of them and didn't toss them out on their ears when it looked more profitable to raise sheep instead?" She paused as if anticipating that he would assure her that was all that had happened. When he instead waited for her to ask the question that he dreaded hearing, she forged on. "Or forced their people to work for free to harvest and process kelp along the seacoast?"

He'd thought she was going to ask if he was one of the ruling class. Instead, she seemed to think he was from one of the crofter families either kept on or put to work at some other job.

He took a deep breath, trying not to let her see how much he didn't want to tell her the truth. He'd thought she liked that he was Scottish, maybe because of the Rampant Lion T-shirt she wore. But now she appeared more likely to see him as the enemy.

He'd never thought he'd have to face someone descended from a line of Highlanders who had been ousted from the old country and resented the treatment. It was in the past, after all. He had a hard time seeing how her family could hold a grudge for so many years, particularly once they'd found living wherever they were now more agreeable than where they had lived in Scotland. At least that would be his assumption. He had to remind himself that, as werewolves, they also lived long lives, so she and her family would be less removed from the experience than a human would have been.

Although battle hardened from years of experience, he felt unwilling for the first time to parry with his perceived foe. Mostly because he had nothing to fall back on to make his stance sound heroic.

"Or worse?" she said, her tone growing more wolfishly dark.

He could feel her eyes steady on him, watching for any expression or body language he might reveal. Wolves were good at reading others' reactions. Even though it was an instinctive ability, he didn't like that she was doing it to him. His family had done what they had for the sake of necessity, and he really didn't feel he owed her any explanation.

So why he responded in the way he did was beyond his comprehension. "Depends on what you might think of as worse. But, aye, we managed the lands, and where we could, we kept our crofters on the land. In some cases, we just couldn't."

"Managed the lands," she said, her voice now full of contempt.

So much for wanting to protect the wolf from anyone who might wish her harm. If he'd tried to clear her off the lands in the old days, he suspected he would have had a real battle on his hands. Wrestling with that body of hers did appeal, though. In truth, if her family had worked for his, he would have kept her on the land, very close at hand, rather than sending her away.

"Well?" she challenged, sounding like she was not about to let up on the discussion until she knew just where his family had stood on the issue.

He glanced at her, arched a brow, and said, "Noble class."

Her luscious lips parted, her green eyes wide. Then she quickly looked away and out the passenger window.

"I'm not the laird of the castle. My older brother, Ian, is."

That made her head whip around. "A castle?" Her words were threaded with a mixture of disbelief and interest. "Your brother is a laird?"

"Aye." He shrugged as if it didn't mean anything. He was hoping that it did. That she would not have as much

animosity for them now. "An American movie crew
filmed at Argent recently." He hadn't a clue why he'd
even mentioned that. He had never planned on telling a
living soul that a movie had been filmed at their home.
That they'd had to stoop so low that they permitted a
crowd of humans to take over a wolves' den without a
battle—or much of one, at least.

"Movie." She really didn't ask it as a question, more
of a statement showing incredulity once again.

He wasn't sure whether that was a good thing or not.

When she just stared at him, her brows arched in astonishment, he added, "I was in it."

He also didn't know why he had told her that. Maybe
because he thought Americans were so enamored with
movie stars—not that he had been anything more than
an extra—that she wouldn't still hold a grudge about his
family kicking crofters off the land. For whatever reason, it bothered him that she was troubled by what had
happened. He wished her family had never experienced
the trauma of the move.

Had they not been with a wolf clan? He suspected not
or they most likely wouldn't have been made to move.
Her family had to have hidden what they were from the
clan chief. That couldn't have been easy for them.

"Not a movie star," she said, sounding as though she
was waiting for him to reassure her that he wasn't someone important.

He stifled a snort. If she was only interested in him
now because he was a star… hell, Sean Connery and
Gerard Butler? Neither could wield a sword like he could.

He sat a little taller. "No, I'm not a movie star, although I got to do what I love best." He glanced at her,

smiling a little, expecting her to figure he was wielding a sword in battle and to ask him something about his prowess with a claymore.

"Seducing lasses?" Her brows were arched in question.

For a second, he was so taken aback by her line of reasoning that he didn't say anything. Then he burst out laughing.

She smiled and he felt the tension in the air dissolve. When he could get his fit of laughter under control, he clarified, "Swordplay."

"Oh. *Then* you seduced the lasses," she teased.

He chuckled. "No, only Ian was able to have that kind of a role in the film."

"Ian, the laird. So he has the castle and the lady, and rules the pack."

"Aye."

She settled back against the seat, looked at the directions she had in her lap, and then glanced up and pointed to a white villa topped with a Spanish tile roof, the area surrounded by palm trees. "That's where I'm staying. Paradise Villa." She faced Duncan. "So when does the movie come out?"

"Next year."

"I'll be sure to watch it."

"Any parts I was in may have been taken out if they weren't important enough." He truly hoped they *would* end up on the cutting-room floor.

"Ahh," she said with a placating tone. "With the way you wickedly wielded your claymore, I'm sure they won't cut any of your scenes."

"It truly would be my profoundest wish that they cut them, not keep them," he clarified. He parked the car in front of the villa and turned to face her. "Otherwise women might recognize me and—"

She cast him a small smile. "Chase after you?"

"Och, lass, not likely. But I could see being recognized and hounded. Not chased."

"Sounds very nearly the same to me." She frowned at him. "I wouldn't think a wolf pack would want a movie filmed within its castle walls."

Not wanting to discuss their financial difficulties, he finally kept his mouth shut—she hadn't asked him a question, after all—and took in the serene surroundings, which would be perfect for a wolf on vacation. The place sat on a private oceanfront with pure white sand leading down a gentle incline to the pristine aqua waters. He wished his clan had the money to put him up at a place like this. Then he wondered where that notion had come from. Being a warrior type, he would have been happy to sleep on the ground surrounded by heather in his native Scotland if it meant he'd get the job done quickly.

"You're only a couple of miles from restaurants and shopping, but won't you need a rental car?" he asked, not meaning to sound like he would be at her beck and call for a ride. He really had to keep his mind on his task. On the other hand, he couldn't help asking. Even hoping she might say she needed his further assistance.

"I'll get a taxi if I feel the need."

Disappointed but irritated at himself for feeling that way, he grabbed her bags and helped her to the front door. "You're staying here alone?"

She turned her head just a little, tilting it, the inference from her posture saying it was none of his business.

He hesitated, waiting for her to say who she was staying with because he couldn't believe she'd be here all alone. He knew it wasn't any of his business, but helping her out made him feel she owed it to him to a small degree. If she *was* a she-wolf all by herself, she had to know he only had her safety in mind.

She finally sighed and opened her door, but she stood in the entryway, silently stating she would take it from here, and he wasn't coming in. "Thank you for the ride."

He didn't budge, still wanting to know if she was staying with someone.

Her stance firm, she smiled just a little, knowing damn well he wanted to learn whether she had a roommate who was a male wolf. "I'll get my bags. Thanks so much for helping us out at the airport."

He set the bags down at her feet and inclined his head slightly. "My pleasure, lass. Enjoy your vacation." Then without further adieu, and not intending to prolong this, he turned and meant to return to his rental car, even though it was killing him to end it like this.

He had it in mind that he'd have to run into her from time to time, given how small the island was, and then he'd learn the truth. Just casually, no pressure, maybe catch her walking along the beach or basking in the sun. The picture that drummed up in his mind, seeing an inordinate amount of bare flesh, made his groin tighten with need. He'd do well to stay far away from the siren.

"I can buy you a drink later, if you'd like," Shelley belatedly offered.

He stopped, turned, and studied the slight smile in her expression. He knew he should decline, but damn if he could. He tried to contain his own smile; once it appeared, he was certain it looked wolfish as hell. "I'll pick you up at...?"

"Seven?"

"Seven."

She glanced around the area. "So... you said your place was near mine. Where is it exactly?"

He grinned. "I'll know as soon as I find it."

Her smile matched his—well, maybe not exactly, as he was sure his was much more wolfish and hers was more amused.

With that, he was off, looking for what he suspected would have been the cheapest place to rent on short notice. Once he was settled in, he intended to find out all he could about Silverman and pay the financier a visit as soon as possible so that he could end this charade and return at once to Scotland, money in hand—so to speak.

But what harm would one drink with an American female wolf do?

—w—

Her stomach fluttering with excitement and apprehension, Shelley wondered if she'd lost her mind. No, offering to buy the male wolf a drink was the right thing to do after he'd given her a ride to her villa. He'd been kind and considerate to take the older couple to their hotel also, when he obviously wasn't overly enthusiastic about it. A castle. Sure. Probably the clan was also a wolf pack. The notion was fascinating.

So then, why had his pack opened the castle to an American film crew? She imagined it wasn't something they regularly did.

What was he doing here alone? So far away from

his native soil? He didn't look like the type who would travel on vacation for no good reason. Not alone. He had the look of a warrior about him, all dressed in black—the boots, the shirt, the pants—and his arms were well muscled. She could tell from the way his pants fit that his thighs were, too. He appeared to be a fighter who probably wielded an ancient claymore and would feel best in a battle where he showed off his fighting skills. An excursion to an island paradise seemed out of character for him.

Putting aside thoughts of the sexy wolf, Shelley took her laptop into the dining nook—a small bamboo table with four chairs situated in front of large windows overlooking the crystal-white sand and clear blue waters.

She felt uneasy. The college grant money was supposed to have already been deposited to her account for this trip. She'd already paid for the trip here and used her credit card to cover expenses for the villa that wouldn't be charged to her until the day she checked out, but she could only afford half the cost on her own. Which was a bad sign. What was the delay?

She'd never had this problem before with the funding for research trips. The cost of airfare hadn't been much. But the villa and groceries—food…

Shelley had nothing to eat for dinner and no way to get to the store to buy groceries unless she got a taxi. Given how out of the way the villa was, she figured it would be a while before she could even get one.

She twisted her mouth in thought. Maybe when Duncan returned for her, she could suggest going to a restaurant where they could have the drinks, and she'd order a dinner for herself, too.

When the Internet access popped up on her laptop, she searched her email messages for anything from the college explaining the money delay. Nothing.

Just an email from her best friend, Wendy.

Hey, let me know when you arrive in paradise! I'll be going out with that guy I was telling you about. I'm not about to stew over Roland. TTYL Wendy

She sent an email off to her best friend.

I arrived, but the grant money hasn't been deposited into my bank account yet. I'll let you know when I hear something. Have fun on your date, but don't fall for the guy! Shel

They always told each other the same thing. They could date a human, but not for the long run. Changing a human into one of their kind could create a mountain of trouble. If he had a family, the problems increased exponentially. So a brief acquaintance was fine. Anything longer, and it could become a real mess.

She just hoped that Wendy wasn't going to do anything foolish. The last time she'd broken up with a wolf that she'd really cared about, she'd gotten a little wild. A werewolf out of control was dangerous, both to him or herself and to others.

Not wanting to borrow trouble, Shelley intended to unpack her bags and put her clothes away. She was excited about studying the plant life here and taking her research back to the university in west Texas for the classes she'd be teaching later next year. She could hardly wait to get started in the morning. What if she could learn of a plant in the ancient forest that could stabilize a newly turned wolf's urge to shift during the full moon? Anytime she could visit new locations and search for such a remedy, she made the best of the opportunity. Of course, the college would never know the true interest behind all her research or why she'd become a botanist in the first place.

In some folklore, wolfsbane could be used to stop the shift. She knew this wasn't true because she'd tested it on a friend of Wendy's who was a newly turned wolf. But only under very controlled circumstances because the plant could kill a wolf or a person or a werewolf. Shelley had always wondered if a *lupus garou* could ingest a *different* plant that could actually stop the shift or bring it on if the person needed to turn into the wolf and couldn't otherwise.

Wouldn't that benefit all of her kind?

A car drove by the villa and she thought again of Duncan and his cocky alpha maleness—the way he had held his head high, challenged her with his gaze, and showed how he was intrigued with her. She envisioned what he'd look like fighting in the movie's mock battles—bare chested, wearing a kilt, wielding a claymore, and vanquishing an enemy fighter with lesser skills or endurance. How would he act in his native Scotland? Superior because he was a laird's brother? Because he lived in a grand castle?

She envisioned Scottish lasses hanging on his every word, hoping for him to act chivalrous with them like he'd done with her. She suspected that if any of the women recognized him in the movie, he'd have his hands full of female admirers chasing and hounding him for more than just his autograph.

He was cute in a dark, sexy way. She loved that he'd driven the older couple to their hotel; anything to get the chance to take her to her villa. She'd been tickled by his insistence that he was staying at a place near hers, so it would be more convenient for him to drop her off last, and then his admission that he didn't even know where his hotel was located. Men rarely did that. Often they were either boorishly brazen and turned her off, or they were too beta to make the effort to get to know her.

Fingers clicking over the keyboard of her laptop, she did an Internet search for Argent Castle. All she found was a small note concerning a castle that was not open to the public and a brief news message that it had been the site of a recent movie project. But there was no picture—it could be small and of little or no consequence, really—and no website, address, or any other information on how to get hold of anyone there. And the castle was not included among any of the important sites of ancient heritage.

Ian MacNeill was laird, and no one else was mentioned. Which confirmed what she'd suspected. His people didn't regularly open the castle to visitors. So why did they agree to do a filming? Even more surprising, why was Duncan in the movie? He didn't seem to have been thrilled with the prospect. She imagined once he had to fight, he'd gotten into the battle scenes with warrior-like enthusiasm. Had Ian also been in the film? She doubted it. He was the laird and would have been above such a thing.

But she'd sure love to see Duncan fighting.

Maybe if she played her cards right, she could plan a tour of gardens in Scotland and stay at a real castle—Argent Castle—compliments of Duncan, and then use what she learned about the botanical displays to show off in her college curriculum. And see if the plant she was looking for might exist in Scotland.

She shook her head at herself. He'd think she was interested in him just because his clan had a castle. Right. Her mother had always warned her about wolves like him. Shelley sensed he had a darker purpose here, and if he could, he'd be wielding a sword, ready to strike down his enemy. He was someone to stay far away from.

So why was she looking again at the clock on her computer? And hoping that seven would come in record time.

Chapter 3

WHEN DUNCAN ARRIVED AT THE HOTEL ON THE LEE-
ward side of the island, he was instantly annoyed to see
ten people waiting in line at the check-in counter to reg-
ister for rooms. Probably all those waiting were from the
airport, and if he hadn't taken the older couple to their
hotel first, he would have been way ahead of most of
these people. Shelley was a different story. Taking her
to her villa had been necessary, to his way of thinking.

He attempted not to tap his foot too much and noticed
a man standing nearby who was wearing a dark gray suit
and had a briefcase chained to his wrist. Duncan wondered if the man was a minion carrying illegal money or
documents to one of the island's banks, which again made
him think of Silverman. Duncan gave the man a steely-
eyed glower. What if he worked for Silverman? The man
with the briefcase held Duncan's glower for a moment, as
if to say he wouldn't be intimidated. Then, unable to hold
the stare, the man shifted his gaze to the lobby.

Beta.

Duncan finally reached the clerk, who was trying to
look upbeat although his rumpled floral shirt and fraz-
zled expression told another story. "You have a room for
me, Duncan MacNeill. My brother, Guthrie MacNeill,
booked the room." He sounded a wee bit harsher than
he'd planned, but he needed to get on with business,
and waiting in line to get his room hadn't figured into

his schedule. Not that a drink with Shelley Campbell did, either.

The man typed away at a computer, then typed some more, then some more. Duncan was getting a bad feeling about this. The clerk finally shook his head and motioned to the units. "No. No room for you. We're booked solid for two months. We don't overbook. Your brother must have made a mistake."

Duncan wondered if in Guthrie's attempt to get the cheapest place available, he'd erred in making reservations for this hotel. Did they often double-book in case tourists didn't show? Or was the hotel's online registration just not adequate in handling reservations? Even so, Duncan didn't trust that the man was right.

"*Look. Again.*" Duncan's voice was so dangerously ominous that the man quickly looked back at his computer screen.

But no matter how ferociously Duncan scowled at the clerk, and no matter how much the man tapped away at the keyboard, he wouldn't budge about the reservations.

"No, sir, nothing for any MacNeill. I'm sorry. If I had a room, I'd give it to you."

The clerk kept his shoulders and posture straight, stared Duncan in the eye, and attempted to look as though he was in charge. But his eyes flicked to the others waiting in line, his jaw clenched and unclenched, and a tiny bead of sweat and then two more appeared on his forehead. Duncan was certain that if the clerk could have found a room, any room, he would have offered it to him.

Scowling, Duncan said in a deep, gruff voice, "My brother would not have made the mistake." He hefted his bag over his shoulder and turned. Everyone immediately moved out of his path as if he were a typhoon intent on their destruction as he made his way outside.

Trying to rein in his irritation but not succeeding, Duncan threw his bag into the rental car and drove to where hotels lined the beach. Tons of places were situated on the beaches—large hotels, family-type dwellings, small hotels. Surely one of them would have a vacancy.

He queried each of them systematically, hearing the same thing over and over: the rooms are all rented. It's the beginning of the tourist season, don't you know? He tried really hard not to look intimidating, but by the last few, he imagined he looked damned dangerous. He finally gave up and went into a bar to get a whiskey. That would likely cost him a fortune, and he had nowhere to sleep the night. Except for the backseat of the compact rental car.

He wondered if Shelley had a roommate. If not, was there any room for him? Even if it was just one night of sleeping on a sofa in the living room. It had to be less cramped than the backseat of the rental car. If she had a roommate that was another she-wolf, she might be agreeable to letting Duncan stay, if he approached them with enough finesse. Having finesse was not one of his strong suits, though.

Seemed the tables were turned. Now Shelley was the crofter descendant with the castle, and he was a member of a noble family without a home.

The bar was dark and small, a total of ten tables surrounded by four chairs apiece, the walls of the place decorated in seafaring stuff—a swordfish, fishnets, a harpoon, colorful glass balls, conch shells, and a mural of the sea, which caught his eye with its voluptuous mermaids lounging on mossy rocks. Their silvery-green tails shimmered in the sunlight, waves breaking across the weather-beaten stones. One mermaid reminded him of Shelley, her richly auburn hair curled over her shoulders, her eyes green and staring straight at him, luring him, and with a mouth that was just as appealing as Shelley's. He could envision Shelley lying on a rock, her breasts bare, her lips damned kissable, her eyes enticing him to join her.

Dragging his gaze from the wall, he noticed a young, dark-haired woman in a sexy red dress seated alone at a table. She looked even glummer than he felt, if that was possible. She was staring at a blue drink with a little umbrella in it, her fingers stroking up and down the slender stem. Misery likes company, aye?

He paid the bartender the exorbitant price, grabbed his whiskey, and sauntered over to the table. "Want some company, lass?"

She glanced up at him and stared with wide, dark-brown eyes. Just stared. As if she knew he was a wolf under the guise of being human. That he had easily had dispatched many men in his youth. He wasn't planning on picking her up, but he might look a little menacing, he belatedly thought.

She gave a soft little snort, looked around the joint, saw all the empty tables, looked back at him, still without smiling, and motioned to the seat opposite. "Feel free to have a seat."

Another American, he thought, only she was human.

She looked back down at the table, and he realized she was reading a text message on a cell phone. She took a deep breath and tucked the phone away in her purse.

He sat, accidentally bumped his knees against hers because the table was so small, and quickly apologized. He definitely wasn't planning to bed the appealing wench. When he looked at her, he thought of Shelley, the way she'd eyed him with surprise, smiled at him, laughed—and yet measured him also—for his family's role in the crofters' fates.

But Shelley was a wolf. So they already had a connection of sorts. That's who he craved bedding, damn it.

"No need to apologize about bumping into me," the woman said, sounding resigned. "You're big and the table's small."

Big. Maybe that was what had bothered her about him as he'd towered over her at first.

"Trouble?" he asked, not intending to burden her with his own problems.

He figured he'd sleep in the car and try to get a plane back to Scotland early the next night, assuming they had a flight leaving then, *if* he couldn't find a place to stay. He could at least spend the day searching for a way to get to Silverman before then. With any luck, more than he was already having, he'd arrange a meeting and make him pay. Then what Duncan wanted to do was drop Silverman in the middle of the ocean to swim with the real sharks and see how much fun that was. But he didn't figure he'd get that lucky.

If he could have the week to wring the money out of Silverman, Duncan figured he'd have a chance. He just had to find some accommodations.

"You might say that I'm having a time of it," she said. "But..." She shrugged. "You know the old saying— when it seems too good to be true, it probably is?"

"Aye, I can relate to that." He leaned back in his seat and figured he'd tell her some of his own troubles. Maybe she knew of a place he could stay off the beaten path. "My brother rented a room for me, and when I arrived, I found the place booked. Solid. For two months."

Her dark brown eyes widened a bit. "How awful."

"Aye. I've checked at the different hotels, but I keep getting the same response. 'Tis the season, you know."

"Oh. What will you do?"

"Get a return flight tomorrow if I can't find a place to stay."

"Oh." She took a sip of her drink. "What are you doing here? Just here for a vacation?"

"Aye, a vacation. And you?"

"I was meeting my boyfriend. Now he's not able to come. At least he's got a rich boss, and my boyfriend can afford to pay for my trips here from Miami and the hotel where I'm staying. Three times I've made this trip to the islands and every time he can't make it."

Sounded like a brush-off to Duncan.

"It's that bigwig Silverman he works for that's all the trouble," she added, her eyes narrowed and lips pursed in irritation. "He had another job for him in the States, and so Kenneth is delayed again."

"Silverman?" Duncan tried to keep his tone of voice light, but she looked harder at him when she heard the telltale sound of anger.

"You're not a cop, are you? Feds or something?" But then she quickly amended what she'd said as if she'd spoken about something she shouldn't have. "Not that *Silverton's* done anything wrong. You just... well..." She didn't say anything more, looked a little red in the face, and began studying her drink as if she wished she could crawl into it.

Duncan made a disgruntled sound. "Hardly." He took a swig of his whiskey, cursing himself for his reaction to the name "Silverman" and tried his damnedest to sound unconcerned. "I just wondered what your boyfriend did for his boss that he couldn't make it here to see you. Seems to me that he's a fool to stand up a bonny lass like you. Especially since he's done it more than once."

He knew he was reaching, but he'd hoped she'd buy his line. He noticed she'd changed Salisbury Silverman's name quickly to *Silverton*, trying to cover up that mistake also. Was that the name he was using on the island, or some other, and "Silverton" had been the quickest one she could pull out of the air? He assumed Silverman wouldn't use a name that similar to his real name.

Continuing to look wary, she stood. "Have a nice flight back."

The one lead he might have had to learn more about Silverman, and Duncan had already blown it. Yeah, "subtle" was not his middle name.

He waited until she left the dark bar. The windows were amber glass, so he couldn't see her through them to observe where she was going. When he thought she'd had sufficient time to get into a car, he headed outside, hoping to follow her and find where she ended up for the night. If she did make contact with the boyfriend, Duncan could then follow him and see if this Kenneth might be a way to learn anything more about Silverman himself.

But as soon as Duncan walked outside, he found the woman standing under the red-and-white striped awning, taking a smoke.

He did not want to appear to be interested in her, but he needed to learn more about her boyfriend and Silverman. He nodded to her and walked down the street. He didn't want her to know about his rental car, in case she intended to tell her boyfriend that Duncan might be looking for Silverman and to keep an eye out for his vehicle.

Seeing a gift shop full of swimwear, sunglasses, floral dresses, shirts, and island-crafted jewelry, Duncan pushed aside the door and entered. He felt like a warrior in a floral shop. Then he noticed a rack of men's swimsuits that weren't covered in gaudy tropical flowers, making him feel not quite so out of place.

Nearly blending in with the merchandise, a college-age clerk was wearing a flowery blouse and seated behind a white laminate counter. She gave him an appreciative smile.

"Anything in particular you're looking for?" she asked, her voice hopeful, and he figured she assumed he was searching for something for his ladylove. Certainly, she couldn't believe he was shopping for anything for himself in here.

He shook his head and looked over the jewelry. Or at least pretended to. He suspected the woman smoking at the bar would be watching to see him exit the shop and where he went next.

He really didn't have time for this. Then he had an idea. "I had reservations at a hotel, but when I arrived, they weren't any good. Do you have any idea about someplace I might be able to stay that isn't as well advertised? I don't need to stay on the beach."

She looked him over as if she thought she might ask him to stay with her, then sighed and shook her head, most likely coming to her senses. "Sorry. All I can say is just keep checking the resorts."

"Thanks." But no thanks. Maybe if he bought a bunch of merchandise, she might change her tune.

He could see trying to explain to Ian why he had spent a fortune on jewelry, floral garments, and perfumes just so he could get a free place to stay. It would be cheaper than paying for a week of lodging. On the other hand, he could see himself buying all that junk and the clerk not offering to take him in.

He stalked back out of the store and saw the woman from the bar still smoking her cigarette, watching the shop just like he thought she might. He wasn't waiting all night to see where she might go or to conceal that the rental car sitting in the lot was his. He headed for the car, got in, and tried again to locate a place to stay. After a good long while, he glanced at his watch, swore when he saw it was 8:30—an hour and a half past when he was supposed to pick up Shelley and have a drink—and headed back to her villa.

He was already in a foul mood over the reservation mix-up, losing the only lead he had for Silverman that might have given him some inside knowledge, finding no other place to stay, and now standing up Shelley. He hoped she wouldn't be too sore, and he hoped he could curb the annoyance he was feeling enough to enjoy a drink with her.

When he finally arrived at Shelley's villa, he found the place dark—not a good sign. Knocking at the door and ringing the bell didn't get any response.

He cursed aloud this time. He still had it in mind to ask if he might stay the night, just the night, on the couch if she would allow it. She couldn't have gone to bed this early. At least, he didn't think she would have. She didn't have a car, so he didn't think she'd gone out.

He didn't smell any sign of any other wolves or strictly humans having arrived, so he was sure she hadn't had any recent company.

He called out, "Shelley, it's me. Duncan MacNeill. Are you all right?"

He didn't believe for one moment that she intended to ignore his arrival just because he was an hour and a half late. Not after he'd gone out of his way to be chivalrous to her earlier, and not without learning why he was so late in arriving.

Able to see with his wolf's night vision, he sniffed the air for anything that would warn him she'd been in trouble, trying to sense another wolf, female or male, or another male visitor. Nothing. But she wouldn't, couldn't be ignoring him.

He paced across the front porch, went around the back, and looked at the white sandy beach. It was void of people, with no one swimming in the dark water, either. Unless she went for a walk along the beach and was way out of sight.

He peered at all the windows, seeing no movement or lights in any of the rooms. To his way of thinking, she was alone, defenseless, and vulnerable, and he had to ensure she was either not at home or was all right. If nothing else, he had to explain why he was so late in arriving.

He knocked again. "Shelley, if you're in there, let me know. Otherwise I'm going to assume the worst."

When she didn't come to the door and let him in or

acknowledge she was there, he pulled out his handy lock picks—standard *lupus garou* issue, unlocked the door, and peered into the dark villa.

He took a couple of steps into the room, looking for signs of a struggle, but saw nothing out of place and shut the door. "Shelley? It's me, Duncan. We had a date to have a drink, but I had trouble—"

He stopped speaking abruptly as he caught a flash of fur. Then turning, he saw a wolf racing toward his left flank, eyes glowing green in the reflection of the front porch light, which was shining in through the living room window where the curtain was slightly parted. Her teeth weren't bared as she leapt at him. Which meant she wasn't truly angry with him or wanting to fight. It was more a territorial show, he thought. This was her place and he had intruded, despite warning her that he would to ensure she was all right.

He understood and welcomed her display of defending her territorial rights.

She was smaller than a male wolf, but the impact of her body and his unpreparedness to handle her jump knocked him back.

He smiled darkly as he regained his equilibrium and readied himself for another attack as she circled around and faced him again. Having wrestled with his brothers and cousins over the years, sometimes as wolves, sometimes as humans, and sometimes like this—human to wolf—he was game. He had to admit he'd never tackled a female wolf in such a manner.

The newness was not only refreshing but momentarily took his mind off his other troubles.

"I'm late, and I apologize, but—"

Her tail waved like a dog pleased to see its master—instinctively wanting to play. Her gaze was on his, watching his reaction, and he knew she was calculating her next move and his, too.

Adrenaline and testosterone raced through his blood, preparing him for the mock fight. When she lunged this time with no warning, he seized the ruff of her neck in a natural reaction to protect himself, and she exposed her teeth, an instinctive response in play or battle. He held on as she snapped and snarled, twisting her head to free herself from his iron grip. Still, she didn't try to bite him, which told him she was only pretend fighting, showing her irritation in a wolf's way for standing her up and breaking into her place without permission.

With a strong jerk of her head, she broke free of his titan grip, jumped aside, and again lunged. Not expecting her attack to follow so rapidly after the first, figuring she'd pause to determine her next strategy, he fell back, tripped over a suitcase, and landed on his back.

He swore she would have been laughing her head off if she could as a wolf. She quickly stood on his belly, triumphant, panting, chest heaving, looking down at him with a proud expression, eyes gleaming, and almost a smile. Yeah, she was damned amused. He'd been bested by a she-wolf and one flowery suitcase.

A beautiful she-wolf at that, with dark red-brown fur covering most of her body and the top half of her muzzle, pale cream underneath, black-tipped ears and tail, and sharp green eyes.

He smiled. He could have wrestled with her further, but he was afraid that, in his exuberance, he might injure her by accident. Besides, he wanted to make it right with her about his being late and breaking into her villa without her permission. She had to realize he had only done so out of concern for her.

"You win." He tried to look as without guilt as he could. None of his people would accuse of him of having that trait, either. Not even when one of his brothers had done something wrong and Duncan had been completely blameless of the infraction. He just didn't have the knack to ever look—*innocent*. "I apologize for arriving at your place late."

She closed her mouth, staring at him with her front paws still standing on his chest, waiting for an explanation.

"My room wasn't available." He sighed. Hell, might as well tell the truth. "I mean to say I don't have a place to stay. The hotel was overbooked. So I've been all over the blasted island, trying to find another place to stay. None of the other places I checked have accommodations. I'd planned to sleep in the car tonight, then take care of business and leave for Scotland tomorrow night if I couldn't find some place to stay in the meantime."

She didn't move, as if considering his words and what she might do.

"I worried something had happened to you."

That's when she finally stepped off him and studied him for a moment more, judging his sincerity as he sat up. She turned and headed into what he suspected was a bedroom, her tail whipping back and forth. He took a deep breath of the sexually enticing smell of female wolf. Their brief physical encounter had definitely turned her on, not that wrestling with her hadn't done a job on his libido, too.

He got up off the floor, and she suddenly reappeared

in the doorway with just a long T-shirt clutched against her breasts and hanging barely to mid-thigh to cover her torso before she shut the door.

He stared at the door that she'd disappeared behind, wanting to see the rest of her long tanned legs, her breasts, and hell, the rest of her.

Trying to get his mind off the tantalizing nearly naked sight of her imprinted on his brain, he finally noted the decor. Everything was light and airy, nothing like Argent Castle in Scotland. All the fabrics were covered in flowers—the sofas, the chairs, the seats at the kitchen table. All the tables were light bamboo, and the curtains over the French patio doors were also floral.

On the kitchen table her laptop sat open, the screen saver scrolling across it showing myriad wolf pictures in woodsy settings, whether wolf-wolves or werewolves he couldn't decipher. What had she been looking at? Business? Emails? Something else? He wasn't going to look, yet he was dying to, which was inherently part of a wolf's curious nature. He wanted to know everything he could about her.

Before he could get himself into hot water by checking out her laptop, she walked out of the bedroom dressed in the clothes he'd seen her wearing previously, minus the silver sandals.

"You have whiskey on your breath," she said, in an accusing tone, her arms folded.

That didn't look good. Either she thought he was a real drinker and had been in a bar all that time, or that he'd lied about his lack of accommodations.

"After looking for places for an hour, I stopped at a bar, aye, lass. Sometimes a whiskey improves the disposition."

She smiled slightly at his comment. "I imagine you looked perfectly lethal to the clerks at every hotel you chanced to query."

"Aye, I did." He liked that about her. That she wasn't afraid of him, even if he might look perfectly lethal.

"You didn't have to break into the place," she said, still sounding peeved.

"I worried about you."

Her head tilted to the side, she gave him a look that said she didn't believe him.

He conceded, "I couldn't believe you'd hold my being late against me, so I began conjuring up all kinds of trouble you might have gotten into."

"Okay," she said, sounding like she did buy that to an extent, or at least wanted to. "So you were a warrior coming to my rescue." She smiled a little, gloating over having knocked the warrior flat on his back with one good wolf lunge and a well-placed flowery bag. "You really don't have a place to stay?"

He felt hopeful for the first time tonight. "Nay. My brother made the reservation, and when I arrived, the clerk said none were available."

Brow wrinkled, she took a deep breath. "Why are you here?"

"You offered to buy me a drink."

"No. I mean, are you here on vacation? Business? Why are you here on the island? You don't appear to be the type who would come here alone on vacation."

He hadn't expected that question, and he was certain if he told her what he planned to do, she wouldn't care for it one wee bit.

"You're right. I have business. Banking business."

She frowned a little at that, then nodded. "I have a proposition for you, since I have a bit of a situation myself."

"Aye?"

"You can stay here with me… *if* you don't cause any trouble."

He wanted to remind her that she was the one who'd attacked him, not the other way around. To his way of thinking, she was the cause of any trouble. Good thing they hadn't damaged the furniture in the rental, and the villa was isolated so no one would have known about their mock fight. All he intended to do was make this his base of operations. Beyond that, he'd be out trying to find a way to get the clan's money back.

"What about your roommate?" he asked, hoping Shelley didn't have one and that he could stay there for the entire week without any problem.

"I got an email from the college that was paying my grant. Seems someone has absconded with a whole lot of the college's money. My grant money isn't coming. I'm a college professor, and I can't afford the villa on my own. I've saved enough money to take some excursions, but paying for the rest of the villa is a little beyond my means. I'll keep the master bedroom suite on the first floor. You can have the guest bedroom with the two twin beds on the second floor."

"Twin beds," he said, figuring his feet would hang off the end of the bed, even though he had to remind himself that his only other alternative was sleeping crunched up in a compact car. Beyond that he'd been hoping for at least a couch.

"Yes. If you'll pay half price."

"Seems to me if I pay half…"

She gave him a pointed look. "I don't have to make the offer at all. Since you seem to be without a castle at the moment…"

She *was* going to hold the grudge about the way the chiefs had cleared the crofters from their lands in the old days.

"How much is half?" he asked.

"You're a true Scot, I see."

He ignored the jibe, not wanting her to know how poor his people were, but also he wouldn't have ever agreed to a price without knowing what it was.

She sighed. "Five thousand."

His mouth gaped. "Per day?"

She gave a little laugh, and if it hadn't been at his expense, he would have loved hearing the melodic sound of it. "Per week."

That wasn't much better than per day. "Each?" He hoped she meant that was the total.

"Ah, yes, each of us has to pay $5,000. I had to have a villa where I would be isolated from others—because of my wolfish nature, of course."

He scrubbed one hand over his face, which he noted was getting more whiskery by the moment. "If you have a grant covering part of your cost, and I'm getting the twin bed…"

"Two twin beds." She stood firm. "You pay half or…"

"Or? You'll be stuck for the whole ten grand," he countered. If he paid $5,000 to stay in the villa, Ian would surely kick him out of the clan.

She chewed on her bottom lip, her eyes narrowed as she focused on him, both of them at a standstill.

"Think, lass, I have a rental car that I've paid for, and as long as I'm not taking care of business—"

"Banking," she said, sounding skeptical.

"Aye, then I could take you where you'd like to go."

"The Mastic Reserve," she said.

"The what?"

"It's an ancient dry forest."

"Dry forest." He envisioned a petrified forest or a deciduous one with no leaves in the dead of winter, but in the tropics, he couldn't imagine such a thing.

"Yes, the reserve has examples of a deciduous semi-tropical dry forest. I want to see it, and take notes and pictures. I teach botany at West Texas A&M, so I'm taking the information to my classes when I start back the fall semester next year. Most of the West Indies have had substantial deforestation, so this is one of the last holdouts that has existed, growing and changing for two million years! You must appreciate ancient things if you live in a castle."

"Dry forest." He did feel the same way about the ancient Caledonian Forest in Scotland. He just hadn't thought of her as a plant kind of person. "Sure. I can drop you off to check out the trees."

"That would work. Tours last two and a half to three hours, but I plan to stay for longer than that to take notes." She hesitated, then added, "If you're to stay with me, it'll cost five thousand dollars."

He couldn't believe she wasn't budging on the price. With her agreement to his taxiing her around the island, he'd thought she'd cut him some slack. Now he was surprised she hadn't tacked on additional charges!

When he didn't respond quickly, she added, "You

were in a movie. Had it filmed at your castle, even. Own a castle, for heaven's sake. Are you trying to tell me that you're the youngest son and your laird brother doesn't support you like he should? You obviously have money or you wouldn't be here doing banking business."

He had never intended to tell the woman what his real business was here. That a wolf had financially taken advantage of his wolf pack, which was downright embarrassing. They had no intention of telling the world.

But he didn't feel he had any other choice. "All right. The truth is that a man stole most of my clan's savings, and I'm here to track him down and get it back."

Her eyes widened. "Your money was stolen?" She was frowning now and seemed uneasy. "How do you plan to get the money back?"

"Any way that I can. He's a wolf."

Her mouth parted in surprise—that sweet mouth that he was wanting more and more to kiss.

But she was still waiting for him to explain his family's predicament, and she wasn't thinking of kisses. "We didn't know it at the time since all the financial transactions were done either through correspondence or phone conversations and wire transfers." He let out his breath, not sure how she'd feel about what he was telling her.

"We deal with our kind any way we have to. I have to admit, my brother, Guthrie, who got us into this financial mess in the first place, had been adamant that I not spend a lot of time or money on this effort. For one thing, he doesn't believe I'd get the money out of one of those secured banks no matter how hard I try. Worse, nearly six hundred banks or trust companies are located in the Cayman Islands."

"Wow," Shelley said. "You're kidding."

"Nay. Not only that, but forty-three of fifty of the world's largest banks are here."

"I would never have imagined."

With only about 56,000 residents on the island, the size of the banking industry was mind-boggling. Especially to Duncan because money and numbers were not his strong suit. Ownership was, though. What was his family's would remain his family's.

"Even though the banks subscribe to anti-laundering money regulations to avoid having proceeds from serious crimes deposited in accounts here, I assume Salisbury Silverman has enough connections he can still make the system work for himself. And he does have a home here. Guthrie had learned that foreign investment in property or homes was perfectly legal."

Her lips were parted in an inviting way, but her brow was furrowed with concern. "Salisbury Silverman? He's been on the news everywhere. He's stolen from major players in several countries." She swallowed hard. "Couldn't it be dangerous? To confront him?"

"Aye. For him."

She looked as though she was fighting a smile as she sat down on one of the floral couches. "I knew when I saw you that you couldn't be here for fun and games. Will you find him before you leave, do you think?"

"I know where his estate is located. I just have to find a way to get to him. I don't have time not to. We can't afford for me to fly all over the world trying to catch up to this bastard."

"What do you do back home? Do you have training in taking down criminals?"

"I am a Highland warrior."

Her lips parted again, then she shook her head, sounding sarcastic when she responded. "I'm sure that will help you with this case."

"If airport officials had allowed me to carry my sword on the plane, I would have ensured that the criminal got my point." He smiled a little at his dark humor.

She didn't smile but continued to frown at him. "You're going to be trouble, aren't you?"

"I won't get you involved in this. I'll just stay here as a stopping-off point, take care of my business, and drive you wherever you want to go to take care of yours when you need me to."

"You say he's a wolf?"

"Aye, an American gray wolf."

The look on her face said it all. She just knew that Duncan was going to be real trouble and she'd regret the day she'd met him.

He attempted a smile that would convince her he was safe and that she had no worries where he was concerned.

She didn't look like she believed it.

Chapter 4

"DO YOU STILL WANT TO GO OUT FOR A DRINK?" Duncan asked Shelley.

Feeling sorry for him and his clan, she was ready to reverse herself on making him pay the $5,000 rent on the villa. Even though she was irritated that he had a castle and was from a family of Scots who had kept their lands while kicking out their kinsmen, she couldn't see using that as a reason to tell him he couldn't stay at the villa. Her mother or uncles might feel a whole lot differently about Duncan's family's situation. She suspected they'd tell him to take a flying leap.

But he *was* a fellow wolf in need, and she didn't like the fact that an *American* wolf had stolen his clan's money.

Besides, she would be out *all* the money if she didn't get him to pay at least $5,000.

"Do you still want me to pay for your drink?" she asked.

He had the balls to look chagrined, and she shook her head. "I'm going for a swim in the ocean. We can share cell phone numbers, and tomorrow you can drop me off at the forest reserve. I'll call you when I'm ready to be picked up."

As far as she was concerned, this was strictly a business proposition. He was subletting the place. End of story. Even if he was one damned sexy hunk of a wolf roommate. Mostly *because* he was one damned sexy hunk of a wolf roommate.

"I meant to buy your drink to thank you for allowing me to stay here, not the other way around, Shelley. And I'll pay the $5,000."

Her mouth gaped, but she needed the money so she quickly snapped her mouth shut.

She got the distinct impression that she'd cut him to the quick and he was displeased about it. She hadn't meant to; her knee-jerk reaction had been due to being rather frugal herself and feeling a little put-out about her own financial woes. But she hadn't expected him to cough up the rest of the money. She bit her tongue when she wanted to ask if he was sure he could afford it.

"But more importantly, nighttime is shark feeding time," he said, looking like he thought the idea of her swimming in the ocean at this time of night was crazy. Apparently the issue of payment for the villa had been settled.

She stared at him in disbelief. "It's an island paradise. The ocean is there to swim in. Day or night."

"Right, and sharks feed more at night. It's a proven fact."

She rolled her eyes, yet she realized that as insistent as he was, he really was afraid for her, so she backed off and offered some of what she'd learned to ease his mind.

"They've got blacktip reef sharks off the east end and at The Maze. But mostly just divers go there and the sharks circle them. Maybe looking for food because the divers used to feed them there until the government outlawed the practice. Nurse sharks were seen on the west and north dive locations. Hammerheads come into the shallows to eat stingrays on the north end. Generally, nurse sharks are in the shallower areas. They don't bite unless you're dumb enough to grab a tail or try to feed one by hand."

He didn't look convinced.

She smiled, reached over, patted his hard chest, and wished he'd go swimming with her so he could protect her from all the sharks. He'd look damned hot in a pair of swim trunks. Unless he hadn't brought any because he was here strictly on business. Did Highland wolves even wear swimsuits? It was too cold for them in Scotland, and she didn't imagine that his castle had an indoor swimming pool.

Did he even know how to swim? Well, sure. He was a wolf.

"I'll be fine. See you in the morning." She attempted to keep any hint of disappointment out of her voice. Swimming alone wasn't all that much fun, but she wanted to work off some of the tension she was feeling over the problem with the grant money, or lack of it.

Before she totally lost her mind and begged him to protect her from all the big, bad man- and woman-eating sharks, or technically in her case, she-wolf-eating sharks, she seized the small floral bag she'd left in the living room. Without another word, she entered her master bedroom and shut the door. Sure that he wasn't going to join her, she fished out her bikini rather than a one-piece, dressed, grabbed her phone and a beach towel featuring a beautiful gray wolf with intense amber eyes, and opened the bedroom door.

Duncan was upstairs in the guest room, talking on the phone and explaining how he had to pay so much more for a room because the reserved hotel room hadn't been available. He sounded angry, and she knew then that he really

couldn't have afforded a lot more. Maybe not even that
much. She paused, wondering if he'd explain he was staying with a she-wolf or say anything more about his plans
concerning the man who had stolen his clan's money.

"One lead," he was saying. "Yeah, a woman whose
boyfriend works for Silverman. The boyfriend was supposed to meet her here, but he said he couldn't come
because Silverman still had another job for him in the
States. The woman wasn't a wolf. I don't know if her
boyfriend is or not. But I lost the trail."

Shelley knew she shouldn't eavesdrop, but she
couldn't help herself. She was curious how he'd manage what he planned to do regarding the crook. Surely,
Duncan couldn't be thinking of breaking into a bank.
Did he even know which bank held the man's accounts?
She was sure Silverman wouldn't give Duncan a written
invitation to his estate.

Her darned phone jingled in her hand, nearly giving
her a stroke. Duncan's conversation suddenly ceased.
His footfalls neared the door to his room, and the door
shut with a clunk.

Caught eavesdropping, sort of. Thankfully, he hadn't
actually seen her, but he knew where she'd been standing because of her traitorous phone and that she'd been
close enough to hear his end of the conversation.

She checked the caller ID on her phone and saw that
her girlfriend Wendy was calling. "Are you with your
date?" Shelley asked, not wanting to explain that she
had found a roommate who was a hot and sexy Highland
wolf, which she knew would concern Wendy. It would
have concerned her if their roles had been reversed.

"The guy's fun but not a wolf."

"I thought for now that would be a good thing," Shelley said.

Wendy sighed heavily over the phone. "Maybe I'm rushing things a bit."

"I think so. Too bad you couldn't have come with me and gotten away from it all."

"You know me. Too much to do, work-wise." Wendy let out her breath again. "How can you afford this without the grant money?" Then after a pause, she said, "I'm sending you the whole $5,000. You can't afford to get stuck with that much of an expense, and I have the loose change to do it."

Wendy was an heiress with tons of money. Her parents had owned a baby-food factory in Canada and then diversified, and she'd inherited the whole lot. Shelley wasn't about to ask Wendy for the money since she'd always managed to come up with the funds to go on trips with her friend when she could afford to and had the time. For once, Shelley had the time, but only because of taking off two semesters from teaching. She hadn't gone on vacation in a couple of years and had really saved for this, but she still meant to be frugal.

"It's okay. I got a surprise roommate." Shelley opened the back door, walked out, and then shut the door and crossed the patio to the sandy beach.

She had to tell Wendy about Duncan, and Shelley was sure her friend wasn't going to approve.

Too bad Wendy couldn't have come along. Shelley figured she and Wendy could have shared the twin beds, and Duncan could have had the master bedroom. His paying for half of the rent would help with expenses, and having two she-wolves working as a unified force against one Highland hunk would help ensure that she kept this strictly a business proposition.

"I don't understand what happened with the grant money," Shelley said, avoiding any mention of Duncan for the moment.

"A guy named Salisbury Silverman happened," Wendy said. "He wasn't just after your grant, but several others, too. He also got into money set aside for salaries. You know… the swindler who stole funds from so many individuals and corporations? It was in the local newspaper, only I didn't read it until I got home from work just now."

"Salisbury Silverman?" Shelley said, not believing that he was the same crook Duncan was after and that she'd been hearing so much about. How could the man be a wolf and risk such exposure?

The sun had set a couple of hours earlier, and the sky was clear. The temperature had dropped from the mid 80s to the high 70s, and one of the cooler, prevailing trade winds swept the beach, ruffling particles of sand in its wake. Trying to feel more serene despite her friend's unsettling news, Shelley took a deep breath of the fresh, salty sea air and loved it.

"Listen, I'm going to be okay." No way could she tell Wendy that the swindler might be here on Grand Cayman, or that she was going to offer any help she could to aid Duncan in getting the money out of Silverman. Wendy would tell Shelley's mother, and her mother would call Uncle Ethan, and he, being the alpha of their family pack, would charge out to the island to return her home pronto. "I got a roommate so I'm pretty well set."

"A roommate? Wow, how did you manage that?" Wendy sounded both surprised and warily pleased.

"Long story. He came here on a business trip but his reservation wasn't any good. He'd been really sweet in giving me a ride to the villa from the airport, so I'd offered him a drink later. Instead, he's staying here, subletting the guest room." Shelley slid her toes through the sand, loving the silky, warm feel of it.

"*He?* Not that I'm all that surprised. I wouldn't think you'd find an unaccompanied woman on the island looking to sublease a room. But wow, Shelley. You're a fast mover. You'll have to send me a picture. Is he cute? He'd have to be if you offered to buy him a drink. But be careful about needy guys. They're your downfall. Next thing you know, he'll be moving in with you in your house in Texas because he was evicted from his own place." Wendy paused in creating her gloom-and-doom scenario, then asked, "What does he do?"

Before Shelley could respond, Wendy was figuring out the situation on her own. "He must have some money to go on vacation in the islands and be able to afford the rent."

"I agree." Shelley skipped saying what he worked at because she didn't have a clue, except that he'd been an extra in a movie. Was he the spoiled younger brother of a laird who didn't have to do anything but live off his older brother's generosity? Maybe that's why he was here trying to get the clan's money back. Maybe if he didn't, he wouldn't be able to live a life of luxury any longer and would actually have to work for a living.

"First, you took in that professor whose wife kept kicking him out of the house."

"That was different. His relationship with me is completely platonic. He's strictly a chemistry kind of guy, but not in the physical sense. Which might have something to do with the problem he and his wife have—not enough physical contact. Besides, I do have an extra couple of rooms. So why should he have had to get a hotel room?"

"Yeah, and when they make the final split?"

"He's on his own."

"What about taking in that woman's standard poodle? And your student's cat because her mother refused to allow it to live in the house anymore?"

"The woman had had a heart attack and needed a home for her dog. So she keeps Misty company. As for the cat, I found a cat lady who had lost two of her own and loved Trixie." Shelley spied a seashell poking out of the sand and bent down to pick it up. "For your information, my new roommate *is* cute. But he's not moving to Texas with me." She paused as she looked at the dark water, wondering if a stray shark or two *were* lurking in the depths. A *lupus garou* would be no match in either human or wolf form against a hungry shark.

"I'm going swimming." The ruffle of the breeze and the sound of the waves slapping against the beach added to the ambience of the island paradise as Shelley made her way to the water. "Thanks for offering to pay half of the money, Wendy. I really appreciate it. Everything's fine for now. I need to swim before it gets too late. You know—the sharks come out to feed at night. I'll call you tomorrow."

"Hey, Shelley!" Duncan called after her.

A prickle of apprehension slithered through her as she whipped around to see Duncan stalking after her. She wondered what he'd heard her say—and what she'd said about him. When she saw the way he was looking her over with predatory interest, she recalled in a flash that she was wearing her bikini and wished she'd worn her one-piece instead.

"Wait up, lass. The least I can do is wrestle the shark off you if one decides to grab some delectable part of you."

He hadn't really said that, had he?

Shelley stared at Duncan, who was now wearing a pair of black Bermuda shorts, the rest of him bare. His toned biceps made her envision him wearing a kilt and swinging a sword, fighting the bad guys in the movie, sweeping up the fair maiden in his arms, and carrying her off to his castle. If women saw him like that in the movie, they'd be all over him when they caught sight of him outside his castle walls.

He didn't say anything more, and Shelley was too stunned to speak. Wendy broke in, dying to know all about him. "That's him? A Scottish hunk? Who sounds like he's already way too intrigued with you? Don't tell me you're wearing that string bikini of yours," she said. Knowing Wendy, she'd want to forget her manufacturing crisis and fly to the island to check him out. She'd let him stay at the villa for free, too. Probably pay for all his meals, excursions, everything. She could certainly afford it.

Forget Shelley taking in needy strays. She figured Wendy would be the one offering a free room stateside for him. Until she learned he was a wolf. Wolves lived by different rules, and they had to be cautious about stepping over the lines.

"Yeah, he's my new roommate." Shelley didn't want to tell Wendy she *was* wearing the bikini, and the

Highlander's tongue was practically hanging out of his mouth. He acted like he'd just shifted into the wolf and come back from a fast-paced run, heartbeat accelerated, adrenaline whipped up, and ready for a lot more exercise—this time one-on-one with a she-wolf. "Got to go, Wendy, and again, thanks for the generous offer. I'll call you tomorrow." Shelley knew she'd get the third degree from her friend, especially when Wendy learned he was a Highland *wolf*, not just human.

Shelley had never dated a wolf, and for the first time, she wondered why the hell not. Because they could be serious trouble, like a commitment forever? And what if she made a wrong choice? Their forever could last centuries.

She clicked off the phone and waved her towel at Duncan. "Didn't bring a towel?"

His sexy mouth lifted slightly, his dark eyes nearly black and the skin beneath them crinkling with good humor. "Do you mind if I share yours?"

Feeling much better about her finances, she cast him a smug smile. "It'll cost you."

—◊◊◊—

Duncan had been looking out the guest bedroom window, watching the waves roll in and the breeze toss the palm fronds like fluttering, dark green fans while he'd been telling his oldest brother, Ian, what he'd learned so far— about the woman he'd met in the bar and her ties to a man who worked for Silverman, the trouble he'd had with his hotel reservation, and his having to pay so much to share a villa with a wolf—when he saw Shelley wearing a shimmering, blue string bikini as she crossed the patio.

Ian asked him more about the she-wolf than about how far he was getting with the investigation. Ian's focus on the female wolf rankled Duncan. Ian had to know a wolf wouldn't sidetrack him. He didn't think that staying with a female wolf should be of any consequence. Until he saw her leave the house wearing barely anything—an iridescent royal blue thong and a barely there halter top that together highlighted the swell of her breasts and her firm ass. He swore when she turned and leaned over to pick up a shell on the beach, and as she spoke to someone on the phone, she nearly fell out of the top.

"Duncan?" Ian said, breaking into Duncan's spell-binding vision of the mermaid headed for the water.

"Uh, I've got to go. My roommate insists on being shark bait, and I need to make sure she isn't food for the fish. We'd never be able to afford the whole cost of this villa if she didn't survive her swim. Talk to you when I have more news."

"Duncan—"

Recognizing the laird's warning tone of voice that would be followed by a stern reminder of duty, Duncan ended the call, unzipped his bag, and dug around in it until he could find the only pair of Bermuda shorts he'd brought on the trip. Now he wished he'd brought both pairs. He didn't own a swimsuit, but he was rethinking that also.

He stripped down in record time, and after yanking on the shorts, he raced down the stairs to reach Shelley before she got into the water. He could imagine one little wave removing the tiny bit of cloth between her legs and the one barely covering her breasts. He smiled at the thought. He'd be there to rescue her. To hell with the bikini.

He tried not to look as anxious as he was to catch

up to her, but when she waved her towel at him, he realized he should have thought to grab one from the upstairs bathroom.

When she told him it would cost him to share her towel, he asked, "How much?"

He wasn't sure if she was teasing, but he was willing to pay anything to stay with her while she swam, whether his clan could afford it or not.

Smiling, she shook her head, the breeze seductively sweeping her auburn hair across her face. "You won't even need it. Too many sharks out there. You won't get wet." She grabbed her hair and held it in abeyance, winked, turned, and continued to make her way through the sand to the water.

He smiled at her sassiness. She paused briefly to lay out her towel, bending over and making him growl low with desire. She didn't look back at him—although she had to have figured out what her body was doing to his—and continued to the water.

When she was only a few feet from the surf, she suddenly dashed into it until she was wading waist deep in the water, her back to him.

He jogged to the water's edge, felt how warm the waves were that caressed his bare toes, not anything like the Irish or North Seas, and ran in after her. Maybe if he got close to her and a wave snatched her bikini away, he'd be able to capture it. Nah, he really wouldn't want to return it to her. Instead, he'd protectively cover her body from prying eyes—not that anyone could see them in the dark like this, except another wolf.

He was within arm's length of her when she was up to her shoulders in water, and she squealed.

"Shelley," he shouted, his heart thudding and adrenaline shooting through his veins at hyperspeed. He grabbed her arm, pulling her toward him, ready to punch the shark in the nose. He'd heard that was a way to keep the sharks from coming back for more.

She laughed but didn't squirm to get loose from him. "Just a school of colorful fish. They nibbled on my legs and startled me."

He relaxed and meant to let her go, but the waves were pushing her soft body against his, and he liked the feel of her curves, the way her breeze-tossed hair caressed his shoulder, the way she smelled so sweet and feminine and wolflike.

He wanted to wrap his arms around her and pull her close, hug all that sweet tanned flesh against him, rub his face in her hair, cup her glorious breasts, and…

He gritted his teeth. He couldn't do any of that and had to satisfy himself with just holding her arm as the waves slowly lifted her off her feet and threatened to pull her away with the current. He remained her steadfast pillar, immovable in the sand beneath the waves.

"You make a great anchor," she said, rising on tiptoes with each swell of a wave.

"If I don't keep you close, how will I get to you fast enough if another colorful school of fish attacks you?"

She chuckled. "If it had been a shark, what would you have done?"

"Socked him in the nose. I'd heard they have sensitive noses."

She laughed and he loved the sound, so airy and light. But he could tell she was very impressed with his plan of attack and rescue.

"So, were you telling your brother about staying with me?"

"Aye. Ian. He wanted to know all about you." Duncan looked down at her. "I think he believed I might be side-tracked, which I never am."

"Not by a woman, I take it," she said, very seriously.

He responded just as seriously. "Never."

"Yet he thought you might be."

Duncan didn't say anything. His brother truly couldn't believe that. Duncan had every intention of checking out Silverman's house, which he would do after Shelley went to bed tonight. Getting their money back was just too important a mission. "And you? Was it your girlfriend who called?"

"Oh, yes. She gave me some… news about the problem with the grant."

She seemed reluctant to tell him what was going on with the missing funds.

"Aye?"

"Someone stole them."

He snorted. "Seems to be a widespread rash of thievery going on."

"Salisbury Silverman."

Duncan frowned at her.

"That's what my girlfriend told me the paper said."

"Bastard."

"Yeah. So I'm willing to help you get your money back—and mine, too."

Duncan shook his head. "No deal. I'll get your money back. But I don't want you getting involved in this."

She looked out to sea.

"Shelley?"

"All right. Just remember I offered if you need any help."

He wouldn't need help. Not from a lovely she-wolf who could get hurt in the process.

Shelley switched topics. "I told Wendy I already had a roommate."

Either her friend would think the situation would work out well, or she'd warn Shelley away from him. "Ah. What advice did she give you?"

A bigger wave nearly toppled Shelley, and Duncan pulled her into his arms, anchoring her silky body against his. God, he was already fully aroused, and having the nearly naked woman in his arms made it worse. On the other hand, he was grateful for the wave that had brought the mermaid to him so fortuitously.

Shelley cleared her throat. "I didn't give her a whole lot of time to offer advice. But she heard your Scottish accent and deep, sexy voice so I'm sure she'll be all questions tomorrow."

"Sexy, eh?"

She blushed a little.

He suspected Shelley hadn't told her friend he was a wolf. She would have been concerned, most likely. "She was all right with my staying with you?"

"She was intrigued. But she did warn me not to take you home with me."

He arched a brow at that.

"I take home strays, according to Wendy. It's not so. I've only taken in one standard poodle that is a companion now to my own and, well, a cat, but I found it a good home. Wendy insists it's only the beginning. I've never taken a stray man home with me ever—except for a good cause."

He lifted a brow at the reference to taking home stray males, and he damn well wanted to know about the men she had taken in for a good cause. In his opinion, a woman should never take in stray males for any reason. Except in his case.

But the comment about her choice of dogs really surprised him. "Poodles." Just like he couldn't envision her studying plants, he couldn't see her with poodles for pets.

She laughed. "All right. Just because we're wolves doesn't mean we don't get along with pets. I suppose you've never had one."

"Irish wolfhounds," he said, proud of having raised generations of them.

"Irish wolfhounds?" Her body slid provocatively against his, silky and warm and so enticing that he was having a hard time concentrating on the conversation.

"Aye," he finally managed to get out, his body tightening with need, his voice much rougher than he intended.

"Well, they were used to kill wolves in the old days," she said, "weren't they?"

Her green eyes looked up at him, her lips so damned kissable that he wanted to taste them and forget about the dogs. "They helped us unseat English knights in the old days," he finally managed to say, every inch of her touching him, sliding and caressing with the gentle push of the waves.

Her nipples were rigid as they rubbed against him, so he knew he was having some effect on her. She had to feel how fully aroused he was. Either that, or she was trying to ignore it, and that's why she kept talking about dogs.

"English knights," she said. "Well, poodles have had a place in Germany, France, and England for centuries as retrievers. They love the water and—"

"I love the water," Duncan said, his voice drenched with lustful intent. He'd never loved the water like this, he thought as he leaned down to kiss Shelley full on the mouth.

Chapter 5

HOW COULD DUNCAN STAND AGAINST THE FORCE OF the current and continue to hold her up as her whole body dissolved while his hot, sexy mouth pressed against her lips?

Shelley had experienced lots of kisses over the years, but nothing this passionate, nothing this unrestrained, hot, and feral. Maybe it all had to do with being in the warm waters, nearly naked in her string bikini, and pressed against a Highlander who was the Rock of Gibraltar, his shorts clinging to his body and every hard inch—his muscles and his arousal—rubbing her as the currents continued to push her against him.

His mouth stole her attention again as he stood with his eyes closed, dark lashes fanning his cheeks, his lips brushing and nuzzling, and his tongue teasing her lips. Her mouth was parted for him, begging him to enter.

He didn't, though, as if that was the ultimate conquest and he was working up to it. Maybe he was afraid to take things too far, afraid they'd end up in bed together. On the other hand, she wondered if that was his ploy. His way to get out of sleeping in one of the twin beds. Seduce the she-wolf and work his way into her bed. She began to frown, and he must have felt her pulling away.

But she didn't want him to stop. She licked his lips and tasted whiskey—like barley and wheat roasted over an oak fire. He paused and opened his eyes, as if curious to see her response. His brown eyes were smoky with lust.

He looked at her as if he'd fallen in love. She knew it was only lust. That was enough, so it seemed. He took her, conquering her mouth and tightening his arms around her as if to say she was his, that the sea couldn't claim her. His tongue entered her mouth and stroked hers as one of his hands moved down to cup her ass. Oh yeah, he wanted her, and damned if she didn't want him right back.

His other hand remained locked around her waist, holding her tight against him so he wouldn't lose her to a wave, but his free hand was doing a number on her needs—caressing her buttock, dipping between her legs, touching her, and making her hot with desire.

Unfortunately, condoms wouldn't work between wolves. Mating meant a permanent relationship, and with their long lives, that could be for a very long time. Abstinence was the only thing allowed between them, or fooling around a little. But if having sex with him had been viable, she would have hauled him right back to the villa and permanently forgotten he was supposed to sleep upstairs.

"Shelley," he moaned into her mouth, his Scottish accent playing with her name in the most sensuous way. "We shouldn't be doing this."

She didn't need him telling her that. She knew she shouldn't be ready to pull off his shorts, strip out of her bikini, climb into his arms, and impale herself on his rigid erection. She was already wet and slippery in preparation for his penetration. He'd stirred up a sweet ache between her legs so deep that she craved satisfaction.

Yet a purely wickedly wolf side of her decided to come out at that moment, taking over her words as she said in a much too heated way, "If you removed your shorts and I pulled off my bikini bottoms and I climbed aboard—that's what we *shouldn't* be doing."

He groaned at her words and held her tighter, his stiff arousal rubbing against her. She felt as though she would burst into flames and sizzle in the water, going up in a puff of hot steam, if they continued the way they were going.

Yet, kissing seemed perfectly acceptable. The idea of riding him in the waves was too delicious not to consider. Not for real, but just to fantasize, she reminded herself.

His mouth curved up as his eyes opened, sparkling with the devil. "Hell, lass, if you weren't a wolf, I'd strip you down and insist you have your way with me." He continued to look into her eyes, wanting more, she knew, as his gaze shifted to her lips. But then as if werewolf reason took hold, he said, "It's time to go back in. I've got to do some work tonight."

"Concerning Silverman," she guessed, knowing that his suggestion to cease and desist this madness was all for the best. Although she hated that it would have to end.

"Aye. That's what I came here for. Bringing our money home. I can't let my clan down. I'll get your college funds back, too."

She sighed, loving that he cared enough about his clan to let go of whatever raging desire he had for her. She gave him a kiss on the cheek, letting him know it was okay with her to end things now. She still craved some kind of release, but it wasn't safe with him. "Let's go then."

He pulled her toward the shore, his hand still around her waist, keeping the currents and waves from taking her away from him, showing he still wanted her and was unwilling to let her go just yet. She imagined that he'd walk with her all the way to the villa like that if she allowed him to. But he was right. Nothing good could come of it. He was on a mission that had nothing to do with finding a mate. He needed to get the clan's money back any way that he could.

Not only that, but he lived in a world completely different from her own. In a castle. With a brother who was laird. Duncan took part in movies, wielding a huge sword. He was Scottish. And had gigantic Irish wolfhounds that would eat her poodles—even though they were the large variety—for breakfast.

They were worlds apart.

So why was she thinking again about taking another trip, this time to see the gardens in England and Scotland? And particularly at Argent Castle, if his clan's home even had gardens.

Apart from him being her roommate and sharing the cost of the villa, she knew that she had to limit her time with him. He wasn't here to entertain her or serve as her companion, and she had her own business to attend to.

So why didn't she pull away from him when they reached the water's edge? Why didn't he release her when he no longer had to protect her from being washed away or attacked by sharks or schools of colorful fish?

She sighed. "Do you have gardens at Argent Castle?"

He looked down at her, his brows both arched. "Aye."

But the question in his gaze said he wondered just what was going through her brain.

She wondered that, too. She looked back at the sand as they made their way to her beach towel, his arm still slung possessively around her waist.

"Why?" he asked, not wanting to be denied her reasoning when she didn't say anything further.

She offered him a small smile, feeling embarrassed that she'd been thinking along those lines, and gave a little shrug. "Someday, I want to see castle gardens all over Scotland and England. I've read that Fyvie has a nice garden. And Crathes Castle, too. I would like to see them for myself."

"Ah."

Yeah, he presumed she wanted to see *his* castle and stay there free of charge, when most outsiders wouldn't be permitted entrance. It had nothing to do with gardens. She straightened a little. "If I ever went to Scotland, would you let me see your gardens?"

He snorted.

"Not worth seeing?"

He chuckled, drew her to a stop in front of her beach towel, released her, and lifted her towel off the sand. After giving it several vigorous shakes, he handed it to her. "It's a garden. What do I know about rows and rows of plants? Ask me about a sword, and I'll tell you all there is to know."

"Oh." Not having realized how disinterested he was in plants, she felt somewhat disappointed as she wiped the water off her shoulders. Not that she truly expected any man that she became intrigued with to be a big plant lover. But it would be nice.

"No one ever stays at Argent who isn't family. It's not open to the public," he said, a glint of amusement in his eyes and the faintest curve to his lips.

"I gathered that would be the case since your clan is also a wolf pack." She was disappointed he'd say that, implying that she was one of the public and wouldn't be welcome.

Then again, his saying so might have more to do with not wanting his people to believe that there was more to their relationship if she all of a sudden dropped by to look at his *garden*. Yeah, his clan would come to all kinds of different conclusions. Like that she'd found this hot Highland hunk on the island and was chasing him around the world to spend more time with him. Or that she thought she'd found a gold mine and a titled family to exploit. Right. As if either would interest her. Unless, of course, his clan had an amazing garden. And then?

She'd be in Highland heaven.

She dried off her belly as he watched her every move. She'd always worn the string bikini at night around her girlfriends, figuring no one else would see them in the dark unless the observer was a wolf. Now, out of the water, she suddenly felt self-conscious about the wet fabric of her bikini showing every detail while she was being observed acutely by a man who could see in the dark as if it were daylight.

She had to offer him the towel, which made her feel even more naked once she held it out to him. He took it, smiled, and then walked behind her to dry her back and all the way down her bare buttocks and calves. The way he gently stroked her was really thoughtful and totally unexpected, but it stirred her craving for him all over again. Just when she thought she'd cooled down a bit from their water moves, too. When he finished, he ran the damp towel over his chest, his eyes again zeroing in on her halter top and bikini bottoms.

He had such an incredibly sculpted chest and perfectly muscled arms—not bulky, but with just the right amount of muscle that made her feel he'd offer real trouble to any man who could be a threat. He had to have chiseled all those great muscles by swinging a sword against an enemy or at least family who served as the enemy in sport. Dark, wet hair trailed down his abdomen to the waistband of shorts slung low on his hips. The trail of hair drew her eye down further to his arousal, to where his ebony shorts were plastered against the sheer size and hardness of it. Man, he was some wolf.

"It's a wonder you don't lose what little you're wearing," he said, noticing the part of his anatomy she'd chanced to get a glimpse of while she thought he was too busy looking her over.

Her face flushing with heat, she glanced back at the water. She didn't normally get caught looking at a man's package when it was in such great form or quite so evident. "The waves weren't violent enough. I've only lost my bikini top once—during rough waters in the Gulf of Mexico off Galveston Island, Texas."

His gaze focused again on her top, and she envisioned him attempting to imagine her without it. Either that, or he was enjoying the view of her taut nipples, which were pressing against the wet fabric and perfectly outlined.

She started to walk back to the villa, and he didn't follow. Too busy watching her backside?

Then he ran to catch up. "If you did come to Scotland

and wanted to see our gardens, you could stay at the castle." A smile lingered in his deep, baritone voice.

"*But*?" she asked, elongating the word, figuring from the teasing light in his eyes that there would be strings attached.

"It would cost you."

She laughed. "Let me guess. Five thousand dollars."

"In pounds, not dollars."

"That would cost me even more." She couldn't help sounding indignant. Highway robbery! Especially since the place was probably fairly big, and she wouldn't take up any space at all. And here she'd taken him in, the stray that *he* was.

"Aye. No twin beds, either." He put his arm over her shoulder and walked the rest of the way to the patio with her rubbing against his hip. "Unless you wanted to share a room."

"How much would *that* cost?"

"Probably too much," he conceded.

"That's what I figured."

He laughed and walked her inside the villa.

"It's too late now, but in the morning, can you take me to a grocery store so we can pick up something to eat?" she asked.

"Aye, lass. Are you hungry? We could try and find someplace that might still be open tonight."

"No, I don't normally eat this late. I wouldn't be able to sleep. I'm fine, thanks. I'll see you in the morning. Good night." She quickly pulled out of his grasp and headed for her bedroom—alone—before she changed her mind and let him sleep with her. She was pretty damned sure that sleeping wouldn't be all they'd be doing if they were together. She'd always thought herself levelheaded, someone who wouldn't do anything that crazy, but around Duncan, she wasn't so sure.

"Good night, lassie." A hint of longing was in his voice—for her or her bed? Or a little of both?

Duncan cursed himself for craving the female wolf so damned much as he drove across the island to Sal's estate. Thinking about her would come to no good, but he couldn't quit envisioning all her curves and the softness of her breasts as they'd pressed against him—all but her nipples, which had become hard little pearls—how her belly had pressed against his erection, the feel of her buttocks tightening as he caressed the smooth flesh, and the way her lips teased and tantalized him, her tongue doing a number on his. That's what he couldn't quit thinking of as he drove around the island, searching for Silverman's house.

He even thought about her visiting and sharing his bed with him back home! That made his loins tighten once again. His mother would say that if he took a female wolf to bed, he was mated, whether he did the deed or not. She was of the old world, where couples did not share a bed without agreeing to a mating. She often quoted his cousin's earlier demise due to his lack-witted dallying with a married lass whose husband had taken it upon himself to kill the interloper. Now, Flynn haunted the castle. Not that Duncan was going to dishonor the family in any way or get himself into a bind like that.

Once again, he reminded himself why he was here. No matter what Guthrie had said, Duncan felt this was their best chance at retrieving the money. Guthrie was still trying to come up with ways to make the castle solvent without the funds. The movie deal had paid off their debts for the short term, but they had to get their investments back from Silverman to make it in the long run.

Ian, the laird of Argent and the eldest of the quads, was busy running the clan and pack and distracted by one sexy red wolf, his new mate who was a werewolf romance writer. The second oldest brother, Cearnach, managed a lot of the details of operating the estate as Ian's second in command. So Duncan was free to do as he pleased.

Simply as a matter of pride, though, he wasn't going to let the bastard get away with the theft.

He finally spied Silverman's white stucco house, a blue iguana running across the red tile roof. A gated entry kept Duncan from getting close to the beachside home, but he figured he could run along the beach and get closer that way. The place most likely had tons of security so Duncan's best bet probably was to wait until the bastard left his estate on some errand or another and then confront him face-to-face.

He parked nearby, got out of the rental car, and began to jog down the beach toward Silverman's house, wearing his black pants and T-shirt and boots. Only another wolf would see him in the dark. Although it was never a good idea to make assumptions about an enemy, Guthrie hadn't found that Silverman had any ties to a wolf pack. He seemed to be a loner who only hooked up with humans. Not having a werewolf pack protecting Sal Silverman's back gave Duncan the advantage, if Guthrie had been correct.

As Duncan neared the house, a couple of dogs barked. Silverman had guard dogs? Lights were on all over the place and security lights all over the grounds also. A couple of men headed for the back patio in the direction of the beach, looking to see what had disturbed the dogs.

Duncan growled and turned around and ran back the other way. No sense in being ID'd by a couple of goons. The guard dogs would be even more of a problem, though, if Duncan wanted to enter the house when Silverman was gone.

The good thing was that Silverman did seem to be in residence. Did he ever leave his estate, though? He might just seclude himself there until he left for some other hideaway.

Duncan had to get to him before that could happen.

Before long, he was driving back to the villa, feeling unsettled about not getting any further with Silverman, when he thought he spied headlights following him. He pulled off the road and killed his car lights, but the headlights behind him turned off down another road, and Duncan continued on his way. Had someone suspected he was trouble?

Whatever happened, he didn't want Shelley involved in this. Tomorrow, he'd change out his rental vehicle in the event that Silverman's people were watching for him, especially if the woman he'd met in the bar had alerted her boyfriend that some Scot seemed interested in Silverman and that she'd made the mistake of talking about him.

When Duncan arrived back at the villa, the lights in the master bedroom were off. A light in the living room had been left on, as if Shelley had meant to welcome him home. He appreciated the gesture, although werewolves didn't need light to see at night. What he'd truly wished she'd done was left her bedroom door open and a trail of discarded clothes from the living room to the bedroom, inviting him to follow her there, close the door, and join her in bed. Not that it would be a good thing for either of them, but he couldn't help wanting it.

He trudged up the stairs to his guest bedroom and the two twin beds, glad at least he had a bed to sleep in. And he stared at the woman sleeping in one of them, her auburn hair splayed across a white pillowcase and the floral bedcover tucked around her throat so that he couldn't tell if she was dressed or not.

He smiled at her. Now he wanted to push the twin beds together and stay just where he was. With her. Forget the queen-sized bed downstairs that would accommodate his size better. *She* would accommodate his size even better.

"You may have my bed," she whispered, half asleep, not even opening her eyes as if that might wake her up too much, but evidently he'd awakened her, or she had not quite drifted off. Probably felt the change in the temperature of the room as he stood next to the bed. Most likely smelled him with the breeze and night salt air on his skin. "'Night," she added softly, confirming that the one-sided conversation was over.

He stood staring at her, not wanting to leave. Wanting to see what she looked like, how she felt underneath the covers. "Are you certain?" he asked. "These beds look pretty good about now."

She still didn't open her eyes, but she smiled her brilliant smile. "Good night, Duncan. I'm not moving downstairs now that I've got the bed nice and warm, and I'm not wearing anything. So run along like a good wolf, and I'll see you in the morning."

"You're not wearing even a string bikini?" he asked, not taking a step from the room. Now he was really trying to envision all that tanned skin perfectly naked.

This time, she opened her eyes, a smile lingering as if to say that surely he knew she wouldn't be wearing anything. "Most of us sleep in nothing."

"Aye, but I don't care what most do about sleeping."

He swore she was fighting back a laugh.

"Good night, Duncan," she said dismissively, her voice sounding amused.

He shook his head, grumbled something about how hard she was on him in a mostly teasing way, and headed back down the stairs.

Shelley chuckled as he stomped down the stairs. She loved his sense of humor and how honorable he was, and she felt like a good Samaritan for ensuring that he would have a restful night in a bed built more for his size.

Very early in the morning, she smelled ham and eggs and cheese cooking, and even a pot of coffee brewing.

"Hmm," she said, stretching her arms above her head. Then she sat up abruptly in bed. He went grocery shopping without her? Not that she was upset about the circumstances—and she truly was glad he was making breakfast because after playing in the surf and having had no dinner, she was starving—but she still wanted to go to the grocery store.

She grabbed her shortie floral satin robe off a chair,

the only robe she'd brought, figuring it would just be her here and no problem. She slipped it on and belted it, then hurried down the stairs. If she weren't so hungry, she would have gotten dressed first. But she didn't want the food to get cold so she wasn't wasting any time in joining him.

Dressed only in a pair of black briefs, Duncan wore a shadow of a beard but still looked as sexy as the devil as he folded an omelet with melted cheese and ham and chives in a skillet in the kitchen. "Look good?"

She looked from him to the eggs. She kept thinking about how *he* looked—damned good, hot, wolflike, wearing only the pair of black briefs—with his perfectly muscled arms and chest, and bare legs. "Yeah, real good," she murmured.

He smiled at her. "I meant, did the eggs appeal. Or would you like me to fix you something else?"

"No, what you're fixing is fine." She thought again about his clothes. He had the ones he'd worn the night before when he went in search of Silverman. So was he just showing off some more? She could handle it.

She studied the way he was working on the omelet, really impressed. No man she'd ever known cooked. "You can cook."

"If you have a chance to speak with Ian, don't *ever* let him know the truth." Duncan's gaze met hers, and she got the impression he was serious. "My brothers and I stick to the principle that unless it's frozen pizza, we can't make it. As long as he believes that, we're happy."

"Or he makes you cook for the clan?" she guessed.

"For him and his new mate when Cook or our cousin Heather is unavailable, aye."

She laughed. "Your secret is safe with me."

He looked down at her and smiled appreciatively. "First one's for you. I'll make another right away."

"Thank you." She took the plate to the kitchen table. "You went to the grocery store without me this morning."

"I had to. You were sleeping so soundly that I figured you'd have quite an appetite when you woke, so I picked up a few items. If you want anything else, we can go out again."

"I'd like that."

"It was the least I could do when you gave me your big bed to sleep in. I had really hoped you might change your mind and come down to join me once I warmed up the sheets a little." Duncan didn't even glance in her direction; he just looked all sexy and forbidding. Getting too close to the flame was definitely going to get her singed.

She had just raised another bite of the cheesy eggs to her lips, but she paused to comment. "I'm afraid it might have gotten a little too hot."

He winked, a look that promised he would have heated her up well and good. "That's what the air conditioner is for."

She laughed, loving his sense of humor.

He finished cooking his omelet and joined her at the table. "I also changed out the rental car early this morning."

A frisson of alarm shook through her. "You didn't have trouble last night when you were investigating Silverman, did you?"

He hesitated a fraction too long for her liking in answering her. "No. I just thought it prudent to swap out cars. Just in case."

"Are you certain?"

"Aye, I am, but I wish to err on the side of caution."

She finished her eggs and set her plate aside, leaning back in the chair and ready to have a serious discussion. "I overheard you talking to your brother about missing a lead in your investigation."

"Aye. A lady said her boyfriend works for Silverman. I must have looked like I was ready to kill the bastard, and she quickly quit talking to me."

That didn't sound good. Shelley sighed and looked at the omelet he'd nearly polished off. "You're a wonderful cook."

"Thank you, but remember it's our secret."

That made her want to meet his brothers, including the laird, and see their interaction for herself. Since she had no siblings of her own, she was curious to see Duncan and his brothers in action. Her friend, Wendy, had four brothers, but Shelley thought that Duncan's family would be different since they were nobility of sorts and owned a castle. And were Scottish.

She smiled, then turned serious. "Are you sure I can't help you in any way with your mission?"

"Nay. I don't want you involved in this. No telling what might happen."

Partly relieved—because she wasn't into spy and criminal apprehension scenarios—but disappointed that she couldn't help him in any way, she looked back at the egg carton, cheese, and ham still sitting out. She was still hungry from swimming and not having eaten any dinner, and she was craving more of Duncan's omelets. Not wanting to sound too greedy, she proposed, "If I promise to clean up after you, will you... fix me another omelet?"

He gave her the biggest boyish grin, and she smiled back, loving that she'd made his morning.

"Aye, it'll be my pleasure."

But he didn't just fix her another omelet. He also mixed her champagne and chilled orange juice. The mimosa was a delightful drink, and she wondered why she'd never tried it before. He also helped her clean up, letting her put the groceries away while he handled the manly task of scrubbing the stubborn eggs off the skillet. She was ready to drag one hot Highlander home to Texas and keep him. Then she'd tell Wendy she was right. Shelley *was* a sucker for strays—but what a stray. Only he wasn't really a stray. He had a whole pack relying on him to do right.

Afterward, they both dressed, and when she came downstairs to join him, she eyed his soft pair of faded jeans and black T-shirt, which had no logo, no design, nothing to take away from his sexy wolfish appearance. He didn't need a smart remark emblazoned across his chest. His whole presence screamed hot male. She liked that she was the one who got to keep him for a while.

Within the hour, he had dropped her off at the trailhead of the Mastic Reserve. She felt the whole world beyond this one place vanish as she quickly immersed herself in taking pictures and notes of the lush, green vegetation. Wearing olive-green capris, a short-sleeved leafy shirt over a peach tank top, and black sneakers to navigate the muddier areas, she carried a lightweight canvas pack on her back filled with a couple of chilled bottles of water—courtesy of Duncan—insect repellent, and sunscreen.

Armed with a notebook and pen in one hand and a

camera in the other, she was all set. She made her way slowly through the black mangrove forest. The long-leggy trees dipped into brackish water with their roots sticking up out of the wet soil, gasping for air, while ferns clustered together in the moisture. Vines crawled up tree trunks, reminiscent of where the ape man had swung through the jungle doing his Tarzan yell.

Snapping shots of all the plants, she was falling in love with the whole place. Normally she would have thought of nothing else, but at the back of her mind, a niggling concern about whether Duncan was all right kept worrying her. The fact that he'd changed out rental vehicles meant he'd been concerned about something. She hadn't wanted to pry, considering he hadn't wanted to involve her. She worried about his continued investigation today, though, and what trouble he might get himself into.

Having opted to take the self-guided tour, Shelley found herself blissfully alone, snapping a picture of a strangler fig, each of its snakelike tentacles like a boa constrictor wrapping around its prey. Not only was observing the vegetation a real treat, but the colorful parrots—with their iridescent green feathers, red cheeks, and white-ringed eyes—caught her attention as they nested in tree holes and twittered about in the foliage. Suddenly one took flight overhead, and she witnessed its brilliant blue wing feathers spreading out as it flew away while a cacophony of birds' chattering filled the air.

A calabash tree towered above with huge, round fruit attached to the trunk—the shell of the fruit so hard that it could be hollowed out into bowls or cups. Thin corded branches drooped toward the ground, weighed down by heavy clusters of purplish and orange ripe mangoes, with others hidden by the thin green leaves.

She was so busy as she moved on to each specimen that she felt as though she was alone in a tropical jungle on an uninhabited island, seeing a world for the first time as explorers to the island might have. A stand of silver thatch palms caught her eye. The tree derived its name from the silver color underneath the fronds and was the only one in the islands with that feature. A blue iguana raced along a fallen tree trunk; a grass snake coiled on a slab of slate. No poisonous snakes lived on the island, thankfully.

Shelley looked up at the thirty-foot-tall palms, thinking how much fun it would be to see the silver reflected in the moonlight. She had read that the palms had been used to thatch roofs in years past, only needing to be replaced every five or six years. If the fronds were cut during the full moon, supposedly they would last for nine years. *The full moon*. It would be out tonight, and the urge to run as a wolf tugged at her senses. Made her want to strip out of her clothes and shift into the wolf to explore this world on four paws, nose to the ground and sniffing the air, running through the thick underbrush, not staying to the path.

She was pondering that bit of folklore about the viability of the fronds cut during the full moon, comparing it with werewolf lore and making plans to come back that night, when she heard the sound of shoes crunching on leaves and heading her way on the winding path.

A woman said in a gratingly syrupy voice, "Ah, come on, Sal. You know how much I love to get away from your house and spend the day taking walks along the beach or here in the forest. I mean, we can have sex there all the time, but I also like to get out and see the island while I'm here."

Shelley did not want to hear about some strangers' sex lives. Why couldn't they have gone swimming at the beach or gone shopping or done anything but come to the forest?

The woman said, "No, before you say it, I wanted to be with you, not by myself while one of your goons followed along."

"Not everyone loves me like you do," Sal said candidly.

The mention of sex had caught Shelley's attention first, but then the woman's comments about goons made her ears perk up even more. Hearing that the couple sequestered themselves at his estate and that not everyone liked him or loved him, according to him, suddenly made her think of Duncan's Sal—Salisbury Silverman. Neither Sal nor his girlfriend had mentioned his last name.

The couple was moving toward her at a leisurely pace. Shelley stood still, not knowing whether to move along the path in the same direction they were headed to try to get out of their way without them realizing she had overheard them, or to step off the path into the jungle so they wouldn't see her. The problem was with the poisonous plants growing in the underbrush.

Maiden plum had sap that could cause serious skin rashes. The Manchineel tree's leaves and fruit were poisonous to the touch, and even standing underneath the tree during a downpour could be hazardous to one's health. The lady hair plant was also to be avoided because of the reaction of skin to the fiberglass-like stinging hairs, so she didn't want to get into any of those. Of course, the last option would be to face Sal and his girlfriend as if they were insignificant in the scheme of things, unless...

Dread bunched in the pit of her stomach. What if it *was* Sal Silverman? The man Duncan was looking for. The one who had stolen the college funds. Could there be another Sal with goons residing on the island? Maybe. But probably not.

Then she took a sniff of the breeze and cursed herself for not noticing. The man was downwind of her so she couldn't tell if he was a wolf or not, which would help her to further identify him as the one Duncan wanted.

But if this Sal was a wolf, he could smell *her*.

Chapter 6

DAMN. SHELLEY WANTED TO CALL DUNCAN AND TELL him she thought she was soon going to be face to face with his quarry, but she knew how well her voice would travel in the forest. Just like Sal's and the woman's did as they sauntered closer to her.

She should have planned this better, made sure she and Duncan had some kind of code to use in the event something like this happened.

Who was she kidding? She never thought she would run into Duncan's target out here. Or anywhere else, for that matter. She thought the guy would remain secluded at his island estate.

But she had to tell Duncan the man was most likely here and let the Scot decide how he wanted to deal with the news. *Somehow*. She pulled her phone out of her pouch and dialed his number.

The footfalls seemed to quicken in her direction. Great.

"Why are we in such a rush now?" the woman said to Sal.

"I thought you wanted to take a dip in the pool. If you wait too long, you'll get burned."

"Thanks for worrying about me but I never burn. Will you swim with me?"

"Not this time," he said.

Shelley dropped back into a crouch with her phone still to her ear. She was pretending to look at a termite hill and wishing Duncan would answer the phone when she heard his voice mail.

Frustrated that she couldn't reach him pronto, she quickly said, "It's me." She figured Duncan would recognize either her voice or her phone number, since she didn't want to say her name out loud in the forest. She had to say something in some sort of code, but she wasn't sure he'd figure it out. Still, she didn't have any other choice. "I just found the plant specimen I know you wanted to locate. It's *really* important. Call me!"

She hung up and was just taking another close-up picture of a mahogany tree when the man named Sal and the woman edged into view. Shelley turned slightly to acknowledge them, get a good look at both of them, and categorize them like she did her plants in the event she saw them again. She was dying to take a picture of them to give to Duncan to verify that this was the man he was after.

Instead, she gave them a half smile in greeting, said a perfunctory "Hello," and began writing in her notebook again as if they didn't interest her in the least.

Sal had light-brown hair with streaks of gray threaded through it and looked to be in his midfifties in human years. He was wearing a white polo shirt and black jeans and muddy, white boat shoes. His face was tanned as if he spent a lot of time in the islands. If this was Duncan's thief, he was using Duncan's family's savings—as well as those of others and the college—to enjoy the island paradise. He was fairly nondescript beyond that, except for his eyes. They were a wolf's eyes—amber, curious, intrigued.

The woman was closer to being in her early twenties.

She quickly wrapped her arm around the man's waist as if she was afraid he might stray as soon as he saw Shelley. Especially because of the way he was showing his interest in her. The woman was wearing hot pink shorts and a hot pink halter top with nothing to hold up her swaying breasts, which had to be enhanced, considering how big they were and how petite the rest of her was. The woman's hair was long and blond, and either the wind had done a number on it, or she thought it looked sexy without being combed after she'd fallen out of bed that morning.

"Hello," Sal said to Shelley, drawing close and obviously interested in or suspicious of her.

Probably interested. Because she was a female wolf. She figured he didn't have a reason to be suspicious of her; her worry about who he might be had probably put her on edge.

She surreptitiously sniffed the air to ascertain if he was a wolf, and a slight smile touched his lips at seeing her check him out. Yeah, he was a wolf, and he liked that she knew he was. *Bastard*. The woman was strictly human and wearing too much cloying perfume. Shelley wondered how he could stand it, considering how sensitive a wolf's sense of smell was. Natural, sweet-smelling soaps and shampoos were one thing, but heavy perfumes or colognes quite another.

"Are you here on vacation?" he asked Shelley, his voice dark and an attempt at sexy, but she found Duncan's voice much more appealing and this guy even more of a lout. Duncan was sexy without trying. This guy was trying way too hard and falling far short of anything appealing.

She suspected the warrior in Duncan, the power to persuade people with a look and a word, made her take notice. This man was more like a parasite, using others' money for power. He wouldn't have been powerful among a pack of wolves and would never have lasted there.

He raised a brow when she hesitated to answer his question about whether she was on vacation, shaking her loose of her thoughts. Maybe he believed she was reluctant to speak with a stranger. A beta wolf who might meekly give in to his every desire. She lifted her chin, showing him she was no beta wolf.

She really didn't want to answer his question, wanted to tell him it was none of his business, but what if she could help Duncan with his mission? Even if he didn't want her help. She didn't want to alienate this man. "I'm here to do some research on plants. I'm a professor of botany."

A definite light shown in his eyes. He was impressed. She wasn't sure if it was because of what she was doing or that she wasn't about to be cowed. "Ah."

From the earlier conversation she'd heard, Shelley could tell Sal wasn't interested in plants, so she was surprised when he said, "I have quite a garden at my place. One in France as well."

The girlfriend looked up at him with narrowed eyes. "You never told me you had a place in France. Switzerland, yes."

Despite not wanting to show any interest, Shelley was intrigued. How she'd love to see gardens in France. Not his particularly, but the great gardens of Versailles immediately came to mind.

He shrugged and said to Shelley, "If you'd like to stop by for drinks later, you could see my gardens."

And what else?

But her thoughts were spinning with the ramifications. *Oh. My. God. Duncan, where are you when you should be right here, right now?*

She stood a little taller, and in a calmer voice than she'd thought she could muster, she asked, "Could you... give me your phone number? I've got to talk to my girlfriend. I'll have to confirm that we don't have any other plans."

Even though she wasn't an undercover-spy kind of girl, what if she could get into his house and learn something? Maybe he'd reveal something that he wouldn't tell anyone else.

She was trying to keep this professional without turning him off or getting in over her head, so she hoped her attempt would work.

"Drinks?" the woman said shrilly, her scowl growing even more rabid. It really wasn't becoming. "With *her*?"

Sal ignored the woman, fished a business card out of a gold card holder, and wrote on the back. His private number, Shelley thought.

Duncan would give her hell for even speaking with the man, she figured. And even more for taking Sal's business card instead of immediately saying she wasn't interested. But she had called Duncan, and he hadn't answered his phone. So what was she supposed to do?

Sal must have assumed she'd throw aside any plans she'd had because he said, "I'll have a limo pick you up at seven tonight."

"If you'll give me the address, I'll drop by... *if* I can make it. But I'll let you know one way or another."

He seemed more amused than perturbed at her reluctance to fall at his feet. He had to know that had to do with her being a wolf. He might even be considering that Shelley wouldn't like his girlfriend tagging along.

He confirmed that when he said, "Lola will be going out for the night."

Lola glowered at him, her lips parted in shock. Before she could say a word, he bowed his head a little to Shelley, a gentlemanly wolf's way of bidding her good-bye, and then quickly pulled Lola past Shelley before the woman started spitting fire.

"What do you mean I'm going out for the night? You didn't even ask what her name was. Did you know her? What if I don't want to go out for the night? You can't do this to me!"

He could and he would. That's the kind of man he was. Loyal only to himself, Shelley thought.

"Be quiet," he snapped at Lola under his breath. The threat in his tone said that if Lola didn't obey him, she'd be out on her ear, flying home at the earliest convenience.

The woman didn't say another word, apparently getting the message loud and clear, and Shelley wondered if Sal had given her an ultimatum before. Girlfriends were replaceable.

Shelley was still thoroughly rattled, partly because she'd met the monster Duncan wanted to take down, but also because Sal wanted to get to know her better. She couldn't think about plants or writing notes or taking pictures as she stared at the path where Sal had disappeared with the woman who appeared to be closer to a daughter's age than a girlfriend's.

When Shelley's phone rang, she stifled a cry of surprise. She pulled out the phone and looked at the caller ID. *Duncan*. What if Sal had heard her phone ringing? Could hear everything she said?

She hurried away in the opposite direction from the one Sal and his girlfriend had taken toward the trailhead. She didn't hear them any longer, but she still was worried that Sal might be watching and listening to her conversation while he made Lola stand silently with him in the forest.

"Hello," Shelley said to Duncan, her voice quieter than it would have been normally, but she knew Duncan could hear her anyway. She just hoped Sal couldn't.

"Shelley, what kind of cryptic message was that?" Duncan asked, sounding somewhat perturbed. "I told you I don't know anything about plants, and…"

"This one you'd want to see. But it's too late. Don't come to pick me up now. I've got more work to do." What else could she say? His target was here? Come now? By the time he got here, Sal would be gone.

"I wasn't scheduled to pick you up for another hour and a half." Duncan sounded slightly incredulous.

She wasn't getting through to him, but she didn't want to blurt out that Salisbury Silverman was here. Particularly since she shouldn't have known his last name, and he might be listening down the path.

"Oh, the dinner cruise," she said, as if Duncan had just told her he was taking her on one, and she'd forgotten all about it. She knew that was not going to go over well with Duncan, who wouldn't know what the hell she was talking about. But she had to have a cover if Sal was within hearing distance.

"What dinner cruise?" Duncan sounded thoroughly confused and a little cross.

Play along, *damn it*.

Shelley sighed. "I thought we were going tomorrow night. I guess I got my nights mixed up. Okay, let me know if you can reschedule for tomorrow night. If not, I'll just have to say no to having drinks at the estate of…" She paused, reading the back of the business card with Sal's name and a personal phone number scrawled on it and then flipping it over to the front to see a firm's name, address, website, and phone number in expensive gold lettering. "Salisbury Silverton of Malicon Investments."

She didn't know if that was a faux name for the guy's business or not, since warrants were out for his arrest and surely he wouldn't pass out cards like that to just anyone. Maybe he hadn't had time to make new business cards that would conceal his beleaguered investment firm and figured she'd be too clueless to know he was a bad guy. That would have been the case if Duncan hadn't told her about him. She hadn't heard of the name of the man's investment company, and he might use several as fronts for his scheming.

Dead silence filled the air waves. That's when she assumed that Duncan recognized the name of the firm or the other name Sal was using.

"I'm coming to get you." Duncan's voice was so dark that she envisioned him wearing a kilt and with a claymore at his back as he rushed to the reserve.

This couldn't be good.

"No! I'm not through cataloging plants!" She couldn't allow Duncan to run into the man right here in the reserve, even though at first she'd thought it might be a good idea. Now she was thinking it might be better if they somehow strung the guy along and Duncan could see him alone, instead of with a human woman clinging to his arm who could serve as a witness to anything that might occur between Duncan and Sal.

"Is he still there, damn it?" Duncan was so angry that she figured he was barely thinking straight.

"Most likely. Pick me up later like we had planned. I still have tons of work to do. All right?"

She just hoped she could get her mind back on her work. She doubted she could. She'd wanted to relish every delectable moment of describing every detail and taking pictures of every new specimen of plant, hoping she might discover one to test and learn if it could have an effect on werewolves' ability to shape-shift. But instead, she was going to be thinking of Duncan and how angry he was. She envisioned him pacing across the villa, ready to kill Sal for even speaking with her.

"All right?" she repeated, having to get his agreement.

Shelley could just see the two men running into each other, ditching their clothes, and shifting. She assumed Duncan would win because he was a warrior at heart. Sal was a businessman who destroyed lives through investment fraud, but physically he couldn't beat Duncan. And Sal's girlfriend? Well, hell, Shelley would have to take care of Lola once she saw the two men shift into wolves.

Humans who saw a werewolf shift had only two choices—death or joining the werewolves. In good conscience, she couldn't add a woman like that to their ranks. The woman could easily give their kind away if she was turned. And the fake boobs would have to go. Genetically when the werewolf kind shifted, they became all wolf or all human. But if a human had fake components like implants, Shelley was certain the silicon wouldn't dissolve with the change. A wolf with silicon implants was sure to cause a stir.

Not that killing a woman was anything Shelley wanted to do, either. That's what she was hoping to avoid.

"All right?" she said again, not wanting to say Duncan's name out loud in case Sal was listening. If she could, she would have said his name in a firm and commanding way, wanting to shake him out of his angry haze. If he had a middle name, she would have used it, too.

"I'll call you as soon as I get there." Then he hung up on her.

Her mouth open, she stared at the phone and swore under her breath. He did *not* just hang up on her.

Okay, so she knew he was the kind of man who set his own rules, but she thought the plan she'd devised made sense. He should have listened to her. He was so angry that he wasn't thinking clearly.

Trying to overcome her own discomfiture and feeling as though Sal was lurking behind every massive, ancient tree, she began taking pictures and documenting the plants again, her heart in her throat as she made her way to a huge, yellow mastic tree with roots stretching across the path.

She tried to pretend the world couldn't come crashing down around her ears if the two men tangled as wolves.

Shelley had thought Duncan would be trouble if *he* stayed with *her*?

Hell, how had this happened? He'd been checking out Silverman's house again, discovering four Doberman guard dogs and two men roaming the place along with a couple of gardeners. All of the men were human, which was a blessing. They couldn't spot him in the dark of night, and they couldn't smell him if the breeze blew in his favor. His survey of the staff seemed to confirm that Silverman surrounded himself with humans. Probably because wolves would have known how risky stealing fortunes from wealthy families would be.

This time, Duncan had joined others at the beach near Silverman's house, swimming with several people of different ages—older men and women, teens, and children—so he looked like one of the tourists. Many were walking along the beach and looking at the large estates. He was walking with some of them when he checked his phone messages and realized Shelley must have called while he was swimming.

The cryptic message about wanting to see a plant specimen had totally thrown him. He almost didn't call her back, being not in the least interested in a discussion of plants of any variety, especially not while he was trying to figure a way to get to Silverman.

But her message sounded so urgent, and something else bothered him about it. He couldn't decide what it was. A deeper anxiety, he thought. And whispered. That's what it was. She'd whispered her message to him like she was in some kind of trouble. So he called her to make sure she was all right. If her call was only about plants, he had intended to set her straight on how much they didn't interest him.

Her response was so thoroughly confusing that he felt as if she'd had a conversation with him that morning and somehow he'd missed the gist of it. Who would have blamed him when he kept staring at that silky, barely there robe and wanting to glimpse the naked flesh underneath?

When had she mentioned that they were going on a dinner cruise?

He thought maybe she'd been out in the sun too long and was dehydrated, but the forest was shaded. He had packed two bottles of water for her because of the humidity in the air. Unless she'd been so excited about the plants that she hadn't been drinking her water.

He couldn't understand it. He was ready to join her, make her drink the water, and get her back to the villa to cool down before she passed out. But then he learned that Sal was there with her. *Bloody hell.*

A red haze had filled his vision, his heartbeat pounded ominously in his ears, and his blood was on fire as he tried to keep his wits about him.

Why in the hell had Sal been at the reserve? Of all the places on the island, Duncan would never have worried about the bastard venturing there. Now Shelley had caught his eye.

She was a female wolf, unmated and a real looker. Damn it.

He tried telling himself she might be right, that he should stay away from the reserve until Silverman left the area. But if he was still there, Duncan didn't want him anywhere near Shelley. He didn't want her seeing Silverman for drinks or any other business later this evening, either. He worried she still might think she could help get the money from the bastard, and he didn't want her involved.

Duncan was already flooring the gas pedal to reach the reserve and make sure Shelley was okay. He could tell from her voice that she was strong, capable, and determined to play any role he wanted, but he wasn't letting her take part in it.

She also had sounded worried—not for herself as much as for him.

He ground his teeth, then pulled his phone out and called her again. As soon as she answered, he asked, "Is he alone?"

"No. Which is why I said to wait to come and get me when I'm through here."

She didn't say who he had been with and her voice was still hushed, which made Duncan believe the bastard was still nearby, possibly listening in. "Okay. A guard with him?"

"No."

"A woman?" he asked, sounding really surprised. How could Silverman have been hitting on Shelley if he had a woman with him? Duncan suspected the woman wasn't his mother.

"Yes."

"Young? Girlfriend?" Duncan asked.

"Yes."

Duncan cursed in Gaelic.

"I love the sound of the words you just spoke, but I'm guessing they weren't love sentiments."

He gave a dark smile. "I'm coming for you. Just continue your work, and when I arrive, I'll call you and locate you."

"I can't dissuade you?"

"No. This man has too much to lose. He could be capable of anything. For your information, we're going on the dinner cruise, so you can't go out for drinks with him tonight or any other."

He heard her take in a deep breath. "Who's paying?" she asked.

He smiled. "I'm sure my brother, Ian, will understand that this is a necessary expense. I'll see you momentarily." He hung up, hating that she was alone in the forest with no protection whatsoever, and drove even faster.

He still couldn't believe the she-wolf had run into *his* quarry while doing *her* job which had nothing to do with *his* job. He saw no sign of Sal Silverman when he parked the car at the trailhead, but he smelled the bastard as soon as he left the vehicle. At least he assumed it was the bastard's scent, male wolf, and no other like it in the area.

He quickly locked the vehicle and strode down the trail, wondering just what he'd do if he ran into Silverman. He'd like to wring the crook's neck, but he had to get the clan's money out of him first. Then he'd wring his neck.

He'd stalked along what seemed an hour's worth of trail when he spied Shelley crouching in front of a flower, camera angled to take a shot. He paused, not wanting to disturb her work. When she was done, she lifted her nose a little, turned suddenly, and nearly fell on her butt when she saw him watching her.

He strode toward her and helped her up. He hadn't meant to do anything more than that, but she threw herself into his arms. One hand still clutched a notepad and pen, while the other was clinging to her camera. Both arms wrapped around him in a lover's embrace, her breasts pressed hard against his chest, and instantly he was aroused.

"I thought you said you didn't want to see me this soon," he whispered into her hair, kissing her on top of her head, hugging her tight, and loving her exuberance, but suspecting she'd worried about his safety more than her own.

With her face buried against his chest, she shook her head. "I had too much work to do," she whispered back.

"Liar," he said, his voice still hushed as he separated from her and looked into her large, green, very worried eyes. "You didn't want me killing the bastard in this special place of yours."

She choked back a little laugh, tears welling up in her eyes. "You're right. So are you going to tell me what you said in Gaelic over the phone?"

"Nay, lass. It isn't something your tender ears should hear."

She smiled at him. "I'm sure I've heard it all. Are you certain you don't want me to have drinks with him?"

"Aye, I'm certain." He gave her whole body a tight squeeze. "Are you done here?"

"No, but you can keep me company. Protect me from anything or anyone while you're at it."

He snorted and released her. "I came to take you away from here."

"I know," she said. She looped her arm around his, since both her hands were full, and tugged him to stroll with her. "I said I wasn't done. He's not here any longer. If you don't want to be here with me, it's all right with me, although it's really nice having you here while I'm working."

He frowned down at her but noted she was serious.

She continued, "If you want me to help with your mission, I'd be willing to do it. It affects me personally, too."

"I'm not willing. It's too dangerous."

"Even for the money?" She eyed him speculatively.

"Even for all the money in the world." He was serious about that.

"All right, but you can't say I didn't offer." She stopped at another tree and said, "It's a giraffe tree. See its winding, odd shape?" Then she snapped another picture. "If I'd needed your rescue, you could have swung through the trees, hanging onto the vines like Tarzan, and swooped down to take me with you into the canopy."

"Ah, lass, now what would a Highlander be doing swinging from vines in trees like an ape man? I would be riding my horse, swinging a claymore at yonder enemy, and then I'd slip you into my saddle and ride off with you."

"Into the sunset."

He laughed. "Aye, into the sunset."

After moving only a couple of inches, she bent down and took several more pictures. He let out his breath hard. "They all look the same. Why are you taking a picture of every leaf in the forest?"

She laughed. "What if I were to say all swords look the same to me? They have a handle and a blade."

He smiled.

"See, so they're not all the same." With that, she continued to take pictures until the filtered light that managed to sift through the trees began to fade.

"We'll miss our dinner excursion if we don't hurry," he finally said.

"Were you serious about that?" She quickly pocketed her camera and notebook in her backpack, grabbed his hand, and rushed him to the parking area.

"Of course I'm serious. If Silverman investigates, he'll find you did go out on a dinner cruise at 5:30. I made reservations on the way over here."

"You should have mentioned it to me earlier. Hurry or we'll miss the sailboat."

He laughed and hauled her toward the parking lot even faster.

They were soon on their way to the boat dock at the water sports center on Seven Mile Beach where they'd pick up the catamaran. He looked forward to wining and dining the wolf on the waves.

She combed her fingers through her breeze-tangled hair and peered into the visor mirror. "I hope I'm dressed all right in capris, tennis shoes, and this shirt."

He glanced at the stretchy peach fabric of the tank top molding to her breasts, only partially hidden by the green leafy shirt she wore over it, and shook his head. No wonder Silverman was interested. "You look good in anything you wear. Too good."

"That's not what I mean."

"It's a catamaran cruise. It can't be too dressy. You're fine. Hell, better than fine."

She smiled. "You know the right words, but if I see all the women wearing dresses…" She pulled off her backpack, dug out a band, and tied her hair back in a ponytail. "How long is the dinner cruise?"

"Three and half hours. I'll have you home and in bed sometime after nine tonight."

She chewed on her bottom lip, not sure where this

was going. Did he mean they were going to share a bed? She really didn't want to ask. If he did want to share the big bed with her, she was already game. She supposed the reason she had changed her mind was that he had been so gallant in coming to her rescue. Not to mention that he was taking her on a dinner cruise tonight. But it was more than that. She really didn't want the night with him to end.

"I guess I'd better call Silverman and tell him I'll be tied up all night."

"As much as I hate that you have to say another word to him…" Duncan cast her a dark look. "Maybe you shouldn't call him. Just leave him hanging."

She shook her head. "I'm never that rude. Even if the guy is a Class A crook. Maybe we should think up a code so that if I run into him again when you're not around, I can give you a call and you'll know what's up."

Duncan scowled at that.

"Ignoring the possibility that it might happen again won't make it go away. If I had given you the code word that said Silverman was on his way down the path coming toward me, you might have called me back faster."

Duncan seemed to ponder that.

She raised her brows. "Well, I couldn't come up with anything else that fit what I was doing at the time. I can't help it if you thought I was crazy."

He smiled a little.

She harrumphed. "So you did think I was crazy. That's why we need a code." She pulled her phone and Silverman's card out of her pack, then flipped the card over to get his number off the back. The drinks engagement hadn't been until seven, so she still had time to beg off. She really didn't want to have to talk to the creep again.

"Hello, um, Sal?" she said when he answered. He sounded way too interested in seeing her again.

She was rethinking what Duncan had said—that she shouldn't have called him back at all.

Chapter 7

SHELLEY SWORE DUNCAN HAD STIFFENED BESIDE HER for calling Silverman by his first name. Maybe just hearing her talk with the crook irritated the Highlander.

"Hello. Is this the pretty wolf I met in the forest?" Sal asked, almost sounding bubbly.

She wanted to throw up, hated having to act, and knew that if she had been asked to be an extra in the film with Duncan, she would have made a real muddle of it.

"Shelley," she quickly said, not liking the way he thought he was ingratiating himself with her with his glib talk. The man was so full of himself that he hadn't even asked her name. "I won't be able to meet you for drinks tonight."

First, there was a stunned silence. That made her smile. Then he began to argue with her. "I've already planned—"

"I *did* have a previous engagement," she said, stopping him from saying whatever he had to say. She didn't want to hear what he had planned. She didn't want Duncan to hear it, either. "I had my days mixed up. I wasn't sure. That's why I couldn't say at the reserve if I could come over for drinks."

Thankfully, Sal must not have stuck around in the forest listening to her phone conversation like she'd worried he might. Probably because he had his girlfriend with him and was afraid she'd open her big mouth again and give away his location and what he was doing.

He tried again with his smooth attempt at seduction. "Is your girlfriend a wolf, too? I could have a friend come over and—"

"Um, no. I mean, I called my girlfriend, but I'm actually going out with a man I'd met who was kind enough to give me a ride to my place from the airport. He's taking me on a sunset dinner cruise tonight."

The silence was palpable. Duncan smirked in a purely wolfish way. He might not have his money back, but he had beaten the wolf at *this* game. Not only was he taking her on a sunset dinner cruise that trumped drinks at the guy's estate, but Duncan had been chivalrous enough to drive her from the airport. Sal also knew she'd just met the guy. Sal was a little late in making a move on her. Having a female clinging to him in the reserve hadn't helped, either.

"I see," Sal finally remarked, sounding extremely vexed.

She was sure that Duncan's offer had more than unsettled the cheat, who she guessed was used to getting his way in most situations. Money could buy a lot of things. But not her.

"All right. What about tomorrow?" he asked, and he truly sounded like he thought he still had a chance with her.

Shocked that he'd ask her out again, she felt her mouth drop open. She'd suspected that once she said she was seeing another man, Sal would get the hint and butt out. Apparently not. He had the arrogance of an alpha male backed by tons of ill-gotten money. If she went anywhere with him, all she'd be thinking about would be how Sal was spending Duncan's clan's money on her. She'd want to shift and tear into him herself to convince him to give it up.

"I... don't know about tomorrow." She hated coming up with excuses on the fly. But even though she didn't want to see the bastard again, she might be able to help Duncan get his money back.

Duncan didn't even look at her, saying louder than he needed to, "We have a pirates' sailing-ship excursion tomorrow, remember? The Jolly Roger?"

"Oh, yeah." Damned if she'd known that. This was getting to be one really super-fun vacation. Except for this business with Sal Silverman.

Again, silence.

"That's in the afternoon, isn't it?" Sal said, sounding perturbed. "Unless it's the dinner cruise again."

She figured he was doubly irritated because he now knew Duncan was listening in on the conversation. Being alpha to the max, Duncan intended to thwart Sal in every way he could, which made her smile.

"Yes, I guess." She had no idea which cruise Duncan had in mind.

But Sal wasn't about to be thwarted, either. "Then we can have dinner later in George Town."

One thing about wolf hearing: they heard. From quiet talks to phone conversations, they heard.

"We have dinner plans," Duncan said self-assuredly.

Of course he was right in thinking that if she wanted to go out, it would be with him. She enjoyed his company immensely. Even so, why was *she* bothering to speak with Sal when the two men were having a fine conversation without her?

She frowned at Duncan and held the phone out to him as if to allow him to talk it over with Sal. Duncan ignored the offer of the phone.

She pulled it back to her ear but before she could relay Duncan's words, certain that Sal had heard them anyway, Sal said, "I'll call you back later." The phone clicked dead.

She slipped her phone in her pocket and folded her arms. "He's angry."

Duncan gave her a self-satisfied smirk as he parked the car at the dock and opened her door for her.

"Well?" she said. "How are you going to get the money out of him if you piss him off over me before you can even ask him about your stolen investments?"

Duncan wrapped his arm around her shoulders and headed down the dock. "You know, maybe now that he's got a little female wolf to pursue, he'll come out of hiding—no goons, no girlfriend—and then I can take him to task one-on-one."

"That could work. You're a genius."

He kissed her cheek. "You should tell my brothers that. But in truth, I don't want you involved."

"As soon as he tried to pick me up at the reserve, I became involved. Are we really going out on a pirate ship tomorrow?"

"Aye, lass. In the 1600s, pirates made port here. So the Jolly Roger excursion is a way to have some sporting good fun with a poke at the past."

She thought he was too broke. She truly believed him in that regard. "But... what about your finances?"

"Ian will understand the necessity. The money I was paid as an extra is mixed in with the clan's money, but even so, I should have some say in this. Besides, the expense of a room is not the same as an expense in drawing out the enemy."

Drawing out the enemy? Or doing whatever he could to protect Shelley from the bastard coming after her? She wished she was swimming in money so she could pay for the extra excursions for both of them. "Does the pirate ship have a gangplank?"

"Aye, what respectable pirate ship would not? Now, if I had my trusty claymore, I'd make all the scurvy pirates walk the plank and take my sea wolf on a nice long sail. You do have sea legs, don't you, lass? You seemed to love the water, but I didn't ask if boats bothered you."

"Oh yes, I love the water and I love to sail." She settled next to him on the catamaran where other couples had found places to call their own for the cruise.

Duncan ordered Baileys Irish Cream for Shelley and a whiskey for himself.

The turquoise waters were so inviting that she wanted to slip into them and swim right beside the boat. "Maybe if we're not too tired tonight, we could swim with the sharks again."

He chuckled and wrapped his arm around her as they sailed out to sea. The lulling feel of the boat cutting through the placid water, with Duncan holding her like this, made her feel as though she was in heaven. About twenty people were on the boat, all having their own conversations and enjoying the wind in the sails and the trip out to sea just like Shelley and Duncan were.

"It might be tempting fate to swim in the water at night again with the sharks feeding more often then. But aye, if you want to risk it, I'll protect you," Duncan remarked.

She smiled and sipped her Baileys. "You are such a brave Highlander. What about stingrays?"

"What about them? I'm not sure punching them in the nose would keep them away from you if one decided to attack." He finished his whiskey and paid for another.

She laughed and squeezed his arm. "No, you can take a boat out to an area to snorkel and feed the rays. Would you want to swim with the stingrays? My treat."

His eyes sparkled with merriment. "When you put it that way... how can a Scot resist?"

"You wouldn't be afraid they'd eat you, would you?"

"Not me. I would be afraid they'd grab one of those bikini strings of yours and..." He frowned at her. "You have to wear something else on the pirate ship and when we go snorkeling with the rays. If any man looked you over for even a fraction of a second wearing so little— and he'd be doing it for a lot longer than that—I'd have to rearrange his face."

She laughed. "I only wear the bikini when swimming at night, normally just when I'm out with my girlfriend. I hadn't expected you to follow me down to the water. If I'm to walk the plank and jump into the deep, blue sea, I definitely would risk losing my bikini. Besides, it's family fare during the day, so I'll dress modestly. Swim trunks down to my knees with a big billowing skirt and a high neckline."

He laughed. "That I've got to see."

But she was certain he'd prefer seeing her string bikini again.

After they finished their drinks, the catamaran anchored, and they were served bowls of potato soup to start the three-course gourmet dinner. Then the main course came. Both chose mahimahi with Cayman-style sauce to enjoy the island experience, rather than selecting the chicken with mushroom sauce. Their fish was served on a bed of rice with steamed vegetables on the side, and slices of white bread and creamy butter. Coffee and rum cake finished the meal.

Everything was delicious, and as they ate each course, the catamaran rocked slightly in the Caribbean Sea. Shelley realized then that she'd never actually eaten on a boat, just sailed a few times. But anchoring and eating at a candlelight dinner shared with Duncan was romantic and casual and unique enough that she'd remember it fondly forever.

Feeling full after eating the last of her rum cake, Shelley didn't think the night could get any better. But Duncan took her to the bow of the boat and pulled her to sit between his legs, well away from everyone else. Loosely draping his arms about her shoulders, he held her like that as they watched the sun sink lower in the sky. It was as if none of the rest of the people on the boat existed, just two wolves enjoying the sunset on a dinner cruise.

The bright ball of fire slipped into the blue water, leaving wide pink, purple, and orange ribbons stretched across the sky as if an artist had stroked his paintbrush across it. Skimpy clouds, a darker shade of purple, floated across the ribbons, growing darker as the sun sank lower.

Duncan wrapped his arms around Shelley's waist, tightening his grip as he leaned down and kissed her ear. She sighed, loving every minute of the colorful display, wishing she had her camera with her to catch the vibrant colors that made the night even more perfect, and loving being in the Highlander's arms. But she'd left her camera in her backpack in the car. "Hmm, Duncan, this beats drinks with Sal at his place any day."

She shouldn't have mentioned Sal when she was having such a good time with Duncan, but she couldn't get the crook off her mind.

"I'm sure he's rethinking his miserly offer of a date with you. Hell, for you, he should have offered the moon. He sure can afford it."

Sal had to be pissed off that Duncan had taken her out. "Most likely women rarely turn him down, no matter what his offer is."

"He's not that outstanding looking," Duncan grouched.

Shelley gave a little laugh. "No, not at all. Distinguished but not movie-star handsome. Not like you. I dare say he's never been in a movie."

Duncan grunted. "I was an extra."

"Right. But he has sort of an appeal, like a man used to getting his way, someone who has money and power." She shrugged. "A lot of women are drawn to that."

"But not you."

"No. I know what a rat he is, but it wouldn't have mattered. The only reason I didn't turn him down outright was that I thought I could help you get to him. So I didn't want to burn bridges right away."

"I don't want you near him. This is strictly my business, understand?" Duncan had the stern look of a warrior who didn't want a woman getting hurt or involved in any way.

"Of course," Shelley said, not about to get into an argument with Duncan. If he wanted her help, she'd do what she could. If not, that was his call. "Will you drop me off at the reserve again tomorrow?"

His mouth parted, and then he frowned. "Didn't you already record every plant there was in the forest?"

She smiled. "More than one hundred species and more than five hundred and fifty plants live in the forest. I think I missed one or two."

He shook his head.

When the catamaran began to sail back to port, Shelley was in wolf heaven, snuggling next to Duncan as if the two of them were on a honeymoon. Or like wolves might do, curled up together under the light of a silvery moon.

She wanted to stay up all night. Run as a wolf with him. Swim as a human. Play until she was too exhausted to do anything but sleep. She wanted to enjoy all of that for now, and nothing more. She'd never had this much fun in her life. Going on a cruise like this with Wendy would never have been the same.

Her thoughts shifted to the problem with Silverman and what his next move might be.

"What if Silverman calls me again in the morning?"

"He's not going to wait."

She stiffened and looked up at Duncan. "What do you mean?"

"You only told him your first name over the phone, right? He hadn't even asked for it before this, expecting you to be blown away by his bold interest in you. He figured he'd learn all he wanted about you when you had drinks with him tonight."

"Yeah, he never did ask, and I wasn't about to offer until I spoke with you. I wanted to see if you thought we could use his interest in me to your advantage."

"That's the thing. He's going to want to know who you are, who your girlfriend is, and who I am before long. He's going to want to find out where we're all staying. He'll think you're rooming with a girlfriend. He'll have the notion of visiting you early tomorrow before I have a chance to pick you up for the pirate cruise. Try to ingratiate himself with you before it's too late. Maybe even attempt to turn your head so much that you'll forget you had a date with me in the afternoon."

"He can't think I'd be that interested in him. You don't think he believes I might consider being his mate, do you?"

Duncan snorted. "Money can buy just about anything. The thing of it is that the man's already got a mate."

Her jaw dropped.

"I wouldn't put it past him to take another, pretending he doesn't have one already and hiding that fact from his first mate while he hides her from you."

"Wolves don't do that."

"Normally, it's not done. Then again, normally they don't pick up other women, wolves or otherwise, once they have a mate. But he's got one, and she's still in the U.S. while he's dallying with some other woman here."

Shelley folded her arms, her back still stiff. It was one thing to pretend to be interested in a bachelor wolf to help Duncan out if she could. It was quite another to pretend to be interested in one who was not only mated but also having an affair with a human woman. He truly was a bastard.

Then another thought struck her. "Does his mate know about the money he's been stealing?"

"Aye, lass. Before he went into hiding from the

authorities, he deposited a whole lot of the stolen funds in her name. She didn't steal any of it that we know of, but she and Sal are attempting to avoid having to give up any of the estates they have all over the world—and luxury cars, two planes, and a couple of ships—by saying it was her wealth and had nothing to do with his stealing."

"It goes against everything I believe."

"The stolen money? Or lacking loyalty to a mate?"

"Both."

"Aye, that it does." Duncan sighed deeply. "I had not planned for things to go this way. What with the devil's interest in you, I will have to stick close to you, and I don't like it one wee bit."

"Sticking close to me?" she queried, her voice and brows raised.

He chuckled darkly. "Nay, lass. You think I would have an aversion to sticking close to you like this? I fear I'm going to have a time trying to learn where our money is while keeping him away from you."

Shelley pondered that for a moment, not liking that she would be the object of such scrutiny by a wolf as rotten to the core as Silverman. Nor that Duncan had to worry about her while he needed to learn what he could about Silverman and where the clan's funds were.

"What if he's waiting at the harbor now? What if he follows us from the harbor to the villa? He'll know you're rooming with me. Then again, maybe that will be the end of his interest in me—once he learns he's not going to be able to get to me alone all that easily. Since most wolves have scruples, he will assume that we're smitten with each other and that he has no chance."

Duncan ran his hands down Shelley's bare arms in a soothing way. "Nay. Over the years, I've learned that a liar believes everyone else lies. A cheat believes everyone else cheats. It's a way to justify one's own actions. He'll believe what he wants to about you. He'll find out soon enough that we're together. But I doubt that will dissuade him initially." Duncan leaned over and kissed her ear.

"That'll be a definite crimp in his plans to get you alone, to wean you away from me. He wouldn't have had time to post anyone at the dock before we left, but I'm almost certain he'll have someone watching now. Maybe even he himself will be nearby, checking me out—his competition—when we arrive back at the island."

They were getting closer, able to see the dock and sandy beach in the distance. She tried to make out anybody who might be watching them, but it was impossible, even though she could see better in the dark than a human could. "Maybe I should have told him I was mated to you."

"He'll know we're not mated, or you would have told him at the reserve. Hell, I would have told him so."

"If he learns who you are, won't he realize you might be trying to have your money returned?"

"No. We had the money listed under a corporation with a different name in the UK. He doesn't know he stole from a Highland wolf pack or he'd be running scared."

She nodded, suddenly understanding. "He'd go to a fancy prison for white-collar criminals if he got caught otherwise. Wolves would have to take him out," she said solemnly.

"Does it bother you?" Duncan wrapped his finger

around a wisp of hair that had pulled loose from her
ponytail.

"No. It would be disastrous if he went to prison. You
have no choice."

"Aye."

"So you're the one who's destined to take him down."

"Once I secure our money."

—◊◊◊—

Once the catamaran had docked, Duncan couldn't help
how protective he felt toward Shelley. He didn't want
Silverman to even think he could get near her while she
was on the island. He glanced around the area, looking
for signs of anyone who might be watching them. Any
of Silverman's hired human goons could see Shelley and
him on the lighted dock. But as wolves, he and Shelley
could also see Silverman's men if they hid in the dark to
observe the two of them.

Duncan suspected Silverman would come himself,
though, wanting to take a look at his competition, wanting to see if he could get a whiff of Duncan's scent and
learn if he was human or wolf. Duncan smiled in a dangerous way. If he'd thought Duncan was only human,
Silverman would soon know he had real competition for
the female wolf's affections.

For the first time since Duncan had met Shelley, he
wondered where the notion of winning her affections
had come from. He appreciated the way she'd offered
to let him stay with her and admired her for her fru-
gality, not caring for the kind who would throw their
money away on everything and nothing. He loved how
she wanted to help him in his quest, despite the danger

that could entail, and agreed with her about how wolves should behave when it came to mates. But competing to win her heart was another matter entirely.

He kept his arm around her waist, holding her close like a lover who couldn't get enough of being with his date. Just like him, she was wary, looking around—but carefully, not like someone who was sure anyone was out to get them. She snuggled closer, wrapped her arm around his waist, and leaned her head against his chest as if to tell anyone watching that she was Duncan's. He kissed the top of her head to show her how much he loved her playacting and to do his own part.

She didn't say anything until they were inside the rental car, away from the others on the cruise who either took a shuttle ride back to their hotels or climbed into their own rental cars. When she and Duncan were on their way back to the villa, she finally spoke. "Did you see him?"

"Nay. I wonder if he knows I'm a wolf yet. Thinking I'm human might be the reason he's still persisting in seeing you. He'd figure he easily had me beat."

"Or not. I might just want to have some fun on my vacation with a human. No ties that way. Since he's a wolf, he may realize I might not want to get involved with him in case he wanted a mating and I didn't. In any event, I'm sure he'll figure out you're a wolf quickly enough, if he doesn't already know." She patted Duncan's thigh and said, "Want to run as a wolf?"

He frowned at her. "I thought you wanted to go swimming." He was looking forward to seeing her in her string bikini again.

"That, too. The night is young."

He thought about them running as wolves in the dark, which did appeal. The moon was at its zenith tonight. He and his family were royals and could shift at will. Even so, the full moon called to him whenever it appeared.

If they shifted back to their human forms on the beach, why bother with swimsuits? He smiled.

She laughed. "So, what exactly are you thinking?"

He shook his head. "I forget how observant a female wolf can be."

"Oh yeah, just keep smiling when you're thinking all those wicked thoughts, and I'll be sure to know you're up to no good."

Chapter 8

As soon as Shelley and Duncan arrived back at the villa, they both hurried into the house, laughing and kissing and putting on a real show in case Silverman or one of his people had followed them. They were only playacting, but it felt real with both of them perfectly comfortable to show each other a lover's affection.

Duncan was again considering taking Shelley home with him. Only this time to meet the family—not just to see the castle gardens. Taking her home would mean the whole family ganging up on them to see who she was and pondering why he was bringing here there.

They shut the front door to the villa behind them, and Shelley headed for the guest bedroom. "I'll be down in a moment. In my wolf coat. You can get the back door. Too bad the villa doesn't have a wolf door."

"I imagine that's because no pets are allowed at the villa."

"Wouldn't the owners be surprised to know what is staying at their place? By the way, I want to return to the reserve tonight."

He frowned again at her. "In our wolf coats?"

"Yup. Silver palm trees shine in the moon's light, and I want to observe it. It's the perfect way to see them. I won't be spending time cataloging plants or taking pictures. I just want to run through there as a wolf before I leave the island. This evening the moon is at its fullest, and the palms should be spectacular." She smiled and hurried up the stairs.

Duncan wasn't a plant enthusiast, but her own enthusiasm made him rethink his interest in vegetation.

He had just finished closing all the blinds when he heard the familiar sound of a wolf running down the stairs. He remembered how beautiful Shelley had looked in her wolf coat when she'd attacked him in a mock battle last night and wished she wanted to do so again.

She headed past him as if his only mission was to open the back door for her, and he hurried to strip out of his clothes. She didn't turn to watch him, just waited patiently, standing at the door like a dog who wanted to play outside, her tail wagging enthusiastically. He opened the door for her, then followed her outside and watched her dash across the sand. He closed the door and summoned the need to shift, to join her and run and play and enjoy the wind in his fur and his face, the talcum-powder-like sand beneath his paws. The shifting was done quickly, his muscles stretching in a smooth, comfortable way to accommodate his wolf change until he was standing as a *lupus*, watching the female still heading toward the water.

He fought seeing her as *his* female, but he couldn't help himself. She *was* his. At least for now when she had no male from a pack who could watch out for her. She was his—to protect and enjoy.

With his ground-eating stride, he raced to catch up to her. She ran so fast that she was like a greyhound, and he loved stretching out his legs to join her. He definitely wanted to protect her from the sharks in the sea some more, but running as wolves was just as exhilarating.

She dashed into the water and snapped at the salty spray, bounding like a wolf pup, jumping and running. For a moment, he just stood and watched, fascinated by her playful side. He wanted to tackle her, but he was used to wrestling with his brothers and male cousins in feral wolf rough-housing with no holds barred, which often accidentally drew blood. He was afraid to play with her like that, afraid of using his brute strength against hers, fearing he'd injure her and she would see him in a different light—savage instead of heroic.

She took off down the beach. He bounded after her.

She ran as if she were in a race to the finish, her tongue lolling to the side as she panted, and his did, too. But running together like this as wolves made him feel even closer to her, their shoulders brushing, their flanks touching. When he felt the overwhelming urge to turn his head and lick her, which he did, he saw the surprise in her green eyes. She smiled a little in a wolf's way. He smiled back and continued running alongside her, pushing their endurance as if they were on a hunt and ready to take down some prey.

If she hadn't been with him, he would have loved to have gotten Sal out here to confront him wolf to wolf.

When Duncan and Shelley reached the Mastic Reserve trailhead, they ran along the narrow path through the trees and vines toward the north of the island. Traveling through the mangrove swamp, they saw the moonlight reflected off the silver fronds of a stand of palms. They both paused to look at the spectacular sight, which seemed magical in the dark forest. They continued on until they stopped at the halfway point up the trail where the majestic mastic tree towered overhead.

He noted colorful parrots, a dove, and even a woodpecker half hidden in the leaves of the trees. And some kind of a furry varmint; he had no idea what it was. As soon as it saw them, it scurried into the underbrush. Lizards appeared on branches and leaves, and disappeared. Shelley ran on, and he raced to catch up.

He often ran in the ancient Caledonian Forest at night back home, sometimes alone, sometimes with his brothers or cousins. Loping through an ancient forest on an island paradise with a woman who made him harden with a touch or a look wasn't something he'd ever thought he'd experience. He didn't think running through the Highland forest would have the same impact on his feral senses as being with her did right now. Running with her as a wolf in his woods was a very appealing thought.

When they came to the end of the trail, she looped around, licked his face, offered him a wolfish smile, and raced back down the path to the trailhead again. The time had come to swim with the mermaid in the sea. He liked that notion better than running in a forest with her as a wolf—even in paradise.

Duncan estimated it was nearly midnight when they arrived back at the beach in front of their villa. He was so intent on watching Shelley's every move that he'd only given Silverman a sliver of thought since they're returned to the villa. Silverman be damned.

Shelley didn't return to the villa to shift into her human form and grab a swimsuit as Duncan had expected. He'd been looking forward to seeing her in that string bikini again. Although he wanted to feel more of her this time, to touch her breasts barely secured in the skimpy top, run his fingers over her nipples erect beneath the shimmering blue fabric, and slip it down beneath the surface of the water so he could touch all of her, feel all of her.

Instead, she dashed into the surf as a wolf, paddled out, and dove under. She nearly gave him a heart attack as he tried to swim after her in his wolf form. Not that wolves weren't great swimmers, but he didn't expect to see her disappear beneath the waves as a wolf.

Before he knew what was up, she surfaced next to him in her human form. He was wolf paddling beside one sexy, naked woman.

She grinned at him as he quickly shifted, the blurring of forms so instantaneous that almost anyone watching would blink twice and know they couldn't have observed what they thought they did. Certainly not if that observer had seen them in the dark ocean or on the equally dark beach.

Intent on dragging Shelley into his arms and kissing her thoroughly, he reached out to grab her. Anticipating his action, she dove under the water again. The chase was on. Fortunately, with his night vision—and the moon so full and the water so crystal clear—he could see her swimming beneath the waves and follow her.

He was a powerful swimmer, having braved the cold Irish and North Seas and the lochs near Argent Castle. But he'd never chased a mermaid in warm waters nearly as dark as midnight, with colorful schools of fish darting about as if Shelley and he were predators in the mix. The currents pulled them down the beach. He allowed the sea to carry him toward her as he stroked the silky water to catch up to her.

He was gaining on her, and by the way she was beginning to panic with her strokes, he suspected she knew he was nearly upon her. He contemplated strategies— grabbing her foot or merely brushing a finger down the sole of her foot, tickling it to see her reaction. Or swimming beside her for a while before he took her in his arms and ravished her. Sooner or later. That was the only question. Would it be sooner or later?

He'd never pursued a female wolf before; human women, yes. Many over the years. But he'd never been so intrigued by a female wolf that he wanted to pursue her. Either the wolves he'd met had been mated or he just had not been interested. This one created problems he wasn't sure he was willing to confront. She was American, living in America. His mate would have to live with him. In Scotland. What would a woman like Shelley think of moving to the ancestral home where her people had lived before being abruptly sent away, forced to pull up roots and move to other countries?

If it went that far, how could he force her to leave her home, give up her job, and live with him?

No, it would never work. But he didn't back off. Damn it. He wanted her. Even if just for a feral wolf's release—as long as she was willing. He'd never played with a female that stirred his loins like she did, either as a wolf or a man. He wanted her so badly that he could barely keep himself in check to let this go at a more leisurely pace with no strings attached.

He wasn't certain where she wanted to go with this, either. He suspected—maybe because she hadn't bothered with a bathing suit this time—she wanted to ravish him back. But maybe that was damned wishful thinking on his part.

He swam closer and ran his hand over her silky calf, up the back of her thigh, and over her bare buttock. She turned to look at him, her mouth smiling in the most seductively devilish way. He truly meant to give her a choice—come to him, kiss him, hold him close—but as soon as she smiled like a wolf who wanted him, that was all that mattered.

He pulled her into his arms and licked the salty water off her lips as he planted his feet on the sand, the warm water lapping at his waist. She gently raked her fingernails up his back like a feline with her claws extended, careful not to scratch, her chin tilted up, her wet lashes tracing her cheeks as she parted her lips and offered herself to him. Her green eyes were closed, her breath coming quickly, most likely in part because of their run and then their swimming, and partly because of the passion flaring between them.

He slid his hands down her backside until he cupped her buttocks and pulled her close, pressing her against his arousal, hard and wanting, showing her just what she did to him. Damned if he didn't want to be inside her tight sheath, thrusting, pleasuring her, and satisfying his own raging desire.

Even though she was breathing hard against his mouth, he gave her the barest of kisses because he knew having a little of her wouldn't be enough, and he'd want it all. But he was trying damned hard to stick with something simple, uncomplicated, and nothing permanent. Just a little innocent pleasuring between two wolves.

Innocent, his ass. There was nothing innocent about the way the she-wolf felt as the currents pushed her soft curves against him, her body sliding provocatively against his with the constant gentle swell of waves assaulting them.

He slid his lips across her parted ones, the invitation raw and inviting. Yet she waited for him to take charge of her mouth, to take control of the seduction. Or else she was just better than him at not jumping into something that was bound to cause them problems if at least one of them didn't put a halt to it.

Again, he licked her lips and then slid his tongue into her mouth, tasting the flavors of rum and Baileys Irish Cream, and she moaned, tilting her head back even more. If he hadn't been holding her, he was certain she would have sunk below the surface of the water.

But her sweet, lusty moan undid him and catapulted him into thrusting his tongue deeper into her mouth while she dug her nails into his back.

Her luscious mouth wasn't enough. He soon had her legs wrapped around his waist so he could lean her back and feast on her succulent breasts. He kissed and suckled a nipple while his hand massaged the other with reverence. Her hands grasped his shoulders, and she leaned back, her eyes closed, her lips parted as she mewled in ecstasy.

The heels of her feet pressed between the backs of his legs as the swells of the sea drew her up and down against his raging erection. It would have been so easy to take her, to satisfy his growing need to find release deep inside her, yet he attempted to keep thoughts about his own needs at bay and pleasure her as much as she was pleasuring him.

He slipped his fingers behind her to find the chasm between her legs and the slickness indicating she was ready for him if he so desired and she agreed. She leaned forward now, her hands clutching his shoulders as he stroked her, but it was hard this way and he whispered, "Turn around for me, lass."

She obliged, unwrapping her legs from around his waist and setting her feet on the sandy bottom of the sea floor. "What did you want to do?" she asked, sounding intrigued.

He turned her around, encouraged her to wrap her legs around him with her buttocks against his arousal, her knees parted wide. Like this, she was much more vulnerable to his touch, like a wolf who would expose her belly to a male wolf she trusted completely. She didn't have any way to balance herself, but he was in control. His arm was anchored beneath her breasts to keep her in place, allowing him to caress her while he kissed and nuzzled her ear, her neck, her throat, and his free hand began its judicious assault on her clit. Her legs around him, knees spread wide, she arched her back against him as he stroked and plucked and tweaked her sensitive nub, enjoying her moans while the winds and waves drowned out her sounds of joy.

"Shelley," he groaned, nearly coming with the way her body rode the waves against him, grinding her buttocks against his stiff erection, the way she arched and twisted and writhed against his touch until she cried out his name with such passion that he realized he'd never heard a woman say his name with so much joy.

He hadn't thought it possible, but her body pressing hard against his pushed his own climax to the top until he was spilling his seed between them, mixing with the Caribbean waters. For a mind-boggling instant, he had the unfathomable thought that he'd wasted his seed. How he could have started his own wolf offspring with Shelley.

He wasn't sure where these crazy notions were coming from. He was a Highland warrior, and wolf pups and babies were not part of the persona of a battle-hardened fighter.

Shelley tried to stand and laughed when her legs nearly buckled. He caught her around the waist again. "I'm not usually this... indisposed after..." She let her words trail off.

He smiled darkly at her. "You've never been with a Highland wolf."

She laughed. "I've never been with a wolf. It's just too dangerous a thing to do. I can see that for myself now."

Out of nowhere, a rogue wave rose behind them, huge, powerful, and ready to suck them under. Before either of them could react, it crashed over them both. He lost his grip on her, tumbling after her in the frothing water.

He grabbed her foot and pulled her to him. Neither of them was in any danger, but he didn't want to let her go, even for the briefest of moments. She was laughing, coughing, and trying to catch her breath as she wiped the salt water from her eyes. He scooped her into his arms and carried her to the shore.

"I hope no one catches us out here like this," she said, clearing her husky throat.

Not a soul was in sight, everyone having retired to bed hours earlier. Besides, it was too dark to see anything. "No one but us wolves." He kissed her cheek.

She snuggled close and purred.

Her snuggling and purring undid him. "About the sleeping arrangements…" he said.

"I was afraid you'd want to make other arrangements."

"Aye. I want us to share the queen-sized bed."

"But will it be safe?" she asked.

"After the day and night we've had? All we'll do is sleep."

"Hmm." She sounded as if she would drift off in his arms before he reached the villa. "Somehow I don't think being with you anywhere would be truly safe."

He chuckled. "Aye. So you see, lass, if you were upstairs in the twin bed, you'd feel the same way."

"Do all Scots think like you?"

Men of any persuasion, he thought grimly, if they had a female wolf like Shelley in their sights.

"Do you have a swimsuit?" she asked suddenly.

"Just shorts."

"We'll have to go shopping and buy you a pair of swim trunks if I'm going to make you walk the pirate's plank tomorrow afternoon."

"Who says you're going to make *me* walk the plank?" he asked, amused at the turn of the conversation.

She laughed. "Surely you don't think you're going to make *me* do it!"

Aye, that's just what he thought.

As soon as he let her down on the patio, he opened the back door for her. She walked inside and froze. She sniffed the air, her heart beating erratically as Duncan caught the same scent.

"Stay here," he commanded, then shifted into his wolf form and raced through the living room and master bedroom, then up the stairs to the guest bedroom, furious enough to rip the crook to shreds.

Silverman *had* been inside the villa while they were away. Had he been watching them while they swam? Or had he just waited until they ran off down the beach in their wolf forms, then checked out the villa and left?

Infuriated, Duncan tried to fight the darkness that swamped him. As a warrior, he couldn't tolerate an affront this blatant. But he didn't want Shelley seeing this side of him.

He wondered why he'd come to that conclusion when before he had been content to be who he was. Even proud to be thought of as a warrior willing to grind any enemy into the ground. A warrior who wasn't prone to having a pretty face turn his head.

The little red she-wolf had turned him inside out. Not in a bad way, either. She'd lightened his mood considerably since he'd spied her in the airport. For the first time ever, he'd felt carefree, like Cearnach always acted. Cheerful and pleased. Duncan knew his brother better. Knew that he was all warrior and business and darkness when the situation warranted it. Duncan wasn't normally the jubilant type, though.

Still hot with anger, Duncan raced back down the stairs, wanting to take the bastard on. He ran past Shelley, who looked anxious, but he wasn't sure if that was because of his behavior or Silverman's. Duncan shifted at the back door and then shut, locked, and bolted it. Turning, he hoped he'd hidden his feral feelings, but the expression of concern on Shelley's face told him he wasn't doing a good job of it.

"He was here," she said softly.

"Aye," Duncan growled, his voice low and angry. So much for attempting to act as though this didn't bother him as much as it did. "He was trying to learn about the sleeping arrangements. He would have discovered from our scents that we slept in separate beds last night."

He had mixed feelings about that. On the one hand, he wanted the bastard to know he'd claimed Shelley. That she was part of his territory. His. Not that she truly was.

On the other hand, he wanted Silverman to know she wasn't the kind of wolf who took up with anyone and probably would be willing to do the same with Silverman. Duncan had no intention of allowing the bastard to think he had any chance with her. He slipped his hand around hers and gave her a reassuring squeeze.

"You don't have to worry about him." He was certain Shelley didn't believe him entirely.

Not liking that the bastard had slipped into her villa and inspected the place, Shelley swallowed hard, squeezed Duncan's hand back to show she appreciated his concern and protectiveness, and then pulled away and headed for the stairs. She would have stayed with Duncan for the night, but Sal's little visit decided it.

She paused at the foot of the stairs and turned, worried about what Sal might have discovered about Duncan. "Did you have anything in your bag that would give away your mission here?"

"Nay. I only had a shaving kit and some clothes. My passport and driver's license won't help him make any connection to the fraud he's committed." He glanced down at her body, shimmering with water and naked, while his glistened with droplets, aroused and ready for action.

Despite being angered by Sal's actions, Duncan

couldn't hide his attraction for her. Her nipples were standing at attention, letting him know she was just as interested in him.

But she knew what she had to do: stay in separate beds or this was going to go further than what they could risk. And beyond that, she didn't want Sal to get the wrong impression about her. "All right. I'll see you in the morning for a shorter trip to the forest so we don't miss our pirate sailing excursion."

Duncan ground his teeth and looked vastly disappointed that she wasn't going to share a bed with him. She couldn't. Not if she was going to keep from getting herself in too deep with him. She was serious when she said she wasn't safe staying with him. Not because he was such a bad boy, but because she couldn't keep her hands off him, either. As tense as he was, she thought he was fighting with himself over doing the honorable thing or trying to convince her to stay with him.

Her phone rang, literally saving the day. She raced upstairs to get it. His heavy footfalls up the stairs made her turn to see him following her, to her surprise. When she crossed the floor to her bag and whipped out her phone, she saw it was just her girlfriend Wendy. She realized Duncan had assumed it was Sal. From his fierce scowl, she assumed if it had been Sal, Duncan would have ripped the phone from her grip and had some words with the creep.

She shook her head at Duncan. "It's just Wendy. I promised to call her and I forgot."

Duncan grumbled a good-night and headed back down the stairs for the master bedroom. She noted he did not offer to switch rooms with her for the night.

"Wendy, sorry I didn't call you earlier."

"Having too much fun? I was feeling bad that you wouldn't enjoy your trip there, just working yourself to death like usual. I knew you'd spend all day every day with your nose in the flora and fauna, but I worried about your nightlife. I guess you're having a good time after all. So tell me all about him."

"First, he's a wolf."

Shelley expected her friend to say something, anything. When she didn't, Shelley thought maybe their phone connection had been cut off. "Wendy?"

"A wolf and a Highlander? All in one? Hell, Shelley, that sounds like a dangerous combination."

Shelley cleared her throat, still a little rough from swallowing some of the ocean water. "Yes."

"Okay, spill, and tell me every detail. If you leave anything out, I will know. You know I will."

Shelley laughed. "Yeah, I know you will, too."

But she wasn't sure what to say about Sal Silverman. She supposed it was best to only mention that another wolf who was a crook was staying on the island. That he had laundered money in bank accounts and was trying to see her. And that Duncan was putting a stop to any ploys the other man might have.

She didn't mention that the bastard had stolen money from Duncan's clan and the college. That he had sneaked into the villa to find out where she and Duncan had slept. Wendy would tell Shelley's mother, and her mother would tell her uncles, and the next thing Shelley knew, they'd be insisting she return home at once.

As to Silverman's little foray into the villa, she was glad she and Duncan had been staying in separate beds so Sal didn't think she'd just sleep with any wolf.

"Oh, wow, two male wolves on one island. Are you sure the other guy is a crook?" Wendy asked, and Shelley was certain her friend really wished she'd come. She was probably envisioning a whole island filled with hunky wolves.

"Yeah. I'll tell you more when I get home. But I'm certain."

"Hmm, so tell me what's going on with you and Duncan."

Way too much, and Shelley wasn't telling Wendy about that, either. She thought it best that no one ever learned what had gone on with Duncan while she was enjoying her island stay. "Did I tell you his brother's a laird and they own a castle? They have gardens, too, and he said I could come by and visit." She thought that information would sidetrack Wendy enough so that she wouldn't probe into how intimately Shelley was getting to know the Highland warrior.

The silence stretched out between them. Uncomfortably so.

"Wendy?"

"Your mother and all her people are still mad about being kicked off the land in the Highlands years ago."

Shelley sighed. Her family held long grudges.

"She doesn't mind that you have your Scottish pride and go to Celtic fests in Texas, because you're sharing your Celtic heritage with other Americans," Wendy continued. Since Wendy had never had a family history like that, she couldn't understand the way Shelley's family was. But she'd heard several of the family discussions about the old ways and knew how adamant they were about holding onto resentments about the past.

Shelley closed her bedroom door, as if ensuring that Duncan didn't hear Wendy's side of the conversation. She knew he couldn't, not if he wasn't in the same room. But the thought made her anxious just the same.

"I'm sure your mother wouldn't mind if you went to Scotland. But she wouldn't like it if you hooked up with one of the noblemen whose families threw crofters off their land like your family was. Believe me."

Shelley sighed again. She'd figured the same. "I've talked to him about it already."

More silence. "And?"

Shelley walked into the bathroom and stared at her wet hair dangling in loose tangles about her shoulders. She needed a shower to wash off the saltwater and sand. "His ancestors were noblemen who did the same to their own people," she admitted, not about to cover up the truth.

"If he were just a poor Scot who managed to stay in Scotland, that would mean all the difference in the world to your mother." Then Wendy quickly asked, "You aren't sleeping with him, are you?"

"No, I'm not."

Wendy let out her breath. "Okay, that's good. If you've spent two nights with him, and you're still sleeping apart, there's hope for you yet. So what did you do all day and night?"

They'd had the most incredible time. She'd experienced heated sexual passion that she'd never felt before and that she wanted to experience again and again. But that she also kept to herself.

Duncan wished he could hear what Shelley's girlfriend had to say about him. He hoped she wouldn't drive a wedge between them. With the way things were rapidly getting out of hand between him and Shelley, they needed something that would keep them from giving in to raw lust before it was too late. He couldn't help how frustrated he was that Shelley didn't stay with him in the big bed tonight, although he understood her reasoning. He still didn't like the arrangements.

When Shelley quit speaking and the shower in the upstairs bathroom came on, Duncan locked the place and took another drive out to Silverman's estate. He didn't like the fact that the bastard had walked into Shelley's villa and searched for clues to what was going on between them. He wanted to do the same to the bastard's estate. But he also wanted to run as a wolf and attempt to catch Silverman wolf to wolf to give him a show of how much the bastard had irritated him. Stealing his clan's money was one thing. But when Silverman invaded Duncan's territory, showing he wasn't backing down on wanting Shelley, the crook pushed Duncan into a different realm of rage. His emotions went a whole lot deeper than he'd thought, Duncan realized.

Money was money, nothing personal, although the missing funds were the clan's and needed to help them keep their ancestral home. But what he shared with Shelley was something personal and intimate, something unique to them, something he treasured. In an instant, Silverman had trampled all over the fragile bond Duncan was building with Shelley. Duncan wanted to retaliate—to show the bastard he wasn't winning this battle.

He parked the car some distance from Silverman's

estate and then jogged down the beach like before, hoping to see Silverman outside his protective estate so he could take him to task. This time, Duncan saw a woman sitting beside the pool with the soft lights around and inside the pool shimmering in the dark. Was she the girlfriend who'd been with Silverman when he met Shelley in the reserve? Or was this someone else?

He doubted anyone Silverman picked up would learn where his money was hidden or how to get to it. Duncan would have tried talking to her, if he thought she knew anything.

Barring that, he was afraid Guthrie was right. Getting the money out of bank accounts wasn't going to happen unless he could convince Silverman to give it up in wire transfers. Despite Shelley's offer of help, Duncan didn't believe that she could coax the money out of Silverman any more than he could—beyond the threat of death—and Duncan even had his doubts that the bastard would give it up then, knowing Duncan couldn't let him live.

Hating that the bastard had stolen so much and ruined so many lives, Duncan felt useless, unable to reclaim their money, unable to do anything. He was used to confronting an enemy wolf to wolf, or human to human, but this business wouldn't allow it, and he wasn't equipped to deal with it.

With a heavy heart, he returned to the villa.

The lights in Shelley's bedroom were off when he arrived, and he pulled out his phone and called his brother. "Ian, sorry if I woke you, but I've got some trouble."

Just as Duncan knew Ian would, he patiently listened and didn't jump to rash conclusions, due to being the eldest of the brothers, the laird and pack leader, but also because of the way he was. At times like these, Duncan was glad for it.

On the other hand, Duncan paced across the living room, ready to kick butt. "The woman I'm rooming with…"

"Shelley Campbell of Canyon, Texas, aye."

So his brother had done a little research of his own. Or knowing Ian, he'd had either Guthrie or Cearnach check into her. For what reason? Hell, she was Duncan's business and no one else's.

"Silverman wants her," Duncan said gruffly, wanting to tear the man apart from limb to limb, not only because of the stolen money, but also because of his insistence on seeing Shelley. Even worse, the man had dared to sneak into the villa to snoop around, invading their privacy and letting them know he'd been there.

Shelley had tried to hide how she was felt about the intrusion, but Duncan knew it had unnerved her.

"And?"

"Well, hell, Ian, he can't have her," Duncan growled.

"What does *she* want?"

Duncan ground his teeth. "To help me bring the bastard down. She doesn't want him, damn it."

"Well, is it a viable option?" The voice of reason.

"No damn way." Duncan's blood was boiling hot with the idea. He was already thinking of sending her to Scotland and his brothers' care to ensure that Silverman didn't get to her.

"All right," Ian said in a placating way. "So what's the plan?"

"I've been taking her on dates, thwarting Silverman, and it's angering him. The more I wine and dine her, the more pissed off he's becoming. But I don't want him thinking he can spend any time with her. I want him to think that she's taken."

"Is she?"

"Is she what, Ian?" He was the laird, and Duncan knew he should show him more respect, but damn it, Shelley was none of the clan's business.

Chapter 9

"HAVE YOU TAKEN HER?" IAN ASKED FLAT OUT OVER the phone, surprising the hell out of Duncan as he paced the living room of the villa while Shelley slept in the guest bedroom upstairs.

Duncan hoped he was keeping his voice low enough, but he figured as mad as he was, he wasn't. He walked into the master bedroom and shut the door. "No, I haven't taken her for my mate. Damn it, I would have told you if this was headed in that direction." He wanted to add it was his and Shelley's business and not the pack's, but he bit his tongue and waited for Ian's response.

Ian didn't say anything.

"I would have said so, if I had taken her as my mate," Duncan said to Ian over the phone, more force-fully than necessary as he continued to pace across the master bedroom.

The more he was with her, the more he wanted to make the relationship permanent. The more he didn't want other wolves thinking they had a chance with her. The more he wanted her for himself, laughing and teas-ing and playing with him. Even the way she scowled at him was appealing.

"All right, Duncan. How will your wining and dining her help the clan?"

Duncan was more than exasperated that he'd have to explain himself. Normally that wouldn't have bothered him, but it damn well did when it had to do with the way Shelley was making him feel. "I don't want to use her as bait to bring the bastard out of his well-fortified estate, but that's what's happening," Duncan said.

"Do you want me to send Cearnach?"

Duncan stopped pacing long enough to stare out the window at the dark beach. "No. I'll handle it. I just don't want Shelley getting hurt."

"You could always bring her here if things get out of control."

That's what he'd wanted to hear all along. Ian was adamant about not bringing strangers into the castle. Duncan wasn't sure how Ian would react if he heard Shelley berating the noblemen who'd kicked her family off the land. But if the situation got out of hand, Duncan did want to bring her home. "You wouldn't mind?"

"Hell, Duncan, of course I don't mind. She's welcome here. Keep me updated."

"Aye, I will." For the first time since he'd learned Sal had an interest in Shelley and wasn't letting go, Duncan felt there was an option—a safe place for her to go if things went downhill fast. He feared that's exactly where this was headed.

The next morning, Shelley came downstairs looking exhausted, circles under her eyes and her gait sluggish. Duncan figured she hadn't slept well. Just like he hadn't. Every sound had awakened him, making him think Sal or his goons were trying to break in to steal Shelley away. Half a dozen times, he'd taken to the stairs and checked on her, found her tossing restlessly, and wanted to carry her back to his bed so he could watch over her. But she was setting the limits, and for now, he'd abide by them.

"You look tired," she said, eating the omelets he'd prepared for her.

Just like she did, but he didn't want to remark on how exhausted she looked, figuring it wouldn't be appreciated. "I checked on you a couple of times during the night to make sure everything was okay."

"Six times," she said, running her fingers through her hair, which looked incredibly sexy. "If you'd come upstairs one more time, I was going to join you in your bedroom. You make too much noise climbing up the stairs and back down again."

He frowned at her. "Why didn't you tell me my seventh visit would have done the trick?"

She chuckled. "I think the wind and the waves crashing kept waking me. Besides you."

"I thought I heard someone breaking into the place several times."

"Hmm," she said, licking her fork.

He groaned under his breath and sat down to eat his eggs. After last night and the way neither of them had slept, he'd made a decision that he was sticking to, no matter what Shelley said. "We're staying together tonight."

She carried her dish to the kitchen and began putting the food away. "You've decided this?"

She didn't sound displeased that he was dictating to her. Maybe that's what she'd needed all along. Someone who would make a firm decision in the matter. "Aye," he said, looking her squarely in the eye. "If we don't, neither of us will get any sleep."

She chuckled under her breath and put the eggs back in the fridge. "All right. But we'll have to make some sleeping rules."

"Aye. No snoring, no kicking, no stealing the covers."

She laughed out loud that time. "Works for me."

He wasn't about to say what they *could* do.

After grocery shopping and dropping off their food-stuffs, they went back out to visit clothing stores so Duncan could buy a bathing suit. He suggested the shop that he knew carried men's swim trunks—the same shop he'd visited the first night. The one where he'd asked the woman about available hotels and she had seemed to consider allowing him to stay at her place—until she came to her senses.

When they walked into the shop filled with sun-glasses, swimsuits, beach towels, and floral jewelry, the clerk's eyes grew huge to see Shelley with Duncan. The clerk was wearing another floral shirt, and Duncan assumed she either bought the merchandise in the store herself or modeled it to help sell the rest. Like before, she virtually blended in with the merchandise.

"I see you must have found a place to stay since you're still here," the woman said, her voice catty as she gave Shelley a brittle look.

Shelley looped her arm through Duncan's. "Oh yes, I had a spare bedroom and was only too happy to share it with him."

He was afraid Shelley would spoil it by saying she'd made him pay for the room, but she only gave the clerk a simpering smile. Duncan felt as though he was about to be in the middle of a wolf and cat fight.

"I need a swimsuit," he said, then quickly started

looking through the first of the racks of swim trunks to get on with the business of purchasing a suit and escorting Shelley out of there as fast as he could.

But he smiled a little as he jerked the swimsuits aside, looking them over and thinking about how Shelley had actually sounded jealous over another woman's interest in him. He'd never experienced such a thing before. He couldn't help enjoying the attention.

"Hmm." Shelley pulled out a pair of Speedos and held them in front of him. With the way she spread the skimpy bathing suit against him and looked lovingly at his crotch beneath the fabric, he was already swelling with interest.

The woman's eyes were glued to his crotch, too, and he wondered if she had wished she had offered to let him stay with her that first night. Shelley wasn't helping him keep his focus on finding the right suit, either. He was ready to try on the suit and Shelley, too, for size.

Before Duncan could find something more suitable to wear on the pirate ship where there were bound to be families, Shelley ran her hand over the Speedo, which meant she brushed against his thickening erection. He jerked back, gave her a look letting her know that he'd pay her back later, and plunged his hand into the rack of swimsuits to pull out something else.

"I don't know," Shelley said, holding up the Speedo. "It might be too small."

"They stretch," the clerk said. When both Duncan and Shelley looked at her, her face blossomed with color.

Shelley made a fist inside the Speedo and stretched it, studying it as if she was comparing her fist with the size of his erection. "Yes, I see. I guess it would work. We'll get this one."

"We'll get this one," Duncan said, contradicting her by pulling out a pair of long swim trunks, more like his Bermuda shorts but these would dry faster.

Shelley smiled agreeably. "We'll get both. This one," she said, moving her finger around inside the Speedo, "for when you swim alone with me and that one for when you swim out in public." She looked over at the clerk whose face was still crimson. "What do you think?"

With the bag of bathing suits in one hand and his other arm draped over Shelley's shoulder, Duncan hurried her out of the shop. "I didn't know you could be so wickedly bad."

"Well, the woman was eyeing you like her next meal, and I wanted her to know that she couldn't have you."

"That you have me instead," he said, his voice thick with lust. Hell, how could the little wolf have done that to him so easily? In public?

"Yep." Shelley tipped her chin up defiantly.

"So... does that mean we truly will sleep together tonight?" He still wasn't sure if she'd change her mind. Even though he had it in mind that they were staying together, no matter what. They needed to get some sleep, and he couldn't if he was worrying about Sal or his goons breaking in and stealing her away.

Hell, she'd made him so hard that Duncan could barely walk. He'd planned to swim with her tonight sans clothes again, but he supposed since she'd bought the Speedo for him, he'd have to wear it to appease her. He wouldn't mind her stuffing her hand in the swimsuit while he was wearing it.

"Swimming and sleeping are two different things. But yes, I agreed that because of your constant running up the stairs to check on me, we'd stay together and *sleep*."

"You have to know, Shelley, that after your little demonstration with the Speedo in the shop, you'll have to pay."

She grinned up at him, and he thought he was going to have as much fun making her pay as she'd have in getting her punishment—of the most pleasurable kind. Then, he had the sneaking suspicion she had every intention of making him pay instead.

Before they went on their pirate cruise, they stopped to have lunch in George Town at a restaurant that specialized in hamburgers with every kind of topping imaginable. That's when another woman caught Duncan's eye. She was wearing jeans and a T-shirt, not the sexy red dress, but he recognized her as the smoker from the bar who was dating Silverman's lackey named Kenneth. Her eyes widened to see Duncan.

Shelley looked over to see what had caught his rabid attention. "Who is she?" She sounded as though she was ready to do whatever it took to keep the new woman at bay.

Duncan hadn't expected to see Shelley acting jealous over another woman so soon. He liked the way Shelley was ready to exhibit her wolf teeth when she thought a woman wanted him.

"She's the woman I met in the bar that first night whose boyfriend works for the guy who wants to take you out."

"Sal… oh."

The woman glanced at the men's room, and Shelley

said to Duncan, "Do you think the boyfriend made it to the island and he's in there?"

"I believe so." Duncan leaned over and kissed Shelley on the cheek. "Trying to get anything out of a human who works for Sal—if this guy is human—won't do any good. Not unless he handles Sal's money. I doubt Silverman allows anyone to handle that but himself."

She sighed. "I'm still the best bet for getting to Sal, don't you think?"

"No," he said flatly, not about to let Shelley be his pawn, no matter how much it might help his cause.

She shook her head. "You are one stubborn Scot. Okay, after we sail on the pirate cruise and swim, we can go home and shower. Then I've got to go back to the reserve. With us spending this morning shopping, eating lunch, and next the pirate cruise, I haven't had a chance to get back to the forest. I have to do research every day."

"All right. I'll take you over, right after we shower."

She sighed. "I know you don't want to spend all that time in the forest. You don't have to, you know."

He grunted.

"I'm serious. No one will bother me. I doubt Sal would force me to go anywhere with him. He's not into kidnapping, just money theft. However, if I could have a dog with me…"

Duncan raised a brow.

"Because of the birds nesting on the ground and other wildlife in the forest, the reserve doesn't allow anyone to walk their dogs. But if I could, you could have joined me and been my guard dog."

He leaned close and whispered, "Only a wolf could adequately protect that hot body of yours."

She grinned. "Now that would be some sight, truly. Brown eyes narrowed, fur all fluffed up in big, bad wolf mode—even if I had you on a leash—"

He tilted his chin down.

"*If* I had you on a leash, even then I'm certain no one would want to cross your path. Not unless it was a kid who might want to pet the big doggy and not know any better."

He grinned darkly at that.

Movement near the woman he'd seen in the bar caught both his and Shelley's attention. They both glanced over as a short, wiry man wearing jeans and a floral shirt headed for the woman. The boyfriend, Duncan suspected. The woman mentioned Duncan and tossed her head in his direction, and the man looked over at him. Duncan met the man's gaze squarely. He wouldn't pretend not to have noticed that the conversation was about him. He also didn't plan to have anything to do with the man. As far as Duncan was concerned, he was a no-account.

He knew the man wasn't a wolf because he was not smart enough to stay put. Instead, he must have thought he'd try intimidation. Maybe tell Silverman how he told off the Scot. Maybe show off for his girlfriend.

Whatever his reasons, the man was way out of his element.

Unlike an aging soldier who had been waging war for years and knew his craft well, Duncan had soldiered for many years but was still in his prime. Not that an encounter couldn't be lethal for a wolf, but this man just didn't know what he was facing. Not knowing the enemy's strengths was the worst mistake any man or wolf could make.

If the man had been a wolf, Duncan would have made the effort to straighten his back and show off his broad shoulders and chest, to display how tall he was even when seated, and to intimidate without even rising from his chair. He didn't bother, which in effect told the man that Duncan didn't feel the need to posture.

Shelley was staring at the man, as if she couldn't believe he'd confront Duncan in the restaurant.

Silverman's man crossed the floor and stood across the table from Duncan. He wasn't getting any closer, Duncan noticed from the corner of his vision. At that point he wasn't making the effort to look in the man's direction, which was another ploy to show that this Kenneth meant nothing to him. It also could show weakness, if the man thought Duncan was afraid of him and seeking a way out of the place in a hurry. Or that Duncan was hoping Kenneth would disappear if he didn't look at him.

But Duncan hadn't seen a waitress yet, and he wanted to at least order Shelley's and his drinks.

"Who the hell are you?" Kenneth asked so loudly that couples at other tables nearby looked over.

Duncan glanced casually at the man, acting almost surprised that he would address him. He was sure that Sal's minion took that for a sign of weakness, too. A wolf would know better.

"Are you speaking to me?" Duncan asked, rising to stand at his full height. His voice was deep and gruff, and he stood at least four inches taller than this man.

Kenneth looked up at Duncan's height and took two steps back from the table. That was the first halfway smart thing that he'd done. The waitress who had started over to the table stopped abruptly, order pad and pen in hand.

Everyone else nearby sat quietly watching the confrontation. Duncan was clearly in charge.

Shelley tried not to drop her jaw at the way Duncan commanded everyone's attention with his very presence and the darkness in his voice. He looked like a Scottish laird, even if his oldest brother was actually the laird. He looked like he could have commandeered battlefields or led one wolf pack against another. He was intimidating, despite the fact that the other man was the one who had cursed at Duncan.

Now the man looked like he was about to pee his pants. His girlfriend looked like she was, too.

Shelley wondered if he'd tell Silverman how badly he'd botched confronting Duncan in a restaurant. She wondered if word of Duncan's behavior would scare Silverman into running, if Kenneth did tell him what had happened.

The waitress broke the impenetrable silence with a half-squeaked question, "Is there anything wrong?" She was young. Shelley doubted the girl had ever had to deal with a situation like this. The best thing she could do was butt out.

Duncan cocked a brow at the man, putting the question to him.

Shelley suspected that he tried to get the words out so that he sounded more gruff and scary like Duncan, but he didn't have the ability. Under his breath, the man said, "Just watch yourself."

"Are you threatening me, laddie?"

Oh. My. God.

If looks could kill, the man would have struck Duncan dead. It wasn't the threatening tone to Duncan's voice, despite how cold and utterly dangerous he sounded, but the way he called the man "laddie" that irked the guy. Shelley felt like she was watching a reenactment of a Western gunfight in Texas, except that neither of the men had a gun, thank heavens. Or at least Duncan didn't. She glanced back at the man. Maybe he did. That wouldn't be good.

The guy wasn't a lad; yet in werewolf years, he was definitely a green lad. But he wouldn't understand the reference.

At two of the nearby tables, a couple of men chuckled. No one else said a word.

Maybe the guy didn't back down because he was dumber than dirt. Or maybe he was packing. He finally said, "You stay away from my boss."

"Who is your boss?" Duncan's eyes sparkled like fire as he put the man on the spot.

The man looked around, finally aware that all eyes were upon him and he wasn't getting anywhere with his paltry attempt at intimidation. "Hell," he muttered under his breath, his face scarlet. Without another word, he turned on his heel and stalked out of the place, leaving his girlfriend behind.

"Kenneth!" She started to leave when a waiter hurried over and stopped her.

"You haven't paid your bill, miss."

She looked like she could kill. But Shelley wasn't sure who—Duncan? The waiter? Or Kenneth, her long-gone boyfriend, who had stuck her with the bill?

———✦———

Duncan was quiet through the meal, while other cus-
tomers talked among themselves, wondering what that
had been about, with all kinds of scenarios popping up
and their voices low as if they didn't want to stir up
the Highlander. But if they had been betting during the
showdown, all of their bets would have been on Duncan.

Shelley had been equally quiet, eating her mushroom
burger, watching the time on a big clock on one wall to
make sure they set sail on the pirate ship, and listening to
the conversations around them. She didn't like Duncan
being so quiet, though. She knew he was making plans
and doing a lot of soul searching. All of a sudden, she
felt that after the brief time she'd been part of his life—
almost the center, in fact—she was once again no one
to him.

She couldn't believe how much she enjoyed being
with him, taking part in his life, and sharing time with
him. Even though she could see his dark, protective warrior side, he always let her choose how far she wanted to
take their relationship.

"Duncan," she said, trying to get his attention without
garnering everyone else's. She felt as though they were
still the center of the world as far as the other diners
were concerned. The scene in the restaurant was probably the most exciting thing that had happened to these
tourists while visiting the island.

They wanted to know more. Wanted to know what
had brought the man to Shelley and Duncan's table and
why he had said the things he had. Why the Scot had
stood towering over the man in battle mode. Why the
man had threatened him, then left his girlfriend behind
with the bill.

Duncan finally looked up at Shelley. His brown eyes were nearly black. He was not happy. "You're going home," he said firmly, allowing no argument.

Several looked in their direction, waiting to see what *she* had to say about it.

She was certain she looked like a fish, her mouth opening, then closing, then opening again. She frowned at him and took a drink of her water, trying to get her annoyance under control. He might be worried about her, but she was on a business trip, not a vacation, and she had work to do. She was *not* going home until she was scheduled to. He had no say in what she was going to do.

Even though she did not want to see him go while she was on the island, he could do whatever he wanted. She wasn't leaving. That wasn't his decision to make. She'd paid for the villa, and she was seeing this trip through to the end.

He watched her, his eyes holding her gaze, his posture saying she would not disobey him in this. He was a man descended from Scottish nobles, and he would tell her where to go. Just like in the old country from which her family had been sent packing.

She shook her head and felt hot tears sting the backs of her eyes as she held them in check, gritting her teeth so she wouldn't say anything to upset herself further.

"Shelley…"

"No, Duncan," she whispered hotly, afraid that if she spoke any louder, everyone would hear. Already the place was damned quiet again. This was surely more interesting than any soap opera could have been.

"I want you someplace safe."

She sat up taller, chin up, eyes narrowed. "I'm fine

here. I've got a job to do. Which I should be doing." She rose, but he reached across the table, seized her wrist, and shook his head.

"We leave together. I'm not done eating."

She scowled at him and sat back down. This was the warrior side of him that she hadn't seen yet. The macho, controlling part. He let go of her, and finished his hamburger and the rest of his milk.

Women narrowed their eyes at Duncan, probably not liking that he was controlling her. Men looked a little like they wanted to speak to him on her behalf, but no one was alpha enough to make the effort. Even if they were alphas, she was sure they weren't certain they'd win in a confrontation with him. He *was* intimidating when he had the notion to be.

She was glad that he had stopped her, though. She hadn't wanted to create any more of a scene or depart the premises without him. But she wanted to get this issue of her leaving settled between them. She was *not* leaving the island. Period.

Duncan motioned to the waitress. She hurried over, not because she expected a big tip but because she didn't dare dawdle, Shelley thought.

Shelley folded her arms and glowered at Duncan.

The waitress looked from Duncan to Shelley, who was so intent on scowling at Duncan that she didn't spare the waitress a glance. But Shelley did see out of her peripheral vision that the waitress's head turned so that she looked at Duncan again.

"Do you want your bill now, or would you like some dessert?" the waitress asked Duncan.

She must have asked because she had been so

indoctrinated about having to mention dessert to restaurant patrons. Couldn't she see that they were leaving? Like now?

Duncan finally shifted his hard gaze from Shelley, softening it when he spoke to the waitress and saying, "What do you have for dessert?"

Shelley couldn't have looked more surprised as her eyes widened and her lips parted again. He couldn't be serious.

To her shock, Duncan ordered an old-fashioned bowl of ice cream buried in hot fudge and whipped cream, with a sprinkle of pecans and a cherry on top. Shelley didn't want anything further. Just to leave and do her work. She'd known that getting tangled up with him would be a mistake.

The dark green bowl of hot fudge sundae and another glass of milk arrived. He told Shelley that the milk was what did wonders for his skin, muscles, and bones. Two women at another table ordered glasses of milk after that.

Shelley eyed the damned sundae.

"Want some?" he asked, poking his spoon into the whipped cream and hot fudge and vanilla ice cream.

He offered her the spoonful but she snatched the cherry off the top, licked off the hot fudge topping, and popped the cherry into her mouth.

His mouth curved up. "I love *your* cherries more."

His comment caused a couple of men nearby to chuckle under their breaths. Her face heated as though she'd just been exposed to several hours of hot sunlight.

"I liked the way you licked that cherry and took a bite," he added, grinning.

Not that she wasn't still upset with him, but she had no reason to let her irritation get the best of her.

"Fine, Duncan. Get your own bowl of ice cream." She took his spoon and bowl to her side of the table and began eating every delicious bite. Chocolate had a way of dissolving grudges.

Duncan waved to the waitress, pointed to Shelley's commandeered bowl of ice cream, and motioned for the waitress to bring him another.

But Shelley still wasn't going home, damn it, no matter what he wanted.

Chapter 10

SHELLEY CALLED *HIM* A STUBBORN SCOT, BUT SHE WAS damned stubborn herself. Duncan was only thinking of her protection, but she wasn't going along with it. In no uncertain terms, he would make sure she wasn't staying here.

She was even talking about canceling their pirate cruise, but he wasn't going along with that. He was going to make her walk the plank. He'd never known anyone who didn't feel intimidated when he was on a rampage. Yet, he saw the sorrow in her eyes, the tears ready to spill when he said she had to leave. He didn't want her to leave, damn it. But he worried about her safety.

Hotheads like Kenneth could easily turn on Shelley as a way to get to Duncan. He didn't fear for his own safety, but Shelley was a different story.

When they finished their ice cream, he escorted her to the harbor, which was within walking distance, his hand around her arm, his body close. He'd changed into the swim trunks in the restroom, and Shelley was already wearing her bathing suit underneath her jeans and T-shirt. He was curious about how sexy it might be. She insisted it was family fare, repeating that it had a billowing skirt, pants down to her knees, and a high neckline.

Thankfully, the dessert seemed to soothe her anger. But he knew that if he brought up the subject of her leaving the island, she'd be angry with him again.

As soon as they got on the pirate ship—with the crew taunting the passengers and teasing with their made-up scripts—the boat was on its way. The cannon fired, the mainsail was hoisted, and a mixture of sweet rum and punch was served to everyone since there were no children on the cruise.

Before long, the pirates were brandishing swords and presenting a mock fight among comrades. Duncan shook his head, thinking how much training the men needed if they were going to pull off a real sword fight. Unable to stand it any longer, he strode forth, seized one of the pirates by the shoulder, and said, "Here, lad, let me show you how it's really done."

The Spanish-looking man was tough and big and mean looking, but he gave a pirate's grin, one tooth appropriately painted gold, and handed Duncan his sword with a low bow.

He had style, Duncan thought. He also didn't figure Duncan knew as much as he did about sword fighting, but the pirate was willing to allow Duncan the opportunity to make a fool of himself.

Duncan swung the pirate's toy sword in the air at no one in particular, measuring its puny weight and reach before he showed the pirate crew a thing or two.

All the pirates watched him with glittering eyes and smirks plastered on their smug faces. He knew they intended to get him back, if he allowed it. The passengers observed in fascination. He figured some wondered if he was part of the show.

For now, everyone was waiting with bated breath to hear what the *master swordsman* had to say.

"First…" he said, taking a stance, his feet apart for

balance. He was used to fighting on ground that did not tilt and roll like the pirate's ship did. "You do not wave your sword around in fancy maneuvers with unnecessary flourishes. You strike your opponent's with balance and boldness."

He thrust and the Spanish pirate swung to connect with the sword and missed. Duncan poked the dull sword at the pirate's torso to show just where the blade would have struck, had they been fighting for real. With an injury to the stomach region, the man would have died a painful death.

The other pirates groaned and ribbed their partners in crime. Another quickly took his place for a demonstration.

The man's coal-black eyes studied Duncan. The pirate's dark brown skin glistening in the sun, and a red-and-white striped kerchief covered most of his curly black hair. He flexed huge biceps, as if warning Duncan that he was not anyone to challenge him. Even if he didn't have the sword skills to fight the good fight, the pirate was muscled enough to wear a man down. A *kill* had to be quick in this man's case.

The man lunged, his heavy bulk barreling toward Duncan, who quickly sidestepped and swung around to skewer the man in the back.

"Ooohs" filled the deck where passengers intimated that Duncan had played dirty, stabbing a man in the back, while the pirates took him to task with jeers.

"Another lesson," Duncan said, bowing his head slightly to the defeated pirate. "When waging war, use every measure available to ensure you are the last man standing. Especially when you are well outnumbered."

He waved his sword at the other pirates waiting their turns. In a real battle, they would not have given him the chance to take another breath before someone else was trying to slice him in two.

The dark man nodded, grinning, his white teeth gleaming in the sunlight.

"Now me, Highlander," another pirate said, really getting into the action. His blond hair was pulled back into a tail, his blue eyes glimmering with good humor and enjoyment, and he held up one hand as if he were a Frenchmen getting ready to dance, his sword outstretched.

Duncan maneuvered around the deck until the sun was shining brightly in the blond's eyes.

The man squinted and thrust his sword. Duncan easily knocked it aside, then attacked just as quickly, his sword point resting at the blond pirate's throat.

"The sun was in my eyes," the blond complained.

"Aye, I planned it that way," Duncan said, and glanced at the last pirate, who watched him with a small smirk on his face.

Everyone laughed, pirates and passengers alike.

"So the Highlander fights dirty, like us pirates," the remaining pirate said. With his red hair and highly freckled white skin, he looked like he could have Scottish roots.

"Have you ancestry from Scotland?" Duncan asked, squaring off with the man.

"Oh, aye," the man said, offering a bit of a brogue in return.

Everyone looked serious, frowns furrowing their brows, as they watched the two men maneuver on deck while keeping the same distance between them.

The pirate crew would talk about this for eons, if they didn't get fired for the insurance risk of having a true swordsman conducting a sword demonstration without prior written permission. At least two of the passengers were making a video of the sword-fighting demonstrations. Duncan thought about being in the movie at Argent Castle. He groaned to himself, hoping that none of this would end up on YouTube for the whole world to see.

"Was your family from the Highlands, then?" Duncan asked the redhead.

"Nay," the man said, smiling amiably, but the gleam in his eye said he was trying to maneuver Duncan into a corner of the ship, wanting badly to best him in front of the passengers and his pirate comrades at arms.

"From the Lowlands?" Duncan asked, distracting the man and forcing him to think about something other than holding his sword at the ready.

"Aye."

"Hmm, you were loyal to the king."

The man raised a red brow, probably not knowing enough about the history of Scotland to know how to respond.

"We were loyal to our clan chiefs." With that parting comment, Duncan lunged at the man, forcing him back.

The redhead quickly parried, falling another couple of steps back, his face flushing red. He hadn't expected Duncan's move. He tried to make up for it with a counterattack. By this time, Duncan had pushed him into a corner. Without anywhere to maneuver, the Lowlander pirate was in a bad position.

Duncan knocked the sword from the pirate's grasp,

sending it flying to the deck. "You should have been loyal to a clan chief and given up your pirating ways."

The pirates and passengers all laughed.

The pirates all cast glances at one another, and in one simultaneous move, three of them attacked. Duncan fought them while the redhead scrambled to retrieve his sword from the deck and join in the fun. In good humor, Duncan slashed at their swords, got poked a few times—how could he not when he was beset by four pirates at once?—and finally raised his sword in defeat so he could enjoy the rest of the cruise with Shelley in his embrace.

Cheers erupted all around, and after a short sail, the ship anchored for anyone who wished to walk the plank or take the ladder to go for a swim.

Shelley was grinning at Duncan and shaking her head as she stripped out of her jeans and T-shirt. That made him want to take her to the privacy of their own beach and do the same with her—only he'd be doing the stripping.

She was wearing a one-piece that was as sexy on her as the string bikini. It stretched across her luscious curves, with the shimmering royal blue just as tantalizing as her bare skin. He pulled off his shirt and jeans and shoes so he stood before her in just his swim trunks.

She smiled up at him coyly. "I can't wait to see you in the movie, Duncan. I can't imagine what it would be like to see you wearing a kilt and swinging a claymore."

Most of the passengers were milling about, intrigued with the Highlander, and finally one ventured to ask, "Do you teach sword fighting?"

"Aye," Duncan said. To the younger boys in their clan, teaching alongside his brothers and cousins. The skill would be passed on forever.

"He's been in a movie," Shelley said proudly.

He quickly guided her to the plank. "I will make you walk the plank for that, lass."

She laughed and hurried down it, stood for a moment looking at the clear blue water below, and then jumped off, holding her nose.

He chuckled, walked the plank, and then jumped in after her. Unfortunately, he was swimming with Shelley in the daytime in crystal clear waters with an audience looking down on them from aboard the ship. That meant he couldn't do what he wanted with her—hold her tight, kiss her until they had to come up for air, and feel that sexy body of hers up close.

Something other than the reaction he had to seeing her, feeling her up close, and tasting her had him wanting more. He damn well enjoyed being with her. The thought that she'd return to Texas and he'd return to Scotland—and they'd never see each other again— bothered him more than he wanted to consider.

"You were tremendous," Shelley said, smiling at him as she paused in the shadow of the boat during their swim, somewhat hidden from curious onlookers. She looked up at him as if he were the hero of her dreams.

He pulled her close. Hell, to pirates and passengers alike, he was a swashbuckling Highlander. It was expected of him. He kissed her.

Aye, he had vanquished the scurvy pirates—well, until they ganged up on him. Truth be told, if they'd been battling in a real sword fight, he'd have still won. But now he had the sweet maiden, having rescued her from yonder ship, and wasn't letting her go.

Their legs continued to touch, their feet sweeping the

water, paddling and keeping them afloat. She wrapped her arms around his neck, while his were around her waist, and they both treaded water while they kissed. Through lips wet from the sea's caress, their tongues teased and tangled as if they were having a sword fight of their own.

She finally broke free of the kiss and looked up at him as if he were some kind of a god. "I can't wait to see you in the movie, Duncan."

He snorted. "I told you, I wasn't a main player. You wouldn't even notice me. I'm just in the background in any of the scenes."

"Fighting."

"Aye."

"If you're there and they didn't cut the scenes, I'll notice you."

"We all wear the same plaids, lass, and my brothers and I share a similar look. Even my cousins do. Only the enemy wears a different plaid."

"You all sound alike, too, I imagine."

He smiled down at her, then kissed her nose. "You would not be able to tell us apart."

"You may be right."

He laughed. "That's not what you're supposed to say, lass. I should stand out among my brothers, and you would never mistake me for one of them," he said with a deepening brogue.

She grinned at him. "You stand out all the time." She moved her hands down to his buttocks and pressed him close, his arousal already thickening with desire. "I doubt I would mistake you for any of them."

That earned her another heated kiss as she wrapped

her legs around his thighs. He continued to keep them afloat as he deepened the kiss. "'Tis a mermaid, I've found," he whispered in her ear, "not a wolf."

"Most wolves love the water."

"I'm liking it better all the time. Are you game for another nighttime swim?"

"You really don't mind the sharks anymore?"

He ran his hand over her buttock. "I'm getting used to the idea."

"I just bet you are."

They swam the rest of the time near the boat, trying to keep from prying eyes. Other swimmers saw them in the water and half watched and half pretended not to. Everyone had to think Duncan and Shelley were newlyweds. He wasn't about to dispel their fantasies.

When they were sailing back to the harbor, he was besieged by questions about being an actor and how he trained others to fight with a sword.

He gave Shelley a raised brow when the movie questions kept coming because she was the one who had told the whole world he had been in a movie. She only smiled, enjoying that everyone was so curious about him. She was not about to let him get away with pretending modesty when he had shown the pirates a thing or two about sword fighting.

If she hadn't been in love with the sexy Highlander before seeing that demonstration, she would have fallen in love with him right then and there. He'd shown how it was done in a humorous, fun way, as if he truly wished to impart some of his long-learned wisdom. The way he allowed them to win the fight at the end, when she was certain he could have bested all of them if he'd truly been in a battle for his life. The way he so gallantly answered everyone's questions—all showed a side of him she truly admired.

Not only did she wish to see castle gardens in Scotland, mostly his, but she also wanted to see him and his brothers practicing with their swords now. To see the battle between equally skilled swordsmen and the outcome.

She had to smile at the way he fielded the questions. He truly was an expert on swordsmanship. Wouldn't the onlookers be surprised to learn he'd used his fighting skills to stay alive in the old days?

But she reminded herself that she and Duncan were worlds apart and soon would go their separate ways. Her love for him could only last a heartbeat, and then… she knew she'd never meet another wolf who'd be anything like him. Despite the way she felt about him and the way he lusted after her, if he was worried about her, he would be ready to send her home, away from him, and that would be the end of that.

When they reached the dock, she was feeling a little saddened. As sensitive as he was, he instantly noticed.

"I talked too much on the ship, didn't I?" he asked, getting her car door for her.

She laughed. "No, Duncan. I loved hearing all about your sword fights and how dangerous they really are, and everyone else loved hearing you talk, too."

"I don't usually get so wrapped up in speaking about it," he admitted, looking a little sheepish.

She grinned at him. "The truth is that I want to see you and your brothers fight against each other so I can see what it's like when all of you are equal in skill."

"Bloodthirsty wench," he teased as he leaned down and kissed her, then shut her door.

Before he reached his door, two men approached. Kenneth stood some distance from them, just watching. The men looked like they might carry guns, not swords. Her heart thundering, Shelley immediately grabbed her door handle to get out of the car so she could hear what they had to say and serve as Duncan's backup.

Duncan recognized the men as two of the guards from Silverman's estate. Keeping his distance, Kenneth observed Duncan angrily with folded arms, his turned-down mouth making him look smug. Now he had the muscle to back up his not-so-tough words.

Shelley had gotten out of the car immediately in an alpha-wolf protective mode. Duncan wished she'd stayed safely inside the vehicle.

"The boss wants a word with you," the bigger of the two men said to Duncan. "The lady can take the car back to her place, and you can ride with us."

Some of the passengers from the pirate ship stood watching the confrontation. Even the pirate crew looked as though they wished to lend support.

"Call your boss," Duncan said gruffly. "After I've showered and changed, he can meet me at Ted's Bar and Grill, if he wants."

"He says you're to come with us now," the man said, taking a step forward.

"Does your boss own a place here?" Shelley asked, as if she didn't already know that.

The man shifted his hateful expression to her.

"If he wants us to come, how about also inviting Duncan's new friends?" She waved at the pirate actors.

They all nodded, looking muscled and lethal. And very willing to help their new Highland sword-fighting friend.

"You should have come alone with us like we said," Sal's henchman said to Duncan. "The boss isn't going to like this at all."

With that, he turned on his heel and headed for a car while the other two men gave Duncan an additional glower and then joined the spokesman.

"Thanks for the sword-fighting tips," the redhead said. "If you ever need backup on the island, just give me a call." He handed Duncan a card.

Ethan McNutt, pirate for hire, crew of the Jolly Roger.

Duncan smiled. "Aye, that I will. Nothing better than having a pirate or two watch your back when you're on an island."

The others gave him nods. "It goes the same for all of us," the dark-skinned man said. "Do you want us to meet you at Ted's Bar and Grill later? If their *boss man* says he'll meet you there?"

"I'll give you a call," Duncan said, "*if* it looks as though it's a meeting he wants."

They all gave him nods and sauntered off to their own vehicles.

Shelley drew in a breath, then returned to the car. Sal had to know Duncan was after him, maybe about the money or maybe not. Maybe the thief wanted to get Duncan out of the picture where Shelley was concerned. If that was the case, she felt a little better about it. She hoped they hadn't spooked Sal into worrying about financial issues so that he'd run for cover somewhere far from Grand Cayman Island.

"What do you think it's all about?" Shelley asked Duncan.

"I want you to go home," Duncan said, his grip tightening on the steering wheel as he drove them back to her villa.

She folded her arms, not about to have this discussion. "Do you think he knows why you are here?"

"Nay. He doesn't like it that he wants you, and I have you."

She smiled a little at his conceit. Duncan didn't *have* her, either. "You truly think that's all there is to this? That it's just about me?"

"Aye."

"But he's got a mate and a mistress."

"Aye, but that doesn't seem to be enough. Like you said, he's used to getting what he wants through his money and power." He flicked a glance at her. "He thought he could have you easily enough, but I'm thwarting his efforts every time he attempts to get to you. With me out of the way, he most likely believes you'd give him a chance."

"Are you certain, Duncan? You said that the woman you saw at that bar thought you might be after him. If that's the case, wouldn't they believe it might have something to do with the money?"

"I'm sure he's already checked me out and learned I'm not with any law enforcement agency. That I came here on vacation, ran into you, and staked a claim. The same claim he wished to stake."

"What about the woman's concern over who you might be? Your reaction to her in the bar?"

"Just as I said to her, I thought it was awful that her boyfriend's boss was keeping him away so he couldn't be with her. Now that I'm pursuing you, that shows I'm a sentimental guy when it comes to women."

She smiled at that, then frowned. "I'm not going home."

He glanced at her. "You understood I'm talking about Scotland, eh? I want you to go to *my* home. Not the U.S. If you return to Texas, he might follow you there. At my home, there's no way for him to breach the castle walls." He gave her a dark look. "I would like for him to try."

She stared at him in disbelief. Was that what he had meant all along?

"Ian mated an American. So we even have ice cubes on hand," Duncan continued, as if he didn't realize what a jolt his words had provided.

"Ice cubes?"

"Aye. I cannot fathom why Americans drink tea with ice cubes in it, but…" He shrugged.

She smiled. "That's because it's hot in places like Texas in the summer and hot drinks aren't as appealing."

"I could show you our gardens."

"I'd love to see them, but what about the cost of lodging at Argent Castle? I couldn't afford it."

"I'm sure we could come up with some mutually agreeable arrangement."

She wondered just what that would entail. Her grandmother had always warned her about Highland wolves.

But she'd never said anything about a wolf like Duncan.

Chapter 11

AFTER DUNCAN AND SHELLEY RETURNED TO THE villa to shower and get ready to go back to the reserve, she went off to the guest bedroom, and he planned to call Ian. She still didn't want to leave the island until she'd finished her work there, but she said she'd be thrilled to accompany him to Scotland to see his gardens. He was glad about that and wished they hadn't had the misunderstanding at the restaurant over where he'd intended for her to go.

At this point, he wanted her to meet his family and to see if she could tolerate his mother, who would not allow anyone to speak unkindly of the clan. Most likely Shelley would tell just how she and her family felt about the nobility and the resettling of the crofters. His mother would not be pleased, and she would let Shelley know it.

For now, though, he just wanted Shelley safe.

"Ian," he said, as soon as his brother answered the phone.

Ian sounded worried. "What's wrong, Duncan?"

"Silverman wants her, damn it."

"Send Shelley here."

"She wants to accompany me home, but only after she's finished with her work here." Duncan knew Ian would find her work ethic as admirable as he did, while also realizing she was a stubborn lass.

"I'll send Cearnach."

"Aye." Duncan knew his older brother and he could ensure that Shelley stayed out of harm's way. But the nagging problem with Shelley's family needed to be discussed. He hated to bring it up, not sure how his brother would view the news. He cleared the sudden frog in his throat. "Ian, she comes from a family of crofters who were ousted during the Highland Clearances."

Ian didn't say anything at first, then finally asked, "She holds this against our family?"

"We did the same to crofters on our land."

Ian grunted. Then as if he finally realized what Duncan had said earlier, he asked, "Has she agreed to come home with you for good?"

"We… haven't really discussed that yet."

"You're mated?"

"Nay, Ian," Duncan said, irritated. Why did his brother continue to assume that? "I told you I would tell you if the relationship was headed that way. I don't even know about her family, her wolf pack. Or whether she'd want to move to Scotland."

A heavy silence ensued, then Ian said, "All right. I'll call you later when we know what time Cearnach will be arriving at the airport, and you can pick him up."

"Aye."

"And, Duncan?" The warning tone was back in Ian's voice.

"Aye?"

"Do not take unnecessary risks. Wait until Cearnach arrives to do anything further where Silverman is concerned."

"I'll wait," Duncan said, but only because he was concerned about Shelley's safety. Otherwise he was ready to take whatever Silverman might throw at him.

"I'll call you later," Ian said.

"Thanks, Ian." Duncan disconnected and headed for the bathroom to shower, hoping they wouldn't have any trouble in the forest while Shelley catalogued more of her plants. He also hoped Cearnach wouldn't make a play for her. His brother had a way with the lasses with his sunny disposition and his air of never being concerned about anything.

Maybe Duncan should tell Ian to send Guthrie instead.

—m—

Shelley finished making the reservations for the snorkeling trip to swim with the rays the next day and found Duncan staring out the window at the ocean. He turned when he heard her approach and gave her an anxious look. "Ian's sending our next eldest brother, Cearnach, to stay with us until you're finished with your work here and we can leave for Scotland."

She was so surprised that she stared at him for longer than necessary. Finally she found her tongue and asked, "When?"

"He's making flight reservations now."

"Oh."

"It'll be safer that way."

Which meant that Duncan was more worried about things getting out of hand with Silverman than he'd let on.

She nodded, but then she smiled. "He can pay half of your half of the cost of the villa."

He laughed. "All our money goes into one account."

"Oh. Sure. Wendy, that's my girlfriend, says most wolf packs do that."

"You don't have a wolf pack?" Duncan sounded surprised but at the same time hopeful. If she didn't have a wolf pack, she might like becoming part of his. On the other hand, she might not be used to being with a pack and have a hard time adjusting. His brothers could be big teases. Especially Cearnach.

"I have a mother and three uncles. It's sort of an autonomous wolf pack. My uncles never mated, and we lost my father many years ago, so whatever we earn is ours to keep."

If her pack was loosely tied together, he assumed they wouldn't mind if she joined his in Scotland.

Then he considered the logistics of their sleeping arrangements here at the villa. That was a more immediate concern and could be a problem when Cearnach arrived. "We'll have to swap bedrooms. My brother and I will share the twin beds, and you can have the master bedroom again."

"Tonight we can stay together so I don't have to hear your footfalls on the stairs all night while you check on me to see if I'm okay."

He gave her a small smile. It would be his pleasure. But if he stayed with her one night, he was certain he wouldn't want to give her up for the next... or any other.

"Did Silverman call to arrange a meeting with you while I was in the shower?" she asked.

"No. He's trying to determine how willing I am to fight him where you are concerned. Ready to go to the reserve before it gets any later?"

"Yes." She grabbed her backpack and headed for the front door. "I made the reservations for snorkeling with the stingrays for tomorrow afternoon. We can swim in the ocean later in the evening, depending on when your brother gets here."

"We'll swim well before he arrives so I can have you to myself. It wouldn't do for him to see you in that string bikini of yours. I've never swum so much in so few days."

"You have to wear the bathing suit I bought you. I want to see how far it stretches." She raised a brow and gave him a sinfully wicked smile.

He laughed, and from the way he did, she thought she might have pushed their relationship into something she might not be ready for... yet.

Duncan pulled the door open for her. She stopped dead in the entryway, her heart skipping a beat. The two burly men who had met them in the parking lot after they had disembarked from the pirate ship—and that damned Kenneth—stood in front of them, blocking their exit. All somber faced.

"Our boss insists on seeing you. Alone," the spokesman of the group said to Duncan. "The little lady can stay here. Kenneth will see to it." The big man turned to look at her. "Sal only wants to talk privately with him. That's all. Don't worry about a thing."

"I'll be fine," Duncan assured her, knowing Sal wouldn't try to make him disappear. Not if this was all about Sal's desire to pursue Shelley, and Duncan suspected it was.

"An hour at the most," the man said.

"I have work to do at the reserve," Shelley said hotly, as if she didn't care what any of them did as long as she got her work done.

Duncan wasn't sure what she had in mind, but he didn't want her coming to harm at the hands of this

Kenneth hothead. Although considering what she could do to Kenneth as a wolf set his mind somewhat at ease.

The spokesman nodded. "Kenneth can go with you."

Shelley looked to see if Duncan was agreeable. He lowered his head, telling her that he thought it would be safe, and then he left with the other two men.

With her stomach tied in knots, Shelley was so close to stripping out of her clothes, shifting, and then tearing into Kenneth that she had to fight the urge to the marrow of her bones. She thought she could reduce the anger and anxiety flooding her system if she went to the reserve and worked. She wanted to call Duncan's brother, Ian, to let his clan know that Silverman's men had forced Duncan to go with them. She was certain Ian would send half the pack to protect his youngest brother. Probably even come himself.

But if she made the call and nothing untoward happened, Duncan would be sorely irritated with her. Especially since the men didn't sound as if they planned to kill Duncan. They must not realize that Duncan knew about Silverman and the stolen funds.

She cradled her bag in her arms, intending to drive the rental car to the reserve and hoping she wouldn't get stopped because she didn't have a special license or insurance to drive on the island. But Kenneth shook his head and made her ride as a passenger.

That made her a little more nervous. She suspected he didn't want her in control of the car or where they were going.

"What's this all about?" she demanded as he drove her to the reserve.

"Sal wants to talk to the Scot. That's all."

"What about?" she asked again, her tongue sharpening.

He shrugged. "None of my business. Are you going to continue to chase after Sal?" A hint of warning was in his voice, which she thought odd, considering who was chasing after whom in this scenario.

"Sal's pursuing me, not the other way around. If you hadn't noticed, I'm happily pursuing a relationship with Duncan."

She still thought it odd the way Kenneth had asked the question, as if he didn't want her involved with his boss. She would have thought he'd want her to agree with whatever his boss wished.

"Tell him you're not interested in having anything more to do with him. You obviously haven't made that clear to him. Like you're playing some damned cat-and-mouse game with the two men."

She wondered if this was a personal issue. Perhaps a woman had played Kenneth for a fool—encouraging both him and someone else to take interest—and he had lost out.

Or maybe he was just worried that his boss didn't have the wherewithal to battle someone like Duncan. That he might be a dangerous man to rile. Kenneth had seen first-hand that Duncan wasn't one to sit back and play into anyone's hands. Maybe he could tell that if Duncan was provoked too far, Kenneth might not have a job at all.

The bottom line was that she was worried about what Kenneth or the other men might be supposed to do to Duncan. Or her, even. "If your boss told you to kill someone, would you do it?"

Kenneth jerked his attention to her. "Hell, no. None of us do that kind of work. Is that what you thought?"

She thought the contradiction was funny. Kenneth could threaten and bully Duncan in a restaurant full of people, but when it came to taking a stand, he didn't have the guts to do anything. He was all mouth, she thought. No real courage. But what if he had a gun? Would that give him enough nerve to put some backbone behind his threatening words?

"What am I supposed to think when you're strong-arming Duncan like you've done and given him no choice in the matter? When you forcibly take Duncan to a private meeting with Sal, and then I'm left with you to guard me?"

He snorted. "It's just so you don't get any ideas. Go to the local police and stir up trouble, saying that we stole your boyfriend or something." He turned his head to ask her, "How does he know Sal? My girlfriend said he has to."

"He doesn't. He just didn't think that any boss should keep a man and a woman who are in love apart. Duncan told me she said she was upset because she keeps trying to get together with you and Sal keeps you from meeting up with her."

Kenneth grunted, as if his job was more important. "She should have kept her big mouth shut."

Hmm, the woman seemed more hung up on the worm than he was on her.

"Duncan's one of the good guys," Shelley said, except that his family had forced Scots off their lands. "So just like he sympathized with your girlfriend, he's not at all pleased with Sal's attempts to hook up with me. Wouldn't you feel the same if some guy asked you to give up the girl you're dating?"

Kenneth hesitated, then finally said under his breath, "For money, hell, I'd do anything." He looked her over and sneered. "I'm sure the Scot will be asking for a lot of compensation, though. The question is: will what Sal offers be enough? What will happen when he pays it? I wouldn't want to be in your shoes, lady."

The threat barely registering, Shelley stared at the creep, his comment about money surprising the hell out of her. "Sal's going to offer to buy me?"

Not expecting where Silverman's men planned to take him, Duncan walked into a bar that was not open for another hour in George Town. They hadn't taken him to Sal's estate like he thought they would. Maybe Sal had decided on this establishment because he didn't want Duncan anywhere near the inside of his estate.

Scowling, Sal leaned back in a leather chair, tapping his fingers on the tabletop with a sturdy rope braiding the edge. A ship's hull with a bare-breasted mermaid masthead jutted into the room, the hull serving as a finger-food bar filled with fried chicken wings, shrimp on beds of ice, sushi, and mushrooms in a sauce, plus salad fixings. The place smelled of beer and whiskey as classical music drifted overhead.

Sal motioned for the bartender to bring them whatever Duncan wanted. "Whiskey," he said, and Sal ordered one, too.

"Kenneth's girlfriend said you knew me," Sal said after the bartender served their drinks, then disappeared.

Even Sal's henchmen who had brought Duncan there waited outside.

"How would I know anything about you? I'm here on vacation. The only thing I know about you is that you're trying to hit on Shelley." Duncan sounded really peeved, which wasn't in the least put on.

"You had trouble getting a room when you first arrived," Sal said, ignoring his comment about Shelley.

"Aye."

"Shelley said you gave her a lift from the airport to her villa."

So Sal was trying to verify everything that had happened between Duncan and Shelley? "She was waiting for a taxi, aye. I gave her a ride and took a couple to their hotel, as well."

"As a good Samaritan."

"As far as Shelley was concerned, aye. I hadn't intended to also take the couple to their rental."

Sal nodded. "Understandable. To attract the she-wolf, you made the effort, especially since you have nothing else going for you. Not even a room to stay at. So out of the goodness of her heart, she allowed you to stay at her villa."

Duncan wasn't going to deny it or tell Sal he was paying half of the cost. That wouldn't look good when this man would have footed the whole bill, although the bastard would have been using Duncan's people's money.

"I'm a very wealthy man. I could give Shelley whatever she dreamed of having. Can you?" Sal asked.

Duncan raised his brows. "Monetarily, nay. In other ways, aye."

Sal stiffened, getting the point of what Duncan was saying. "I'm interested in seeing Shelley further, and you seem to be an impediment."

"Aye." Duncan fought smiling. For the first time, Sal was squirming. Duncan liked to see Sal squirm since he didn't figure the man did that often.

"How much would it take for you to leave the island and give her no further thought?"

Duncan pondered the question. If he mentioned the amount that Silverman had stolen from his clan, he predicted the man would not connect it to any one individual account. Duncan wanted to say the entire amount, plus the interest that should have accrued. He wasn't greedy; he just believed in justice. Not that he could be bought off to leave Shelley to the snake.

But he did tell him what Sal owed him, wanting to be up front and honest with the man when Sal himself could not be. "Two hundred and fifty million pounds sterling," Duncan said.

Sal looked aghast for only the briefest of moments. Then he had the nerve to smile, figuring Duncan was making a joke. "That's a lot of money for one little female wolf."

"She's a hell of a lot of wolf." Duncan suspected Silverman might have seen Shelley and him frolicking in the ocean. Although he couldn't see this stiff-necked fool doing anything of the sort, who knew what Sal was capable of when it came to women?

"What makes you think I have that kind of money or that I'd want to pay it for the privilege of seeing a wolf without your interference?"

"You're the one who said you were wealthy and asked how much it would take to buy me off."

Sal liked money too much. Duncan didn't think the bastard would kill him to keep the money and get the girl. He also believed Sal thought he might be able to give Duncan a pittance, and he would go away. Now the thief saw that he couldn't.

Duncan downed his drink and rose from the table. "Two hundred and fifty million pounds," he reiterated. "She's worth every farthing. But even if you paid me off to leave, she would decide whether she wished to see you or not."

Sal looked a little sick. Duncan was beginning to think Shelley was right. Because of the money and power he wielded, the man was never denied anything he wanted. For the moment, Duncan was completely dumbfounded.

He slammed the door to the bar as he exited and said to Silverman's two thugs, "Take me to the reserve where Shelley is."

The spokesman opened the door and said to the boss man, "Is it all right to take him to the girl at the reserve?"

"Yeah. Take him," Sal growled, and Duncan had the feeling that this business concerning Shelley wasn't over between him and Sal.

The situation got Duncan thinking about Sal's mate and how she would feel if she knew he was trying to see another wolf. She might know about his interest in human females and not care, although most *lupus garou* mates would. Maybe she was satisfied to live well and ignore his indiscretions with human women.

With a wolf? She might not be so forgiving.

Ian had Guthrie research everything he could about Duncan's new she-wolf friend. It was the first time Duncan had ever been interested in a female wolf. He denied he had any long-term interest in her, but Ian knew his brother better than that. At least he thought he did. He assumed they would soon have a new American wolf living in the castle.

He would have kept this to himself, only telling his new American mate what he was thinking. But since he was sending Cearnach to be with Duncan, he wanted Cearnach to know that if he attempted to work his charms on the lass, he and Duncan might come to blows. They needed to work together, not fight over a female wolf.

"You sent for me?" Cearnach asked, stalking into Duncan's office, his shoulders back and his countenance serious for once.

Of all the brothers, he was the most cheerful, no matter what the circumstances, so Ian figured his next eldest brother assumed Duncan was in trouble and was ready to rescue him.

"Aye. I need you to fly to Grand Cayman Island to assist Duncan. Guthrie's arranged a flight that will get you there tomorrow night. Duncan will pick you up at the airport. You'll be staying with him at a villa with a Shelley Campbell."

Cearnach's posture changed from stiff to relaxed in an instant. He took a seat across from Duncan's desk. "Tell me about this lass. Scottish?"

"American."

That didn't faze Cearnach in the least. "Human?"

Ian hesitated too long to say. He knew his brothers would have words over the wolf.

Cearnach smiled broadly. "A wolf?" He didn't say it as a question to Ian, but more to himself. He looked delighted with the prospect.

"She's Duncan's."

Cearnach's brows arched. "He's taken her as his mate? Mother will have a conniption that she wasn't consulted."

"Nay, he hasn't mated her."

"Ah, but it's in the making. Hmm, maybe I need to show him the error of his ways."

Ian straightened. He didn't need the additional aggravation. "You will do no such thing. Leave her alone. I don't need the two of you coming to blows over the woman."

"He's serious, then. *Duncan.* I can't imagine. She must be a warrior maiden to be able to handle him."

"I believe she's more of a maiden in peril, the way Duncan tells it."

"Well, it will be interesting to meet her and find out all about her. I just can't see Duncan falling all over himself for an American wolf." Cearnach folded his arms across his broad chest. "What about Sal Silverman and our money?"

"He's now after Shelley. Duncan hasn't made any headway about the money."

Cearnach's mouth dropped open. "Bloody bastard."

"Aye. I'm thinking we might all need to take a vacation on Grand Cayman Island. For now, I'm sending you to scout out the situation. Duncan's getting in way over his head with this."

Cearnach chuckled darkly. "Because of a lass." He shook his head, stood, and added, "I take it no one knows of this latest development concerning Duncan and the lass?"

"Nay."

"Why not, Ian? If he's as serious as you think he is—"

"It's his decision to let the clan know what he plans to do about her. I'm not sure he's come to any decision of his own. Until then—"

"I have a sporting chance."

"Do you want me to send Guthrie in your stead?" Ian asked harshly. He would not be disobeyed in this. If Cearnach even considered making a move for the wolf Duncan was interested in—

Cearnach grinned and waved his hand as if dismissing the notion. "Nay, I will keep my hands and my thoughts to myself."

"Aye, and watch your tongue. That is the worst of it."

Cearnach laughed, turned, and left Ian's office. Ian was wondering again if he should send Guthrie instead.

———

When Duncan reached the reserve, he stormed down the path, trying to keep his blood pressure from going through the roof and hating that Kenneth, the mealy little bastard, was alone with Shelley. If he so much as touched an inch of her skin, Kenneth was a dead man.

One of Silverman's goons followed Duncan, trying to keep up with his long strides to make sure Duncan didn't kill Kenneth if he was doing something he shouldn't to Shelley. As angrily as Shelley had looked at Kenneth at the villa, Duncan was fairly sure that she was ready to shift and take care of the creep herself.

She'd gone much farther into the forest than he'd thought she might. When he finally reached her, she was standing before some kind of tropical tree, photographing its leaves and huge gourds hanging in clusters.

Kenneth was watching until he heard Duncan stalking up the path, and then he turned to see the rampaging wolf in human form headed for them.

Even though Kenneth was a couple of feet from Shelley, he instantly stepped back a few more. For the first time, Duncan thought the man might have half a brain. Shelley looked over to see Duncan approaching and smiled brightly at him. Her smile was like a brilliant shaft of sunshine piercing the thick leafy canopy, striking him, and instantly heating him to the core. She didn't look stressed or concerned, just happy to be in her element, as if she absorbed pleasure from the plants themselves, the oxygen they gave off giving her peace of mind.

She reached for him as if to kiss him in greeting. He had been so anxious to see she was safe that he gathered her into his arms, hugged her like a grizzly, and kissed her smiling mouth. It wasn't enough. He had to taste her, claim her, let these men know that she was his and that Sal could drop dead. As soon as he released the money he'd stolen, Duncan would take care of him.

Duncan's mouth sealed with Shelley's, his tongue ravishing hers, unable to get enough of her. Wanting to get inside her, to claim her, to connect. His hands roamed down her back, sliding her shirt over her warm skin while she wound her arms tightly around his neck. Her breasts were pressed hard against his chest. He felt her arousal, her nipples beaded and enticing, as he knew she felt his erection stirring, growing, craving her as if it had a will of its own.

Her tongue slid over his, her eyes closed as she squirmed a little, not to get free or because she was uncomfortable, but to rub against his straining cock, to show how much she wanted him back.

Vaguely aware they had an audience—he had wanted Sal's men to understand in no uncertain terms that he wasn't giving Shelley up for anyone or anything—he cursed under his breath.

"Wow," Shelley said, coming up for air, licking his lips, and smiling at him. "You missed me."

He gave a disgruntled sound, wrapped his arm securely around her shoulders, and began to escort her away from Silverman's men. He didn't bother to ask if she was finished there because as long as the men hung around, she was done with this spot of the forest. She had to realize just how concerned he'd been about her welfare, even though he'd done his damnedest to appear unaffected when he'd spoken with Sal.

Duncan could just imagine what Sal's goons were thinking as they'd watched his and Shelley's heated exchange. Forget giving the woman to Sal; they wanted a piece of the hot little wolf themselves.

"Well? What are we supposed to do?" Kenneth asked the other man, his tone annoyed and breaking the silence that filled the air.

Not that the birds and bugs didn't make a lot of racket, and the breeze sifting through the trees rustled the leaves in its path. But the men's silence had garnered Duncan's attention. No one spoke for a moment. Duncan was certain the men were having a time getting their own lustful thoughts under control.

"We did what we were supposed to do," one man growled. "Drop him off and leave. Come on. Let's go."

Sal's minions headed out of the reserve, tromping through the forest, one stumbling over a tree root in the path, which made him curse and kick it at the same time.

Duncan shook his head and continued to walk Shelley in the opposite direction while Sal's goons returned to the trailhead.

Shelley talked about the various plants she'd photographed and showed Duncan a picture of a rabbit-sized rodent on her camera. The creature had long, thin legs and hoof-like claws, and she called it an agouti. Duncan recognized it as the shy little beast he had seen the first night he had run with Shelley as a wolf.

She was talking nonstop. He wondered if she was nervous about the men still being nearby and gave her shoulder a reassuring squeeze. She smiled up at him as if to say she wasn't concerned in the least.

A heron took flight nearby. They both watched it soar over the trees.

"Well?" she finally said when they figured they were alone, "what did Sal have to say to you?"

"He wanted to pay me to stay away from you."

A leaf had caught her eye, and she leaned down to photograph it. "Oh."

"He wouldn't meet my price."

Shelley looked from the leaves she was taking pictures of to Duncan. "What was the price you were willing to hand me over for?"

"Two hundred and fifty million pounds."

Shelley had been relieved that Duncan had returned to her unharmed and surprised at the way he had so amorously greeted her. But she was even more astounded by this bit of news and she gawked at him. "That can't be how much he stole from you," she said softly.

"It is."

She didn't know why she hadn't realized how much

the crook might have absconded with. But then again, she couldn't imagine having that much money. Then to lose it all. She supported only one person, she reminded herself. The money Sal had stolen supported a whole wolf pack. At that point, she was even more resolved to help Duncan.

"You have to get the money back."

"Aye, I do, lass."

She took a deep breath and tried to lighten the somber mood. "I'm glad to know you thought I was worth so much."

He gave her a dark smile. "If only you knew just how much."

Oh yeah, she knew how much, just from the way he'd kissed her into the ground with Sal's thugs looking on. She didn't mind, knowing they would tell their boss that Duncan didn't look like he had any intention of giving her up. But she knew Duncan was playing for keeps.

"Are you done here? We need to talk. Privately." His voice was gruff, but she thought that had more to do with his arousal than anything else.

"Yeah, let's head back to the villa."

On the drive back to her place, Shelley wondered if Duncan was going about this all wrong as far as Silverman was concerned. What if dealing with his mate might have better consequences? "Duncan, I was wondering—what if we get Sal's mate involved?"

Chapter 12

LOOKING ASTONISHED THAT SHELLEY WOULD SUGGEST involving Sal Silverman's mate, Duncan frowned at her as they drove back to her villa. "Why would we do that?"

"I don't believe she'd go along with him having another mate, do you? You said that you thought he'd try to keep her and me from knowing about each other, but I don't think that would work. For one, we're both wolves. So if I'm with him, surely she'd realize he'd been with another wolf by smelling me on him or something. And if I were interested in being his mate and he'd been with her, I'm certain I would know that he'd been unfaithful."

Duncan seemed to consider what Shelley was saying, then replied, "Aye, could be. But since it doesn't bother him to cheat on his mate, he may believe you wouldn't be bothered, either. And his true mate may not care if he takes up with you, as long as she continues to live extravagantly off his ill-gotten gains."

"Is she my age? Older? Younger?"

"His age."

"Hmm, then she might not like him being interested in a younger wolf. Money may be her only care in the world, but women don't often give up their mates easily. Especially she-wolves. She might not care about his human conquests, knowing there's nothing permanent in the relationship and the connection isn't like between wolves. But his wanting another wolf? That's a different story."

She pondered an uglier alternative. "What if Sal thinks the best option would be to get rid of her? Permanently. Before she even learned about me. Or... before I might learn of her. If she found out about me, all she'd have to do is—"

"Put a hit out on you," Duncan growled. "Hell, Shelley, you could be a prime target for her wrath. Both because you might be the cause of her losing her mate and because he might consider getting rid of her for good so he can have you instead. She's got the money to hire anyone to do the job, too."

Shelley considered that for a moment. "I hadn't thought of that. You're right. What if we clued her in on the fact that Silverman stole from a wolf pack? She'd know that he was a dead man. A werewolf can't go to prison. She'd realize he's only living on borrowed time."

"She'd still have her money. *Our* money."

"Right. But what if she thought the wolf pack would go after her next? It's your money, after all. You're not going to play nice by the Fed's rules, allowing her to pretend that it was her money and not the funds that Sal stole. You'll want them back, or else. She might even be worried enough about her own life to agree to give up your money. If we let her know that Sal is trying to take a new wolf mate—if that's his intention with me—she won't care what happens to him. Wolves can be protective of their mates. But she won't be if she believes he's planning to eliminate her first."

Duncan pulled into the driveway of the villa. "That brings us back to her wanting to get rid of you. She might figure that we'd take care of Silverman, and considering what he's pulling with you, that might be fine with her as long as she's got the stolen funds stashed under her own name. But she might be so angry about you that she'd want to get rid of you for even thinking of taking her mate away from her."

Shelley smiled brightly and patted his hard, muscled thigh, thinking of Duncan wearing his kilt and readying his sword. "That's why I have you, a brave Highland warrior, to protect me."

He gave her a look that said he didn't care for the idea. "I don't like it."

"I can't think of a better way to go about this. I truly believe that if she thinks she could lose her life, she'll be willing to give up your money. She wouldn't bother trying to protect her mate if she thought he was having an affair with another wolf behind her back."

"I'll discuss it with Ian first."

She wasn't sure why that bothered her. She and Duncan were the ones involved in this fiasco, not his brother, Ian. Maybe she was annoyed because Ian was the laird of Argent Castle and very much like the one who'd thrown her people off the land in Scotland long ago. She didn't like it that this laird was still calling all the shots. Well, she wouldn't wait to see what he had to say. She kicked off her shoes, sat at the kitchen table, opened her laptop, and began looking for anything she could about Sal Silverman's mate.

Meanwhile, Duncan pulled out his cell phone and called his brother. He didn't know what she planned on doing, but he was certain that letting Sal's mate know he was wooing another wolf could prove deadly for Shelley.

Duncan wasn't going to allow it. He noted that she'd kicked off her shoes, and he couldn't help wanting to see her naked and in his arms again. But then his brother answered the phone, breaking into Duncan's lustful thoughts.

"Ian," Duncan said without preamble. "Shelley has an idea I'm not entirely satisfied with."

She cast him an annoyed look, but he only raised his brows. Then he explained to Ian what she thought would work and why he thought it was too dangerous for Shelley to risk it. Afterward, he waited for Ian to consider the plan while he watched Shelley search for something on the Internet.

When he drew closer, he saw her looking at news releases concerning Sal Silverman.

Ian finally said, "It might work, Duncan."

"But—"

"Hear me out. We'll need someone from outside our pack to call Sal's mate, Carlotta Silverman, and let her know the situation with Shelley. Otherwise, Sal will assume the Highlander who's on the island—which is you—is associated with the pack and may decide to come after you. Maybe my mate can have her father call Carlotta, since Julia's father is American—or at least has lived there long enough to sound mostly American. If Carlotta confronts Julia's father about the wolf Sal's trying to seduce, Carlotta might decide to plan a hit on Shelley for mucking everything up."

"Aye, so that means the plan won't work. If his mate confronts him about a wolf pack coming after him, he will try to flee. At that point, he might not care anything about what happens to Shelley or his mate, just about his own wolf skin, and go into hiding again."

Ian didn't say anything for several minutes. "Wait until Cearnach arrives tomorrow night. The two of you can make sure Sal doesn't leave the island."

"Aye," Duncan said, but he was determined to develop a different plan. One that didn't make Shelley the focus of a hit.

When Duncan ended the call with his brother, he considered the news stories Shelley was reading on her laptop at the kitchen table.

"What's Sal Silverman's mate's name and… wait, I found it," Shelley said.

Here she was, willing to risk her life when the leaders of his clan had sacrificed her people to improve the quality of their own lives. He wouldn't let her be the clan's pawn to make their lives better again.

He wanted to tell her that this wasn't his clan's way—making one of their women bait an angered wolf. He wasn't having it. That's when he realized just how he saw her. As his. His woman. His mate. Even if they weren't mated yet. It was only a matter of time. He knew then he would never let her go. That he had to somehow forge the link between them that could never be broken.

He wasn't used to waiting for what he wanted, either. He hadn't planned to let Silverman get away with the theft, and he wasn't planning for defeat as he waited for Shelley to acquiesce and say she wanted him like he wanted her.

His thoughts were in turmoil, like a man about to propose to a woman, except that wolves didn't marry. There was no time to back out of the deal, no wedding preparations, no concern of either not showing up at the altar. All they needed was to agree to consummating sex, and the mating was a done deal.

A wolf's way of saying "I do, forevermore." A wolf's way of keeping the promise to have and to hold from this day forward—for better, for worse, for richer, for poorer, in sickness or in health, to love and to cherish till death do us part. And to pledge their faithfulness.

Well, *normally*. The MacNeill brothers were potentially titled, so each of them would be required to have a wedding in their kirk on the castle grounds or in the gardens, if the lass so preferred. A wedding was a necessity in the event that Ian didn't have a son, nor Cearnach or Guthrie, leaving Duncan to have an heir to the title.

He glanced over her shoulder to see what Shelley had found.

Normally, werewolves kept their names out of the press. But with Silverman's worldwide theft, his name was easy to Google. When his name came up, so did his mate's in a few instances.

"Hmm," Shelley said, reading the news. "It says here that Carlotta Silverman had substantial savings in her name only and that the Feds aren't considering her as suspect in the thievery."

Duncan's gaze hardened as he read all the news stories, refreshing the memory of how he and his clan had read through the breaking news releases, concerned that the bastard would get caught and thrown in jail—and create a whole new scandal. One that werewolves couldn't live with.

"Nay. She just deposited all that stolen wealth into accounts in her name, not to mention showing ownership of all the properties they have. Of course, none of that has anything to do with her mate's dirty dealings," he said sarcastically.

"I doubt she'd stand up to you or any of your clan if you took her to task about the money, Duncan. Certainly not once she realizes he stole from a wolf pack. He must never have associated with any other packs, or surely someone would have tried to take him down. I really believe this will work. What did your brother say?" She looked up at him with such expressive, large green eyes, willing him to allow her to help him with this, willing him to trust her.

He pulled her from the chair and studied her parted lips, which she immediately licked. Whether that was in response to what she knew he wanted or because his reaction was making her nervous, he didn't know. And didn't care.

He held her shoulders with a desperate grip as if he was afraid she might say no, that she might back away, that she might slip free, and he pressed his mouth against hers.

She melted beneath his touch, which propelled him forth, drawing him deeper, dangerously so. Her hands clutched his waist, not pushing him away but holding herself up, holding him close. Her mouth fused with his, heating his lips and begging for more. His erection jerked to attention, hard and ready to follow his orders. He wanted to lift her and carry her to the master bedroom and ravish her first on the soft mattress and later that evening in the ocean, bringing her fantasies and his to fruition.

"It's forever," he mouthed against her lips, his pressed tenderly, hoping she'd agree, afraid she would not.

She licked his lips with the tip of her tongue, teasing them. As soon as he opened his mouth to draw her in, she swept her mouth against his hard jaw, not taking his bait. She ran her hands over his back and pressed her belly against his raging erection. "Mating? Or something else?" she asked, her voice ragged with lust.

Her tone was sexy, heated, making his temperature rise even more.

"When I saw you at the airport," he rasped out, "hell, saw you wearing all that silver, I wanted to grasp the chain at your waist and drag you to me and hold on tight."

She gave a low, throaty chuckle. "I thought you looked like a damned hungry wolf—dangerous and all alpha. I guessed right."

"If another man had approached you, human or wolf, and even if you'd planned a rendezvous with him, I doubt I would have permitted it."

She laughed. "Wouldn't he have been surprised if a man he didn't know had approached and told him to butt out when he and I already had a date?"

"But *you* wouldn't have been surprised." He traced her jawline with a tender touch that seemed at odds with the gruffness in his voice.

"No, I would have expected as much from a wolf like you." Then she sighed. "I don't know enough about you—nor do you know enough about me—to make anything permanent."

"I know that if I don't return to Scotland with you, I will forever regret the decision. Tell me you feel the same way."

He could feel her heated skin against his, her body soft and yielding, not stiff and pulling away. He knew she wanted this as much as he did.

She coiled a finger around his chest hair, staring at it, not lifting her gaze to meet his, unable to deny what he knew they both felt. "My mother and my uncles…"

"Aren't mating me."

She looked up at him then, smiled, and took a ragged breath. "They'll want my happiness. They still hold a grudge against the Highland chief who threw us off the land."

"I'm not him."

"No, but your family did the same to your own people."

He ran his hands down her arms, then wrapped them around her back and hugged her tightly, showing her he didn't intend to let her go. "Eons ago. Think of this as making amends."

"You don't have to do this for my…"

"Hell, Shelley. Do you want me to get down on bended knee?" He was serious, but he wasn't sure she was taking him seriously.

She grinned at him. "A warrior like you begging me to say yes?"

He shrugged, unable to maintain a serious expression, his mouth curving upward some.

She shook her head. "No, don't bother. I'd laugh too hard and spoil the moment."

He caressed her soft cheek and tipped her chin up with his fingers so he could drown in her green gaze. "So you'll say yes?"

"If I don't, you won't give up trying, will you?"

"Hell, no." With that, he took her response as a yes, swept her up in his arms, and headed for the bed.

But she wasn't done protesting. "What do we really have in common?"

"You and I love swimming together."

She chuckled at that. "You make a damned good anchor."

"You make a damned good mermaid wrapped around my anchor."

She smiled up at him with a devilish gleam to her eye, but then she sighed. "There has to be more."

"Aye, lass, there is. I love running with you in the woods and intend to take you running in the Caledonian Forest anytime your heart desires. I love playing with you in the water and tackling you in wolf play in the house."

"You're afraid to tackle me," she said, as he put her down on the bed.

"I'm used to rough-housing with my brothers and male cousins. I'd never wrestled with a she-wolf before, and I was afraid I might get a little too physical."

She reached up and grabbed hold of his shirt. "You're going to have to wrestle with me, Duncan MacNeill, and get a little physical. It's all part of a wolf showing who's boss. When I win too easily, it's not as much fun."

He growled with impatient need. "I'm all for getting a lot more physical with you, lass. Believe me."

"We've already wrestled some. I stood on your chest in triumph when you broke into the house without invitation, but I would have liked to have worked harder at it."

He slid his hands under her shirt and fondled her breasts, covered in a silky bra, making her nipples harden like rough diamonds. "Next time, I won't be so easily cowed."

She laughed. "You? Cowed?"

"Only with you. And only as a means to an end."

He lifted her shirt, exposing her lace-covered breasts, and then reached behind her to unfasten her bra. "You love to watch me sword fight," he added, getting back to everything she loved about him, hoping he could think of enough common areas of interest that she would capitulate. "You love my cooking."

"Hmm. I do love both." She copied him by sliding her hands up his shirt and running her fingers and palms over his pecs. Having her touch his skin ratchetted his heartbeat up several notches.

"You like that I'm a movie star," he said, barely able to repress a smile.

"But you said you were only an extra and didn't even get the girl."

"Aye, which is good for you, because I'm free to pursue the one I really want." He stared at her shirt, her bra unfastened but not going anywhere unless he peeled everything off. But she was just as sexy half undone as she was totally naked. He slid his hands over her breasts, pushing the bra cups up and out of his way.

"You don't like plants," she said in an accusing tone. "Don't deny it."

"I have offered to show you our gardens at Argent Castle, a guided tour even. I don't doubt that in your capable hands, I could become quite knowledgeable about plants. We even have a secluded arbor in the rose gardens and a gate that can be secured for privacy."

"Where I could teach you about the different varieties of roses?"

"Where I could teach you what else can grow in a garden."

She laughed. "I love your sense of humor."

"See? You love lots about me already. When we get home, I can show you my sword."

She slid her hand over his crotch, making his arousal jerk with enthusiasm. "I've seen your sword, and it's mighty impressive."

"So say yes," he said, unzipping her pants, then tugging them down her hips. If she didn't say yes, he was going to die an excruciatingly agonizing death. At least for the moment, because no matter what, he wasn't giving up on her.

"I have poodles. Your Irish wolfhounds will eat them."

He laughed. "They will romp through the castle together as one big happy family."

"You don't like poodles."

"I will learn to love them."

"What about my job?"

"What do you think about teaching the clan's children about plants? I know it's not the same as teaching at a college, but we don't have anyone who teaches the subject, and we homeschool all our children."

"But I bet you teach them sword fighting."

"Aye."

"Not the girls, though."

"If any want to learn…"

"I want to."

He laughed. "I would be happy to show you how to swing a sword." He could imagine holding her back against his chest as he leaned forward and held her arms and helped her swing. He'd have to take her somewhere private as he was certain anything he did with her would get him into the mood for another bout of this kind of play.

She seemed to consider her options, her gaze focusing on nothing in particular, her fingers stroking his chest in a tantalizing way. If he didn't get her stripped and naked soon...

"All... right," she said slowly, and he could see some apprehension in her eyes. She would move in with his clan, his wolf pack, an American who wasn't familiar with their ways. And she was willing.

Not about to allow her to change her mind, he pulled off her capris, threw them aside, and then began to slide her shirt and bra off. She wrapped her legs around his thighs, and he was reminded of the mermaid and the anchor and smiled.

"Wait until I get you back in the water," he said.

"Just as long as you follow through on your promises."

"Oh, aye, lass, 'tis what I'm good at."

"And sword fighting."

"Aye." He jerked his shirt over his head and threw it to the floor, then reached for his belt, taking in her contemplative expression, her full breasts, and her extended nipples that looked like mouthwatering cherries waiting for his kisses. He thought about the way she'd eaten the cherry from his hot fudge sundae.

"You're not in a rush, are you?" she asked, leaning forward and running her fingers over the swelling in his jeans.

Her touch made his erection jump again. He marveled at the way the she-wolf could make him react so quickly.

"Aye. The next time, I'll try to take it slower."

"All right, then. Hurry up before I see reason and change my mind."

"You *are* seeing reason, and you *won't* change your mind."

He stood before her naked, only long enough for her to take a good lingering look, which was killing him. She swept her gaze all the way down him as though he were prime meat and she was ready to sink her teeth into him.

She smiled and sighed at what she saw, her gaze shifting to his face. "Maybe we should wrestle first. Make sure that we're suitably matched."

"We *are* suitably matched," he said, and before she could say another word, he was moving her into the middle of the bed, his knees planted on either side of her thighs, his head dipping for a long, slow—*painfully* slow—kiss on her lips as his arousal prodded him to go faster.

He didn't let the rest of his body touch hers, not yet. Every time she touched him, he wanted to thrust between her legs, claim her for his mate, and keep her with him forever. That was another reason why he hadn't removed her panties despite the temptation to just take her.

Her hands cupped his face as she kissed him back, her moistened lips teasing and sweeping across his, but it soon turned to something much more passionate and fiery, her tongue exploring his mouth, his penetrating hers. Her hands quickly shifted to his shoulders as she steeled herself, her heartbeat thundering with need as he smelled her pheromones. They instantly kicked up a firestorm in him.

The way she raised her thigh and rubbed gently against his cock and balls really got his attention. He shifted his mouth from hers to a hot nipple and lathed it with his tongue. He knew without even touching her that she was wet and ready for him. He wanted more. He wanted to hear her beg him to follow through, to force the issue. This time he kneed her legs apart.

But of all the damn times to get a call, Shelley's cell phone rang. "Leave it," she said, as he looked over the mattress to the floor where her cell phone was in her pants pocket.

"After I turn it off." He climbed off the bed, fished the phone out of her pocket—not intending to look at the caller ID but noting it was from an Ethan Campbell—and then shut it off.

He retrieved his phone and turned it off also, just in case.

When he returned to bed, he thought she looked as though she half wished he'd tell her who was calling and half wished he'd keep it a secret. Duncan didn't want her kin getting between them, whoever Ethan might be, so he didn't say, figuring he'd abide by her wish not to know.

Her legs were still spread, the patch of curly auburn hair between her thighs taking his attention before he moved in between her legs. He began to stroke her swollen nub with his finger, his tongue licking her navel, his libido cooled somewhat from the phone call.

She was quickly aroused full tilt again, her fingers sliding through his hair, her body arching beneath his strokes. It wasn't enough to have her begging for more. He had to possess, to conquer, to give in to her needs as well. His mouth covered hers and his body did the rest—his penis nudging at her entrance, entering, allowing her heated velvet sheath to accommodate him—until he was all the way in. Tight. Hell, she felt as though she was virginal the way she hugged his penis so constrictively, and it felt damned good.

He thrust deep inside, penetrating her deepest chasm. That connection meant she was his, just as he would always be hers, his mate, forever.

"Love me," she whispered, her voice soft, warm, and husky like a breeze on a summer's night.

He did, with every ounce that he possessed. He loved her, pumping into her with an enthusiasm he'd never felt before with any woman, creating a union that was not just sex but an unbreakable link between them that would last through the ages.

"Duncan," she said, barely able to say his name.

He sensed she was climbing to the peak, her body feverishly stretching out to reach the climax as he thrust into her deeper, seeking the pleasure that only came from a permanent mating.

He couldn't respond, couldn't say her name, and suspected she didn't care that he was so wrapped up in the way her muscles clenched around him and her supple body arched against him, gyrating a little as if to allow him deeper access, that the headboard was banging against the wall.

The moment she cried out in the ecstasy of their union—of their bodies grinding and arching and thrusting as if they were a well-oiled machine, two parts as one—he came, explosively spilling his seed into her womb.

He at once thought of how he would deal with babies and wolf pups—him, a dark warrior.

He sank down on top of her for a moment, trying to

catch his breath, all the blood having run straight to his groin. For a moment, he couldn't think of anything but holding her beneath him, just like this.

He stirred and felt himself hardening again, but he fully intended to get off her, not wanting to crush her with his weight.

She kept him in place. "Stay," she said, "just like this, inside me, on top of me, all around me."

Then she went to sleep, and he thought life couldn't get any better.

Chapter 13

SHELLEY KNEW THIS WAS EXACTLY WHAT SHE'D AL-
ways dreamed of when she woke to find Duncan still
sleeping soundly, her body now nestled against his. She
wondered when he had changed position, enabling her
to sleep half on top of him so that he wouldn't crush her.
He didn't crush her, though, when he was on top of her,
instead making her feel protected and loved.

He was wonderful, a considerate and consummate
lover, passionate, yet tender at the same time. She knew
beyond a doubt that he loved her.

She couldn't help worrying about what her family
would say concerning her mating with him without their
input. She didn't need anyone's approval. But knowing
her uncles, she was certain they'd think otherwise. She
could imagine them worrying that Duncan had forced
her into agreeing to a mating, as alpha as he was, and
because he was the kind of man who, when he decided
something, went into battle mode to get it. She liked
that about him, liked that he cared so much about his
family's financial troubles that he had intended to take
on Sal Silverman alone—and anyone else the bastard
hired to do his dirty work.

She was anxious about what would happen with the
money Sal had stolen, though. Even more so now, she
was determined to help Duncan get it back. Maybe she
had a selfish reason for wanting the money returned.

She wanted the college to pay for her grant like they'd promised. And she wanted the money returned that the college would have used to pay salaries. What was she to do now, though?

Maybe if Duncan and his family were wealthy enough, and she was now part of the family, she could visit every palace garden in the world. Maybe she could afford to travel to more exotic places like the Amazon to locate a plant that might help newly turned werewolves to control their shifting.

She smiled at the thought and ran the tip of her finger over Duncan's taut pecs. God, he was gorgeous.

But more than that, he cared about her, even from the moment he'd seen her at the airport and wanted to yank the silver chain around her waist to draw her into his arms. He'd wanted to do so not only for a purely sexual reason, but because he wanted to protect her from anyone who might wish her harm. Sure, from sexual encounters also. She had been a wolf and alone, and she knew that had bothered him from the start.

She loved the way his dark chest hair rubbed against her sensitive nipples, loved the way his mouth kissed hers, hot and fiery one moment, and brushing tender kisses the next. The way his hands gripped her hips when he was thrusting into her, working her against him in perfect sync. The way his dark brown gaze clouded with lustful intent. Even the way that all she had to do was look at his crotch and his cock would begin to stir.

She was serious about wanting to play with him as a wolf, just like all wolves did, testing their mettle and finding their position in the pack. She'd never had much of a chance to do that when she was younger. Not with three grouchy uncles who had nipped at her when she was a pup, forcing her to quit biting at their swishing tails or tackling their legs as they stood patiently watching their surroundings, wary of anything that might be a danger to her. Both male and female wolves produced the hormone prolactin, known as the nurturing hormone, which induced them to take care of the pups, to play and feed and teach them. However, her uncles had been more concerned about her welfare.

She had no interest in frolicking with her uncles now. With Duncan, that was a different story. She knew he could be gentle even if he was afraid he might not be— the big brave Highlander who no doubt always fought to win. She was certain he could tone down his aggression enough to give her a workout without injuring her. If he fought at full strength, or maybe not quite that hard, he'd still give her the sense that she'd had some chance to best him.

She wouldn't mind if she had to resort to tackling him unaware or using strategically placed suitcases to help in her conquest. Part of being a wolf was using cunning to rule the day. She smiled and kissed his nipple, then licked and watched as it tightened.

He didn't open his eyes, just growled something low under his breath as his hand clamped over her shoulder. Then he said more audibly, "Does the sleepy little wolf want to play some more?"

"I should check my missed phone call, and we should take a swim before it gets too late, and…"

"Too late," he said, his voice already rough with need, as he rolled her over and spread her legs.

That was one way to wake the sleeping dragon.

—∿—

After an evening of delight, napping for a while, and a meal of shrimp and scallops and a salad, Shelley finally changed into her bikini. While Duncan was changing into his Speedo, she checked her phone to learn who had called her. She figured it was either that bastard Sal or her girlfriend Wendy. But when she saw it was her Uncle Ethan, she was furious. Not with him but with Duncan. Why hadn't he told her that her uncle had called?

Not that she didn't know the reason. Duncan probably assumed that if he'd told her, she might have had second thoughts about mating him right then and there. She wouldn't have. Well, maybe she would have. If she'd talked to Uncle Ethan, he would have tried to convince her to wait a while longer. The sizzling, sexy mood between her and Duncan would most likely have fizzled. She sighed.

Still, he could have told her after they'd made love the second time, damn it. While they'd had dinner. Sometime. Her uncle was not going to go away.

That made her wonder why Uncle Ethan was calling her. He couldn't know about Duncan.

She paced across the living room floor with her turned-off cell phone in hand. She'd only turned it on to see who had called her, then got the shock of a lifetime and hurriedly shut it back off in case her uncle tried to call her again. He wouldn't have called her unless…

Wendy, damn it. Wendy had to have told Uncle Ethan that Shelley was rooming with a hunky Highland wolf. She might not have done it on purpose, maybe letting it slip because Uncle Ethan was worried about Shelley being alone on the island.

Great. Just great.

Duncan's footfalls padded along the carpeted hallway, and she steeled her back. This would be the briefest wolf mating in history before a big-time fight occurred.

Duncan knew as soon as he saw Shelley glowering at him—arms crossed beneath her breasts, back stiff with indignation, and cell phone in hand—that he was in deep shit. Yet, he was still having a devil of a time concentrating on her anger, as he took in her barely there bikini. He'd had his hands and mouth and tongue all over her breasts just an hour ago, but that didn't matter. He was ready to slip the small scraps of shimmering blue material down and start all over. Already her nipples were poking against the fabric. He knew, without even smelling her arousal, that his eyeing her was preparing her for another bout of sex with him.

Trying to get his mind back on the issue at hand, he didn't regret not telling her that her relative had been the one to call when they were getting ready to consummate their relationship.

No sane man, no matter how noble, would have been dumb enough to tell her that a relative was calling, and did she want to speak with him? That they could have sex some other time.

Or had she already talked to Campbell? Had he upset her? Hell, no way was one of her relatives going to tear apart their newly formed relationship.

"Shelley—"

She shook the phone at him. "You could have told me that my Uncle Ethan called."

So it had been one of her three uncles. "I forgot. After we made love…" Twice. "I'd planned to tell you about it. Did he counsel you that he intended to make me pay for taking advantage of you?"

She gave a little huff of a laugh. "Get real. I haven't talked to him yet."

The tension drained from his tension-filled posture.

She noticed. Wolves noticed every physical reaction, no matter how slight. She also relaxed. "He's going to be pissed."

To Duncan's relief, she seemed to have lost her irritation over the whole issue.

Then she looked down at his Speedo. Hell if he didn't react to her perusal. Instantly.

"If you want to play out our fantasies in the ocean before we don't make it that far, come with me," he said, his voice damned rough with feral need. He hated how little control he had over his body when he was around her.

Even if she wasn't about to move, he was ready to grab her in his arms and force the issue. He wanted to play out the water fantasy—the one she'd suggested before they had come this far.

As small as his swimsuit was, the fabric was expanding to accommodate his growing arousal. But he figured he'd pop right out of it soon.

She gave a little snort of laughter, left her phone on the table, and murmured, "I've never seen a man this close up in a Speedo, but I don't think it's going to hold you for long. I want to play wolf to wolf with you. That'll teach you to keep my phone calls from me."

He lifted her into his arms and stalked outside and across the hot sand, the dark enclosing the island and sea. "Wolf to wolf?"

"Not in a sexual way. Just in play. I want to let my inner child out."

He chuckled, darkly amused. "Whatever would please you, Shelley," he said, leaning down to nuzzle her cheek. "Anything at all."

"He's not going to like this," she said softly. "My Uncle Ethan, I mean."

"As long as *you* don't regret what we've done."

She smiled at Duncan, flicking a nail lightly across his nipple. "I'll let you know after we try to fulfill our water fantasies."

"I won't worry, then."

She laughed. "I doubt you worry about anything with regard to facing another wolf or man."

He was very serious when he said, "I worry about your happiness, Shelley. If this causes problems with your family and it upsets you, it upsets me."

She gave him a rueful smile. "I wanted this as much as you did, and I'm *not* changing my mind, no matter what any of my uncles say."

With her body rubbing against him, he couldn't concentrate on the conversation any longer. "I think I picked the wrong-sized swimsuit. This feels like I'm about to burst out of it at any minute."

She grinned up at him. "That makes me think it's just the right size."

They'd barely made it into the surf where the water rose to Duncan's waist when his fingers were sliding her bikini top down, exposing her breasts to his mouth and tongue as she wound her legs around his thighs to hold on while he tortured her exquisitely.

She tried to reach for his Speedo, to free his straining cock, but he wouldn't let her. "Wait," he said, so raggedly that she knew he was ready to erupt.

Whether it was the warm sea, the friction between their bodies as the gently rolling waves moved her against him, or their scanty clothes that turned her on so much, she was ready to climax with barely any help from him.

She leaned away from him as he yanked her thong down, dipped his fingers deep inside her, and stroked her nub until she was ready to jump backward into the waves. Oh God, this was a fantasy come true.

He growled her name and jerked his Speedo down only enough to release his cock. Before she knew it, he was inside her. She was riding him up and down, the buoyancy of the water making this one sexual encounter she wanted to repeat over and over again until they left the island.

"Tell me you have an indoor swimming pool with doors that lock where we can spend every night before we retire to your room in the castle, Duncan," she huskily said.

He moaned something under his breath—something Gaelic, she thought—that sounded beautiful to her ears, even if he was only cursing again. She rode him as he held her hips and brought her down on him as forcefully as he could, considering the way the water contradicted the motion. Their mouths kissed, and their tongues tasted and tantalized, licking the salty spray from each other's skin.

She knew she'd never experience sex like this again, not anywhere but with him here. She vowed that if they got the money back from Sal, she and Duncan would come here at least once a year to relive the heady experience of sex in the warm waters of the Caribbean. They would take leisurely walks in the forest with colorful parrots chattering in the foliage, swim with the rays and schools of brightly colored fish, fight pirates on sailing excursions, sail on catamaran dinner cruises designed to celebrate a sunset at sea, and just enjoy each other in a bed built for two.

She dug her fingers into his back and bit his lower lip with a gentle nip as she felt her blood heating, her climax nearing. She felt his impatience as he drove into her, his own body surging close to completion. Just a little higher, just another thrust, his pelvis rubbing hers until she clenched so hard, the intensity of pleasure driving her to the swell of the peak. She felt she was going to implode if she couldn't reach the top soon.

He quickened his thrusts, deepening as he licked her chin, one hand shifting, slipping around her bare buttock, touching her between her legs where his cock was thrusting inside her. He suddenly growled out her name as she crested the wave, shooting his hot seed inside her. She shattered in his arms, her muscles clamping down on him with heady contractions. Her body limp and sated, she clung to him, head against his chest, tongue licking salty drops of the sea collecting on his skin.

"Hmm, lassie, you keep that up, and I'll have to start all over again."

"Is that a threat or a promise?" she said, her voice thready, raspy, tired.

He chuckled darkly. She hoped he hadn't planned for her to walk through the sand to get back to the villa, not as boneless as she felt. Nor that he expected her to tackle him as a wolf now. She was ready to snuggle and cuddle with him for several hours before she did anything else.

He held her for a moment, letting her ride him for a few more seconds, then slipped out of her, yanked up his Speedo, and tried to retie her string bikini top, without much success. She laughed. "Just hold me while I do it."

If she'd tried to stand on her own two feet and tie her bikini with the waves pushing against her, she would have been swept away, as unsteady as she was. As it was, she had a difficult enough time retying the top. Having him eye her with predatory interest didn't help. She swore he was ready to make her come all over again, with very little rest in between.

"Do you still want to play wolf to wolf?" he asked, his eyes smoldering with lust.

She was too limp to play well and couldn't believe he'd be raring to go. She wondered just what would happen if they did play wolf to wolf, because from his hungry expression, she didn't think he meant just to play.

"Maybe later," she said, smiling up at him.

"Later?"

"Yeah, after I've had time to sleep a little. Then I'll be ready for you."

"Hmm, all right. It's a date."

After they returned to the villa and took quick showers, they went back to bed to snuggle and nap. When she woke later to find he was no longer in bed with her, she peered around the room and saw Duncan sitting on his wolf haunches near the door, watching her, panting, and waiting to play.

He was a large, sturdy alpha male with his brown eyes observing her and his ears perking up as his gaze met hers. He was ready to frolic with her as wolves would.

She laughed, loving that he was willing to give in to her wishes. "Are you ready to get beat?"

He smiled.

Naked, she climbed out of bed and stretched her arms, his gaze taking in every inch of her. The way he was observing her, she figured that if he hadn't been in his wolf form, he'd have dragged her back to bed.

Her muscles heated, and she felt gloriously exquisite as every fiber in her body stretched to accommodate the swift change and the freedom it gave her for a brief couple of seconds before she shifted into the wolf.

She dropped to her pads to face Duncan on all four paws. He was standing now, preparing for her, tail wagging, mouth closed, the slightest smile in his expression, but he didn't attack. Gentleman that he was.

She bounced around him first, excited to play as he grinned at her. She lunged, jumping on top of him. He fell back as she bit into his neck with a playful bite. He growled and snapped at her in a mock fight. She jumped away from him, then dove again, impacting with his body. He stood his ground, letting her tackle him, allowing her to bite him. He grabbed at her nuzzle, more in a love bite than real battle. She wanted to throw back her head and laugh, but she growled instead, wanting him to give her real competition.

His tail was wagging, his ears perked, his tongue lolling to the side. She jumped to tackle his neck and hung her forelegs over his back. With high spirits, Duncan dislodged her, tackled her, and brought her down, licking and chewing on her neck and muzzle. She loved it, loved that he was pinning her down and forcing her to fight him, but still in a sweet way. She doubted he would be half as gentle or loving with his brothers or male cousins. She wanted to see him play with his male siblings, to see how vigorously they fought in mock battle.

Growling and snapping, she kicked at him with her feet until he lay crosswise on top of her and licked her muzzle, and she gave in. As soon as she shifted into human form underneath his furry body, he licked her nipple and she laughed. Then he shifted also, still on top of her, only skin to skin as humans. "Lass, you are no beta female, if that's what you're worried about. Are you ready to retire for what's left of the night?"

She lay on her back on the carpet smiling up at him. "You have to fight harder next time."

"Aye, I will," he promised with a sparkle in his eyes, but she presumed he wouldn't really. Not like he would with his brothers, in any case. Maybe that was just as well.

He pulled her up from the floor and kissed her lips, his hands roaming down her back and buttocks. "When you crawled out of bed before you shape-shifted, I nearly returned to human form and carried you back to bed."

She laughed and squeezed his ass. "I'm glad you didn't and played with me as a wolf instead."

She retrieved her phone and turned it back on.

"Put it on vibration, in case we get frisky and someone wants to call and annoy us in the middle of the night," Duncan warned. He slipped into bed with her, spooning her and intending to wait until her breathing was soft and slow—like that of a sleeper who was dead to the world— before he left her.

He couldn't tell her what he intended to do, because knowing her, she'd want to go with him. He wasn't having any of it. This business with Silverman was his job, not hers. He wanted her safe and sound and sleeping until the next time they made love.

Forty-five minutes later, Duncan was finally able to slip out of bed, believing she was asleep. He watched Shelley for what seemed an eternity, waiting to see if she woke and noticed he'd left the bed. She didn't stir, too tired from all their love bouts. He breathed in her fragrance one last time—the feminine, musky, sweet scent of her—and damn if his libido didn't ratchet up a couple of notches.

Before he changed his mind and began to make love with her again, he headed naked for the back door of the villa, opened and closed it, then shifted. He hadn't thought he'd be scent-marking his territory on the island, nor would he have if he'd actually had a room at a hotel like he'd first planned. Everything had changed when he had gotten involved with a sizzling hot she-wolf. He was playing for keeps.

As he loped around the perimeter of the villa, he only thought to show Sal that Shelley was his—as well as the villa, the territory surrounding it, and even the beach and the sea that caressed it. That any wolf who crossed that line was in serious trouble. Wolves killed other wolves that were not of their pack and invaded their territory. The need to do so was just as strong with a werewolf who was protecting his own.

Instinctively, the wolf half of him had to do his bit to

ensure Sal knew it beyond a doubt. Sal hadn't done so around his own property, which had surprised Duncan. He wondered if that was because Sal didn't often release the wolf side of his nature. Or maybe Sal didn't feel the right to claim territorial possession because the money that had undoubtedly paid for it all wasn't his. Or maybe Sal just didn't feel he needed to prove anything to anyone.

Duncan left a few calling cards around Sal's estate also. With a smile.

After all, with all the money Sal had stolen, this could very well have been Duncan's pack's estate. Marking it as his own enforced the claim that it was theirs, not Sal's.

What Duncan hadn't expected when he returned to the villa—with his she-wolf sleeping soundly inside— was to discover two men snooping around the perimeter.

Two men who were wolves.

Chapter 14

As soon as Duncan smelled the two male wolves in human form near the villa, the fur on the nape of his neck stood on end. Truth be told, his whole wolf coat fluffed with aggression, making him appear even larger than he was.

If the men had seen him, they would have known he was a hair's breadth short of attacking them. However, he was afraid that as soon as he attacked, his growling and snapping jaws and their frantic cries would awaken Shelley. He didn't doubt she'd come out to help him. Somehow, he needed to draw them away from the villa before he showed them what he was made of.

They had to smell his scent markings and realize he was damned serious that any wolf in the vicinity should know to keep his distance. These men probably assumed that Duncan was snuggled in bed with the she-wolf, not standing out here in the dark and sensing them while they observed the villa.

"I don't have a good feeling about this," the first man groused. "I know you said he's got to be inside with her, but, hell, I swear he's just remarked the area with his scent, as fresh as it smells. If that's so, he might very well be out here still… *with us*."

The other man didn't say anything, just crept toward the house, his eyes glued on the villa. Either he wasn't afraid of meeting Duncan out here, so he wasn't looking

out for him, or he was like Sal might also be, not used
to being a wolf. That would make him more wary and
cautious, constantly on the alert when faced with the
danger of a wolf fight. The other man's head kept swiv-
eling around like an owl's, peering into the darkness and
watching for any signs of Duncan.

Two male wolves to one were not good odds in wolf-
to-wolf combat. In his wolf form, Duncan could handle
a couple of humans, but only if neither was armed with
knives or guns. He could manage one of these wolves
before the other responded, though.

Still, he waited, listening, anticipating their next
move and trying to determine what they were about. If
they thought he and Shelley were in bed together, what
did they hope to accomplish?

They came into view around a stand of palms, both
men slightly bent in a crouch to be inconspicuous. Were
they armed?

Both wore black jeans and black boots, but one had
on a button-down, charcoal gray shirt with the sleeves
rolled up, while the other had a crinkled black polo.
Neither looked to be carrying a gun, but they could easily be sporting knives. They were muscular, tall, and
looking for trouble.

"Wait," the talkative one said, the one in the polo
shirt. He was dark haired, yellow eyed, and wearing a
two-day growth of beard, with a long, hard jaw. He had
a swagger to his step, like he owned the world, as if
the other man's silence and steady approach toward the
house assured him that they'd run into no trouble.

They must not have dealt with a Highland wolf before.

Big Talker suddenly stopped, lifted his nose, and

took in a deep breath. "We're just supposed to scout the area. We don't need to get any closer to the house. Not right now." So a case of nerves was finally melting his steel exterior.

Again, Duncan wondered what the hell the two planned on doing.

The other man paused, his dirty blond hair streaked with red highlights, his chin smooth and stubby, his gray eyes narrowed as he studied the house. They were still a good three hundred yards from the back porch. The waves crashed along the beach, the wind flapping the palm fronds about, particles of sand shifting, a bank of clouds obscuring the moon as the two men remained half-hidden in the stand of palms.

Duncan hadn't seen either of these men before. He thought they must have arrived at the island today or been in hiding all this time. But he suspected the former was true. Sal must have figured that since he couldn't persuade Duncan to leave Shelley for a small amount of money, maybe some wolf muscle would do the trick. Sal didn't have the strength to fight Duncan on his own.

The dirty blond took another step toward the house. "I don't want to wait. We don't get paid if we don't take care of business. The sooner we take care of this, the sooner we're outta here."

Duncan let out a very low threatening growl, warning them not to get any closer. The natural instinct erupted before he could even think further of the consequences. He wasn't worried about the villa or the territory around it. Shelley being inside the house concerned him the most. Big Talker stood rooted to the ground as if he'd become one of the palm trees he was standing between.

The dirty blond twisted his head in the direction he heard the ferocious growl come from. Both men's eyes were wide as they tried to see Duncan in the dark.

Neither man said a word. Neither moved an inch.

This was when they'd pull weapons—if they had them—and stand and fight. Or begin yanking off clothes to shift into the wolf with the same intent, only planning to fight wolf to wolf. Or back away slowly so to not further antagonize one pissed-off wolf, which was the only way they would get out of here alive.

Duncan needed to wait and see how each of them reacted. For now, the two men couldn't see Duncan; they could only hear another rumble of menacing ferocity slip between his bared teeth.

He was concentrating so hard on the men's reactions, although he seemed to have turned them to stone, that he didn't at first notice the smell of her—Shelley—somewhere in the direction of the men.

He stood up straighter, frowning, smelling the air. The men slowly turned, realizing that she was behind them and they could smell her scent. They didn't move quickly, maybe concerned she might take anyone's sudden movement as a threat to her well-being. Duncan's heart instantly leapt with distress as he realized she was behind the men, meaning they were between him and his mate.

Damn it to hell. He didn't want her out here in any danger.

The men had to be concerned, even though she was a smaller female. She still had one hell of a mouthful of sharp teeth if they tested her strength or willingness to attack—and they were still in human form.

She quickly let Duncan know she was with him—part

of his team, so to speak, and not there needing his protection. Her deep growl pierced the sounds of paradise, of the breeze tossing palm fronds and the waves beating and sliding over the beach, of the shuffle of sand. Her growl was a discordant sound like his had been. It didn't belong in the idyllic islands, a predator's threat that had to have rarely been heard here, if ever.

She growled again at them, as if her first wolfish statement hadn't had the right impact, warning them to disappear or else. She wanted to be taken seriously. Duncan knew beyond a doubt that she intended to attack if they made any move to harm him. But he didn't want her anywhere near them.

"Shit," Big Talker said, half looking over his shoulder in the direction of the she-wolf's growl and unable to see her, just like Duncan couldn't. The men had to recognize her voice was not as deep as a male's. That she was half the threat that Duncan was.

She was playing it safe, though, keeping out of view. Duncan was damned grateful for that.

The other man turned his attention back in the direction of Duncan, the bigger threat.

"Shift," the man said under his breath, undoubtedly figuring Big Talker could hear him while Duncan was too far away to make out the whispered word. Or maybe thinking Duncan would mistakenly believe he cursed instead of giving the order to shape-shift.

Duncan knew Shelley would fight them. He just didn't want her getting hurt.

He lunged for the man who had taken charge of the situation and knocked him to the ground, growling and threatening to rip him to shreds.

The other man tore off toward the road where Duncan suspected they'd parked a vehicle. Shelley didn't take chase, for which he was glad. Instead, she moved in closer to the remaining man, watching Duncan as he bit at the man's hands, his teeth exposed for a killing blow. The man was trying to keep Duncan from reaching his throat while grabbing for Duncan's muzzle. Duncan was considering his options as he snarled and snapped and cut the man's hands with his sharp teeth. Kill him, maim him, let the bastard go.

The bastard held up one arm to block Duncan's teeth. With his free hand, he slipped a dagger from beneath his shirt.

Knowing the man was armed, Duncan was certain that if he let him go instead of killing him, he would come back to murder Duncan and take Shelley against her will.

It didn't matter that the man hadn't had time to shift. He'd intended to murder Duncan, and if Duncan had given the two men a chance to shift, Shelley would have gotten into the battle and could have been seriously hurt. He made the decision, the correct one as far as a werewolf's thinking went, and bit into the man's hand, gripping the knife to neutralize the threat to himself. The man screamed in pain. Duncan lunged for his throat one last time, severing the spinal column in a killing blow.

He wished he hadn't had to do so in front of Shelley. He suspected she hadn't ever seen a wolf kill a man before. Or at least he assumed she hadn't. He hadn't wanted her to see him like this, in such a black mood with only one thought in mind—to kill before being killed.

He glanced up at her. Shelley looked in the direction

of a car engine rumbling. Duncan sidled up to her, nuzzling her to come with him. He wanted her in the house before he made his next move. This time she was *not* leaving the villa if he had any say about it.

Proud of Duncan for taking care of the threat but unable to clear her head of the image of him killing the wolf-man, Shelley locked the villa, per Duncan's instructions after he made her go back inside. She had wanted to come with him, but he'd refused. What if the other man returned, and she was alone? But in truth she was part of this and didn't want to be left out. She needed to stand by him, no matter what happened. She needed to be with him in wolf form and help if he needed her.

Her argument fell on deaf ears.

After Duncan had shifted, cleaned up, and dressed, and she was locked inside, he left her alone in the villa.

She'd watched him through the back patio's glass doors until he'd disappeared from sight, headed in the direction of the dead man. She expected to hear the rental car engine start after several minutes and that he'd take the body away to some other location. The car never moved from the driveway. She was left wondering what Duncan had done with the dead man. Hauled him into the ocean? Swam out with him into the surf? Fed him to the sharks?

If Duncan had, they'd better not swim in that part of the ocean again. She couldn't help worrying about his safety if he did swim out into deeper water with the bloodied man, potentially drawing sharks into the area.

She wasn't sorry for the man. She'd known as soon as he whispered to his partner in crime to shift that they intended to fight and kill Duncan. He was only one wolf against two. Not that she wouldn't have done her part, but she would have been at as disadvantage against the bigger males. The man had been armed with a knife, and even though werewolves had faster healing capabilities than humans, she knew that if he had cut Duncan in a lethal place, he could still have died.

She knew that's why Duncan hadn't hesitated to attack the man who appeared to be in charge and that he'd worried if he didn't survive, she'd be left on her own. His mate.

She was glad the other took off running like a scaredy-cat. Unless he got more backup, she really didn't expect he'd return anytime soon. But what if he ran to Sal and the two of them came back seeking revenge?

She knew that Duncan had to have taken the wolf-man's body somewhere, but not where. Shivering as the adrenaline spiking her body and readying it for a fight began to drain from her bloodstream, she waited and paced, anxious that Duncan was taking way too long to return to her. A million scenarios raced through her mind. The police would catch him carrying a dead body over his shoulder. Sal's other wolf would have changed into his wolf form and caught up to Duncan to avenge his buddy. Sal himself and the other remaining wolf would gang up on Duncan. What if there were more than just the two?

She so wished Duncan had allowed her to watch his back. They were in this together, as far as she was concerned. But the warrior in him insisted that he take all the risk, damn it.

Nearly an hour later, Duncan materialized out of the dark, stalking toward the villa, his face grim with

a warrior's stern expression, a battle obviously fought
and only partially won. It would only be done when his
clan's money had been returned.

She opened the door for Duncan, and before she could
do anything or say anything, he locked the door, seized
her hand, and hauled her back to the bedroom. "I'll join
you in a minute," he said, leaving her next to the bed. He
looked displeased, but she didn't think it was with her.
Unless he was pissed off that she had approached the
men in her wolf form from behind and growled. Yeah,
she imagined that he planned to take her to task for that.

She wouldn't have done anything differently. She
had been staying downwind from Duncan the whole
time he'd been scent-marking their territory around the
villa—and even around Sal's as a heightened threat to
let the man know Duncan was serious about Shelley
being his. She had added her own special scent to ensure
that everyone knew they were a pair. Duncan wouldn't
have been aware of it. When he went wherever he did to
dispose of the dead man, Duncan would discover what
she'd done.

Maybe *that's* what he was pissed off about it. She
wouldn't have reacted in any other way.

She hadn't believed Sal would send some wolf muscle their way.

Without another word, Duncan went inside the bathroom and shut the door, the shower coming on again.
Not to wash away the blood, though. He had already
done that in the ocean, and his clothes were salty and
wet from the sea. Now he was removing the salt and
sand from his skin and hair and clothes.

She wanted to wait for him before she undressed and

crawled into bed, wanting to hear what had happened. She figured he needed to think about what had occurred and what he thought best to do next without talking it over with her first. So she did what she thought best. Took off her clothes and returned to bed and waited for him to join her.

He soon left the bathroom but he didn't join her right away. With a towel wrapped around his waist, his skin glistening with water droplets, he said in a low, reassuring voice, "I'll join you in just a few minutes, Shelley. Sleep. I won't be long."

He lifted his phone from his pants and stalked out of the room. She knew then he was calling his brother to tell him the news.

That meant she wasn't part of the package when it came to dealing with the bad guys. In his estimation, she was only the maiden in distress. Annoyed to the max, she harrumphed at that and decided she wasn't about to wait for him to join her in bed. She was going to go to sleep, damn it, and pretend she didn't care what he'd done.

Closing her eyes didn't shut her brain down. Not until he climbed into bed with her and pulled her against his hot, hard body—and knowing tomorrow would bring all kinds of new trouble—did she finally fall asleep.

Early the next morning, Duncan seemed to be in deep thought, his expression dark as he went about preparing breakfast before he got a call from Ian. Was his brother telling him Cearnach's arrival time that night? Duncan and Shelley hadn't made love since the previous night, not that she hadn't been in the mood, but Duncan seemed so absorbed in what had happened that she didn't feel he was interested.

He hadn't talked to her about the men last night. She didn't bother broaching the subject because she figured she'd get a lecture. If he even thought about lecturing her, they were going to get into a fight.

Shelley's phone began ringing, and she hurried to get it. Good thing they had both turned off their phones last night, or she was sure she would have been awakened way too early. When she answered the phone and saw it was Wendy, Shelley was not happy. "Wendy, did you call my mother and tell her I was rooming with a wolf?"

"I didn't mean to tell her anything, but she was upset about the grant money. You know, heard all about it on the news. She knew you couldn't afford the cost of the villa on your own. I had to explain that you were okay, but not… exactly alone. I told her you had a roommate, and he was helping to pay for half of the cost. I didn't mean to tell her he was a *he*. But you know how she is. She started grilling me. She told your Uncle Ethan. He started in on me, trying to learn all the details. Somehow I let it slip that your roommate was a wolf. From Scotland."

Shelley glanced at Duncan, expecting him to be doing anything else but watching her. She was wrong. He was observing her expression like a wolf would, watching closely and looking for signs of trouble.

She took a deep breath. Things were bound to get worse in a hurry. "Great."

"I tried to call you, to warn you, but your phone must have been turned off. Your Uncle Ethan is on his way to the island."

Oh. My. God.

Forget Sal and his thugs. Her Uncle Ethan would kill Duncan.

Chapter 15

WHEN SHELLEY GOT OFF THE PHONE, SHE KNEW SHE had to tell Duncan that her uncle might be on a rampage and that he was headed their way, but Duncan looked like he still had a bucketful of worries of his own. "What's wrong?" she asked as she joined him for breakfast.

"Cearnach's not arriving tonight as planned, but tomorrow instead."

"Oh." It wasn't good news. Now that Sal was sending wolves to deal with Duncan, she figured they would be safer if at least one of Duncan's warrior brothers was staying with them.

Duncan was so tense, so feral looking, that she was fairly certain he was angry with her because she'd been nearby when he'd confronted the two wolves.

"How long were you following me last night?" Duncan finally asked. His gaze was dark, his eyes focused on her, watching her to see her reaction.

She raised her brows, not about to be intimidated. "You went out in the middle of the night without me. We're mated, you know. So I followed you. All the way to Sal's estate, if you must know." She smiled a little. "I liked that you claimed his territory. I did also."

He ground his teeth, then let out his breath in an exasperated sigh. "Yeah, I found that out. The two wolves were out scoping the area, meaning you could have been in danger. Why didn't you return to the house when you saw them? Let me deal with them on my own?"

"They intended to shift and fight you, most likely to kill you. You needed my help."

His expression lightened a bit. He must have thought she wasn't serious. She *was* sincere, though. And highly annoyed that he wouldn't take her seriously.

"I always go out, Shelley, marking the territory to let Sal or anyone else that has wolf genes know to back off. It's instinctual and necessary. I don't want your enticing smell out there, too, encouraging any male wolf around to come sniffing for you."

She was his mate now, and he wanted everyone to know she was off limits. She wanted everyone to know they were together, too. She was glad to see his mood shift to something more agreeable and less testy, though.

"Who were they?" she asked.

"I don't know for certain. Since they were close to the villa snooping around, I assume they work for Sal." He slid a plate of sausage links and hash brown potato patties over to her.

She loved how he cooked. Everything he fixed tasted great. She couldn't imagine how he hid his cooking talent from Ian so well.

"What happened to the other man? The one who got away?" she asked, wondering if the guy who was really talkative would return anytime soon. Maybe not. Without his sidekick to help give him courage, he probably wouldn't come near them. She wondered if the man knew what had happened to his buddy. Hell, she didn't even know what had become of him.

"I don't know. The guy didn't go to Sal's house."

Duncan sat down with his own plate of sausage and po-
tatoes and began to eat.

So Duncan had tried to track the second man down
and eliminate him as a threat?

"Maybe he didn't go to Sal's house because he was
afraid of what Sal would do if he learned the guys
botched the job. What happened to the one you killed?"
Shelley still envisioned the man floating face down in
the ocean, the sharks taking big chunks out of him, just
a little way down the beach or wherever the tide would
have taken him. Maybe even lying on the beach with
the hermit crabs nibbling on him. Either of which would
be bad news if someone on the island came across him.

At least if the sharks were enjoying him, no one would
think he might have been chewed up by a wolf. Actually,
since wolves had never existed on the island, she figured
no one would assume that anyway. More likely they
would think a vicious dog had attacked him instead.

Duncan set down his empty mug. "He took a swim
in Sal's pool."

Shelley had nearly finished her breakfast, but at
Duncan's last comment, she nearly dropped her fork.
She meant to say something, but nothing came out. She
cleared her throat. "His pool?"

"Aye. If it was Sal's man, he can dispose of him. It
would clue him in on what happens to wolves who get
out of hand."

She stared at the table, envisioning Sal going outside
to the pool for an early-morning swim. She half suspected his girlfriend would sleep most of the day. Most
wolves loved the dawn and dusk, their natural time to
hunt. A human woman would probably still be sleeping,

if Sal had had sex with her during the night. Unless she was naturally an early-morning riser. Another thought occurred to Shelley. What if Sal went outside and saw the body, and didn't know who the hell it was?

"What if Sal didn't send the men after you?" Shelley asked very quietly.

Duncan rose from his seat, came around the table to Shelley, rested his hands on her shoulders, and gently rubbed in a soothing manner. "That's one possibility I don't want to consider."

His voice was so grave that she feared the worst. "Carlotta might have hired a hit."

She assumed Sal hadn't intended to kill anyone. At least she didn't think so. That made her wonder why he would have sent the men, except maybe to scare Duncan off.

Then again, what did she know? A man who could buy anything he wanted was butting up against a Highlander who wouldn't bow down to money or some other man's will. So maybe he was resorting to other means to get his way.

But a woman scorned could be doubly dangerous.

"Aye. What if Carlotta Silverman already got word about Sal's interest in you and she's the one who sent the men? It's entirely possible."

Shelley stood but her body felt like one big, wet noodle. Duncan wrapped his arms around her and held her tight. She appreciated the heat of his warm body wrapped protectively around her.

"So, if that was the case, what would Sal think about the dead man in his pool?" she asked. She couldn't quit thinking about who might find him and what Sal would say about it to his men, or to his girlfriend if she saw it and began screaming.

"If the guy wasn't his man, Sal probably figures his wife learned about his attempt at picking up a she-wolf. If he's never strayed with a she-wolf before, he might not have realized how mad his wife could become. Most likely, he would assume I wasn't about to let any wolf harm a hair on your head. In which case, I don't know what he would do. Flee the island? Presume Carlotta might order a hit on him next, and he has to do it to her first? I think we've started a war."

"Good. Make them give us the money. They can kill each other off afterward. End of everyone's worries. No more taxpayers' money spent on trying to apprehend the bastard and bring him to trial, or if he got convicted, to house and feed him for whatever time he got behind bars—even though that's not an option for a wolf." She sighed. "What will happen with the dead wolf?"

"Sal will most likely take him far out to sea. I'm certain he has a boat that he can use to get the job done."

"As long as he dumps it where it's not close to our beach. What did Ian tell you last night when you called him?"

Duncan rubbed her back, not saying a word. Shelley pulled partly away and looked up at him. "What did he say, Duncan?"

"You're to be on the next flight out with Cearnach as soon as he arrives. He's to fly back to Scotland with you tomorrow."

Thinking they'd already resolved this issue, she scowled at Duncan and stood up. "No."

"You don't want to go to Scotland?" Duncan asked, sounding astounded.

"Of course I want to go to Scotland. But not with your brother! With you, when you get your money."

His expression darkened like that of a brooding warrior. "You can't be here. Not with whatever's going down. It's the only way I can make sure you're protected."

She pulled completely away from him, paced, and then collapsed on the couch, bouncing slightly in not too ladylike a fashion. "You're my mate now. I'm not leaving you behind."

"Lass…"

Her brows deepened even further. "Don't you 'lass' me. No. I'm not agreeing to it, and you can't make me. We're in this together. A wolf team." She rose from the couch before he could say another word, returned to the dining room, and opened her laptop. "It's time for Plan B."

As soon as Duncan told Ian that he was involved with a she-wolf, Ian knew that the situation would get out of hand. He knew because Duncan would never have even mentioned the woman if she hadn't distracted him something fierce. Being distracted in battle was a deadly scenario all the way around. Ian had never expected the little American female wolf to get into this much trouble. That reminded him of his own mate, come to think of it.

He sat at his desk in his solar, motioning to Cearnach—who'd just arrived at his older brother's summons—to take a seat. "Cearnach, we're going to have a fight on our hands," he told his second oldest brother as he explained the change in the flight plans and what he expected him to do.

"Aye, Silverman's called on some wolves, and we're going into battle." Cearnach nodded agreeably, always ready for a fight.

"Nay. The girl is the one who's going to give us real trouble."

Cearnach smiled, enjoying this a little too much.

"Hell, Cearnach, the situation is too serious to be amusing. How can you always see humor in every situation?"

"Sorry, Ian." Cearnach didn't look in the least bit apologetic. He spread his hands in an appeasing way, a humorous light still gleaming in his eyes. "What is it you want me to do? I can't force the lass on the plane if she won't agree. If you tell Duncan to return with her, leaving the money behind while I try instead to take care of the situation, you know he won't do it. He's honor bound to both protect her and get the clan's money back. He'll want her on the plane and out of danger. He'll want to remain on the island. We can't force her to leave. Not unless we had our own pilot and plane. Which we don't."

For the first time since he'd ruled the pack, Ian wasn't certain what to do. He usually had no trouble making decisions. This time, his youngest brother's happiness and life were at stake. "I'd send my mate to try and talk some sense into her, but I'm afraid Julia would then be at risk."

"I agree. As a romance writer, Julia doesn't belong in the middle of a fight like this. What if this is Carlotta Silverman's doing? What if she paid the men to go after Duncan, or maybe not even him but the lass? It might not have anything to do with Sal."

"That's entirely possible. All right. If Duncan and

you can't convince her to leave, you'll stay with them. Maybe between you and Duncan, we'll turn this nightmare around."

Ian was rethinking the situation once again, wondering if he shouldn't send a larger contingency. The problem was that keeping their wolf identities secret on a small island would be difficult enough. If all four brothers and some of their male cousins arrived, hell, no telling what kind of catastrophe that could be. Yet, he was still considering it.

Duncan watched over Shelley's shoulder as she searched the Internet for email addresses for Sal and Carlotta Silverman, wondering what her Plan B entailed. He had already decided that he wouldn't agree to it. Mostly because he had the sneaking suspicion that she was thinking about being used as bait.

Instead of asking her about her plan, he asked her about the call she'd gotten from Wendy. Whatever her friend had told her had undoubtedly upset her, judging from the distressed look Shelley had had when she was speaking with her. "What news did Wendy have to tell you?"

He said it conversationally, but as soon as the words left his mouth, her fingers paused above the keyboard and her whole body stiffened.

His hands went to her shoulders. He began to massage the tension out of them. "What, Shelley?"

"My mom learned that the college lost a lot of money to Silverman, including the grant money they should have paid me for this trip, which meant that I couldn't afford to be here alone. When Mom grew worried about it, Wendy let it slip that I was rooming with a Highland wolf—male type."

"And?"

She let her breath out in an exasperated sigh. "My Uncle Ethan is on his way here."

Hell. Her uncle was bound to get in the way. "The one who called, then. Did you return his call?"

She gave a little snort of laughter. "No. Are you kidding? He'd give me the third degree and come here and kill you anyway."

Duncan smiled. "He'll have to get in line."

"I'm not going to Scotland with your brother, Duncan," she said, looking back at him. "If nothing else, if I stay here, I might be able to stop my uncle from wanting to kill you."

"We'll talk about it later." He meant to get her on the damned plane no matter what. No sense arguing with her about it right now. "What is your Plan B?"

"Well, it was to email Sal or Carlotta, or both, and let them know that I'm in the picture, but I can't find an email address for either of them." She pulled out her cell phone and Sal's business card. "I guess I'll just have to call him and see what's up, even though I really don't want to talk to him on the phone any longer."

Duncan frowned at her. "What are you going to say?"

"Not sure until I hear his voice." She smiled not so innocently.

He wanted to take away her phone privileges and return her to bed instead. Duncan pulled her from the dining room chair before Shelley could make her phone call. He took her to the couch, where he sat down and settled her between his legs, then wrapped his arms around her waist. "Go ahead."

"Just be nice and quiet while I try to figure out what to say, all right?"

He grunted, which meant he wasn't buying it. She frowned at him, then punched in the number for Sal's phone. At first, there was no answer. The answering machine came on. She hesitated, not sure what to say. She wanted to hear what Sal had to say first, and then she'd wing it.

Speaking into an answering machine made her tongue tie in knots. "It's Shelley. I… guess you're not in. I'll… call back later."

She'd just managed to snap her phone shut and open her mouth to tell Duncan she'd try back later, when the phone rang in her hand. She dropped it in her lap. Heart thudding, she looked at the caller ID and saw it was Sal's phone number. No name listed.

"Hello?" she said very sweetly, like she hadn't a clue who was calling her. In truth, until she heard his voice, she wasn't sure it would be him calling her back.

"Shelley," Sal said, his voice silky smooth. "To what do I owe the *pleasure* of your call?"

As soon as she heard Sal's voice, she stiffened with apprehension.

She didn't care how much he tried to sound like some Casanova. She didn't find him sexy in the least. Put on? Definitely. "Duncan and I had a visitor in the middle of the night. Was he a friend of yours?"

A long silence passed between them.

Listening in on the conversation, Duncan began massaging Shelley's shoulders again. She was grateful, trying her damnedest not to moan in ecstasy as he helped ease her tension.

"Only one visitor?" Sal asked warily.

Either he *knew* there were two wolves, which meant he had to have sent them, or he *assumed* they had come as a pair. So which was it? She took another tack. "Duncan was pissed. He said you tried to buy him off to see me, so why did you send a friend to… persuade him to go away?"

"I didn't know the man who visited you. Is that what Duncan told you the man said?"

She hesitated for less than a second before she responded. "He wouldn't tell me what the man said. He told me it was best if I didn't know." That wasn't exactly the truth, but since Sal was one of the biggest liars around, she didn't feel obligated to tell him anything that he didn't need to know.

"Is Duncan around? Let me talk with him."

She raised her brows at Duncan. He nodded and held out his hand for the phone. "Yeah, Sal?" He didn't sound friendly in the least, rather like he was ready to take Sal as he had the other guy. Just one false word or move on Sal's part and he'd be a goner.

Sal didn't respond at first, but Shelley figured he'd assumed Duncan had to be nearby when she'd called, particularly after what had happened in the middle of the night. Unless Sal had thought she'd called him privately to see what he knew about the whole ugly affair. Sal's hesitation to respond to Duncan's answering the phone surprised her. Maybe Sal was losing some of his bravado around Duncan, now that he knew what the Highland wolf was capable of.

"How many men were there?" Sal asked Duncan.

"Don't you already know?" Duncan's voice was dark and growly, threateningly menacing.

Sal had to realize that Duncan was seriously angered.

"I didn't send the men," Sal quickly said.

"But you knew there were more than one."

Shelley was holding her breath until Duncan leaned over and ran his hand over her belly.

"I assumed no one would send only one wolf after you. That whoever had done it would have sent at least two." Sal was talking faster than he normally did, not cool and collected this time. "So, what happened to the other one?"

"If he's smart, he's swimming home," Duncan said, his voice low and hard.

Shelley smiled up at Duncan. He kissed the tip of her nose and winked.

"Why the hell did you leave the other one's body in my pool? My…" Sal abruptly stopped speaking.

"Your girlfriend might have seen him?" Duncan prompted with dark humor.

"I sent her away last night on a flight back to Miami. I didn't send the bastard to your place, all right?"

So, he sent his girlfriend home because he still thought he had a chance with Shelley? But now Sal sounded as though he was running scared. Maybe thinking if Duncan could kill a wolf like that and thought Sal had sent him, Sal could be next. So why wasn't he packing his bags and leaving? Maybe this was the safest—or had been the safest—place for him to hole up, away from the various agencies that wanted him in prison. Maybe Sal was afraid to make a move for the time being.

Shelley wanted to tell Duncan to ask for the money again, but she didn't want to be part of the bargain, even if it was a ruse. On the other hand, she was afraid that if they did tell him that he had stolen money from Duncan's wolf pack, Sal would make a run for it, no matter how afraid he was of the Feds. *They* wouldn't kill him. Not like the wolves would. He would have to know that.

"So if you didn't send the bastard to see me, who did?" Duncan asked.

Again, Shelley held her breath, waiting for Sal to tell them that his mate had sent the men. Then he'd have to let them know that he had a mate. Sal had to be thinking that if they learned he was the one who had stolen so much money, that he was *the* Sal Silverman of Miami, they'd realize the danger he would be to the werewolf kind.

Even if Duncan hadn't been one of the people Sal had stolen from, he was still a wolf, and once a wolf knew of a crime committed by another of this magnitude, the wolf or any other had to take care of the perpetrator as soon as possible. That made her think Sal must have isolated himself from wolves all along.

Sal would have to know the trouble he would be with any wolf pack. He kept quiet.

"If you didn't send the men, and I can't imagine any-one else who would do such a thing, who did?" Duncan growled. "Believe me, if I get hold of the other man— and this is one damned small island, considering square footage to hide in—I'll be sure to find out all the details from him."

Duncan was letting Sal know that he was vulnerable, despite his guard dogs and bodyguards.

Sal still didn't speak. Duncan mouthed to Shelley, "Carlotta." His eyes were nearly black. She knew Duncan was concerned even more now about her own safety.

"Hell," Sal said. "I'll take care of it."

Yeah, he'd take care of the other wolf because he didn't want Duncan to learn who sent the men. But for once, Shelley smiled. How had the tables turned so quickly that now Sal was on their side, in a manner of speaking?

Not really, of course. Because not only had he ruined so many financially, but Shelley had learned from the news stories that at least four individuals had committed suicide over the losses. Two because they'd lost their jobs with their firms over it. Two because their life savings had been tied up in those funds and they were losing everything they owned. So in essence, he'd committed murder by suicide. Shelley was certain that none of the men would have considered killing themselves if Sal hadn't brought them to financial ruin.

At least Sal would make every effort to get rid of the other wolf who had come to the villa. She suspected that the wolf was trying to get a boat or plane ride off the island pronto before he was shark bait, too.

"Did you break into my house?" Sal finally asked.

Duncan frowned. "I'm sure you have it heavily secured if you're worth so much. Your estate is probably filled with priceless treasures. Why would I attempt such a thing? Why would I feel the need?"

Long silence filled the airwaves. Shelley wondered what had happened. She mouthed back to Duncan, "Carlotta?"

Duncan said silently, "Possibly." He turned his attention to Sal. "What was stolen?"

Again, an unfathomable silence. Then Sal cleared his throat. "Were you at the airport anytime last night?"

He'd evaded Duncan's question, which made Shelley wonder what was missing at his estate. But the airport question really threw her.

Duncan raised his brows at Shelley's surprised look. "Why would I have been at the airport? I was taking care of wolves who threatened me and my own. After that, I returned to Shelley and stayed with her the rest of the night, if it's any of your concern."

Sal swore under his breath.

"What happened at the airport?" Duncan asked, sounding more curiously amused than concerned.

Chapter 16

SHELLEY WONDERED WHAT COULD HAVE GONE DOWN that had Sal worried about Duncan breaking into his estate. Sal didn't say anything for a couple of minutes after Duncan's question about what trouble might have occurred at the airport, which made her wonder what had happened there, too.

Sal finally said, "All right, listen. I want you to know I had nothing to do with the two wolves that came to your place. As far as Shelley goes, she's yours, beyond a doubt. But I'm going to need some protection. Do you have any training in that? Beyond what I've seen you can do as a wolf to a man?"

Duncan and Shelley's startled gazes met. *Protection?* What had happened?

"Protection?" Duncan asked, his voice betraying his surprise.

Duncan couldn't offer to protect the bastard. Not when Sal owed so many millions in stolen funds. Sal had to disappear after that—permanently. He'd caused deaths. It wasn't just a matter of stealing money from wealthy folks. He had ruined people and led some to commit suicide. The bastard had lived like a king off their money without any remorse whatsoever. More than that, once the Feds caught up to him, he'd go to prison. There was no escaping that eventuality.

Moreover, she didn't think Duncan could promise to

keep him safe, then go back on his word. Not as honorable as he seemed to be.

What if Duncan asked for his clan's money again?
What if Sal agreed to pay it? Then Duncan would feel
obligated to protect the bastard.

From what or whom, though? Carlotta? Or was he
thinking Duncan could protect him from the Feds? Had
the government learned he was here?

No, she thought, it was someone else. One pissed-off
mate, a woman scorned. Had she heard about Shelley
and now planned to feed her mate to the wolves? If she
had to get rid of her mate, Carlotta would no doubt keep
trying to eliminate Shelley also, perhaps being angry at
her for having to kill her mate.

"Three of my bodyguards have gone missing. I have
no idea what happened to them. None of them have
taken a flight out of here. They were just... gone this
morning when I walked out to the pool and found the
dead man floating face down in the water." Sal sounded
tired and anxious.

"I called for my bodyguards. No one came. My guard
dogs were all gone, too. Vanished. My private plane is
gone. Hell, I need protection. I know we've gotten off
on the wrong foot with each other, but after you took
on the two men, well, you're not one to piss off. So I'm
willing to pay good money..."

Shelley and Duncan exchanged dark looks.

"...to ensure that I don't meet with an untimely
death," Sal quickly finished.

"Who would want to eliminate you, and for what
reason?" Duncan asked coolly.

"It's none of your damned concern. The woman is

yours. I won't even hazard a glance in her direction. I need a damned reliable bodyguard and am willing to pay top dollar, depending on your worth. You'd be in my employ. My reasons for anything I do are my concern, not yours."

"I'm not for sale. If you didn't send the wolf goons to eliminate me last night, then who did? The same people who are giving you grief? I'll take my chances protecting Shelley here. You're on your own."

"Damn it! How much do you frigging want?"

Duncan smiled, but the look was pure evil.

Shelley could imagine just what Duncan wanted—his clan's money and for this scum to never take another breath.

"Kenneth," Sal said, sounding shocked, but he wasn't talking into the mouthpiece of the phone now.

"Hell, boss, where is everyone? No dogs greeting me, no guards anywhere. Are you leaving the island?" Kenneth asked, speaking in the background.

"Where the hell have you been?"

"With Rose. You said I could have the night off to be with her. She's been giving me grief for leaving her alone so much."

As if Sal finally remembered he had been having a phone conversation with Duncan, he said into the phone, "Think about it. I'll pay you a thousand dollars a week to guard me until I can leave the island."

The phone clicked dead.

If Sal wanted to leave the island, even though his private plane was no longer available, why not just book a commercial flight out? Carlotta must have sent a pilot to fly the private plane home, taking Sal's bodyguards and guard dogs with him.

Still why wouldn't Sal have just hopped on a pedestrian flight with the rest of humanity? No passport? Had Carlotta had someone steal his passport? Even with his money, it would take him some time to get another one.

Duncan shook his head. "This is bad, Shelley. Really bad."

"Do you think Carlotta's just trying to scare him? Or do you think she's hoping you'll kill him now that he has no protection?"

"Either could be a distinct possibility."

"So what do we do? If you ask for the same amount again, he's going to get suspicious. Even if he felt his miserable life was worth it and he could hand your clan's money over to you, then what? You can't let him get away. The Feds or Interpol or someone is going to pick him up eventually. Then they'll put the wolf in jail, and…"

"Right now, all I care about is protecting you, Shelley. If Carlotta is behind this, and I highly suspect she is, she's not only after revenge for her wandering mate, but also after you, not me, for breaking up the family. As far as I'm concerned, you're all that matters. She had to have sent the two wolves. When she learns they didn't accomplish her mission, I wouldn't put it past her to send more."

"But your family's money. If Carlotta kills her husband, then she's…"

"Got control over all the money. Sal's too greedy to realize he's stolen from a wolf pack, and she may not realize it, either. If he dies, we go after her."

She sighed. "All right. I guess that means I need to cancel the trip to swim with the stingrays today."

"No, we'll go. She can't do anything to you or me while we're in the public view. Since I've taken care of one of her men, all we have is one left to deal with. From the way he ran last night when I tore into his companion, he's not as alpha as he tried to act."

Another thought made her shudder. "The other body-guards all disappeared. Would the two men have killed them before they came to see us?"

"Maybe. Or maybe his bodyguards were bribed to leave on a boat. Carlotta might have even paid them to leave on the private plane. The thing is, money does talk. Carlotta's got enough of it to do whatever she wants. Sal should have realized that before he began to play this game over you."

Shelley figured Sal thought he was invincible. Maybe he'd always fooled around with human types, and as long as Carlotta was floating in dough, she didn't care. Picking up another wolf? That might have earned her ire, something Sal hadn't anticipated.

"If Sal is alone, he won't be able to take down the other wolf. I doubt he's much of a wolf fighter. Since Kenneth is human, Sal can't let him suspect what he is, so he can't solicit his help," Shelley said.

"I halfway suspect Sal might know where the other man's hiding. Or the man might have slipped away with the rest of the bodyguards when they left."

"Do you think Carlotta would let the man come home with the others after he failed to do her job?" Shelley asked, not believing Sal's mate would be that kind. Not when she was setting Sal up and most likely wanted Shelley dead.

"No." Duncan rubbed his chin in thought. "I have

to stay with you, so I'm not running all over the island looking for the guy. Sal can deal with him. I suspect once Carlotta learns that her play for you didn't go as planned, she'll be sending more of her people. That's why I think it's time I got you to Scotland."

She didn't respond to his comment but instead pointed to the clock on the living room wall. "We need to rendezvous with the boat that's taking everyone out to snorkel, if you're game."

"Let me get my swim trunks."

She smiled. "No Speedo?"

"Later. When I'm with you, it nearly strangles me, and I definitely don't want to be swimming with you in public wearing that stretchy swimsuit."

Duncan had assured Shelley that no one would bother them during the day. But as they made their way to the boat that would take them out to the Stingray City sandbar, they both watched for signs of danger while pretending they weren't worried in the least. Shelley noticed Duncan surveying the area for any sign of trouble as they left the villa, on the road to the boat dock, and around the area when they parked.

He became a little less vigilant when they had climbed aboard the boat and were headed out to the sandbar to swim with the stingrays.

"How long is the excursion, Shelley?" he asked, settling down to enjoy the trip with her. She was wearing a T-shirt over her bathing suit and had already slathered a good amount of sun protection on her legs and arms.

As a wolf, her fur would protect her from the sun's

rays, but as a human? Although she was lightly tanned from working in her garden, and despite the smattering of clouds beginning to clutter the sky, she still was vigilant about using a good sunblock. She glanced up at the darkening sky, frowning, and sniffed the air. A storm was coming. Maybe later tonight.

"The trip takes three and a half hours," she said. "It's about a mile out off Rum Point so it's like being way out in the middle of the ocean, but it's supposed to have a sandbar that makes the area really shallow."

He shook his head and whispered to her, "I've done a lot of things, but something's not natural about this—a wolf swimming with a bunch of stingrays."

"Two wolves," she said back.

He smiled at her, a heart-thumping, want-to-take-you-back-to-bed smile. "You're only a wolf in disguise. You're really a mermaid."

She grinned back at him. "Don't tell me you have a thing for mermaids."

"Only this one." He squeezed her hand, then kissed it.

When they reached the sugar-white sandbar in the North Sound, they slipped into the aqua water wearing fins and snorkels. Shelley was surprised at how shallow the area was. Only about three feet deep. She remembered reading how the hammerheads fed on the rays in the shallower water. That made her twist around, looking for any sign of a shark.

"For years, local fishermen cleaned their fish here before they brought the catch to shore. The rays learned it was a good place to find easy food," a guide said. He pointed to one of the rays. "Stubby. See he has no venomous barbed tail? Sharks like to eat rays. Stubby got away from one but lost his tail in the process. In fact, one hammerhead managed to grab ninety-six stingrays' tails. None of the venomous spikes were digestible, so when he was caught and opened up, the fisherman found all of them."

All of a sudden, a herd of flying stingrays descended on them, circling close and vying for the food they knew the snorkelers had. Swooping in, the rays competed with one another for the food, bumping the swimmers, brushing against them, and jostling for a better chance.

Several of the people were feeding the rays bait, but being the predator that Duncan was, he wouldn't do it. Shelley was more interested in reaching out to run her hand over one of the large Southern rays' wings. The skin felt like velvet-covered muscle as the ray glided by, reminding her of an underwater version of a *Star Trek* Klingon Bird of Prey warship. Some of the rays were huge, and she knew they could get to twelve feet across their wing spread. She enjoyed watching them dive and turn on the proverbial dime in such a graceful manner to feed, like giant gray birds in sweeping slow motion.

It was interesting to see that as much as they wanted the food, they were like floating acrobats as they dove and veered. She also noticed they had a pecking order— like wolves.

When she turned to see what Duncan was doing, she saw to her surprise that he had taken a bit of bait from the guide. With his hand outstretched flat, keeping his fingers from being bait, Duncan offered the bait to a hungry ray. The stingray glided over his hand, and the food vanished, the gentle creature twisting away to look for his next morsel. She smiled at Duncan as he watched the ray with an expression of wonderment, and then he caught her eye. He looked a little chagrined that she'd spied him feeding the ray.

He swam over to join her and pull her into his embrace as a man nearby said, "Hey, look at this."

In the clear glass-like water, they could see the ray wrap itself around the man's thigh, and then he said, "Ow." The stingray skated away, leaving a round bite mark on the man's leg that was already bruising.

The man proudly announced, "He gave me a hickey."

Sure enough, the man's thigh sported a stingray hickey. He seemed delighted with his bruised badge of courage. Shaking his head, Duncan took Shelley's hand and swam with her toward some breakers. She wondered if that was the extent of the snorkeler's man-against-nature trial of his life.

That's when she started thinking about Duncan and how many times he might have fought against other wolves in life-and-death situations. She hadn't even considered that. He wasn't a warrior in appearance only. Not just an expert swordsman because he'd liked to wield a sword.

For now, she wanted to enjoy this other world, a marine world she'd never before explored. She figured he was just like her, in uncharted—for them—territory. She poked her face into the water to see the brightly colored yellow-and-white fish as Duncan kept hold of her arm, not letting her drift away from him. She loved how she could relax while he took care of her.

Despite the problems they were having with Sal and probably now Carlotta, Shelley had never had this much fun. It wasn't just being here, which wouldn't have been half as special if she were by herself. Being with Duncan made her feel so alive—even seeing him steadfastly deny he wanted to feed the stingrays, then doing so with such awe.

When she lifted her face from the water to see where they were, she realized they'd gone some distance from the boat and the ocean stretched for miles around them. For a minute, panic filled her. The water was deeper where they were now, and without the stingrays to distract her or the boat close at hand, she realized how far they were from any shoreline. Duncan might think she seemed like a mermaid, and she did love the water— especially this water—but she was still a wolf who felt a bit out of her element.

"They're beginning to load the boat," Duncan said in a deeply reassuring voice. "Ready to go home?"

She didn't want to sound or look anxious, but he knew. He could tell by the way her heartbeat had accelerated, saw the way she'd scanned the horizon as if looking for a safe haven, and felt a light sheen of goose bumps on her arm, which he tried to smooth away.

"I'm feeling a little waterlogged myself," he said. "I'm ready for a meal and anything else we can come up with." He gave her a smile that said he meant to take her back to bed.

"You're not going back out by yourself to scent-mark the area again, are you? Or to look for the other man?" She wanted to clear that up now as they swam back toward the boat. The rays had drifted off to other areas now that no one had anything to feed them, leaving only schools of colorful fish darting back and forth.

"No. I'm staying with you. Until Cearnach gets here—"

"I'm not leaving for Scotland with your brother."

Duncan shook his head, waited for her to climb aboard the boat, followed after her, and then set his flippers, snorkel, and mask aside as he sat beside her on a bench. "You're not related to Julia Wildthorn, are you?"

"No, why?"

He smiled and wrapped his arm around her. "You remind me of her."

Shelley was shocked. "You know her? The romance writer? Personally?"

"Aye. She mated my brother, Ian."

With incredulity, Shelley stared at him for a couple of heartbeats, then smiled. "Oh my God, she's famous."

"You read her books?"

"No, but that doesn't mean I don't know of her." Shelley couldn't quite fathom why Duncan was still smiling. "Do you read her books?" She couldn't keep the astonishment and amusement out of her voice.

He cleared his throat and said in a disgruntled way, "Nay, they're romance."

She studied him further and didn't think that the sun had anything to do with the way his skin was reddening. "I guess if she's going to be a wolf sister, I'll have to read them." So had Duncan sneaked a peek at Julia's books? She suspected so. "Did she say anything in her books that you think might be interesting to try?"

He laughed. "You are not a mind reader, are you, lass?"

He pulled her close, their bodies wet and warm. She couldn't wait to shower, eat, and maybe even discover what he'd learned from Julia's books that appealed to him.

Chapter 17

AFTER THE DAY TRIP TO SNORKEL WITH THE STING-rays and a meal at one of the local fish eateries, Duncan and Shelley arrived back at the villa to settle in for the night, the sky growing more ominous by the moment. She'd been relaxed, feeling like taking a nap with Duncan before they did anything else, but as he walked her to the front door, both of them were at once on alert. The door was locked, but she swore she smelled the telltale scent of the man who had fled the scene the previous night when Duncan attacked his companion.

And Sal. It smelled like he'd been there, too. Not that they left calling cards, but she smelled their scent just the same.

"I want you to get back in the car," Duncan said slowly.

She understood his concern as a smattering of chills beset her, but she wasn't sitting in the car and acting like some cowardly beta while he could be putting his life on the line. "Why don't we go around back? I'll shift, you open the door, then you shift. We can check the place out together."

"I'd prefer you'd return to the car," he said gruffly.

She wasn't about to let him go by himself. "I'm not going to leave you to face two wolves alone."

He took a deep breath and exhaled it in an annoyed fashion. "Are all American she-wolves this stubborn?"

"Only when we have to deal with equally stubborn males of any country."

He shook his head. "Okay, you open the back door while I shift. I'll go in first, and you can shift, then follow me in."

"Sounds like a great idea," she said, since it sounded very much like her idea, except that he would shift first. She didn't care as long as she got to go with him.

"The greater idea would be that you stay in the car." He moved around to the sheltered back patio with her. Once there, he quickly ditched his clothes and then shifted.

For *his* information, the greater idea was that she'd stick by her mate.

She stripped out of her clothes, unlocked the door, and pulled it open. Before she could shift, he bolted inside, tail held straight like a warning flag, ears perked, and hackles raised. He paused in the living room, sniffing the air. He could have waited for her, but she knew he hadn't wanted to. That he wanted to protect her from anyone who might be waiting just inside the door. She loved that protective alpha male quality in him.

The adrenaline raced through her blood as she shifted and followed him inside, expecting to be in a fight—most likely against two wolves. She smelled both Sal and the other wolf's scents that indicated anger and fright mixed together. She wondered who would have been the more terrified? Sal or the other wolf? Had the wolf been in Sal's employ after all? If so, why would either be afraid?

Maybe of the notion of actually tackling Duncan. They did have something to fear when it came to him.

She didn't hear any sounds of a couple of wolves

or men searching for anything, if they were doing that upstairs or in the master bedroom. Then again, Sal and the other man would have heard Duncan's rental car and might be waiting to jump them at just the right moment. The men's presence in the villa probably had more to do with an ambush than a search mission.

The men had to know that both she and Duncan would have smelled them and be warned they were here. She and Duncan would be prepared for an attack.

In his menacing wolf form, Duncan turned to look at her, his expression telling her to stay. Which was ridiculous. He needed her to watch his back. She wasn't staying.

She let him take a slight lead to appease him somewhat, then followed behind.

Apparently sensing her close proximity more than hearing her, as soundlessly as she was walking, he turned his head to look at her, again giving her a silent warning to stay put. She stood still, matching his narrow-eyed expression.

He shook his head at her, figuring his order would be ignored, and then turned and headed for the master bedroom. She followed him and stood in the doorway, watching his back like a good mate would. The men had both been here. They didn't appear to be here now unless they were hiding in the bathroom or the narrow closet. Nothing looked out of place.

The bedcovers were disheveled, but that's the way she'd left the bed this morning. She felt guilty that she hadn't straightened them. Not because it would have mattered otherwise—she was on vacation, and she and Duncan were going to make a mess of them again anyway—but she hated that anyone else might have

seen the way she'd left the bed. Even if they shouldn't
have been here in the first place.

After checking the bathroom, Duncan headed back
to the bedroom door, waited for her to get out of his
way, and then took off for the stairs. Again, he looked
at her, willing her to stay downstairs. She did this time,
figuring there wasn't a whole lot of room to maneuver
upstairs. If the bad guys were up there, she'd hear their
growling. She'd race up the stairs and help Duncan then.

In reality, she figured neither of them were up there.
Most likely, they had come, looked around—maybe trying to find something out about her and Duncan—and
left. Maybe Sal wanted to show them he could come
and go as he pleased, especially once he discovered
Duncan's scent markings around his estate. It was a
testosterone contest between alpha males.

But then she smelled the faint odor of blood. She
sniffed the air again, then the rug, and found it. Drops of
fresh blood, a wolf's blood, on the riser of the carpeted
bottom stair. Her breathing suspended, she looked back
up the stairs.

Duncan appeared in the upstairs bedroom doorway,
glanced at her briefly, and then loped down the stairs,
looking ready to kill somebody. She moved out of his
path, and he headed for the back porch. She glanced
up at the guest bedroom, wanting to explore upstairs to
see if it was like the rest of the house—nothing touched
and only a scent reminder that the men had come and
gone. She hoped that one of them had simply cut his
paw on something outside the villa and left the blood on
the carpet by mistake.

Her gut instinct—along with Duncan's angry

expression and the fact she hadn't seen or smelled any other signs of blood—warned her it was much worse than that.

Before she could go upstairs to look, Duncan stalked back into the house in his human form, wearing his damp swim trunks. The rest of the clothes they'd discarded when they'd hurried to shift were crumpled in his arms. "The other man's dead up there. Looks like Sal killed him."

Her heart skipped a beat. Since she wouldn't have to use her teeth to fight a battle, she knew it was safe to shift. She quickly summoned her human form and, naked, rubbed the chill bumps on her arms as she realized she should have turned off the air conditioning before they went to swim. She knew that was an odd thing to think of, considering that a dead man was lying upstairs. The chill bumps weren't just because of the air conditioner, either.

With a look of concern, Duncan handed her clothes to her and ran his hand over her bare arm in a consoling caress. "Are you okay, lass?"

She nodded, hurrying to slip on the pair of shorts and T-shirt that she'd worn over her swimsuit on the stingray cruise. "Yeah, I'm all right."

He let out his breath in exasperation, sounding as though he didn't think she was and he was worried about her. Then he stalked into the kitchen and returned with wet paper towels in hand. Surprised at what he was planning to do and before she could even help him, she watched as he washed the spots of blood off the carpet at the foot of the stairs.

She eyed the stairs above it, looking for more spots.

"What happened?" she asked, her voice hushed, having to know but not wanting to, either.

"They had both shifted before fighting. Patches of wolf fur are all over the place. Nothing broken… thankfully. A little blood."

She shuddered, partly from the chill in the air and partly because one of the men had died in the upstairs bedroom. She was glad she was sleeping downstairs now. If she hadn't been before, she would be now. Not that she was afraid of ghosts or anything. Although the idea that the man had met a violent death did make her wonder if she and Duncan would be in for a little haunting.

She ground her teeth. "So Sal killed the other man and carried him away, leaving us with the mess to clean up," she said under her breath.

"No." Duncan leaned over to kiss her cheek, then went back to the kitchen to dispose of the bloody paper towels.

"What do you mean, 'no'?"

"The dead man's still up there."

That meant the man had been a wolf while fighting, but once he died, he would have reverted back to his human form. Naked. Dead.

Barely breathing, she looked up at the landing at the top of the stairs. She wasn't sure why she should have been so shocked. Sal was a real bastard, anyway you cut it. "Sal left the body for us to dispose of?"

"Aye. He was ticked off because I left one of the men dead in his swimming pool, not to mention that I wouldn't agree to be his bodyguard. Plus, this is a way to show me he's not a sniveling beta wolf. He can take care of himself."

"Can he? Take care of himself?" she asked.

"He did this time." Duncan ran up the stairs.

"What are you going to do?"

"Give Sal another swimming buddy."

———

As angry as Duncan was about having to carry yet another body to Sal's estate in the dark of night—figuring that was safer than transporting the body in the car and chancing getting blood on anything—he was more worried about leaving Shelley by herself.

He thought one reason why Sal had left the second man's body was that he couldn't have carried it all the way back to where he could readily dispose of it. That meant Sal might have followed this man to the villa and didn't have any other choice but to kill him. Then he'd left the body for Duncan to take care of. Or Sal had arrived, wanting to meet with Duncan face-to-face to try and secure his agreement to be his bodyguard, and caught the man here. If that was the case, the man probably had come here to lie in wait for Shelley and Duncan's return, figuring they'd be in human form and more vulnerable.

The hired assassin couldn't face Carlotta or any of her wolf assassins—if she had any more on retainer—without worrying he'd be next on her list, so maybe he figured he might as well try for a sneakier confrontation.

They'd fought as wolves, Sal and this man; that much was evident. Scraps of wolf fur clung to the floral cover at the foot of one of the twin beds. A chunk was on the carpet, and scattered remnants lay all over, as if they'd both had a sudden shedding frenzy.

Sal had left the man naked, but his clothes were lying near the first of the twin beds where evidently the man had stripped, then shape-shifted. Hating to bother dressing him, Duncan had jerked the man's clothes on him, not wanting to carry a naked dead man to Sal's place. Not that it would have mattered a whole lot if anyone caught him at his task. He would be in a hell of a lot of hot water, no matter what, if anyone discovered him.

In the dark, Duncan trudged through the sand with the man tossed over his shoulder, wanting to wring Sal's neck. He didn't need this aggravation. He certainly didn't want to leave Shelley alone at the house without protection, in case Carlotta had more men on the payroll or Sal was waiting for Duncan to leave her alone while he disposed of the body. The only good thing was that Carlotta probably hadn't had time to secure another couple of wolf hit men. The dead man might not have informed Carlotta his partner was dead, afraid of what she might do to him next for failing his mission. In which case, she wouldn't be sending another hit team right away.

With every step Duncan took in the sifting sand—he swore the dead man was getting heavier—he couldn't quit worrying about Shelley. He vowed he'd make Sal pay.

Before he'd reluctantly left the villa with the dead man slung over his shoulder, Duncan had made sure Shelley had locked and bolted the doors, even though she'd wanted to go with him to run interference if he needed her to. She belonged inside, doors bolted, safe from harm. She told Duncan she'd clean up the mess upstairs before he returned, even though he said he'd take care of it, insisting he didn't want her to be responsible for it. He meant what he said.

Over the years, he'd had his fair share of battles, seen plenty of dead men, and done his part in cleaning up after the fact. He wasn't immune to it, but he figured he was much more experienced at it than Shelley. He didn't want her upset any further than she was already. Despite her saying she was all right with everything that had happened, she hadn't been.

He admired her for offering to take care of the mess and for wanting to stick with him to protect him. No matter what, though, he didn't want her forced into a situation where she felt the need to do the protecting.

Damn that bastard Sal. If getting the clan's money back wasn't so vitally important, Duncan would kill Sal as soon as he saw the crook again.

When he finally reached Sal's estate, Duncan realized that when he'd dropped the other body off at Sal's pool last night, he should have noticed there were no guard dogs barking and no guards roaming the grounds chatting, smoking, and watching. He guessed that was because he had been so bent on dumping the other body without anyone seeing and then getting away from the house.

Surely, Kenneth was staying around the place now that Sal had no one else to guard it. Not that Duncan believed the guy would offer much protection. Duncan tossed the body over the low wall and then catapulted over it. After lifting and carrying the dead man to the pool, he dumped the body in with a splash. Then he propelled himself back over the wall and stalked back across the sand toward the villa. He was already out of sight of Sal's place when he heard the patio door squeak open.

Sal cursed out loud. "Damn you, Duncan!" Then he turned and shouted, "Kenneth! That son of a bitch did it again! Get the boat ready."

Duncan smiled smugly, feeling some satisfaction from the whole vile matter. That would teach Sal to leave a dead body in Shelley's villa.

He wanted to run as a wolf because he could reach the house much faster. But he hadn't brought a lot of clothes with him on this trip. He couldn't afford to ditch what he was wearing, especially since he might need to wear the swim trunks again. Having worn just his swim-suit to avoid getting blood on his clothes, he jogged into the ocean, washing off whatever blood he might have gotten on his skin, and then left the water to continue jogging down the beach.

The wind was blowing now, whipping around him with a slight undercurrent of cool mixing with the smell of rain. The clouds that had been building earlier now covered every inch of sky, blocking out the moon, the stars, and every speck of light in the universe. By the time the villa was in sight—with lights on only in the downstairs part of the house and the guest room upstairs dark—a light rain had begun to fall, trickling over his heated skin.

Before he reached the back patio of the villa, the rain was flowing in a mighty torrent. He was soaking wet.

When he was at the back door, he knocked a couple of times. The seconds passed like a lifetime as he worried that something untoward had happened to Shelley. Kenneth and Sal were at Sal's estate so she couldn't be in any danger from them. Unless Carlotta had managed to get another goon...

Duncan didn't have any lock picks with him, but then he remembered Shelley had dead-bolted the door. Maybe she didn't hear him because of the torrential downpour sliding off the roof onto the granite patio.

The bolt slid open, and she turned the knob and stood before him, one towel wrapped around her body and another around her hair in a turban.

She gave him a worried smile and looked damned sexy. He wanted nothing more than to sweep her up in his arms and take her back to bed. He had to shower first, though, and didn't plan to touch her until he was truly clean.

Even so, Shelley kissed his lips lightly. She had to know by the way he stood so rigidly just inside the doorway, dripping water on the tile floor, that he couldn't give in to the lust he always felt when he was around her. He didn't want to take this any further just yet. She pulled the towel off her body and wrapped it around him, teasing him with the lush sight and fragrant scent of her, when she could just as well have removed the towel from her hair and not given him such an eyeful.

Siren.

He cast her a wicked smile as he wrapped the towel around his waist. That garnered a mischievous smile from her, and then she relocked and bolted the door. "Wait for me in bed. I'll join you momentarily," he said, his voice already husky with need.

She sighed and slipped her arm around him as they headed for the bedroom. "I never went to the reserve today. So I need to do some more research tomorrow."

Plants. He couldn't believe that she was still thinking about plants after what had happened. On the other hand, maybe they gave her a sense of peace and tranquility, no matter what else was going on. He had to admit that when he ran through the Caledonian Forest back home, he loved being immersed in the wild and nature.

"If you won't return with my brother to Scotland, we'll all three go to the reserve." That was the only way she was going back there, he decided, given the way things were going. He was certain they'd only get worse.

Shelley was half asleep when Duncan finally joined her in bed. He'd not only showered and smelled of her tangerine body wash, but he'd called his brother to apprize him of the latest news. She'd heard him talking in the kitchen, unable to make out what he was saying, and nearly drifted off to sleep. At first, his duty to his brother had bothered her, when she felt he really only needed to talk to her since she was here with him and they would face whatever they had to alone.

But when he returned, she realized how much more relaxed he was. Discussing their situation with his brother, who *was* the pack leader, helped to ease the tension Duncan was feeling. For that, she was grateful. He tugged the covers aside and slid in beside her, pulling the covers back over them as if they were just going to sleep.

There was something sexy about the way he did that, skimming his hand underneath the covers and softly over her belly without seeing what he intended to do next. As if he were sliding his fingers up a nightgown—if she'd worn one—caressing and maneuvering until his fingers touched the underside of a breast and cupped it. She gazed into his beautiful dark eyes and saw the love in them but the worry, too. She smiled wearily up at him, tilted her chin up, and said, "Kiss me, Highlander."

He actually grinned at her, as if that was the last thing he'd expected her to say and it both amused and pleased him. She knew the latter was true as his hand moved over her breast, molding to it as his lips pressed against hers in a way that said he wanted to block out the whole world and just experience this.

Her hands swept over his back as he leaned closer, his mouth partly open, his tongue slipping over her dry lips and moistening them for another assault. She greedily surrendered, shifting her hands lower until she was cupping his buttocks and squeezing the firm muscles.

His breathing instantly grew ragged, his eyes smokier, his tongue and mouth more insistent. She felt him already on the edge, his cock rigid with arousal as he pressed against her thigh. He was a considerate lover. She knew he wanted them to meld together as one and wouldn't think of putting his own needs before hers.

He continued to touch her where it counted, her skin sensitive to his caresses, preparing her for his ultimate conquest. His fingers teased her nipple as she ran her fingers lightly over his backside, her touch making him move his fingers lower over the curls between her thighs, parting her feminine lips and stroking her into a fevered pitch.

She moaned against his mouth, his tongue flicking at hers. His fingers stroked her clit faster as her fingers dug into his buttocks. She rocked with the motion, arched against his fingers, trying to quicken the feeling aroused in her.

The sensation felt like the strong rising tide, drawing on strength, building, and promising to carry her away on a sea of ecstasy. The rain pounded on the tile roof, but inside they were warm and dry, except for their exertion and how slick and wet he was making her in preparing her for his penetration. She cried out as she came, her words drowned out by the wind and rain and thunder booming overhead.

As if he couldn't hold on a second longer or wanted to feel her arousal gripping him with spasms of delight, he centered himself between her legs and pressed forward with a deep thrust that sent her thoughts reeling.

Duncan needed to bury himself in Shelley's sweet flesh, making her moan with sensuous surrender as he drove in deeply, feeling her inner muscles clamping around his cock in a steady rhythm as if gripping him in welcome. Just hearing her call out his name while the storm raged around them, he felt his own storm-filled thoughts subsiding, given over to her sweet, appealing nature, to the way she surrounded him in silky heat.

Nothing else mattered when he was with her like this, loving her as she loved him back. Spirited and tenacious, she was his match, his mate, and he cherished her.

He kissed her soft, pliable lips as she arched against him and deepened his thrusts. His tongue stroked hers as her hands swept up his back in a tantalizing caress. "Shelley," he murmured against her mouth, feeling her tense as she clenched her muscles around his penis, tightening like a slick satin glove.

He pulled halfway out, wanting to prolong the heightened sensations, and then plunged in again, barely able to maintain control. She drew her fingernails down his buttocks like a sexy cat resting on her back, purring and lightly scratching in rapture, inciting him to finish this quickly.

She was all wolf—growly when she didn't get her way, and loyal and protective like a *lupus garou*. She was all his.

He felt the tumultuous end coming and let go. He filled her with his hot seed, bathed her deep inside, and kissed her again, saying sweet nothings to her in Gaelic that made her smile.

—⁂—

Falling asleep in Duncan's arms as the storm raged outside was almost as wonderful as waking up in his arms in the wash of early afternoon sunlight. She would have felt guilty for sleeping so long, if she *had* been sleeping so long. Their repeated bouts of lovemaking wouldn't count as sleeping—just being in bed.

His hand was caressing Shelley's breast, his mouth nuzzling her ear, when a violent pounding on the front door nearly gave her a heart attack.

"Sal," Duncan growled, guessing it was the bastard. "Maybe something else has happened—he found Kenneth dead or something—and he wants to offer me more for my services as a bodyguard."

"Don't agree to do it, Duncan." Shelley began to pull the cover aside.

Duncan shook his head as he slipped his Bermuda shorts on. "Stay right where you are. We'll finish what we had begun after I get rid of him."

Bare chested, wearing only his shorts, he shut the bedroom door and stalked down the hall.

The banging started all over again. For an instant, Shelley thought it couldn't be Sal. Wouldn't he just have called? Also, she didn't see him as the rough, violent type.

Except that he had killed the other man as a wolf.

Her heartbeat quickening, she was torn. Get dressed and monitor what was going on? Give Duncan aid if he needed it?

Or stay where she was and wait for Duncan to return to bed? She didn't trust the situation. What if Carlotta had sent more hit men?

Shelley wasn't one to wait things out if she had any other option. She yanked the covers aside.

A familiar booming voice at the front door made the hair on her skin stand at attention. "Where the hell is my niece, Shelley?"

Uncle Ethan.

Chapter 18

DUNCAN STARED AT THE BIG, SCOWLING SCOT, WHO was standing like a riled-up grizzly in the villa's doorway. The man's gruff, angry voice was still tinged with a brogue, although living in America had taken away some of it. This had to be Shelley's Uncle Ethan, his hair as auburn as hers and eyes just as green, only smaller and narrowed and angry. He was wearing buff-toned cowboy boots, a black Stetson, blue jeans, and a blue-checked Western shirt, like he was getting ready for the rodeo or to rope some cows on the ranch. Only he looked more like an enraged bull, come to think of it, and somebody needed to rein him in. That's when Duncan remembered Shelley was from Texas.

Then he noted the engraved silver tips on the toes of Campbell's boots and the belt with fancy silver trimmings. He thought of Shelley and the silver belt and sandals she'd worn at the airport.

"Where is she?" Ethan Campbell bit out.

Duncan moved aside to let the man enter, not backing down but not wanting to be antagonistic, either. The man was Shelley's uncle, after all. Duncan didn't want to create ill will with her close family.

"I'll tell her you're here. If you'd like to take a seat in the living room, I'll be right back," Duncan said with conviction.

"No, *I'll* get her."

Duncan knew that wasn't the best idea. Campbell would smell his and Shelley's sex fests in the bedroom. Before he could explain that he and Shelley were mated, he was sure her uncle would attempt to kill him.

"We're mated," he quickly said before Campbell could storm farther down the hall than the several steps he'd already managed.

Campbell swung around. "It will be the shortest mating in wolf history." He stalked back toward Duncan. He knew this was going to be bad, no matter how it ended.

He didn't want to strike the older man, not when he was Shelley's uncle. Campbell took a swing with one large-fisted hand, and Duncan blocked the blow by throwing his arm up and knocking the man's arm aside. His quick action didn't deter her uncle. He rapidly swung his fist for another killer blow.

"Uncle!" Shelley screamed, rushing down the hall, a T-shirt and shorts covering her, but her hair was as tousled as if they'd made love half the night—which they had—and her feet were bare. "He's my mate! If you kill him, I'll never forgive you."

She really didn't believe her uncle could get the upper hand with Duncan, did she?

Her uncle glowered at her. "What have you done? Disgraced our name after all that went on in the old country? Aye, 'tis a shameful day when one of their kind takes one of ours like the users they've always been."

Duncan knew that her uncle's words cut deep by the way Shelley's face crumpled. Her family must have filled her with horror stories all her life about the old days. No wonder she initially had not liked what he and his family had represented.

"Sir," Duncan said, trying to take a more appeasing stance and to draw her uncle's ire away from Shelley.

The man turned and growled at Duncan. "You should be ashamed."

"For loving your niece?" Irritated that her uncle would make the statement, Duncan walked past her uncle and put his arm around Shelley's shoulders in a comforting embrace.

Ignoring Duncan's comment, her uncle said, "You're not taking the lass back to Scotland with you."

"Oh, aye, I am," Duncan countered, his back bristling with barely controlled anger. "She can visit the States anytime she likes, but she's living with me at Argent Castle." He was even thinking that when the clan got their money back, he might suggest to Ian that they build an indoor swimming pool. He was fairly certain Ian would say no, but swimming with Shelley was something he didn't want to give up.

"A castle, is it?" Campbell glanced at Shelley, a bit of calculation gleaming in his eyes.

She cast Duncan an anxious look, then quickly said to her uncle, "I'm sure that Duncan's brother, Ian, who is laird, would say you and your brothers and my mother are free to visit anytime."

"Aye," Duncan agreed. He was certain that as hotheaded as her uncle was, things were sure to heat up between his family and hers. Why did taking the lass as his mate mean taking in her whole family?

At least they lived across the ocean.

"Your brother is the laird? Not you?"

As if Campbell truly hadn't known, Duncan thought. Campbell frowned at Duncan, as if he were thinking of allowing the mating, which was a moot point because once it had been done, it was for a lifetime. Campbell finally said, "I'll let you keep her."

The hell if Campbell had any say in it! His tone wasn't conciliatory, either. An unspoken condition hung between them.

Duncan knew he wouldn't like the condition, but he also didn't like Campbell believing he had any say in whether Shelley stayed with Duncan. Shelley's back stiffened with her uncle's declaration.

"Aye." As if Duncan would allow anyone to take her away from him.

Campbell folded his arms across his broad chest and gave the most evil smile. "We'll move in with you."

Shelley's jaw dropped.

Duncan was just as stunned, unsure of what to say and knowing he couldn't decide such a thing without Ian's approval. Nor did he want to upset Shelley. He wasn't sure what she wanted—her family far away or close at hand.

"She'll be having children. My grandnieces and grandnephews. They will learn everything there is to know about their family roots from their uncles and their grandmother." Campbell looked unmovable from his stance.

So that was what this was all about? To continue passing on the discontentment he and his family felt about how they'd been mistreated in the old days—the years of holding a grudge about something that should have been let go eons ago?

"Surely, you haven't discussed this with your brothers or with my mother," Shelley said, sounding stricken.

"They do what I say."

"Laird Ian MacNeill would have to have a say in this. It's his castle, his clan, his pack after all," she quickly said, as if she was afraid Duncan would jump into the fray and cause the situation to get even more heated.

But Duncan knew when to let the she-wolf have her say. Right now, that was definitely something she had to do. If she grew quiet, unsure what to say, Duncan would again take on Campbell.

Campbell smiled slyly again. "Aye. We are a generous sort. If Duncan MacNeill wants you badly enough, he'll agree to our terms. Either we all move back to Scotland, or your mate can have a home with us."

"I have my own home," she said, her voice angry now.

"Aye, which is fine. You don't live far from us, which is my point."

Duncan wanted to know if Shelley was all that close to her uncles. But he could see that her uncle was all business, no matter what the outcome. He was proud of her for being fiercely independent. She wasn't letting her uncle get away with bullying her into what he wanted, either.

"I'm going to Scotland with Duncan," she said firmly. "We could plan to return to Texas…"

Her uncle shook his head, then took a seat on the couch and motioned to Duncan as if Campbell was the king and Duncan served him. "Call your laird brother, lad. Call him and tell him he meets my conditions or *else*."

Shelley opened her mouth to protest. Duncan gave her another squeeze and kissed her cheek. She looked up at him with regret swimming in her eyes. He gave her half a smile. "I'll call Ian, lass." He was doing it for Shelley, not her pretentious uncle.

When he headed for the door, Shelley caught his arm, and with her back to her uncle so he couldn't see what she was saying, she mouthed the words to Duncan, "You don't have to do this."

Appreciating that she said so, but knowing he did indeed have to do this if he was going to make any inroads with her family, Duncan smiled, wrapped his arms around her, and kissed her mouth with all the wolfish passion he possessed. He was stating that they were mated, she was his, and there wasn't a damn thing her uncle could do about it.

When he released her, she clung to him, a little unsteady on her feet. He smiled, loving how he could make her melt against him just from his kisses.

He tried to put on an everything-is-under-control expression, but she looked too anxious for him to believe he was successful. Fighting the bad guys was easy. Trying to smooth over the situation with her uncle in a way that was satisfactory to all parties concerned was quite another thing.

Hell, didn't they have enough trouble already? Duncan couldn't believe he had to call Ian about this mess with Shelley's uncle. But he didn't want to tell her uncle the difficulties they were having with Sal Silverman or he feared Campbell would feel it was his duty to escort Shelley home to Texas at once.

Duncan walked outside while Shelley tried to talk reason to her uncle while fixing him a cup of coffee.

Ian answered on the first ring. He had been closely monitoring the phone, worried about what all was going on in the islands. Duncan told Ian about the second dead man and about Sal wanting Duncan to protect him.

"I said no to his offer," Duncan said.

"Maybe you should agree to be his bodyguard," Ian said seriously.

"What the hell for?"

"If Carlotta has him killed, then we've lost a chance to get the money through him."

"Then we go after her." It didn't matter to Duncan who had their money.

Ian sighed. "Yeah, we'd have to."

"I can't agree to protect him, get the money, then kill him."

"All right. Do what you have to do."

"There's something else." Duncan hated to bring up Shelley's family's request more than he hated the discussion about protecting that bastard Sal. "It has to do with Shelley's three uncles and her mother. The one in charge of her pack, her Uncle Ethan Campbell, wants to move the family in with us. Or else he doesn't want her to leave the States and I'm to move in with her near where her family resides. The family has close ties. They want to get to know our children, their grandnieces and grandnephews, when they're born." Duncan knew his brother wouldn't like being dictated to, not by anyone.

"How do you feel about this?" Ian asked.

Duncan stared out at the ocean, not even truly seeing it. His brother had never asked him how he felt about anything—or anyone else that Duncan could remember, for that matter. Maybe being mated to Julia Wildthorn, romance author, had changed Ian.

"I will kill every one of them to have the right to keep my mate," Duncan vowed fiercely.

"Aye. How would you feel about living in the States

and not here, if it means staying with her to keep peace with her family?"

Duncan ground his teeth. Taking Shelley for his mate shouldn't mean he'd have to forsake his own family, his clan, his pack. "With the deepest regret, Ian," he said, nearly choking on the words, "aye. I would stay with Shelley in Texas."

Ian didn't say anything for what seemed the longest time, then spoke up again. "How does Shelley feel about it?"

"Shook up, no doubt, Ian. This has all come as a shock to her as well."

"Let me talk to her."

"Shelley?"

Ian chuckled darkly. "Aye. I promise I will not upset her."

Duncan frowned and opened the door to see Shelley showing pictures of all the varieties of plants at the reserve on her camera to her uncle, excited as if nothing had come between any of them. She was like a young girl showing off a treasure to a parent. For an instant, he saw that she was indeed close to her uncle, and he was with her. Campbell wasn't looking at the pictures as if it was a duty but smiling like he truly enjoyed seeing her work.

Duncan cleared his throat, not wanting to interrupt them since her uncle seemed pleased to observe her findings. He didn't want to set the older man off again. "Shelley, my brother wishes to speak with you."

"I will speak to his lairdship as well," Ethan said with a disgruntled tone, casting Duncan a dangerous look.

Duncan handed the phone to Shelley and gave her a

heartfelt embrace, then whispered into her ear, "All will be well."

She nodded, but from the guarded look she gave him, he didn't think she believed him. He wasn't sure he did, either. Families could be good for a mating, but they could also be destructive. This one seemed to be off on the wrong path already.

He shut the door to let Shelley have some privacy with his brother and said to her uncle as he motioned to the camera he was now holding, "She's dedicated to her work."

But Ethan only gave him another glower and said, "What will she be doing in Scotland, pray tell, *if* you take her back there?"

———∽∽∽———

Shelley swallowed hard as she took Duncan's phone and took a deep breath, hating that her mouth had become a dried-up desert before she spoke to Ian.

"Hello?" She tried to sound like someone who was worthy of being mated to a laird's brother, but all of a sudden, with her family's interference in her life, she felt like a two-year-old with no say in anything.

Not that she would allow her uncle or her family to have any real say over what she did. On the other hand, she truly had believed they'd be as happy for her as she was for herself. Never had she expected something like this to happen.

"Hello, Shelley? First..." Ian said to her over the phone. He put her at ease at once with the way he sounded so much like Duncan when he was in a heroic, endearing mood. "I want to welcome you into our family. I understand your uncle's concern about parting with you, and I would feel the same way if one of my own was leaving to live someplace else so far away."

The tension remained in her spine. She appreciated that he could feel the same way as her uncle did and understood some of what was feeding her uncle's animosity, but Ian wasn't resolving the issue, either.

"I would welcome your family to visit you here at any time," Ian continued.

Which was just the problem. She'd expected Ian to be generous in welcoming her family on visits, but the matter went beyond visits. She cleared her throat. "He doesn't want to just visit."

"My understanding completely."

Duncan had told him, and Ian wasn't perturbed?

"What I want to know is how this will affect you. Do you want to stay with us here? Live in the States? Visit back and forth?"

Now she knew why Ian was the laird of the clan, the leader of their pack. He definitely had leadership skills that weren't dictatorial.

Ian said, "Duncan has already stated that he will do anything that makes you happy."

Shelley glanced back at the house, an overwhelming feeling of love and pride in Duncan filling her. She knew he couldn't have said he'd do so without feeling regret that he'd have to leave his own family and pack behind. "He did?"

"Aye. You must know that giving up his family wouldn't be easy."

"Oh, no, I never wanted that." She truly didn't. Even though she had a loose-knit pack of sorts, Wendy had a close-knit family and pack, so Shelley knew something about the dynamics in her friend's family and how they wouldn't want to lose her like that, either.

"But he's willing to do so if that's what you want."

"But I don't," she insisted, feeling horrible about her uncle's stand.

"All right then, if your family comes to live with us, I have rules that they must abide by. Everyone works, just like in the old days. They might not have the same jobs as eons ago, but we all support the clan, the pack. For that, they have our protection and our loyalty," Ian said sternly.

"Which is what they're disgruntled about—the past, about getting kicked off the land after being loyal to their laird."

"Aye. But it's different now. I'll do anything I can to make this work. Your family will have to understand that I make the decisions ultimately as to the pack's concerns, though."

"I understand." She knew that it would be hard for her Uncle Ethan to give up ruling their own small pack, yet he would have to if her family wished to join Ian's.

"Then if this is agreeable to you, let me talk with your uncle."

She didn't want her uncle to screw things up with her and her new family and Duncan. If he did, she would be true to her word and never speak to him or the others again. Even if that would be difficult to do as well. Still, she had to live her own life. They might not understand how she felt, not any of her uncles at least, since none had been mated.

"Thank you."

"My pleasure, lass. It's about time someone gave Duncan something to think about other than bashing heads."

She laughed, the tension instantly dissolving. "Thanks," she said, feeling much more lighthearted about meeting Duncan's older brother in person when she had the chance. "I'll let you speak with my Uncle Ethan now."

When Shelley entered the villa, she waved the phone and said, "The laird wants to speak with you, Uncle Ethan." She hoped to God everything would be all right.

He grunted, shoved the camera in Duncan's hands, rose from the couch, and took the phone, then stalked outside and shut the door.

Shelley pulled Duncan into her arms, breast to chest, and began kissing him. He jumped right in, not one to let a chance get away.

He smiled against her lips. "Ian must have said something that made you happy."

"Oh, yes, Duncan. He told me what a wonderful, caring, loving individual you are."

Duncan looked down at her frowning. "Ian did?"

Then she laughed. "Oh, yes, and I already know I'm going to love him and the rest of your family." If only she could get her own family to toe the line.

After speaking with Ethan Campbell, Ian called his little American werewolf mate into his office and pulled her into his lap. He nuzzled her soft neck and said, "Julia, you don't happen to have any relatives named Ethan and Shelley Campbell, do you?"

"Not that I know of," Julia said. "We have a connection to the Duke, but there are so many branches of Campbells that I wouldn't know if we had any other ties. Why?"

"Duncan has mated with a Shelley Campbell."

Julia smiled. "Here he was so grouchy about going to an island paradise. Sounds like it was just the place he needed to be." Then she frowned. "You seem worried, Ian."

"Her uncles and mother plan to live here."

"Oh."

"Aye. They were crofters forced to move away in the old days and still resent it."

Julia's eyes grew big. "Oh."

Ian ran his hands over her belly. "Aye. Her Uncle Ethan is quite outspoken about it."

"What happens when your mother and aunt learn of it?"

Ian sighed. "I want to see Duncan happy."

She gave Ian one of her self-assured smiles. "He will be. Your mother and aunt can take care of the uncles. How many are there? Most importantly, do they have mates?" She arched a brow, and her eyes sparkled with an intriguing thought.

"Nay, do not even think of any of them making a match. We will be lucky if we have any peace around here at all."

⁓

Duncan couldn't decide what to do about Ethan Campbell, who was staring off at the ocean, no longer speaking to Ian, the phone in his hand at his side. Duncan didn't think that if Ian had said Shelley's uncles and mother could move in with them at Argent Castle, Ethan would just hop on a plane and return home to Texas. Which meant Uncle Ethan most likely would cause trouble once he learned Shelley was in danger and would want to take her right home.

Shelley seemed to be thinking the same thing, and she said, "We have to tell Uncle Ethan what's going on."

"He'll take you back to Texas."

"No, he won't. Not any more than you're sending me to Scotland with your brother. But I doubt he'll go home right away. Cearnach will arrive, and how will we explain all this? Uncle Ethan needs to know. He is family after all."

Duncan didn't want to explain any of this to Campbell. Particularly how they'd lost their money to a master thief. He could just imagine Campbell being smugly amused that after all these years of owning the land, Duncan's people could lose it because of a swindler of vast proportions.

"We have to tell him," Shelley said.

"Tell me what, Niece?" Ethan asked, walking in through the back door, then shutting it. "That you need protection?"

Shelley closed her gaping mouth. He knew. Ian must have told him.

"That a woman might have ordered a hit on you for attempting to steal her mate? That the MacNeill is close to financial ruin? *Tch*, now it is the Campbell who will save the MacNeill's arse."

At that, Ethan Campbell set the cell phone on the kitchen table, folded his arms, and gave Duncan a conceited smile.

Chapter 19

"So what is the plan?" Ethan asked as Shelley served up the rest of the baked chicken wings at the kitchen table. She was hoping her uncle wouldn't get into a fight with both Cearnach and Duncan once Cearnach arrived because they needed to be a unified force against Silverman.

Duncan couldn't help being amused at the way the man had taken it upon himself to join the battle against Sal Silverman, as if the money was Ethan's own. Already, he was offering his loyalty to the pack and clan.

That's when he knew Shelley's uncle was a good man, a lot rough around the edges but willing to make some concessions. Most of all, he wasn't insisting that Shelley go home to Texas and out of harm's way. Not that he hadn't brought it up at once, but Shelley had, in no uncertain terms, told him no.

"After we finish eating, I'm leaving for the airport to pick up my brother. We can all go, or you and Shelley can stay here and wait for us," Duncan said, picking up another wing and taking a bite.

Shelley stirred her soy beans, miniature corn, water chestnuts, and snow peas, thinking over what would be best. Neither Duncan nor Ian had been able to tell Cearnach that her uncle was here. It might be best for Duncan to have a word in private with his brother. She wasn't even sure he knew Duncan and she were mated yet.

Ethan motioned with his hand as if waving away what was happening next. "I don't mean with your brother. What are we doing about Silverman?" He shook his head. "Who would have thought the most newsworthy financial crook would be a wolf?"

Shelley was glad to see that her uncle seemed more interested in taking down Silverman than in saying anything further about her mating Duncan. "If he knows any wolves, they might not realize he has a residence here."

"Aye," Duncan said. "I imagine that's the truth of the matter. Guthrie, another of my brothers, learned of it. The house is not in Silverman's name but under some alias he must be using."

"Maybe we should all offer to be Silverman's body-guards," Ethan said. "While I'm guarding your back, you can get the money out of the bastard."

Shelley didn't like the idea that they would have to be dishonest in what they had to do, pretending to protect Silverman when they knew they had to eliminate him.

"Nay," Duncan said. "Silverman has no one else to watch his back, save the human Kenneth. I wouldn't take on the job of providing a protection service for him. The only reason I haven't taken him to task yet is that he had a force protecting him. When Carlotta sent her goons after Shelley, she became my priority. Now that my brother is coming, you are here, and Silverman's hired thugs are all gone, it should be an easy matter. After I pick up Cearnach at the airport, we'll all see Silverman and talk to him about the money."

"Along with Shelley," Ethan said. "She can't stay here alone."

"Aye." Duncan reached over, took her hand, and squeezed. "We'll go together, all as family."

Shelley's heart nearly burst with pride to hear Duncan include her Uncle Ethan in the declaration. She knew he did it in part to please her. Her uncle was making inroads, too, just by offering to work on Silverman himself to ensure the money was returned. It might have something to do with him now having a castle to live in, but if they didn't get the money back, then what? Maybe the MacNeills would all have to live with her uncles in the States. Talk about turning around the scenario of the crofter pushed off the land in Scotland. Then she was certain Uncle Ethan would rule the pack. Or at least try to.

Duncan glanced at the clock. "Nearly 9 p.m. Time to get my brother. Will you come with me or stay?"

"We can wait for you, if you think it will work well that way. Then you can bring your brother here first, and we can feed him a bite to eat if he didn't get enough of a meal on the plane. We can talk over the plans to see Silverman, then call on him," Shelley said.

Clasping her hand still, Duncan looked as though he didn't want her to stay alone at the villa with her uncle, that he might say things to her that would upset her. She suspected Duncan also was worried about her safety. Even so, she thought that his having time to speak alone with his brother was important.

Despite looking like it was killing him not to butt in and make a decision for them, Ethan held his tongue.

Shelley turned to him and asked, "Uncle Ethan, what do you think?"

His eyes sparkled with admiration because she'd

included him in the decision-making. "I think it will kill your young man if you stay here alone with me." Ethan smirked. "He doesn't trust me to protect you. But I fought just as well in the old days, like his kind did when the time came."

He hadn't fought like that in years, she suspected. Not like Duncan did in keeping up his swordsmanship skills to teach those in his clan. Duncan was a skilled warrior. Seeing how much it pleased her uncle, she was glad that she hadn't left him out of the decision-making.

"All right. We go together," she said.

They left the villa and climbed into the car with Duncan driving, Shelley seated beside him, and Ethan riding in the backseat. They'd barely pulled onto the road when a truck roared up behind them and, without warning, rammed them off the asphalt, barreling them past the villa and shoving them across the sand toward the ocean as if the truck was a tank in a battle zone and they were the enemy.

Anger heated Duncan's blood instantly.

"You don't happen to have a gun to blast them with, do you?" Uncle Ethan growled, glowering out the back window.

The vehicle was no match for the truck, and although Duncan tried, applying the brakes was of no use.

"I don't know what they hope to do," Shelley said. "They can't shove us very far into the surf before the car floats off, and we'll just get out of the vehicle."

He knew what the bastards planned to do. Catch them in a more vulnerable position—unable to fight back as easily. "Can you see if anyone in the truck is wearing their wolf coats?" Duncan asked, his voice dark with fury.

"Can't see any of them, just the driver, and he's a steely-eyed bastard, itching for a showdown," Ethan said. "Can you swerve out of their path and let them deal with the breakers?"

"Nay. I can't drive in this sand at all. They're propelling us straight through it."

"Should we jump from the car first, Duncan?" Shelley asked. "Before we get into the surf?"

"Nay. We go together. If we leave the vehicle, they'll release a truck full of wolves, and we'll be at a decided disadvantage." He meant Shelley, not himself or Ethan.

"But it will be harder to get out of the car when it's in the water," she said, jerking off her clothes.

"Shelley." His tone indicated that he didn't agree and was full of dire warning.

"I'm shifting, and I'm getting out. Now." Shelley gave him a small smile, kissed his cheek, and then shifted.

"I second that, lad," Ethan said, still watching out the back window. He began stripping out of his clothes. "We're better off standing our ground as wolves since we have nothing but our teeth to protect us."

"Hell. I meant for Shelley to stay in the vehicle while you and I tackled the wolves, damn it."

"If you think Shelley will stay in the car and watch us fight, you sure don't know her very well." Ethan grinned. "Maybe you should have learned a little more about her before you took her for your mate."

Duncan glanced at Shelley, who was wagging her tail, looking eager to please and not in the least bit like a vicious wolf that could tear into a bunch of big males. He let out his breath and released the steering wheel, since he wasn't doing much of anything anyway, and then reached over his mate to get the door and opened it for her. And prayed he wasn't making the biggest mistake of his life.

She jumped out of the moving car, though with his foot pressing hard on the brakes, they were going slow enough for her to lunge safely onto the sandy beach.

Ethan jumped over the backseat into the front and bounded out of the car to join Shelley. Duncan hoped to God the guy in the truck behind them was a wolf, because otherwise... well, he guessed there was no otherwise. The guy was a dead man one way or another. Without a weapon and in human form, he wouldn't have a lot of options. But for now, Duncan had to get out of the driver's seat where he couldn't easily yank off his clothes and shift. All he worried about, though, were Shelley and her uncle. He sure as hell wished Cearnach was here already.

The car still barreled toward the ocean, propelled by the bulldog of a truck behind it. Duncan was trying his damnedest to haul himself over the console in the compact car. For a man, it was hard to clear the steering wheel and slip over the blockade with any ease. Growling in frustration, he finally managed it, ripped off his clothes, and shifted. Cursing himself, Duncan jumped out of the vehicle as a wolf before the tires hit the first wave. He had to get word to Cearnach.

As soon as his paws hit the ankle-deep water, he saw the wolves. They must have gotten out of the truck while Duncan was busy removing his clothes and shifting. Three damn big males. When Duncan was out of the car, the driver of the truck stopped and opened his door. Duncan knew they'd have another wolf to face in short order. He raced up the beach and tore into the first of the wolves immediately.

Ethan had only been waiting for Duncan to join him, while the offending wolves seemed to be waiting for the driver of the truck, their alpha male. Ethan attacked the closest wolf to him. That meant Shelley had her own male wolf to tackle. Duncan felt cold chills race down his spine at the thought, especially since the driver would soon be joining his comrades in the fight.

The wolf he attacked was almost a golden color, an Arctic wolf who had somehow gotten himself mixed up with a gray pack. The wolf snarled at him, snapping his jaws and trying to get Duncan's throat.

He heard the wolf growling and the enamel of Ethan's and the enemy's teeth making contact. He didn't hear a peep out of Shelley. He couldn't look to see where she was—not when the other wolf raced around the truck to aid his companions, then stopped and looked in the direction of the ocean.

Glancing that way, Duncan saw the one wolf chasing after Shelley. She was headed straight for the water. Damn it. The wolf he'd been fighting had paused to look, too. Then the truck driver raced out with the other wolf after Shelley. Damn it to hell.

He swung his head around, catching the wolf he'd been fighting by the neck, but he only tore the skin, nothing vital enough to fell the hefty wolf. The Arctic wolf screeched with fury and attempted to bite Duncan, who dodged out of the path of his snapping canines. He wanted desperately to go after Shelley. Ethan hadn't made any headway with the gray wolf he was fighting, either.

Duncan couldn't spend any more time looking to see

what was happening to Shelley. His fight had to be with the wolf trying to take him down. He lunged again, only to clash with the white wolf's teeth, missing his throat once again.

Shelley hadn't been sure what to do, but she knew she couldn't outfight the male wolf. When she saw the truck driver shifting, she was certain he'd come after her. Easier to kill a female and be done with it. She also figured she was their primary target so they'd think they might as well finish her off.

She was fast like a greyhound, her family had always said. She was swifter than the whole lot of the bulkier males. So she ran, not feeling cowardly in the least. Not when she would have been at such a disadvantage if she'd had to fight them. This way, she could draw two of the wolves off Duncan and her uncle until they were ready to tackle them.

She knew any of them could run as wolves for hours, although she didn't have hours. Plus she was afraid that despite the dark, someone might see three wolves racing behind the lighted resort hotels on the beach, if they weren't careful. Not that people would think they were wolves. They'd figure they were a pack of wild dogs.

She'd started to run into the ocean, but she didn't believe paddling in the surf would help her. None of them would be able to fight well in the rolling waves, but they might be able to herd her back to shore and give her the killing blow. With their longer legs, they'd be on firm ground before she could manage. So she ran for the only refuge she could think of. At least she knew the Mastic Reserve fairly well. They probably had never been there.

With her greyhound speed, she flew across the sand and headed for the reserve, hoping she might save herself there. Then she had another thought: what if…

She glanced back at the wolves running after her, noticing that their heavier weight bogged down more in the sand. She had a much greater lead on them. If the forest didn't work, she'd head to Sal's place. As long as no one was there trying to kill him, maybe she could secure his protection. At least he was a male wolf and could aid her against the other two. He might even have guns in the house.

But what if Carlotta had sent men to his place also? What if he was already dead?

—⁓—

Cearnach and his brothers had one thing in common— they were all punctual. So when his flight arrived and there was no sign of Duncan but the smell of other male wolves permeated the airport terminal, Cearnach wasn't about to hang around. He knew his brother was in trouble.

He called Ian to let him know what was happening as he headed for a waiting taxi. As late as it was, taxis were no problem, and he had the driver take him to the villa. Over the phone, Ian told Cearnach, "Duncan's taken Shelley for his mate."

Cearnach smiled. "I don't believe it."

"Believe it. Her uncles and mother are coming to live with us. Her Uncle Ethan's there now, and he'll be helping Duncan with any fight headed their way."

"Aye, Ian. Good to know. Looks like I'm here. I'll call you back as soon as I know something."

When the taxi drove up into the drive, Cearnach saw no lights on in the place and no vehicle out front. As soon as he opened the taxi door, he heard wolves growling on the beach behind the villa. Adrenaline surging through his blood at racecourse speed, he hurried to pay the driver, slammed the door, and tossed his bag at the front porch. Then he ran full out around the back of the villa.

In wolf form, Duncan was fighting an Arctic wolf, while another male wolf fought a gray. Since the one was close to Duncan, he seemed to be on the same side. Was it Sal Silverman? No one else was here. Where was Shelley? He hoped she was in the house, safe from the fight. That's when he saw the car in the surf and the truck with the driver's side door open as it had been left, engine rumbling at the edge of the water.

Hell.

Thankful he'd arrived in time, Cearnach stripped out of his clothes and shifted. Then he ran straight for the wolf that Duncan was tackling. When Duncan saw him, a hint of relief shown in his eyes. He did the damnedest thing—turned his back on the wolf, which was a dangerous course of action, and ran north along the beach.

Duncan had to have gone after Shelley. Another wolf must be trying to run her down. Damn it. The white wolf didn't go after Duncan because he'd seen Cearnach as a much bigger threat and turned to face him. Cearnach was fresh, hadn't been fighting, and was ready for the kill.

As soon as he tackled the Arctic wolf, Cearnach

recognized that the wolf was tired. Too bad. He had to help Ethan Campbell next so he quickly put the Arctic wolf down. Easy enough to do since Duncan had already worn the white wolf out and his stamina was spent.

Cearnach tore into the other enemy wolf, and with two against one, the wolf quickly collapsed, sucking in his final breath. Cearnach didn't wait to see the wolves shift into their human form. He tore off after Duncan, hoping he found his brother before it was too late.

Ethan was loping close behind him, breathing hard and sounding a little out of shape. Cearnach would have expected that since he was older. He might not be used to fighting wolf to wolf. He had hoped Ethan would take care of the bodies while he helped Duncan. It wouldn't do for anyone to run into a couple of chewed-up, naked men on the beach. Ethan seemed intent on helping him to save Shelley, though. Cearnach couldn't blame him. Not since Shelley was the man's niece.

As soon as they took care of these wolves, Cearnach would deal with Sal. With no one watching his back any longer, the man would give up their money or else. Problem was, he would still have to die. So there wasn't much of an incentive for him to give up the money... *or else*.

Cearnach glanced back at the older wolf, who raised his head in greeting. He must have known that Cearnach was Duncan's brother, coming to lend some muscle to the cause.

Not hearing any sounds of growling, Cearnach had to follow his nose, which told him four wolves had gone this way. A female—had to be Shelley—and three males, one being Duncan. Damn it to hell. No wonder

Duncan had given up the wolf he'd been fighting to Cearnach so he could deal with the spent wolf. The she-wolf had two male killers on her tail.

That meant Duncan still had two male wolves to deal with, not just one. Cearnach had to reach him before that happened.

—◆—

Shelley was doing great, having arrived at the reserve well ahead of the other wolves attempting to chase her down. Even though poisonous plants could cause skin irritation, she figured her wolf coat would protect her. She darted off the path and deeper into the forest. Following her scent, the wolves could still track her. If she could shift and climb a tree, maybe she could lose them. But as soon as they lost the smell of her foot pads leaving a scent on the forest floor, they would return to the spot they'd last smelled her and realize she'd shifted and scrambled up a tree. Too bad she couldn't use the vines to swing through the forest and navigate it like Tarzan, minus the yelling.

Not figuring she could evade them in the forest after all, she headed toward Sal's beach resort. With any luck, he was by himself and Carlotta hadn't sent a hit team after him. If Kenneth was there, as soon as he saw her as a wolf with two more wolves on her tail ready to kill her...

He would be a dead man.

Chapter 20

WHEN SHELLEY SAW SAL'S ESTATE, SHE FELT CHILLS race up her spine. The house looked dark and dead. Had Carlotta already murdered Sal?

Or maybe he was sleeping, although it seemed a little early for that.

She didn't slow her pace, knowing the wolves behind her would soon catch up once they figured out where she was headed. She leapt over the fancy wrought-iron fence surrounding the swimming pool. Spying a doggy door in the bottom panel of the back door, she assumed then Sal must run as a wolf some nights. She dove through it.

That's when she heard the two angry male voices in another part of the house.

"You son of a bitch, Kenneth. All this time you've been working for my wife? Who the hell pays your salary?" Sal growled.

So Kenneth had been the traitor all along. Shelley figured that both were paying the man, only Carlotta was paying more.

A soft light was glowing in another part of the house—the light-blocking curtains on the front windows blocked out the light from within.

"No, Mr. Silverman. I didn't tell her about the woman you'd tried to pay the Scot to give up. I thought she already knew about Lola, and Mrs. Silverman didn't seem to care. Why would I think she'd care about this other woman, Shelley, then?"

"Even though you said you hadn't told her?"

Something crashed where the two men were speaking. Shelley jumped a little. She glanced back at the pool. No sign of the other wolves yet.

"You've been telling her about the women I've been seeing all along, haven't you? Spying for her?" Sal said, his voice so harsh that he sounded like he was ready to kill Kenneth.

"No, no, I haven't done anything of the kind. I've got lots of women on the string so I see nothing wrong with it."

Bastard.

Kenneth was backing up, his voice getting closer to Shelley, but he was facing in a different direction.

Sal had to be stalking him. "But it doesn't matter if you're spying for Carlotta. Telling her what I'm doing. I pay you. She pays you more. Is that it?"

"No, I'm just on *your* payroll."

"Her money is my money," Sal growled.

So now the truth was coming out. The money was all Sal's. Every stolen bit of it.

"No," Kenneth said, groveling.

"So you do it for your love of her? What? Don't tell me that you're doing it for free, knowing if I learned of it, I could terminate… your employment with me."

"Terminate you" was what his pause meant to Shelley. He would, too, she thought, although at first she'd believed Sal didn't have it in him. Stealing money was his forte. Killing was becoming a side venture.

Something banged on the back patio. The wolves

who had been following her. One ran into a pool chair and knocked it into the other wolf. He growled. Shelley raced into a formal dining room adjoining the living area where Sal stood stock still.

For a second, he just stared at her, then he must have realized she was Shelley. Probably had watched her with Duncan on the beach shifting after all. "What the hell?"

One wolf bashed through the dog door, followed by the other.

Shelley raced around behind Sal, expecting him to shift and help her fight the male wolves. Instead, he shook his head at the two wolves as they came into the room. "Where are the others?"

They shook their heads.

Her heart nearly stopped. *He* had sent the wolves to kill Duncan? Not Carlotta?

"Hell, didn't you kill Duncan? He can't have killed the others."

Stealing the show for a second, Kenneth choked out, "They're... they're wolves. Trained killer wolves."

"Yeah," Sal said, motioning to one of the wolves. "Kill Kenneth, the lying bastard."

Not believing that Sal—and not Carlotta—had been the one to sic the wolves on her and Duncan, Shelley tried to sort out her options to get herself out of this predicament. She couldn't move past the other wolf to get to the wolf door. She couldn't do anything about the front door—not while she was in wolf form. Once Kenneth was dead, the two wolves would deal with her.

Carlotta wasn't the one who had wanted her dead. What about Sal's guards who had already left his estate? Had Sal staged the whole thing to look like he was without protection? Had he wanted to get the humans away from here so he could deal with Duncan, a wolf and much more of a threat?

One of the wolves lunged at Kenneth. He threw up his arms to protect his throat from the wickedly bared canines, screeching in abject horror.

Seconds later, Kenneth was sprawled on the tile floor, his throat ripped out, dead.

Shelley was panting from all the running and her heart tripping over itself, her body heated, but chills still ran up her spine.

Sal folded his arms and looked crossly at Shelley. "So, Duncan MacNeill believes I've stolen his clan's money, eh? That's why he asked for that much money for you. It wasn't for you at all."

So he knew. How long before he'd finally figured out that Duncan and his people were after their investments? That had to have been why Sal had ordered his men to kill Duncan. It had nothing to do with her.

Shelley inched away from Sal. If she could get to the front door, maybe she could shift in time, run outside, and shift again. Even though she was tired, she'd had enough of a rest that she felt she could run back to see Duncan and still outdistance the other wolves. The adrenaline was still pumping rapidly through her blood.

Hopefully Duncan and her uncle were all right. The three of them could take these two wolves on. Sal also, if the bastard decided to shift.

"You could have been mine. But you were in on this, trying to trap me, weren't you?" Sal's brows rose. "Now you came here for my protection, didn't you? A little too late." He shrugged.

Not having much of a choice, she knew her next move might not work, but she had to give it a try. She bolted for the front door and found to her profoundest relief that it had a wolf door. She rammed it with her nose and dashed outside.

"Get her!" Sal yelled.

As soon as she raced around the front of the house, she saw three wolves headed straight for her, while the two Sal had commanded to go after her were catching up to her from behind.

Duncan was in the lead with another wolf racing after him. She didn't recognize the second wolf as one they'd been fighting. Had he been a latecomer? Her uncle was off in the distance, running to catch up to them. So it would be Duncan and her against the two wolves behind her and the one following him.

She just hoped Sal would stay out of it.

But the wolves behind her began to slow down. Maybe not so confident when they saw Duncan. *She* sure didn't intimidate anyone.

What truly amazed her as she ran to join Duncan was that the wolf behind him didn't seem intent on fighting him.

Then she didn't hear the wolves behind her. Not running toward her anyway. They were suddenly moving away from her, back toward the safety of the house.

Duncan reached her, brushed his body along hers in greeting, and kept running after the two wolves. The other wolf that had been following him dipped his head slightly at her, almost smiling, and she wondered...

It couldn't be Duncan's brother, Cearnach, could it? How did he get to her rented villa? They'd missed him at the airport! A taxi. He must have realized they were in trouble.

Her uncle finally reached her and nuzzled her face, catching his breath. As much as she wanted him to rest, she knew they needed to kill as a pack. Together, she and he followed Duncan and his brother into the house, where Duncan began fighting one of the wolves who had chased her, and Cearnach was battling the last of the wolves. Another wolf was waiting for Duncan and Cearnach to wear down before he got into the fracas. That coward Sal.

Damn Sal that he cared more for his blasted money than for werewolf lives or human life, she thought, as she glanced at Kenneth's dead body.

Duncan growled and bit at the big alpha male that had driven the truck. Cearnach was seeing to the other. Her Uncle Ethan had Sal pinned to the floor, not killing him, knowing they needed to get the money out of him.

Cearnach and the other wolf crashed into a table, a porcelain lamp falling and smashing to the floor. Then the wolf yelped and Cearnach stood over the dead man, panting, then shifted his attention to Duncan, ready to lend aid if his brother needed it.

Shelley would have helped Duncan, but the two wolves were snarling and running into tables and couches, their attacks so vicious that she knew if she got in the way she'd get trampled by the much bigger males.

The wolf turned his back on Duncan and tried to escape. Fatal mistake. Duncan leapt on him, ripping into him, and killed him.

Shelley knew Duncan wouldn't have let the wolf live, not after he had tried to kill her, his mate, his to protect.

Even if he had only wanted to leave and save his own skin at that point.

Duncan glanced at Shelley, making sure she was okay, that his brother was fine, and that Uncle Ethan wasn't having any difficulty with Sal. Then he loped into another part of the house. Within minutes, he was stalking back into the living room, wearing a pair of jeans too short for his tall height. Lamps and candy dishes were broken all over the floor. Chairs and couches were overturned. Kenneth and two dead wolves, who had reverted to their human forms, lay sprawled on the floor nearby.

"Enough," Duncan said to Sal. "It's over. You've taken a wolf clan's money, which you *will* return. You will also return monies owed to the many others you stole from."

Sal growled.

"If you do this… although it kills me to make such allowances because I'm certain she's as guilty as you are, we'll consent to allowing your mate to live. She'll be penniless, but she won't be dead."

Shelley located Sal's bedroom, found a closet full of women's clothes, and willed her wolf's form to shift into her human one. Then she pulled out a pair of fancy pink sweats trimmed in rhinestones. She wondered if these were Sal's mistress's clothes or Carlotta's. She hurried to dress.

Uncle Ethan and Cearnach remained as wolves, able to attack easier with lethal effect if Sal gave them any more heartburn. Sal had shifted and was now sitting in a bathrobe at his desk in his office with a spectacular view of the beach and pool. Shelley could imagine him accessing and transferring his money with a touch of the keyboard while gloating over the gorgeous view.

Sal snorted and crossed his arms, giving Duncan a steely-eyed glower. "You can't get the money out of a dead man."

"Perhaps not." Duncan motioned to a painting of Carlotta on the wall. "But I have no qualms about going after your mate. The Feds have already stated that they don't believe she was involved in your crimes. Whether she was or not, she'd have access to the money."

Shelley thought Duncan was bluffing about Sal's mate knowing how to get to the money. How would he know for sure?

Sal shook his head. "My mate loved the thrill of the game. Loved wining and dining men with money, wrapping them around her little finger, getting them to agree to grand investment schemes. The greedy bastards were asking for it."

"She didn't entertain my brother," Duncan said hotly.

"Unfortunately, no. If she had, she would have known he was part of a wolf pack and would have left well enough alone."

"We'll get our money one way or another. As your mate, she'd have access to all the money, all that has been stolen and in your custody and that which she has control of in the States."

"I spent a lot of the funds," Sal said, as if that would get him out of the grave he'd dug for himself.

Neither Duncan nor Shelley believed it. He couldn't have spent the billions he had purportedly absconded with.

"This reminds me of a time I was in a night class teaching, and all of a sudden all the electricity went out,"

Shelley said. "No storms around, nothing to have caused the sudden electrical outage. The next morning I read in the paper how a man had stolen money from a bunch of lawyers, doctors, a judge even, a big-time business man, with a deal that was too good to be true. So all these high rollers invested in his get-rich scheme. Just like yours.

"The thing of it was, ten years earlier, he had murdered his wife, saying she'd just up and decided to leave. Right in the middle of helping her daughter with wedding preparations. He had a mistress and wanted to get rid of his wife. They never found a body, so the police could never pin a murder on him. Everyone knew he had murdered her. The men who had invested in his fraudulent schemes. Even his grown son and daughter knew he'd killed their mother.

"They even went to that show that looks into unsolved murders. But they couldn't find enough evidence to prove he'd done anything wrong. So disgustingly, he got away with murder. Then a decade later, when he was going to trial for embezzlement and tax evasion and having stolen so many of the local prominent citizens' money, he couldn't deal with it. He ran his car into a telephone pole. Killed himself outright so he wouldn't have to face imprisonment."

Mouth agape, Sal stared at her. "You think I should commit suicide?"

"Others you've ruined financially have done so because of how you've destroyed their lives. Their only crime? Believing in your get-rich-quick schemes. Do you feel remorse for any of it? No, you've got your beach estate and other residences all over the world, a mistress, God knows how many more, and you're looking to have another she-wolf for a mate. Do you think Carlotta will be happy about that when she learns of it?"

Sal turned a little gray. For a moment, she wondered if he felt bad about that.

"So after you give up the money, why not do everyone a favor?" Shelley continued.

Sal stared at his computer, a picture of a hammerhead shark prowling the sea filling the screen.

A shark. A predator who was like an eating machine. Who ate the little fish and grew and grew and grew. Who didn't care about anything or anyone but himself.

"Why did you do it?" Shelley asked. "You were wealthy already. Why would you cheat so many people, make them lose everything they had?"

"They were greedy. None of them had enough. They wanted easy money. They made for easy targets. I wasn't always well-to-do." He shook his head. "My dad did the small scams. Taught me everything he knew, then died in a barroom brawl. I wanted to prove that I could do what my dad taught me, except on a much grander scale." He finally lifted his head and looked Duncan in the eye. "You won't hurt Carlotta."

"I give my word," Duncan said. "She won't keep any of the money, though. She won't benefit from your ill deeds or her own. She won't be hurt unless we learn she's continuing your scam."

Uncle Ethan nudged Shelley's hand. She reached down and petted her uncle's head, barely breathing, waiting for Sal to touch the keyboard.

"Wire my clan's money to my brother, Guthrie, who's in charge of finances. Then, you'll be wiring the rest of the money to this account and sending an email with attached files containing the information about the accounts you stole from and the amounts," Duncan said, hovering over Sal. He glanced over his shoulder at Shelley. "The college where you worked also."

Then as she and Duncan watched Sal work his magic, Duncan used Sal's phone to call Ian. "Ian..." He hadn't gotten anything else out when she heard whooping and hollering in the background at Argent Castle as if some huge celebration was taking place.

Ian laughed, then shouted over the din, "Hell, Duncan, what did you do? Guthrie just gave me the word. The news is spreading like wildfire through the pack. We've got our money back. Guthrie has already transferred it to another secure account."

The sound of all the laughter brought home to her how much this meant to Duncan's pack. She felt caught up in the overwhelming joy with them. For her college, too, and the staff that would also be celebrating once they knew the money had been returned.

"Just a little wolf persuasion, Ian. We'll be home soon," Duncan said over the phone.

Ian said, "Expect a warrior's welcome." Then the connection went dead.

"What about all the bodies?" Shelley asked.

Cearnach had disappeared, she realized, and she peeked out of the office door to see that he was hauling a body out the door.

"My brother will take care of them. We can't let anyone find men that have been killed by wolves," Duncan said.

Her Uncle Ethan hurried out after him and disappeared into Sal's bedroom. Then he returned, dressed in a pair of shorts, and helped Cearnach with the remaining bodies. More shark food.

"Show me the balances of each of your accounts," Duncan said to Sal. When they were all zeroed out, he said, "How do you want to handle this?"

Sal opened a desk drawer and pulled out a gun.

Afraid he'd use the weapon on Duncan, Shelley's heart lurched. But instead he kept the gun in his lap, pointed at the desk, looked at Shelley, and offered her a bittersweet smile. "I don't believe your mate will allow me to drive off to locate a telephone or electric pole to run into."

Every muscle tensed, Duncan was ready to grab the gun, not about to let Sal use it on Shelley or himself.

Sal turned to Duncan. "We could fight wolf to wolf, but it would be no contest. I'd be better off fighting your mate."

"No deal," Duncan said.

"I didn't think so." Sal raised the gun and pointed at his head.

Bang!

Not expecting it to happen so quickly, Shelley was so startled when he actually pulled the trigger that she jumped and gasped. Sal slumped over his keyboard.

Duncan touched Sal's neck, feeling for a pulse, waited, then nodded. "Dead."

They left him there for the police to find.

The time had come for Shelley and Duncan to go to his home in the Highlands. She hoped that she fit in with the rest of the pack and that her Uncle Ethan wouldn't stir up all kinds of trouble with Duncan's family.

Which… she was certain he would.

Chapter 21

AFTER THE WIRE TRANSFERS AND GETTING PLANE TICK-
ets for the return to Scotland, Shelley, Duncan, Cearnach,
and her Uncle Ethan finally arrived in Edinburgh in the
morning after an all-night flight. Then they drove for
several hours from the airport to Argent Castle.

Exhausted from not being able to sleep on the plane
like everyone else was able to, Shelley had gone to bed
as soon as she arrived at the castle with the others. She
barely noticed that Duncan's room was so darkly decorated. All that mattered were the big bed and climbing
into it, enjoying his masculine smell on the sheets where
she promptly drifted off to sleep.

Shelley woke to the sound of something clang-
ing in the distance and realized that it was already late
afternoon—and she'd slept for some hours. She rolled
off the high mattress—thinking that if she ever got
pregnant, she'd never manage by herself—and looked
out the arrow slit of a window. She saw a group of men
sword fighting, and boys nearby practicing their skills.
Everyone was decked out in kilts, no shirts or sashes, just
muscled backs and chests and arms as they swung their
swords at each other. Her heart did a few triple beats.

She threw on a pair of jeans, a sweatshirt, and tennis
shoes, and then rushed through the hall and down the
stairs. She didn't want Duncan to give her any lessons in
sword training while everyone was in the courtyard, but

she did want to get a front-row view of Duncan battling with his clan. How long would they be at it?

She was afraid she'd make it to the inner bailey in time to see them quit for the day. They might not practice all that often.

She flew through the great hall where Ian's mate, the werewolf romance writer Julia Wildthorn, was speaking with Duncan's cousin Heather. Shelley had met Heather briefly when she first arrived—so sleepy that she had barely greeted anyone, though they were all smiles and welcoming her to the family. There was talk of a great feast and celebration, a Highland wedding, though werewolves didn't get married, and the return of their money had everyone in high spirits. Except for Shelley, who'd barely been able to smile and nod before she fell asleep on her feet.

They both looked over at her a little in surprise because of her abrupt appearance as she dashed through the room, not bothering to wish them good morning or anything.

She bolted through the door as she heard Julia say, "She's worried about Duncan's training."

No, not worried. She just wanted to see him fight with men who knew how to wield a sword better than the pirates had on their afternoon cruise in the Caribbean. Well, maybe she was a little anxious, too.

She stalked across the inner bailey, trying not to distract anyone and hoping to observe them unobtrusively. Being wolves and wary of their surroundings, several turned to see her approach and smiled.

Her whole body instantly warmed. She wasn't used to being around a whole pack of male and female wolves. Even though she was already mated to Duncan, several seemed to appreciate having another female wolf in the pack.

Duncan was fighting Ian farther away, concentrating so hard that neither of them noticed her. Cearnach sauntered over to have a word with her. Guthrie stopped in his fight with another man and watched Cearnach approach her, a small smile on his face. She loved how Duncan's family had taken her in as if she were one of their own.

"The only one who fights better against Ian is me, lass," Cearnach said, wiping the sweat off his face with the back of his arm. "Duncan will be all right."

She'd loved how he had come to Duncan's and her uncle's aid on Grand Cayman Island, instead of waiting at the airport for them. She swore he'd worn a small smirk ever since he'd caught sight of her at Sal's house. She'd been a distraction in Duncan's mission to return their money, but she had aided him by leading the other wolves off until Duncan and her uncle could kill off the first two wolves.

"He showed me a little of his skill fighting pirates in the Caribbean," she said, wincing when Ian swung so hard that she could see the shudder of the impact race up Duncan's arms.

"Pirates of the Caribbean, eh?" Cearnach said, watching his brothers battle it out. "He never said anything about it to any of us."

"He won. I have to admit when he was fighting four at once, he was a bit outnumbered."

Cearnach raised a brow as he continued to observe Duncan and Ian. "He's a warrior at heart," he admitted. "We couldn't have been more surprised to hear that he was not only planning to bring home the clan's money, but also a mate—who he swears is not all wolf."

She glanced at Cearnach, wondering just what he meant by that. Certainly she was all wolf. A royal. Barely any human roots at all.

He smiled in a way that would have had all the women he encountered swooning at his feet.

"He said you were part mermaid." Cearnach let his gaze drift over her. "He made us all curious about what made him think so."

She smiled and looked back at Duncan and realized he'd become aware of her talking to Cearnach. Duncan looked ready to take Cearnach on next and stalked toward them.

Cearnach only grinned. "I believe my younger brother wishes a rematch." With that last comment, Cearnach went to join Duncan in battle.

Ian and Guthrie came to stand on either side of Shelley as if in protective big-brother mode. She really found it endearing. Ian said, "Cearnach is just being Cearnach, but Duncan is too enamored with you to see that he means nothing by his flirtations."

Shelley sighed. "Duncan has my heart, no other."

"Aye, and in time, Duncan will know that he has nothing to worry about where you are concerned." Ian offered her a knowing smile. "Worrying about you will keep him on his toes."

Guthrie laughed. "Duncan's temper will keep Cearnach on his toes. He fought vigorously against you, Ian, wanting to best you as always. Now that he knows his mate is watching and Cearnach had the audacity to speak with her alone, he's fighting more aggressively than I've seen him do in a good long while, especially after having been out here for an hour in training already."

Maybe Duncan could show her some moves once everyone finished their training, if he could demonstrate some private place where she could practice a little. She really would like to see what it felt like.

"We want to thank you for helping Duncan to have our money returned," Ian remarked. "This was the first time we were able to pinpoint where Sal had ended up, and when he learned we were after our money—well, we couldn't have done it without you. We understand that your mother and other uncles will be here within the month and are looking forward to their arrival."

"Thanks, my laird."

It seemed odd to call him that, and Ian quickly said, "You're family. Call me Ian, please."

"Thanks," she said, but she still couldn't call him Ian, not when so many referred to him as their laird. "I'm sure they'll love it here and I will, too."

Ian and Guthrie cast her knowing smiles.

Shelley sighed deeply, grateful that everything had worked out all right.

Her gaze was riveted on Duncan and Cearnach's swordplay.

Cearnach wouldn't give an inch as he swung his sword at Duncan, just as stubborn at putting on a good show as his brother. He finally motioned that he'd had enough and said, "I concede, Duncan, but only this once because your ladylove is waiting expectantly for you."

She was, too.

"Duncan was lucky to find such a resourceful young woman to be his mate," Ian said.

She smiled. "He proved to be a handy roommate, despite promising he'd be no trouble at all."

Ian and Guthrie laughed.

Duncan bowed slightly with good grace to Cearnach, then jogged over to join Shelley and his other brothers. His whole body was red with exertion, his muscles glistening with sweat, his eyes and lips smiling at her with joy because she'd come to watch him battle with his clansmen.

He didn't say anything but handed his sword to Guthrie and motioned to two male teens to give up their practice swords to him. Shelley opened her mouth to object. She was not going to fight here in front of everyone.

He grinned at her, as if he knew she was ready to protest, and said to his brothers, "We'll be in the gardens if you need me." His tone was more like—*Don't even think of interrupting us*.

That made her wonder just what he had in mind.

Heather ran out to join them and handed Ian a piece of paper with a smile and a wink at Shelley. "By the way, Cousin," she said to Duncan, "we just saw you had your own screen appearance."

Duncan frowned at her.

Heather smiled and waved a phone at him. "YouTube—Highlander fights pirates on the Jolly Roger. We'll have to use it as a training video."

He groaned.

Shelley laughed. She couldn't wait to get to know Heather and Julia better. Duncan tucked the paper into his sporran. Then taking Shelley's hand in his, he hurried her to the garden gate.

"Where are we going?" she asked, as he moved her

so quickly that she nearly had to run to keep up with his lengthy stride.

She heard men's laughter and a couple of ribald comments about just what Duncan planned to do with her. Heat crept over every inch of her skin all over again. Back home in Texas, no one would notice her much. Here in Duncan's clan, she felt she was the center of attention.

"We are going to the heart of the gardens, lass," Duncan said, not missing a step.

Having just awakened at Argent Castle, this was the first time that she and Duncan managed to slip away to see the gardens, or anything else for that matter.

She quickly realized that he wasn't letting her stop to see any of it. "Oh," she said, spying heather and wanting to take pictures of it and everything else blooming in the garden. If only she'd brought her camera with her, but it was back in his room.

"Later," he said, sounding amused and pulling her through a hedge maze where benches were secreted away and hidden fountains flowed.

He pulled open a gate where the yew hedge rose over the top in a full arch. On the other side, he bolted the wooden gate.

Bolted it to keep everyone else out. To sword fight in a Garden of Eden. Or, maybe not.

"We'll have the wedding in the kirk or here, whatever you prefer, lass."

"Wolves don't have weddings," Shelley said, surprised.

"Titled wolves—or wolves that could someday be the recipient of a title—wed. We'll have a nice Highland wedding here as soon as the rest of your family arrives."

"A Highland wedding," she said.

"Aye. Your people can wear Campbell plaid, and we'll wear the MacNeill. There will be much feasting, dancing, drinking, and playing of games."

"A wedding," she said, not believing that she'd ever be married in such a fashion. She had girlfriends who were not wolves who had talked about being princesses at their weddings, but she'd never thought she'd partake in such a fantasy.

"Aye, the women are already planning it. But you can make any changes you wish."

"No, I've… well, never envisioned having a wedding of my own. Whatever anyone wants to do is fine with me." She smiled, knowing that her own Highland family would be as pleased with the notion as she was. As long as no one said she had to wait to share a bed with Duncan until after the wedding.

She heard water flowing. In one corner of the garden, a man-made waterfall flowed into a shallow pool, maybe four feet deep. He hadn't mentioned that to her.

She looked up at him questioningly. He smiled. "You wanted to sword fight, aye?"

She had hoped he wanted to do something else. Instead, she smiled back at him, hoping she wasn't too transparent. "Absolutely."

He showed her the right stance as she faced him, how to swing her wooden sword, how to attack and parry. "Are you sure, lass, you must go back to America next fall and teach for the year?"

"Yes, Duncan, but you'll be with me. Then my contract's up, and we'll return here."

He sighed, and she realized he didn't want to leave his own home. While she had him in the States, she'd show him as much as she could—starting by taking him to the steak house in the Panhandle where the steaks were bigger than the plates. She'd drive him to where the eccentric Texas millionaire buried ten Cadillacs with their tail fins pointing to the sky.

He'd most likely enjoy a real Texas cowboy outing with a meal served out of an old-style chuck wagon in the Palo Duro Canyon. She'd have to take him to the outdoor show *Texas* so he could see just a fraction of what Texas was all about. She was also thinking how much she'd like to take him down to South Padre Island for more water play.

Before long, he had his arms wrapped around her, helping to perfect her sword swing. His face was in her hair, against her cheek, nuzzling and kissing. She felt his erection pressed hard against her back, showing her just how much he wanted her. Then he tossed the wooden sword aside.

"I've missed my mermaid of the sea," he said, his voice rusty with lust as he swept her into his arms and carried her to the falls, the sword practice forgotten. "I'm ready to return to paradise when I would never have thought to have enjoyed the experience. Ian insists. Says that since we brought the money home, we deserve another stay in paradise, only this time to strictly enjoy it. His orders."

"Ah, Duncan, have I told you how much I already love your family?"

He smiled and hurried to strip her of her clothes. When he pulled his kilt off, she stared in wonder. He was ready for her, all glorious, hard, ready.

"You were naked under your kilt," she said. Had every man been who'd been sword fighting?

Duncan laughed and lifted her into the falls.

Naked, his kilt and her jeans and sweatshirt cast aside on top of the rocks surrounding the man-made pool, he held her tightly in his arms under the falls.

"Were you naked under your kilt when you were in the movie, too?"

He smiled and kissed her wet cheek. "Aye."

She grinned. And kissed his mouth back. "I will have to watch the movie exceptionally closely then."

He chuckled. "You will never see the small part I played in the background."

"I will see you, Duncan MacNeill." She sighed. "I thought you said you wanted Ian to build you a pool, but you already have one." She ran her hands up his wet chest as the water from the falls poured over them.

"I was thinking of an indoor pool that we could enjoy year round. After a while, this one will be too cold."

The water was cool, not warm like the Caribbean, but that didn't keep them from heating up.

He set her on her feet in the pool of water and kissed her, his fingers tangling in her loose hair, hers gripping his narrow waist. She loved him, loved how he'd brought her here to this special place to make love to her.

"You're gorgeous." She licked his nipple and then the other as he groaned, the falls drowning out the sound. "And so very hard."

He smiled and cupped her face, kissed her mouth, and parted her lips so he could stroke her tongue with his. He didn't stop until they were breathless and ready to sink into the pool. "Mermaid. Siren," he said, lifting her against him.

Here, there were no waves to knock them over, no

fish to nibble at their legs, no saltwater to caress their skin—just fresh, cool water running down their bodies in a steady, welcoming stream.

He reached down and lifted her under her thighs, wrapping her around his body. Before she knew it, he was inside her, thrusting, kissing, savoring her like she was savoring him.

Never in a millennium did she think she'd be in the heart of the most beautiful Highland gardens, making love to a warrior Highland wolf. In a few weeks, she'd be marrying him dressed in traditional Highland clothes.

She thrust her tongue deep into his mouth, and he groaned, moving her around so that she no longer faced the rock wall behind him. All that she could see was his beautifully sculpted chest. What was he doing?

She felt her buttocks slide onto a smooth ledge, and his fingers moved to stroke her clit while the water rushed deliciously down her body, making her nub even more sensitive until she was arching against his fingers, begging him to finish her off.

His eyes were dusky with need as he dipped his head and again kissed her mouth, thrusting his tongue into it until she was gasping for breath, the climax so close she felt as though she were being swept up the falls and ready to go over the edge.

"Ahh, Duncan," she moaned against his mouth, straining to draw on every bit of pleasure he was giving her, making it last until the cord broke. She felt the release and his immediate need to take her again.

At first, he thrust inside her as she sat on the ledge, but he wanted more. Again he lifted her, hugging her close, penetrating her to the core, ramming hard, in and out. Her body shuddered with release around him until he burst inside her, groaning her name, speaking in Gaelic, cursing her or offering loving sentiments—she didn't know and didn't care.

He was hers and she was his, and she wanted to do a lot more of this before the day was through.

She sighed, expecting that she'd have to work for a living here, teaching everyone who wanted to learn about botany before long. For now, she hoped everyone would let her and Duncan have a nice long honeymoon of sorts.

After they dressed, their skin and hair still wet—next time they'd bring towels—Duncan pulled the piece of paper out of his sporran and said, "Now I'll give you a tour of the gardens, lass."

She was ecstatic. When she explored the gardens again, she fully intended to bring her camera and notepad.

True to his word, he gave her a grand tour of the gardens, stumbling over Latin names for the plants as he led her through each of the special gardens—herb and vegetable garden, the flower garden, more of the hedge maze and sitting gardens, and the greenhouses where flowers and fruits and vegetables were growing. What tickled her most was that his cousin Heather had made up the list of all the gardens and what they contained so Duncan could give her a proper guided tour.

"Do you have any wolves here who are not royals?" she asked.

"Aye, a few."

"Have you noticed that any plants they might have ingested could have affected their desire to shift?"

He shook his head. "Why do you ask?"

"I'm searching for something that might help them to fight the change or to shift when they need to."

His mouth parted, then he raised his brows. "That's why you were in that forest?"

"I'm thinking that the Amazon might have such a plant."

He looked at her with new admiration and hugged her close. He actually looked like he was enjoying sharing with her everything about the different kinds of plants and what they were good for, too, which she loved.

"I'll speak to Ian about us going there sometime later, if you'd like," he said.

"I'd like that."

"Jaguars are the predators there, you know. Wolves don't rule in the Amazon."

She raised her brows. "We'll make do. They undoubtedly have never seen a brave Highland wolf and what he can do."

He laughed.

Before they could reach the gate to leave, they heard Duncan's mother arguing with Uncle Ethan beyond the walled garden. Shelley stiffened a little. Duncan kissed her cheek and wrapped his arm around her shoulders, as if to tell her that whatever her uncle or his mother said or did had nothing to do with Shelley or him.

"Are ye never going to let go of the past, Ethan Campbell? 'Tis a shame you canna appreciate what you've had since you left Scotland and what you have now," Duncan's mother scolded.

"'Twas fraught with hardships," Ethan complained. "Several died who had to make their homes in the States."

Shelley had heard that old tale forever.

"Aye, well, several died who stayed in Scotland as well. You should learn to appreciate the present. Look at my son and your niece. They are happy together. You should be well pleased to see the match."

Uncle Ethan and Duncan's mother stopped walking, and so did Duncan and Shelley. Her uncle and Duncan's mother didn't know they were in the gardens. Neither couple could see the other, and Shelley wanted to hear what her uncle and Duncan's mother said to each other—good or bad. She wished they'd quit bickering. They'd been at it since Ethan and Shelley had first arrived and Duncan had escorted Shelley to his bedroom to sleep.

"Duncan's Aunt Agnes said you were in a movie," Ethan said.

Shelley flicked a quick glance at Duncan. He smiled. "Aye," Duncan whispered to her. "She rushed into the great hall during the dining scene and armed Julia with a dagger. The camera caught the scene, and they kept it. Apparently the director loved the realism."

Shelley's mouth gaped. "Why would your mother arm Ian's mate with a weapon during the filming of a movie scene?"

"An enemy clan had breached the walls. Ian couldn't get to Julia in time to protect her, and neither could Cearnach nor I."

Shelley couldn't believe he hadn't told her that the fighting in the movie had been for real. "You're kidding. Why didn't you tell me this? What happened?"

Before Duncan could say more, his mother finally said to Ethan, "Aye, well, someone had to protect Ian's mate. I told Ian not to allow Julia to be in the film. Stubborn men. You are all the same."

Shelley's brow quirked up at Duncan.

Duncan smiled at her. "Some lasses are more stubborn than *us*. A couple come to mind."

"Ha," Shelley said.

Duncan changed direction. "We'll go to a different gate."

"To avoid my uncle and your mom?"

"Most definitely."

"And?"

Duncan wore the most devilish grin.

"And?" she repeated, as he tightened his hold on her.

"I didn't get enough sleep last night, did you?"

He was just a wolf, always wanting to nap... and more. Which totally appealed to her own wolfish desires. She hurried him on their way.

Shelley sighed. She looked up at Duncan's wet hair, water droplets speckled on his cheeks and naked chest, the way his kilt was slung low on his hips, the way he was smiling at her, the way he was moving her fast through a secret passage to his room. She slipped her arm around his waist and hugged him closer. One hardcore warrior wolf—and he was all hers.

Now that the clan had its money back and Ian said they could make the trip, she was planning a return to paradise soon. This time it would all be for fun. She just hoped while she and Duncan were gone, her uncles and mother would behave themselves at Argent Castle. She hoped her beloved standard poodles would behave, too, and didn't get too frisky with Duncan's Irish wolfhounds. She could just see a bunch of little Irish-French wolf-poo hounds running around.

Wendy was planning a visit, too, and Shelley thought

she wanted to look over some of the available bachelor
Highland wolves.

It had nearly killed Duncan when he'd first arrived
at Argent Castle with his mate in hand, and he'd had to
leave her off in his bed—alone. She had been so tired
that she couldn't last another moment without sleeping.
The whole of his clan had wanted to hear about Shelley,
her help in getting their money back, that she was now
his mate, and how important she was to his people.
They'd regaled him with plans of how they'd conduct a
marriage ceremony, too.

Tonight, the first celebration of their union and the
return of the clan's money would take place.

Until then, he was joining his mermaid in bed, and
nothing—short of the castle being under siege, and
maybe not even that—would change his mind.

Read on for an excerpt
from Terry Spear's

A Highland Werewolf Wedding

from Sourcebooks Casablanca

1785, St. Augustine, Florida

THE HEAT OF THE OCTOBER DAY MADE ELAINE
Hawthorn wilt as tears blurred her eyes. She choked
back a sob as men shoveled the dirt onto her mother's
and father's coffins. Never again would she see her
mother's bright smile or her father's raised brow when
she did something he thought was not quite ladylike.
Never again would she feel her mother's and father's
warm embraces, telling her how much they loved her. A
fateful carriage accident had brought them to this.

Barely an hour later, her uncles Tobias and Samson
pulled her away from the reception to speak with her
privately. From their weary expressions—and the way
Kelly Rafferty, a pirating wolf himself, had leered at her
at the funeral—she was in for more dire news.

"Lass, you must have a mate," Uncle Tobias said,
towering over her like an Irishman ready to do battle. He
was a seasoned fighter, sailor, and pirate—or as he often
reminded her, a privateer, like his twin brother. Tobias
never took any guff from his men. He and his brother had
been born while their parents were crossing the Irish Sea
from Ireland to Scotland so she believed seawater ran in
their veins. They were also shape-shifting gray wolves.

"He has the right of it, Elaine." Uncle Samson lifted his grizzled, tanned hands in an appeasing way. "At sixteen, you need a mate. Kelly Rafferty has the only wolf pack in the area and has asked for you to be his mate. We have concurred."

The air rushed out of her lungs, and she felt lightheaded. She grasped the side table to steady herself. Gathering her wits, she responded with outrage. "You did not even ask *me*! I will not marry that arrogant, conceited wolf! He has never been interested in me. Never! Not until he thought he might gain my parents' properties!"

That made her wonder if *he'd* had anything to do with her parents' carriage accident. Wasn't it a little too convenient? Her family had been in competition in the pirating business with Kelly Rafferty all these years—and suddenly her parents die when Elaine is old enough that Kelly can mate with her and take over her parents' estates.

"Take me with you. Let me see the world first. Then when we return to St. Augustine, if I have not found my own wolf mate by then, we will see if Mr. Rafferty is still interested."

Over her dead body.

After much arguing with her uncles, Elaine convinced them to allow her this one boon. With great reluctance, they had their solicitor arrange to have her estates managed until she returned.

—⁓—

Two days into the ocean voyage, Elaine heaved the contents of her belly into a bucket while attempting to rest in the captain's quarters, sicker than she had ever been.

Everything went from bad to worse as soon as they

arrived at the port city of St. Andrews, Scotland. The ship carried a new name and her uncles dressed as respectable merchants, but someone must have recognized them for who they truly were.

Word soon reached the authorities that the notorious, pirating Hawthorn brothers had returned. As armed men hurried toward them, her Uncle Tobias signaled to one of his sailors, who shoved her to the cobblestones as if she was in their way.

Men grabbed her uncles and several of their crew, led them away in chains, and tried them with barely any representation. To her horror, her uncles were hanged in the town square at the behest of Lord Harold Whittington who owned a fleet of merchant ships and claimed her uncles had sacked three of them.

Scared to death that someone would see her, believe she was part of her uncle's crew, and hang her, too, she hastily wiped away the tears rolling freely down her cheeks and tried to slip away unnoticed in the chilly breeze. Her best hope was to return to Florida and her family's estates.

As she started to steal away, she spied a broad-shouldered man observing her. He was wearing a predominantly blue and green kilt, the plaid gathered over his shoulder and pinned, a sporran at his belt, and a sword at his back—and he looked fierce. Her heart did a tumble.

She had dressed as plainly as she could in a dark-green muslin gown with a fitted jacket and a petticoat of the same color. With a cloak covering these and the hood up over her head, she had hoped to be shielded from the view of the men and women milling about. She thought she had been obscure in the crowd, but the stranger was watching her as if he knew she had been involved in her uncles' pirating ways. As if he thought she should be swinging from the gallows alongside her uncles and some of their men.

He appeared to be a Highland warrior of old, someone who had fought in ruthless clan battles and come out a survivor. Maybe a loyal friend of Lord Whittington who would want a noose around her neck, too.

He lifted his nose and appeared to take a deep breath. As if he was trying to scent the wind. As if he was trying to smell her. Which immediately made her think of a wolf. Her skin prickled with unease.

He *couldn't* be a wolf. Maybe that's what made him appear so dangerous, feral, and determined.

His eyes widened and he headed in her direction. The other men he'd been with followed him.

Her heart pumped wildly as she tried to reach an alleyway, thinking she had gotten away. She was slipping down the narrow brick alleyway when a large hand grabbed her arm and effectively stopped her.

Barely able to catch her breath, she bit back a scream.

"Lass," the man said with a distinctive Highland burr, his voice low, "where are you going in such a hurry?"

His dark brown eyes were narrowed, focused on her, yet a small smile curved his lips. As if he was amused that she thought she could evade a wolf. Because that was just what he was.

A gray wolf, tall, muscularly built, but more wiry than bulky. His hand was holding her still, not bruising her but with enough pressure that she knew he was not about to let her go. He was handsome as the devil, the crinkle lines beneath his eyes telling her he was a man who liked to smile, his masculine lips likewise, not thin and mean like Kelly Rafferty's, but pleasingly full with a curve that made her think he enjoyed life in a jovial rather than a cruel way.

His wind-tussled hair was an earthy shade of dark brown with streaks of red, and he had no hint of facial hair, as if he had just shaved. He was lean and hard, not an ounce of fat, and determined, his jaw set, his brows raised a little now as he examined her more closely. He was taking a good long look, not in a leering way but in a way that said he was memorizing her distinctive appearance, maybe comparing that to her uncles', and not speaking a word as if she'd stolen whatever he was going to say right from his lips.

The three men who had been trailing behind him were now immersed in a brawl outside the alley, fists swinging as they were caught up in the fight.

"Are you here alone, lass?" the man asked, his voice seductively low. He was an alpha, in charge, wanting answers.

"Let... me... go," she growled. She was trying not to make a scene in case any of Lord Whittington's men were nearby and could overhear her and grow curious about her. *If* this man was not already one of Whittington's men.

"Come with me and my brothers, and I will protect you," he offered.

A shiver stole up her spine. He must know she was related to the hanged men. The fight was growing closer—she could hear men's shouts and cries of pain, scuffling, and thuds as some went down.

"If Lord Whittington learns you were one of the Hawthorns' kin, it willna go well for you," the man said. "My name is Cearnach MacNeill, and those behind me..." He glanced over his shoulder, then turned back to her and amended, "Who *were* following me are my brothers. We will see you to safety."

She shook her head. "You are mistaken about me, sir. Release me at once."

He did not seem inclined to do so, but a beefy half-drunken man came up behind him, skirted around the Highlander, and slugged Cearnach in the jaw. He immediately released Elaine so that he was free to pelt the drunk.

She darted down the alleyway, glancing back to see Cearnach struggling to rid himself of the brigand. He took a swing at the drunk, and when he had knocked him back several steps, Cearnach looked for her. And spied her getting away. Her heart did a flip. He appeared both troubled and exasperated.

She ran out of the alley, dashed down the street until she found another alley, and ducked down it. She would find a ship and return home on her own.

Somehow she had to figure out a way to deal with Kelly Rafferty next.

———

Present Day, Scotland

Cearnach MacNeill had promised Calla Stewart that he would show up at her wedding to lend moral support. Friends did that for friends. He would attend because she had asked him to. Even though he knew his being there could stir up real trouble.

Why did she have to marry into the McKinley clan? Pirates, every last one of them. Even though the pirating stopped a century ago. As far as he was concerned, they were still a bunch of ruthless brigands.

He drove through the open castle gates and then through the outer bailey. Out on the main road, he tore off in the direction of the church and cursed the wind for impeding his progress.

Trying to get his mind off the drive ahead and the dwindling time, he thought about Calla and the regret he felt that he couldn't have been the one for her. They just didn't have what it took to be a couple.

No matter how many times he told himself Calla understood what she was doing, he knew Baird McKinley didn't deserve her. She was making a big mistake.

An hour later, only halfway to the church and with the strong headwind thwarting his progress, Cearnach came around a bend in the hilly road to see a black Mercedes hogging the pavement in his lane. Since the other driver wasn't budging, Cearnach jerked his car off the road before they collided head-on.

Hell and damnation!

With the rate of speed he was going, the car sailed over the rocks littering the terrain, ripping up the rear tires with a boom! And another boom! The tires exploded before he could brake the car enough to stop it.

Cursing a blue streak, he cut the engine and climbed out of the car to see who the idiot driver was. Probably someone who had been celebrating a wee bit too much. He grabbed his sheathed sword and strapped it around his waist.

The black car had pulled to the side of the road, the driver hidden behind tinted windows, the engine purring.

When the driver's door opened, a long-legged

brunette stepped out of the car. He had a hell of a time shifting his gaze from those shapely legs and a pair of sexy high-heeled pumps—her clingy red dress having risen to mid-thigh before it settled lower—to see how good the rest of her looked. Especially since he'd expected some sloppy-drunk male type.

His gaze traveled upward to take in the rest of the package. The wind blowing in her direction forced the dress's red slinky fabric to cling to her shapely legs, hips, and everything in between. The dress screamed hot and available. At least to him.

The neckline wasn't all that low, just enough to show off the swell of her breasts, but her reaction to his perusing her was what made him direct his attention upward while he bit back a smile. She folded her arms beneath her breasts, lifting them a little and making him wish he could do the honors, and then she let out an annoyed huff of breath.

More than anything, he loved her reaction and wasn't beyond pushing her a bit after she'd forced him off the road and ruined two of his tires.

"Done looking?" she asked. The hint of sarcasm amused him when he should still have been furious about what she'd done to his vehicle.

She was American, not a Scottish lass, which meant she was trouble if she was anything like his brothers Ian and Duncan's mates, except both of the women were wolves, Julia of the red wolf variety, and Shelley, a gray.

"All right," she said, now sounding *really* annoyed. "I get it. You're a big, bad Highland warrior type of wolf, and you have to present this image..."

She knew he was a *wolf*?

Only *one way* she'd know that. She smelled his wolf scent. Only one way she could do that. She was also a wolf.

After getting over his initial shock, he crowded her as a wolf would, checking her out, sensing her response to him, learning if she truly was a wolf. She nearly folded into the car, trying to back away from him. He seized her arm to keep her close and moved his face in to get a good whiff of her.

She-wolf. Gray. A hint of a seductive floral fragrance.

He took in another breath, attempting to learn how she felt about him, trying to see if she was angered, intrigued, scared. He frowned. She smelled familiar somehow. From the scent he gathered from her, she *was* angered, intrigued, and a wee bit scared. Just as she should be around an imposing Highlander of the Old World like he was.

"Bloody hell," he said, quickly releasing her, not wanting to feel any interest in the lass. But he continued to remain in her space, continued to suck in the air around her, continued to enjoy the essence of the wolf. He couldn't help it. When a female was *this* enticing, he was all male wolf.

"What's your name?" he asked.

"Elaine Hawthorn." She stared him down like a wolf that wouldn't be cowed, but she didn't ask his name or act as though she wanted it.

He eyed her more closely, sure he had seen her somewhere before. A long… *very* long time ago. That was the problem with living for so many years. He wasn't good at remembering new names and faces in the short term. Long term? Even worse.

Something about her appearance and something about her reaction to him had him wondering.

Acknowledgments

Thanks to my fans who asked for more of the Highland wolf hunks before anyone had a chance to read the first of the Highland wolf stories, *Heart of the Highland Wolf*. To my editor, Deb Werksman, who makes it possible for me to share more of my wolf tales, and now even some jaguar shifter tales! To Danielle, my publicist, who is my marketing inspiration, and to the editorial staff and the cover artists who design such beautiful covers, creating praise for the characters well before they're even available to the world, and make me proud to say that these books are mine.

And to the Rebel Romance Writers critique partners—Carol, Judy, Vonda, Tammy, Randy, Pam, and Betty—for being a super support group that has helped me immensely throughout the years. And to my fans who offer suggestions for titles and which characters they want to see get their happily-ever-afters next, send pictures of hunky men and of wolves and jaguars, and who tell me why they've fallen in love with my wolves—you are my inspiration!

USA Today *bestselling author Terry Spear has captured hearts worldwide by wrapping the realities of nature into the glorious romance of the wild. Now, she turns her award-winning imagination from the sexy werewolf hunt to the intense sizzle of jaguar shape-shifters.*

Savage Hunger

by Terry Spear

—⁓—

He saved her once...

When Kathleen McKnight was caught in the crossfire during a mission deep in the Amazon rain forest, a mysterious man saved her life then disappeared. Kathleen returns a year later in hopes of finding her mysterious savior...

Now he wants to claim her...

Jaguar shape-shifter Connor Anderson is instantly intrigued by Kathleen's beauty and courage and thinks about her constantly. When she comes back to the Amazon to seek him out, he knows he has to act fast if he's to keep her for his own...

—⁓—

"Time after time Spear delivers, giving paranormal fans plenty of action, plenty of mystery, and, of course, love and romance aplenty." —*The Good, the Bad and the Unread*

For more Terry Spear, visit:

www.sourcebooks.com

Untamed

by Sara Humphreys

An ancient race of shapeshifters has lived secretly among humans for thousands of years... they are... the *Amoveo*

Her worst nightmare is coming true...

Layla Nickelsen has spent years hiding from her Amoveo mate and guarding a devastating secret. But Layla's worst fear is realized when the man who haunts her dreams shows up in person...

He has finally found her...

William Fleury is as stoic as they come, until he finds Layla and his feelings overwhelm him. She won't let him get close, but then an unknown enemy erupts in violence and threatens everything Layla holds dear...

"Compelling... Deft world-building and sensuous love scenes make this paranormal romantic thriller an enjoyable journey."—*Publishers Weekly*

"Humphreys's spectacular talent is on full display... You will feel as if you are entirely immersed in her world... This series is getting better with each book." —*RT Books Reviews*, 4.5

★ ★ ★ ★ ★ ★ ★

For more Sara Humphreys, visit:

www.sourcebooks.com

About the Author

USA Today bestselling author and an award-winning writer of urban fantasy and medieval romantic suspense, Terry Spear also writes true stories for adult and young adult audiences. She's a retired lieutenant colonel in the U.S. Army Reserves and has an MBA from Monmouth University. She also creates award-winning teddy bears, Wilde & Woolly Bears, that are personalized and designed to commemorate authors' books.

When she's not writing or making bears, she's teaching online writing courses. Her family has roots in the Highlands of Scotland where her love of all things Scottish came into being. Originally from California, she's lived in eight states and now resides in the heart of Texas. She is the author of *Heart of the Wolf, Destiny of the Wolf, To Tempt the Wolf, Legend of the White Wolf, Seduced by the Wolf, Wolf Fever, Heart of the Highland Wolf, Dreaming of the Wolf, A SEAL in Wolf's Clothing, Winning the Highlander's Heart, The Accidental Highland Hero, A Ghost of a Chance at Love, Deadly Liaisons*, the start of a new jaguar-shifter series, *A Savage Hunger*, and numerous articles and short stories for magazines.

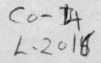